To Viol[...]

Best Wishes

SHADOWS

Alan

Bartlett

X

The author was born seven miles from Swindon in the Oxfordshire village of Ashbury. The early part of his life was spent in nearby Watchfield – from where he attended Shrivenham Primary School and Faringdon Secondary Modern.

Initially employed in administration at RMCS Shrivenham he transferred to an IT post in Bicester before moving to MOD (Navy) Bath as a systems analyst in 1993 – where he is currently employed in the same capacity by Boeing UK.

Married to Lynn (nee Wilson), the couple lived in Swindon for seventeen years before moving to Brackley, Northamptonshire. Their current home is Melksham in Wiltshire. Alan and Lynn have two daughters – Kim and Nikki – and a grand-daughter Mistee.

Alan's interests include writing, poker and chess. He also enjoys the musical theatre and period drama. In the dim and distant past he once completed a London Marathon – but his sporting activities are now restricted to a squash court and the golf course. He still suffers an occasional match at the County Ground where Swindon Town FC were followed on a regular basis for twenty-five years.

SHADOWS

Alan Barrett

SHADOWS

Olympia Publishers
London

www.olympiapublishers.com
OLYMPIA PAPERBACK EDITION

A CIP catalogue record for this title is
available from the British Library.

ISBN: 978-1-84897-192-9

This is a work of fiction.
Names, characters, places and incidents originate from the writer's
imagination. Any resemblance to actual persons, living or dead, is purely
coincidental.

First Published in 2012

Olympia Publishers
60 Cannon Street
London
EC4N 6NP

Printed in Great Britain

In memory of Mum and Dad

Acknowledgements

The feedback and encouragement from my two daughters and Melissa (Kirk) have played a large part in the completion of this book.

I'm also indebted to Amy (Fletcher) – for her 'SHADOWS' artwork – and to Steve Fice-Noyes for his help in verifying certain day-to-day police routines contained within the story.

Thank you to Olympia Publishers for giving me this opportunity.

FOREWORD

Over a span of ten million years the human brain still retains much of its original mystique. Despite huge advances made in the field of neurological research, twenty-first century man is still striving to fully understand its many complex and subtle nuances. The genetic building blocks of a savage and un-structured beginning, suppressed over the centuries, are capable of re-surfacing at any time. Just a simple physical act or emotive reaction can activate cells buried deep in the human psyche and be responsible for triggering the most violent of acts. The sudden emergence of a serial killer or homicidal maniac is clear evidence the manifestation exists.

For the vast majority of us primitive rage is controlled – a momentary surge of temper – but when the brain is permanently jolted from its original niche the changes to cell patterns make it unpredictable – never fully under control. The primeval killing instinct, resurrected within the sophisticated and cunning mind of modern man, is a weapon out of control. A civilised populace does not understand the phenomenon, or know how to deal with it. All the ancient taboos and fears from a bygone era can sweep across whole communities, causing them to panic and stampede.

A base instinct of our early ancestors that still survives today is the absolute protection of their young. Identify the predator, isolate it, and with chilling savagery, disable or destroy in the shortest possible time.

The ancient hunter-gatherer suffered neither conscience nor remorse, just a feeling of exhilaration in the blood lust that eliminated an immediate threat – and ensured at least a temporary survival for the young of his species.

CHAPTER 1

Sixfields Housing Estate: Friday 19 January 2007: 09.10 pm

It was late evening. The man stood perfectly still, his elbows resting on top of a low wooden fence. Ten minutes passed. He continued to look up and down the narrow alleyway, monitoring it for any sign of movement. Above him a single street lamp did its best to light up the thoroughfare's natural gloom.

The man routinely checked his back garden for intruders every evening, and his vigil would continue until ten o'clock. Fifty yards in length, with a small shed positioned just inside the fence, it provided individuals with sufficient enough privacy in which to pursue their activities. Discarded cannabis stubs, hypodermics, used condoms and empty bottles were just some of the items that Robert Milner regularly came across and had to dispose of.

A bitter, icy, blast barrelled its way through the deserted alleyway, carrying scraps of litter along the readymade wind tunnel – there was little sign of any trespassers tonight. It was cold. Thin layers of ice had formed on the surface of nearby puddles as temperatures continued to plummet. Milner hunched deeper into his coat. It was a miserable evening.

The view he looked out on did nothing to lift his depression. Two rows of grey, nondescript houses stretched away either side of the alley, disappearing into a vast, suburban, concrete sprawl that was the Sixfields Community Housing Estate. Two high-rise tower blocks, added in the late sixties, had done little to enhance Sixfields' image. The estate's current population of ninety thousand inhabitants ground out their daily routines in an area that now covered over six square miles.

Established after the Second World War, as a result of Birmingham's inner city slum clearance, Sixfields was promoted as a model blueprint for post war community housing across the UK. That it eventually failed was undoubtedly due to the estate's sheer scale and size of operation.

Despite attempts to administer the community through smaller, self-contained neighbourhoods, years of neglect and decline had gradually taken its toll, making the estate's ageing properties uneconomic to maintain.

Latterly, despite increased funding to finance and initiate modernisation programmes, the concerted efforts to lift Sixfields from its present demise remained largely unsuccessful. Abandoned building projects and un-developed wasteland remained common features throughout the estate. The community's problems were not just confined to its property and buildings, a nationwide increase in crime and social breakdown was inevitably magnified on an estate the size of Sixfields. Teenage gangs ran rife on its streets, unchecked, seemingly given free rein to intimidate and harass the majority of residents at will.

Challenging the gang's actions were usually met with reprisal attacks – on property and individuals – a shrug of the shoulders from local police – any physical retaliation by the victims would result in them being pursued by the full might of a liberal and disapproving state.

Safe in the knowledge that their actions would not be punished gang behaviour flourished, and those disadvantaged groups forced to live in Sixfields – the poor, the old, the unfortunate and the misfits – were left to fend for themselves, co-existing against a permanent background of anti-social behaviour and continual abuse.

It hadn't always been like this for Milner. He once pursued a high-income career, lived an expensive lifestyle, enjoyed the support of a close and loving wife. Then he was dumped from his job, and the close and loving wife dumped him, too.

A painful divorce, and the failure to match his previous career resulted in severe clinical depression. The continuing, downward spiral landed him in Sixfields ten years ago. Little wonder that his spirits were as mean and low as the neighbourhood he looked out on.

Milner's thoughts were cut short by movement from one of the gardens opposite. Twenty yards to his left a young woman emerged into the alley, pulling a child's buggy. Milner recognised Janet Sterne, a single mother who lived further along the lane. A young girl, three or four years of age, clutched the woman's hand. Wedged into the buggy was a small toddler.

The mother looked cold, harassed. Milner watched her struggle to close the garden gate, a short, lightweight coat providing little protection against the biting wind. Leaving her mother's side the young girl ran across to one of the puddles and began stamping on its thin layer of ice.

Her mother's impatience carried over to Milner's side of the alley 'Stop pissing around Zoe! It's too cold!'

A stampede of running feet caused the woman to look up sharply.

From one of the alley's side entrances a group of youths appeared, quickly filling its width. All of them wore hooded tops pulled up over their heads, black scarves covered the lower half of their faces. Only the eyes remained visible.

They made no attempt to move out of the woman's way, staring her down – Milner could feel the intimidation from thirty yards away. The young girl ran back to her mother's side. When one of the hooded youths flicked a lit cigarette at them Sterne attempted to push her way through, but the gang formed around her, a foot on one of the buggy's wheels, halting its progress.

The toddler looked up at her mother, as if it didn't quite understand the new game they were playing. The other child clung instinctively to her mother's coat, old enough to know it wasn't a game.

The woman panicked. 'I'll scream this fucking place down!' she shouted at them.

A grey-hooded figure, presumably the gang's leader, stepped in close 'You'll shut the fuck up!' A long-bladed knife appeared in front of the toddler's face. The woman froze. Behind his shed, camouflaged by the darkness, Milner watched it unfold, unable to move or react.

The gang-leader, older and more heavily built than the others, motioned to one of them 'Check her pockets!' Milner was surprised to see that it was a girl who stepped forward – no more than fourteen years old. She rifled through the woman's pockets before feeling under her coat. When the girl's hands brushed against Sterne's breasts the gang started to shout and jeer.

Playing to an audience the girl dropped her hand down to the woman's crotch, and held it there. A different mood descended. The gang fell silent. Sterne, frightened now, tried to turn away but the girl punched her hard in the face. A thin trickle of blood ran from the woman's nose, but she kept her eyes on the gang-leader, and the knife he was still holding.

The girl stood back.

'Anything?' the grey-hooded figure asked her impatiently.

'No!'

Grasping the buggy's handle he tipped it forwards, pitching the toddler out onto the ground. Milner could see it was a baby girl. The mother immediately moved to pick her up.

Stooping down, the gang-leader laid his knife against the baby's neck, drawing a small pinprick of blood. Milner instinctively straightened. The mother backed off. Distressed at its rough handling the child began to cry.

'I haven't got any money!' Sterne shouted at the gang-leader, 'Please don't hurt my baby.'

Still gripping the child's arm he motioned with his head. The teenage girl stooped down, running a hand around inside the buggy's storage areas. She stood up, shaking her head.

One of the watching gang lit a cigarette. Milner watched it flame and flare in the semi-darkness. Cannabis. The glowing tip was passed around between them, until it eventually reached the gang-leader. Pinching an end between his thumb and forefinger he sucked deeply at the loosely packed roll, continuing to hold the child.

The group waited.

'Fuck you!' the gang-leader finally said to Sterne, stubbing his cigarette against the baby's hand.

The woman flung herself forward as the child cried out in pain.

Sterne's screams ripped down the alley, literally jolting Milner's head backwards. The group scattered. Milner drew back into shadow as the grey-hooded gang-leader and two others raced past. Vaulting the low fence he padded instinctively after them, following their laughter along the alley. Milner couldn't identify the deep growl that muffled his hearing, but it remained alongside him as he trailed his quarry. A predator had been identified. It had to be isolated and destroyed.

Despite their constant backward glances, the cover of deep shadow allowed Milner to keep all three gang members in full view. When two of them disappeared into one of the alley's side exits Milner's attention remained fixed on their leader, who continued forward onto a stretch of rubble-strewn wasteland.

Although the man had lowered his hood a strong wind masked the rapid progress that Milner was making behind him. He quickly closed the distance between them. Without breaking stride Milner stooped to pick up a fist-sized rock. The all-consuming rage climaxed. A powerful adrenalin surge suffused his face with blood.

A split second too late the gang-leader sensed someone at his shoulder. He half turned. With all of his bodyweight Milner smashed the rock down onto the man's shaven head, cracking a section of outer skull as it buckled inwards.

Pitching forward onto his face the gang-leader's nose split open as it hit the ground. Scrabbling blindly around on all fours, completely disorientated, he desperately tried to focus about him. Blood poured from both his broken nose and a three-inch gaping wound at the base of his skull.

Milner looked down at the archetypal lout that represented all the abuse he'd suffered from gang behaviour over the years. Stepping back he kicked him hard in the face.

Feeling the gang-leader's teeth break against the toe-end of his shoe Milner experienced the near sensation of a physical orgasm. He stood back and kicked the face again, spraying his own jeans and trainers in a fine red mist.

When the gang-leader tried to curl himself into a ball Milner lifted both of his legs and dragged him across the icy waste ground. As the grey-hooded top gradually rucked up around the man's neck, razor-sharp ridges of frozen mud shredded strips of skin from his bare back.

Milner reached a short flight of concrete steps. Aware of his location he knew the steps would take him down into an abandoned children's play area. He turned to check for signs of anyone on the waste-ground. Satisfied they were not being watched Milner grabbed the man's foot and hauled his dead-weight behind him, each downward step resounding with a dull thud, as the shaven head flopped against frozen concrete.

Despite the sub-zero temperature Milner was sweating heavily. He left one of the gang-leader's legs propped against the bottom step. Placing a foot on top of the man's knee Milner applied enough downward pressure to feel the bone resisting his weight. He lowered his head, 'Do you understand what's happening to you big man?'

The gang-leader tried to move his lips. He was barely conscious. Milner's face remained close to his ear, 'Do you understand why?'

No response. The leader's mouth was a soft pulp, his senses scrambled.

Milner increased downward pressure on the outstretched leg. 'Do you feel intimidated big man?'

The gang-leader moaned. He tried to look up, but the blood running into his eyes made it impossible to see anything clearly.

Milner pushed down on the leg again. 'And you can tell all those other little bastards who think they run this estate that I'll be coming for them as well,' he stepped back to give himself some space. 'If you survive.'

Using his full body-weight Milner stamped down on top of the braced knee, snapping the leg completely in two. A short, high-pitched scream echoed around the sheltered hollow. Before it died away the gang-leader had passed into a state of deep unconsciousness.

Milner heaved the inert body onto a dilapidated, old roundabout and set about stripping off the blood-stained clothing. Finding a mobile phone Milner dropped it into his coat pocket. Sheathed and concealed in the man's waist-band was a long-bladed knife. Milner used it to slice away the remaining clothes. When he'd finished the gang-leader lay fully naked, his penis hardly visible – the acute pain and shock had caused it to shrink completely into his body.

Milner fussed over the inert form, re-arranging it into precise angles.

Before leaving he took hold of the roundabout and spun it forcibly on its axis.

Halfway up the concrete steps Milner looked back. A bright moon lit the surreal scene. On top of the slowly revolving roundabout, stretched out like a ritual human sacrifice, the man's fleshy white body lay facing the sky, his arms and legs positioned in the shape of a star.

Milner took a few moments to admire his work. With a satisfied nod he finally turned and re-crossed the empty waste-ground. Now that the fleeting savagery had disappeared his first instinct was to get home. Milner checked the house keys were still in his pocket – he couldn't risk using the back alleyway.

Mapping out a return route in his head Milner quickly exited the waste-ground and headed away from the alley. He ignored the recurring, subconscious images of what had just happened and concentrated on keeping his face turned away from passers-by.

After what he considered was a suitable distance Milner dropped the gang-leader's knife into one of Sixfields drainage outlets. Ten minutes later he was standing in a small copse of trees looking towards the front of Silver Street.

To reach his garden Milner had to cross the stretch of common that led up to a road in front of the houses. Unable to tell if the soles of his trainers were still bloodied Milner took them off. He couldn't see anyone on the pavement. There were no headlights on the road. He had to go now. At his front gate he checked neighbour's curtains for signs of movement. Nothing. It was a few steps to the front door. He quickly inserted his key and pushed open the door.

Now he had to hurry. Standing on a mat, just inside, Milner stripped off his blood-stained clothes. Dropping them onto the mat he retrieved a roll of black bin liners from the nearby stairs cupboard. Ripping one off, Milner quickly stuffed clothing, trainers and gloves into it, along with the doormat.

After dropping in the gang-leader's mobile phone he tied the bag, hoisted it over his shoulder, and went upstairs. In the bathroom Milner turned both taps full on before retrieving a small stepladder from the spare bedroom. Climbing up to the attic flap he pushed it open, shoved the bag inside, replaced the flap, came back down the steps, returned them to the spare room. Slow down. Deep breaths. The clothes were a worry but there was nothing he could do about them until tomorrow.

Sitting in the bath Milner soaped and scrubbed at his nails. After shampooing he ducked his head beneath the water several times. In all it took less than five minutes. Milner pulled the plug and quickly dried himself, cleaning the bath thoroughly afterwards.

There were other jeans, T-shirts and trainers in the wardrobe. He quickly dressed and headed downstairs. Milner didn't risk looking out from the window that overlooked his garden and the alleyway.

He hurried downstairs to the lounge where his television was still on – football – England playing a euro qualifier. Milner had been watching it when he'd left the house to check his garden. He glanced at the clock. It had been less than an hour ago. Sit down. Concentrate. Janet Sterne's child had been assaulted outside his house. The police would be here at some point. Maybe tonight.

Milner leant back and closed his eyes. He waited for the shock waves. Nothing! Although he'd nearly killed a man there was no feeling of guilt. No remorse. He looked down at his hands. Not a tremor. There was something though. Difficult to define. Not satisfaction. More a feeling of exhilaration. A small frisson of excitement sparked in the pit of his stomach 'Shit!' Had he actually enjoyed it?

The night's violence re-surfaced, a swollen, bloodied face came into sharp focus. Milner felt another rush of blood. He wanted the bastard to survive. Wanted him to suffer.

The referee's whistle blew. Milner picked up his remote and turned the television off. No score. Remember it.

Milner remained in his chair, the gang-leader's face continuing to float in and out of his sub-conscious. He may have drifted off to sleep. Three loud raps sounded at the front door.

CHAPTER 2

Sixfields Housing Estate: Friday 19 January 2007: 10.00 pm

Detective-Sergeant Frank Crosby pulled up behind the flashing blue light. Once out of his car he took a moment to scan the immediate area. His level of awareness was always sharper here. Sixfields, especially in recent years, was not a district where the police were entirely comfortable.

It felt bloody cold. Silver Street was deserted, just one or two passing cars. With temperatures down to below freezing most of the estate's residents had remained indoors tonight.

An operator at the comms-centre had called his home at nine-thirty that evening to report details of an assault. As these were fairly common-place in Sixfields the prompt appearance of an officer from CID was somewhat unusual. Police at the scene however had reported that an eighteen-month old baby and a knife was involved, making the response immediate. Crosby had just about seen it all during his thirty-five years with the force, but ill-treatment of babies and young children still had the capacity to upset him.

Light from a full, high moon allowed him to look down along Akers Lane, the back alleyway that ran between Silver Street and Wassom Avenue. Fifty yards down the lane Crosby could see PC Stewart in his high visibility yellow tabard – a small knot of bystanders gathered around him. The detective turned up his collar and headed into the alley, not feeling any initial enthusiasm for the investigation. Crosby had attended enough calls in Sixfields to know that if estate gangs were involved then assistance from other residents would be minimal.

Before leaving home Crosby had called his senior officer, Detective Inspector Oliver Rees-Bramley – but the DI didn't consider an assault in Sixfields was of high enough profile for him to turn out in this weather, and had indicated so in his usual brusque manner.

The Detective Inspector had a degree in Criminal Psychology, acquired by pounding the beat around Oxford University's colleges and lecture halls.

Crosby had served his apprenticeship out on the streets, gaining a promotion to Police Sergeant before eventually transferring to CID.

The Department's obsession with higher education and fast track promotion saw twenty-six-year-old Rees-Bramley already heading a small team of officers within CID. He was impatient to climb higher. His superiors thought him forthright and dynamic. Crosby considered him rude and arrogant.

He neared the small group of residents gathered around PC Stewart.

Tall, gangly and looking about fifteen years old, Peter Stewart had only recently graduated from police training college. The young PC's body language was not of someone in complete control. He looked relieved at Crosby's arrival.

The detective took him to one side. 'What have we got son?'

Stewart almost came to attention. 'Sir!' he consulted his pocketbook. 'At precisely nine-thirty this evening PC Jennings and I were requested to investigate reports of an assault on the Sixfields Estate. Cancelling a routine call we turned at the next available opportunity and proceeded in an easterly direction towards Sixfields by direct route,' Stewart spoke quickly. A prominent Adam's apple bobbed nervously up and down in his throat.

'Forget the route,' Crosby interrupted. 'What have you got on the assault?'

'Sir!' Stewart returned to his pocketbook. 'Mother and two young children, accosted by a gang of youths at approximately twenty minutes past nine this evening in Akers Lane. One of them had a knife.'

'Injuries?'

'Cigarette burn to the baby's hand. A small nick to her chin.'

'Who reported the incident?'

'A Mister Brown made the initial call. He telephoned emergency services to report an attack in the alleyway that ran adjacent to his rear garden.'

'Address?'

'Wassam Avenue Sir. Number thirty-one. To your immediate left. Mister Brown was waiting inside the gate on our arrival.'

'What did he have to say?'

'Mister Brown told us he was standing in his kitchen when he heard a number of screams coming from outside. Not wishing to open the door he went upstairs to look from his rear bedroom window.' Stewart's voice had quickened again. 'A woman and two young children were standing in the lane looking very distressed.'

Crosby held up his hand. 'Slow down.'

'Yes Sir!'

Stewart continued at the same speed. 'Mister Brown opened his window. The woman was screaming that her baby had been stabbed. He couldn't see anyone else in the alleyway. After telephoning the police he went downstairs and brought all three of them into the house. PC Jennings is with them now, trying to get a statement from the mother,' he snapped shut his notebook. 'That's all we've managed to ascertain at this point Sir!'

'Where's this lot come from?' Crosby jerked his head at the small crowd.

'Nearby residents Sir. One or two passers-by.'

'Did they see anything?'

'No Sir!'

'There's a surprise. Any sign of the knife?'

Stewart shook his head. 'We did make a cursory search of the surrounding area initially but couldn't find anything.'

Crosby nodded. 'OK! I'm going in to see PC Jennings. Clear the area. Get in touch with Central-Ops and let them know what's happening. Return to the car. Stay with it. Belongings tend to disappear if you leave them unattended around here. I'll get back to you as soon as I can.'

'Yes Sir!' Stewart wheeled away from Crosby and strode purposefully towards the small crowd of bystanders. 'That's it then ladies and gentlemen. Show's over. I'm sure you've all got homes to go to.'

'Give me bloody strength,' muttered Crosby, turning away. He opened the nearby garden gate and made his way up towards the house. PC Stewart continued issuing instructions to his group of residents – who showed no signs of moving on.

PC Jennings opened the back door before Crosby had a chance to knock. The detective had worked with Phil Jennings on a number of occasions. An experienced officer, he secured a crime scene quickly and efficiently, making sure witnesses were identified and placed in readiness for CID to begin their investigation. Solid, dependable, with over thirty years in the force, Crosby had a lot of time for Phil Jennings.

'Late one for you Frank,' Jennings said.

Crosby shrugged. 'What's new?' he remained outside the door. 'How are the baby's injuries?'

'Tiny cut to her chin,' Jennings said. 'The burn on her hand is superficial. I've applied some first aid but she'll need a hospital visit – ambulance is on its way.'

'Is the mother talking?'

'Some,' Jennings lowered his voice. 'Name's Janet Sterne. Single

24

mother. Two young children. They live five doors away. She was returning home when the gang jumped her. One of them held a knife to the baby's throat. When Sterne couldn't come up with any money he stubbed his cigarette out on the kid's hand.'

'And they all disappeared when Sterne screamed?' Crosby asked.

Jennings nodded. 'Evil little bastards. Local vet would be better employed by putting one or two of them down every so often.'

Crosby offered no comment. 'How old are the children?'

'Tracey's eighteen months old. Zoe's four.'

'How's the mother's state of mind?'

'Aggressive and agitated!' Jennings replied. 'She's a bit of a rough diamond – needs careful handling. Mrs Brown is well out of her comfort zone.'

'Thanks Phil,' Crosby said. 'I'd better see her then. Are you checking on your partner? It looked as if he was having problems.'

Jennings moved over to let the detective step inside. 'He'll survive. It's a steep learning curve. You remember what it was like.'

'He seems keen enough,' Crosby said.

Jennings shrugged. 'We'll see what he's like after his balls have dropped.'

The two officers passed through a small kitchen that was in urgent need of modernisation. A deep, square, white porcelain sink, with tin draining boards on either side, took up most of the room's space. Both doors on the kitchen's solitary cupboard were wide open, displaying a haphazard jumble of pots, pans and unmatched crockery. There didn't appear to be a washing machine or dishwasher, just a small fridge that trailed its cable half-way up the wall to what looked like a dangerously overloaded wall socket.

PC Jennings ushered Crosby into the living room.

An elderly couple sat joined together on a large overstuffed settee, the woman nervously twisting a small handkerchief in her fingers. Crosby judged them to be in their late seventies. They looked up with some relief at his arrival. The atmosphere felt strained. A young woman, extremely thin, her hair dyed a dark red, sat opposite. She didn't look up. The baby on her lap seemed bright enough, looking around the room with wide eyed interest. An older child stood quietly alongside them, staring up at PC Jennings in his police uniform.

Crosby turned to the elderly couple. 'Mister and Mrs Brown! My name is Detective Sergeant Crosby, attached to the West Midlands Criminal Investigation Department. I just need to have a few words with Janet here and then we can see about returning your home to you.'

Sterne's head jerked up, her eyes red and swollen. The piercing she wore through her lower lip looked uncomfortable. 'Don't fucking well come in here treating me like a child. You call me Ms Sterne. And I want more than a few words. My Tracey's just been assaulted.'

Crosby recognised the symptoms of shock and waited for Sterne's outburst to peter out. Mrs Brown looked down at the carpet, her fingers twisting the handkerchief ever more vigorously.

'Took a knife to her he did. Burnt her hand,' Sterne began to cry again. 'Bastard!' She hugged the baby closer. Zoe leant over and put an arm around them both.

Crosby lowered himself into a chair alongside. He gently picked up the baby's hand and examined an angry red mark just above her wrist.

'You do know that Tracey will need a thorough examination at the hospital,' he replaced the baby's hand. 'There is an ambulance on its way. Are you up to travelling with her? We'll arrange for transport home.'

Sterne nodded. The tension eased.

'What about Zoe?' Crosby asked. 'Is there anyone she can stay with?

'I'm coming with you Mummy,' the older child interrupted.

Sterne ignored her. 'She can go to my mother's.'

Crosby nodded. 'OK. PC Jennings will make sure Zoe gets there safely.' Sterne seemed a lot calmer. The detective risked probing a little deeper 'Did any of the gang use names?'

She shook her head.

'Would you recognise any of them again?'

Sterne nodded. 'I'd recognise that bastard with the knife. He had to pull his scarf down.'

'Would you be able to pick him out of an identity line-up?'

Yes!'

'Are you sure?'

'I was fucking well there wasn't I?'

'Have you seen him around before?'

Sterne hesitated. 'No!'

Crosby didn't push it. 'How would you describe him?'

'I've told him all that,' she jerked her head towards Jennings.

The policeman took out his notebook and turned the page. 'Well built. Not that tall. Wore a small stud in his left ear. Shaven head. He was older than the others.'

Crosby turned back to Sterne. 'Unusual clothing? Distinguishing marks?'

The woman thought about it. 'His sleeve came up, when he was holding the knife,' she replayed it in her mind. 'He had a tattoo around his wrist – those crosses you see painted on the walls around here.'

'Swastikas!'

Sterne nodded. 'Does it help?'

'It might.' Crosby was only too aware that most of the estate's white yob culture sported tattooed swastikas in one form or another. 'Which wrist were they on?'

She thought about it again before holding up her right hand.

Crosby eased himself out of the chair. 'OK Janet. We'll leave it for now. You've had a shock and Tracey needs that check-up. PC Jennings will look after you until the ambulance arrives.'

The detective stooped down next to Zoe who had remained alongside her mother, continuing to stare at the considerable bulk of PC Jennings and his uniform. 'And what about you Zoe? How are you feeling now?'

Large blue eyes in a wafer thin face turned towards him. 'I was scared of that man with the fucking knife. Is he coming back?'

'No he isn't. So you be a good girl for your Nan tonight.' Crosby shook his head. It wasn't the kid's fault. They just absorbed the everyday language of their environment. It was difficult not to be affected though – he had a grandson the same age. Zoe went back to staring at PC Jennings' uniform.

Crosby turned to Mister Brown. 'A quick word Sir. In the kitchen perhaps?'

The elderly pensioner was slow out of his chair. He followed both policemen from the room. Crosby waited until they were in the kitchen.

'Will you and your wife be OK tonight Sir? I can get someone to stay with you.'

The pensioner shook his head. 'I was just trying to help see,' his voice wavered. 'We usually keep ourselves to ourselves.'

Crosby put a hand on his arm. 'The ambulance will be here shortly. PC Jennings will stay until then. You go back in and keep your wife company. I'll tie up any loose ends tomorrow.'

Brown shuffled away. The pair of baggy old brown trousers he was wearing may have fitted him several years ago but they hung halfway down his thin hips now, the bottoms concertinaed around his slippers. He didn't seem to notice, and didn't bother trying to pull them up.

Crosby waited until the lounge door closed. 'I'll brief young Stewart as to what's happening,' he said to Jennings. 'We can knock on a few doors while we're waiting for the ambulance.'

'Do we need to get the Families Liaison Officer involved tonight?' Jennings asked.

Crosby nodded. 'Can you get in touch with her. It'll be PC Black. She can baby-sit Janet Sterne at the hospital and report back on the child's injuries.'

Jennings got busy with his radio. Crosby opened the back door and headed down to the alley. He half-expected to see PC Stewart still surrounded but the lane was clear. Crosby dug out his mobile and punched in Rees-Bramley's home number. He got the answering service. Not bothering to leave a message Crosby headed up towards the silhouette of Stewart's thin frame, clearly illuminated against the squad car's flashing blue lights. The PC smartened to attention as Crosby approached.

'Lose the lights son. They attract moths.'

'Moths Sir?'

'The two legged variety. They get very curious around here.'

'Yes Sir!' Stewart doubled around to the driver's side. Reaching inside he flicked one of the switches and extinguished the lights.

Crosby updated him about the arrangements for Janet Sterne.

'Shall I stay with the car Sir?'

Crosby shook his head. 'We're going to see what the neighbours have got to say. You take Wassom Avenue. I'll work my way along Silver Street.'

Stewart took out his pocketbook. 'Do we haul them back to the station if they're un-cooperative Sir?'

It was late. Crosby's patience was wearing thin. 'We're in the middle of Sixfields. It'll soon be midnight. Most of the residents won't even bother answering their doors at this time of night. Those that do will be less than helpful or downright abusive. We'll compare notes tomorrow. OK with all that?'

The PC closed his pocketbook. 'Yes Sir!' He went to turn away.

'Stewart!' Crosby called after him.

'Yes Sir!'

'You might want to lock the car.'

Crosby swore underneath his breath as he re-traced his steps back down the now deserted lane, stopping outside the Brown's garden gate as a start point. He dug a small torch from his coat pocket and switched it on. House numbers, crudely daubed in white paint on resident's fences, showed up clearly in the beam's light.

Not that hopeful at finding anything Crosby shone his torch into the adjoining gardens. Even under moonlight most of them looked a mess – untended tracts of mud and grass – one of which was completely covered in dog faeces. The last fence he looked over revealed a whole scrap-yard of abandoned household items, including an old iron bedstead complete with rotting mattress. Crosby gave it up.

He cut through one of the alley's side exits and emerged onto a pavement running along the length of Silver Street. The first door he knocked at brought movement to the adjacent front window. A small round face peered out from between the curtains.

Crosby stepped closer to the window. 'It's the police madam! We're making enquiries about an incident in Akers Lane earlier this evening.'

The face continued to stare at him.

He raised his voice, 'Is it possible to have a few words?'

'You're not wearing a uniform!' the woman shouted back at him.

Crosby located his warrant card and held it flat against the window. 'CID madam. We do not wear uniforms.'

'You'll have to come back tomorrow. We don't open our door to anyone after ten.' The woman closed her curtains.

Crosby muttered underneath his breath and walked around to the next house. He rapped at the door. A bedroom window opened above him

'What!' The face that leaned out was clearly irritated.

'Good evening Sir. I'm Detective Sergeant Crosby from Studwell CID.'

'Fuck Off!' The window closed.

Crosby wasn't in the frame of mind to pursue it. Continuing to work his way along Silver Street, the detective found house-lights being switched off at his approach.

He arrived at number sixty-nine. Another grey head bobbed at the window. Crosby flashed his warrant card. 'Apologies for the late hour madam. I am a plainclothes police officer from Studwell CID making enquiries about an assault that took place earlier this evening in Akers Lane.'

The woman disappeared. Crosby was surprised to hear a chain rattle at the front door. It cracked open. 'Could I see your identification again please officer?'

The detective pushed his card against the gap. Another rattle of security chain and the door opened. Crosby was momentarily taken aback that the figure in front of him was male. He quickly recovered himself. 'Detective Sergeant Crosby Sir. Can you spare a few moments?'

The man's personal appearance had startled Crosby. He was thin, almost skeletal – the T-shirt hanging loose on his tall frame. Deep creases ran down both sides of a long, angular face, the shock of thick, white hair, contrasting vividly with his thick, black eyebrows. It was difficult to estimate an age but he looked fit and alert, his eyes a piercing, intense blue.

'You're welcome to step inside Officer. It must be freezing out there.'
A well-educated voice. No accent.

The detective declined. 'I've a few more calls to make.'

'You mentioned an assault,' the man said.

Crosby nodded. He took out his pocketbook. 'A young mother and her children were accosted in Akers Lane about an hour ago. Can you recall hearing or seeing anything unusual at that time?'

The man shook his head. 'I've been watching the football all evening. Our rear gardens are unusually long. You'd have to be standing in the kitchen to hear any noise coming from the alleyway,' he paused. 'Was the assault serious?'

'Serious enough,' Crosby replied. 'We're waiting for an ambulance. Just a precaution hopefully.'

'Happens around here all too often,' the man said. 'And it's on the increase. A higher police profile wouldn't go amiss.'

Crosby didn't respond. 'Could I trouble you for a name Sir?'

'Certainly Officer. It's Milner! Robert Milner.'

Crosby made a note. 'Thank you for your time Mister Milner. There may be some follow-up questions at a later date.'

'I'd be disappointed if there wasn't Officer.'

'Disappointed?'

Milner smiled. 'Disappointed if the investigation was left to gather dust after a few cursory questions. Another common occurrence.'

The flashing blue lights of an ambulance appeared in the distance. They watched its progress along Silver Street before it turned and disappeared into Akers Lane.

'The Emergency Services seem to take longer and longer these days,' Milner said.

'I believe the original call was downgraded from an emergency.' Crosby was aware the man's remarks were beginning to annoy him.

Milner stepped back. 'If that's all then Officer?'

Crosby nodded. The door closed on him.

He continued along Silver Street for another twenty minutes or so but the response was minimal. He turned back. By the time Crosby returned to his car he found a completely deserted alleyway – both ambulance and police car had left.

On the drive home, and for no particular reason, Crosby registered that Milner had razor sharp creases ironed into the front of his jeans. 'So what!' the detective muttered to himself. He turned the car's heating down and concentrated on keeping his eyes from closing.

Looking out from his rear-bedroom window Robert Milner watched the two paramedics assist Janet Sterne and her baby into the ambulance parked opposite. Sterne's other child and a policeman stood alongside. In the distance he could see a squad car waiting at the alleyway's entrance. Milner stayed at the window after both ambulance and police car had left. A third vehicle remained. He continued to wait. Fifteen minutes later, the detective who had spoken to him earlier returned to his car. He wasted no time in turning the engine over and pulling away.

Milner stood in the darkness. The clothes would have to be moved, and he didn't want to be seen carrying a large, black plastic bag out of the house tomorrow morning – it would register with his neighbours.

He quickly made a decision and acted on it. Retrieving the bin-liner from his attic Milner pulled on a grey fleece and collected a small torch from the kitchen drawer. Hoisting the bag of clothes over his shoulder he opened his back door and headed down the garden path.

The lane looked deserted. Milner turned left outside his gate, reaching the alleyway's entrance without seeing anyone. Across the road, directly opposite, were two blocks of garages. Milner took a few moments to make sure the area was clear before crossing to his own garage. Unlocking the metal door he pulled it up and over before stepping inside. After retrieving the gang leader's mobile from inside the plastic bin-liner Milner quickly exited the garage and re-locked its door.

Moving into an adjacent patch of deep shadow Milner switched on the mobile and punched in three nines on the keypad.

'Please state the service you require. Police, Fire or Ambulance.'

'Police!'

The connection was made. 'West Midlands Police Communications Centre. Please state your name and current location.'

Milner put a hand to his mouth, 'A man has been attacked and left unconscious on waste ground at the northern end of Akers Lane in Sixfields.'

'Please state your name and current location caller.'

Milner broke the connection and walked around behind his garage block. He dropped the mobile onto a concreted area and crushed it into tiny pieces beneath his heel. After using his torch to pick up all of the fragments Milner scattered them into nearby bushes.

Back at the road-side there were no headlights and the pavement was clear. Milner crossed over and disappeared down the alley. Two minutes later he was un-locking his back door.

Milner set about scrubbing the linoleum flooring – laid throughout the house apart from his two bedrooms – he considered the covering hygienic. Completely absorbed in his cleaning routines Milner also vacuumed the bedroom carpets and took an anti-bacterial spray to all flat surfaces above floor level. The obsessive cleaning had nothing to do with removing traces of forensic evidence, it's what he did on a regular basis, or whenever he was agitated and stressed. The comforting routines were familiar, they had a calming effect on him.

When Milner undressed and laid his clothes in a neat pile on the settee it was one o'clock in the morning. He sat upright in an armchair with a blanket around him. Sleep wouldn't come. His mind was too active.

Milner was due to meet his daughter in Birmingham later that day, a regular lunch date – he had to ensure there were no changes to his routine – nothing to raise suspicions. Loosely formed plans continued to dominate his thoughts. He also had a headache. Even during his breakdown he'd never suffered from headaches.

Sheer physical exhaustion finally forced him into a deep sleep. Shortly afterwards the wail of a nearby ambulance siren registered somewhere in his subconscious – it didn't wake him.

CHAPTER 3

Sixfields Housing Estate: Saturday 20 January 2007: 07.15 am

07.15 am: Milner woke with a start, instantly aware of what had happened the previous evening. Still no feelings of guilt. He knew there wouldn't be. For the first time in ten years there was a purpose to the day. A purpose to his life. Plans to be made. He felt refreshed and energised, anxious to get started. Milner checked the time. The first test this morning was to hold his nerve.

After his phone call to the police last night he had to assume the gang-leader had been found. Initial investigations would have already identified the victim as Janet Sterne's assailant, and that would result in more door to door questioning, probably this morning. What time though? He couldn't leave the house until eight thirty – anything earlier might be noticed and passed on. Even at this stage Milner knew that police attention would focus on anyone who suddenly changed their routines.

07.30 am: Another hour yet. Milner got up from his chair, carefully replacing and re-aligning the cushions. He took his blanket and clothes upstairs. Selecting a fresh disposable razor from the bathroom cabinet Milner shaved with meticulous care. As was his habit he shaved again with the same razor, before dropping it into a small bin. Stubble irritated him. It was not allowed to develop. Squeezing out an exact length of toothpaste onto his brush Milner counted to one hundred whilst he cleaned his teeth. He dressed in a plain white T-shirt and blue denim jeans before going back downstairs.

Breakfast consisted of porridge and a glass of water. Bowl, spoon and glass were washed up, dried thoroughly, and put away. Milner was aware of his routines, a result of the breakdown. Resisting all attempts by doctors to embark on various courses of medication Milner had survived well enough, and come through the other side. After ten years he'd learnt to live with the symptoms, and to a certain degree control them, an achievement he was still proud of. Milner finished wiping down his worktops before returning to the lounge.

08.00 am: The on-going wait was unnerving. Although logic told him there were no speeding squad cars only minutes away, the bag of clothes still sat in his garage. He fretted. Until they were removed he was not in control of the situation. Milner forced himself to sit down. He rehearsed his responses to the next round of questioning. When the investigation did return he would enjoy the verbal sparring.

08.30 am: Milner opened the front door. Before he was able to close it there was a cry from the stretch of open common, opposite his house. Milner spun round. Donald was heading across the green towards him. He'd probably been waiting outside the house since first light. Milner slowly exhaled. He watched Donald amble across the common, uncoordinated, like a young child trying to manoeuvre an adult's body.

The two of them had first met three years ago, when Donald proudly told Milner that it was his birthday, and he was twenty-five years old. The following day Milner had presented him with a belated birthday card, and the bond between them was sealed. Thereafter, Donald told anyone who cared to listen that his two best friends were Spike and Mister Milner.

Spike was an overweight cross-bred Labrador, Donald's constant companion and always at his owner's heels. The pair were inseparable.

Milner always tried to find time for Donald. He recognised a certain affinity with him. Both had suffered abuse within the community – from those elements who neither tolerated nor understood the differences that life can throw up.

Spike and his equally overweight owner laboured up a slight incline towards the roadside. Milner crossed over to meet them. It would give him a better view of the garage block to his right.

Donald's big, round open face was flushed from his exertions. He held a poop scooper in one hand and a small black plastic bag in the other. 'Hello Mister Milner. Are you driving your car today?' Coming from his adult frame, the voice was unexpectedly child-like.

Milner glanced towards the garage block. It looked to be all clear. 'I am Donald. To meet my daughter.'

'Can we walk to the garage with you?' Donald's weak eyesight had focused on a point beyond Milner's shoulder.

'I'm in a hurry this morning Donald.' Milner continued to monitor the garages. 'Maybe next time.'

Donald produced a wrap-around purse from his pocket and pulled at the Velcro fastening. 'Could you get Spike some more of those doggy chocs

Mister Milner? Our shop doesn't sell them.'

'It'll be my treat Donald.' Milner scanned the street. 'Put your money away.'

Donald's large round face lit up. 'Did you hear that Spike?'

Panting heavily, the dog plonked himself down, a large, pink tongue lolling from the corner of his mouth. He wagged his tail furiously as Donald bent to tell him about the chocolates.

Milner extricated himself and crossed back over the road, towards the garage-block. He sniffed the morning air. Even at this early hour the temperature was appreciably higher than yesterday – an overnight frost had turned to heavy dew on the grassy stretch of parkland.

The block was deserted, his garage door intact. Although most cars on the estate wouldn't appeal particularly to Sixfields' young joyriders, vehicles were still routinely hijacked and abused on a daily basis.

Milner unlocked the garage's swing door and pushed it upwards. The black, plastic bin-liner was where he'd left it the night before. Opening his boot, Milner placed the bag inside. He closed the lid. There was very little space in the garage, and Milner had to carefully edge his way along the car's length, before he could open the driver's door and ease himself inside. Milner's old Rover had been well maintained over the years and it kicked into life at the first turn of his key.

After reversing the car outside Milner left it idling whilst he closed and locked the garage door. Trying not to appear hurried he climbed back inside and snapped on his seat belt. Taking a couple of deep breaths Milner manoeuvred the car around. Nearly there. A few more seconds and he would be clear of the area.

Donald and Spike were still standing by the roadside. Milner raised his hand as he drove past. Donald saluted. He continued to follow the car's direction as it disappeared up towards the shopping centre.

08.40 am: After watching Milner's car disappear into the distance Donald set off for home. He lived with his parents on the far side of the common and had strict instructions to be back for breakfast by nine o'clock.

When two squad cars suddenly screeched to a halt across the road, Donald and Spike turned to watch several uniformed police emerge from their vehicles and gather on the pavement.

08.45 am: Milner eased the old Rover up through its gears as he followed the main route out of Sixfields. He approached the nearby Park-Gate Shopping Centre. As the precinct lay barely half a mile from Silver Street Milner was familiar with its layout – identical, two-storey retail units shaped around the large pedestrianised square – a design that certainly hadn't stretched the imagination of its architect.

Inside the pedestrianised square, occupying its centre, was a large concrete fountain, long since dried up. The empty pool now served as a convenient receptacle for shoppers to dump their litter and empty bottles.

Although the precinct looked fairly quiet as Milner drove past it was a natural gathering place for Sixfields' anti-social elements to meet – groups of them would congregate there at all times of the day and night. Local dealers would soon be busy in its large car park, servicing a steady stream of customers from inside and outside the estate. 'Bastards!' muttered Milner.

He glimpsed shutters and grilles being removed from window fronts as the precinct prepared to open its doors. The car's slipstream scattered empty cartons and paper cups into the road as Milner passed two fast food outlets near the Shopping Centre entrance – discarded pieces of half-eaten chicken and burger meat lay beneath the overflowing waste bins.

As ParkGate disappeared in his rear view mirror, the local comprehensive loomed into view. During the week DeneValley's entrance gates had to be manned by two high profile security guards. At weekends and holidays, the tall, wrought iron entrance gates were secured by padlock and chain. Most pupils who made it to their final year at DeneValley would have long since been co-opted into one of the many gangs that controlled Sixfields.

Fed by an irregular police presence, Sixfields' gang culture flourished. The gangs in turn were manipulated and controlled by a well-established drugs trade, its aggressive marketing techniques addicting members from an early age. Victims that weren't able to fund their habit by acting as runners or lookouts turned to petty crime and prostitution – offences largely ignored by the authorities.

Although an overstretched police force still reacted quickly enough to violent crime within Sixfields it would probably admit to losing routine day to day control of the estate many years previously.

Milner reached the estate's original six meadows, where the first houses had been constructed, and after which Sixfields was named. Row upon row of neglected, rundown facades passed in a blur, the occasional, well-maintained property, few and far between. As the streets became busier Milner's progress slowed. The estate was beginning to wake up and go about its business. Colourful saris and the more severe burkha appeared as he wound his way through areas populated mainly by Hindu and Moslem cultures. Milner smiled to himself. It didn't seem to matter where individuals were initially allocated – all minority groups with a similar ethnic background eventually ended up living next door to each other.

Sixfields' majority white population rubbed shoulders uneasily with its black and Asian immigrant communities – a recent influx of east European refugees from the war-torn Balkan republics added to the volatile mix. Prejudiced abuse, not surprisingly, was an everyday occurrence, routinely carried out by all sides.

09.00 am: Milner had been driving through Sixfields for about fifteen minutes when the blur of concrete came to an abrupt end, giving way to rural villages and open countryside. Clear of the estate he joined a busy dual-carriageway and headed towards the suburbs of Birmingham.

CHAPTER 4

Studwell OCU HQ: Saturday 20 January 2007: 08.30 am

In 2007 the West Midlands Police Force was made up of twenty-one Operational Command Units (OCU), administered by a central headquarters based at Lloyd House in the city of Birmingham. Each OCU covered a specific geographical area headed by a Senior Superintendent, who was responsible for day to day policing within that area.

Divisional HQ for Studwell's OCU was based at the old police station in Stoney Lane. The tall, red bricked, Victorian building was home to over two hundred uniformed police officers and a Criminal Investigation Department. Housed in a separate annex behind the main building, Studwell's CID consisted of two small, inter-dependant teams, each one headed by a Detective Inspector.

DI Oliver Rees-Bramley, who led one of the CID teams, swept into his place of work at exactly eight-thirty am. Carrying a leather attaché briefcase in one hand, and slimline laptop in the other, he strode briskly through a narrow corridor of unoccupied desks towards his office. Five foot six inches tall, with thinning fair hair, his short purposeful stride covered the ground with deceptive speed.

Crosby watched his approach with grudging admiration, the man exuded a supreme air of self-confidence. There was no concession to the fact it was a weekend either, dress standards had been maintained. Detective Inspector Rees-Bramley didn't do casual. The suit was made to measure, a single breasted, blue worsted pinstripe. A dark red silk tie reflected vividly against the crisp white shirt, and his black Oxford brogues had been polished to a mirror shine.

He reached Crosby's desk. 'Good morning Frank. My office! Ten minutes!' the voice was clipped, short.

'Yes Sir,' Crosby replied, as his DI breezed past. Rees-Bramley closed the office door behind him. His predecessor had always left it ajar.

Crosby had been Rees-Bramley's Detective Sergeant for six months now but had still not warmed to his DI's brusque manner. It was especially irritating this morning as Crosby had only managed four hours sleep last night, and that always left him feeling generally tetchy and out of sorts.

Crosby continued to nurse his mug of black coffee, still waiting for the three sugars to kick in. He looked along the row of functional, standard issue desks, in-trays piled high with half-completed forms and reports. Although state of the art IT equipment now stored data gathered at all levels of an investigation, the department was still drowning under a sea of computer printouts.

'Paperless offices!' Crosby muttered. He checked his watch. As there were no high priority investigations currently running in his section very few desks were due to be manned this weekend – the extreme violence of the second assault that Crosby had attended last night might change all that. It certainly had the attention of his DI this morning, who was responsible for the bulk of criminal investigation on the Sixfields estate.

The attack would have also registered with those responsible for the region's Major Investigation Units, who retained ultimate responsibility for investigating all homicide and suspicious deaths in the West Midlands area.

The office door swung inwards. Detective Constable Paul Berne, dressed in jeans and white T-shirt, wandered casually into the room. Six foot tall, with closely cropped black hair, Berne had only been with Studwell CID a short time. Previously with The Met in London, he had opted for a tour in the provinces as a means of transferring to the rank of Detective Constable. Crosby still had reservations about him. 'Bit of a Jack the Lad,' was one expression that sprang to mind, always first with the easy chat and ready opinion. The male chauvinist was never too far away either – 'Persuading a woman into bed isn't the problem, it's getting them to leave afterwards.'

Although competent enough Berne certainly didn't measure up to the high regard he had of himself. Crosby was keeping a close eye on him.

Reaching his desk Berne shouted a cheery, 'Morning Sarge,' down the office before throwing an expensive-looking leather jacket over the back of his chair. Crosby contemplated his own regulation sports jacket and grey slacks. Twenty-three years old, unmarried, attractive to the opposite sex – maybe that was the problem Crosby had with him.

As Berne hadn't originally been rostered for duty today he must have also been summoned in by Rees-Bramley. The DI was obviously keen to make some early progress regarding last night's major incident.

The office door opened again.

Crosby nodded a greeting to DC Taylor.

Twenty-one years old, with a figure that turned heads, Grace Taylor was third generation Jamaican, her paternal grandfather having emigrated to Birmingham in the late fifties. As she negotiated her way through the narrow corridor of desks Crosby caught himself watching her progress. He noticed Paul Berne doing the same. Although Taylor was far too level headed and professional to develop close relationships with work colleagues DC Berne's male chauvinism had yet to work that out, and he persisted in his attempts to impress her.

Crosby thought Taylor had every chance of rising through the ranks. A disciplined mind, that paid attention to routine and detail, she was also gifted with the flashes of inspiration that detectives rely on to develop leads.

Taylor stopped at the large desk she shared with Berne. Switching on what he considered his most winning smile Berne received a nod of the head and a formal, 'Good Morning,' in return.

Crosby drained the last of his coffee and wandered down to join them. 'DI arrived five minutes ago. Better not keep him waiting.'

'Sounds serious Sarge,' Taylor said. 'I've been listening to radio reports on the way in about an assault in Sixfields last night. Is that why we're here?'

Crosby nodded. 'Not a good night to be on call.'

Berne and Taylor followed him along the room towards Rees-Bramley's office. He knocked at the DI's door.

'Come!'

Crosby ushered the two detectives inside. Rees-Bramley's office was bare and impersonal, completely devoid of any clutter. No photographs on his desk and no pictures on the wall, apart from his framed university degree. Taking up most space in the office was a long rectangular table, positioned at right angles to Rees-Bramley's desk. From his viewpoint he was able to look down the table at whoever was sitting in the two rows of evenly spaced chairs.

Rees-Bramley continued to peck away at the keys on his open laptop.

'Take a seat!' He didn't look up. The three officers pulled out chairs from the table and sat down. When Rees-Bramley finally snapped shut the lid of his laptop he took a moment to look at each detective in turn.

'For Christ's sake get on with it,' Crosby muttered inwardly. He thought the practice was ill-mannered and unnecessary, along with the DI's other habit of swivelling in his chair to look out of the window when you were talking to him.

'Frank!' Rees-Bramley eventually said. 'You had to attend two incidents in Sixfields last night.'

Crosby nodded. 'Both within half a mile of each other,' he opened his pocketbook and placed it on the table. 'The first call-out was Akers Lane, a rear alleyway that runs between Silver Street and Wassom Avenue. One of the local gangs confronted a young unmarried mother and her two children. The assault took place at approximately nine-fifteen.'

Berne and Taylor began making notes.

'The mother's name is Janet Sterne. Zoe's four years old. Tracey is eighteen months. They live in Wassom Avenue, number twenty-seven.'

'Do we have a motive?' Rees-Bramley asked.

Crosby shrugged. 'Money? Intimidation? One of the gang held a knife to the baby's throat before stubbing out a cigarette on the back of her hand. When Sterne became hysterical and woke up the neighbourhood they all scattered.'

'Would she recognise any of them again?'

'She seemed confident enough about identifying the ringleader when I took her statement. That might change. An ambulance arrived at eleven o'clock to take mother and daughter to Millfields Hospital. The Families Liaison Officer has since reported the baby's injuries as superficial.'

'Any witnesses to the incident?'

'No Sir, but PC Stewart has left a name and address to follow up on as a result of his enquiries last night.'

Rees-Bramley nodded. 'And the second call-out?'

'A particularly brutal attack on an unidentified white male.' Crosby turned to another page of his pocketbook. 'Fractured skull. Broken kneecap. Severe facial damage. Deep lacerations along the length of his back. Surgeons at the hospital have operated on him but he's yet to recover consciousness. His condition remains critical.'

'Any weapons involved?'

'A heavy, blunt object to the back of his head caused the skull fracture. Doctors at the hospital who examined him reported several rock fragments embedded in the wound.'

'Where was he found?'

'The Akers Lane alleyway leads directly onto undeveloped waste-land and a derelict children's play-area. He'd been stripped of all his clothes and staked out on top of an old roundabout there.'

'What have Scene of Crimes turned up?'

'Nothing as yet.'

'No one saw anything presumably?'

Crosby shook his head. 'There may be something from the house-to-house we're carrying out at the moment.'

'Who raised the alarm?'

'Our comms-centre took an anonymous call at eleven thirty last night.'

Rees-Bramley looked up. 'Anonymous?'

Crosby nodded. 'From a mobile. And the positioning of masts in that area means we can't get a precise fix on where the call was made from. The mobile itself is no longer emitting a traceable signal.'

'What about the registered owner?'

'Leonard Duggan. Lives about three miles from where our victim was found. He's an eighty-five year old widower.'

'You've checked him out?'

'Sent someone round last night. He wasn't even aware the phone had gone missing.'

Rees-Bramley got up from his desk and walked across to the office's white board. 'Anything else?'

'The waste ground victim's right wrist has a bracelet of small swastikas tattooed around it,' Crosby said. 'Janet Sterne reported a similar tattoo around her assailant's wrist.' The detective shrugged. 'If it is the same person then location and timings would indicate he was attacked shortly after carrying out the assault on Sterne and her child.'

Rees-Bramley nodded. He turned to Berne and Taylor. 'Initial thoughts?'

Berne was the first to speak. 'There's a lot of friction between local gangs at the moment. He could have been jumped by one of them.'

Taylor shook her head. 'Those confrontations are usually hit and run affairs. Staying behind to strip and display your victim is the handiwork of someone working to a different agenda.'

Berne looked slightly annoyed. 'Some of these gangs do have their own resident psychos.'

'Not only that,' Taylor continued over the top of him, 'there'd be guns or knives involved. Being struck on the back of the head with a rock sounds more opportunist.'

Rees-Bramley lifted his eyebrows a fraction, waiting for the exchanges to finish. 'Lines of enquiry then,' the DI said. 'First we need to establish the identity of our hospital patient.' He turned to Crosby. 'Frank! Alert the usual media outlets with a description. Someone out there must know him. There will be interest – the local press have already been tipped off with details of the circumstances he was found in.'

Crosby made a note.

'Grace!' Rees-Bramley picked up a marker from the whiteboard's shelf. 'Arrange a one-to-one with Janet Sterne. See if she's still prepared to carry out this identification? He must be practically unrecognisable at the moment but I need to know what her mind-set is. And see what else you can turn up on that stolen mobile.'

'Sir!'

'Paul!' Rees-Bramley continued, filling up the board. 'Check your sources in Sixfields. If our man is attached to one of the local gangs your contacts should be able to tell us who's disappeared off the streets since last night. And get in touch with the hospital. See if anyone's turned up to claim him.'

'Guv!' Berne responded.

Crosby stopped himself from glancing across at Grace Taylor's reaction. He always found it amusing that the formally correct Rees-Bramley never corrected Berne for occasionally addressing him as 'Guv!' He assumed that his DI thought it conjured up some kind of macho television image from the seventies.

'Frank!' Rees-Bramley turned back his way. 'Have a look at our workload and see what we can re-prioritise. I'll need some extra manpower. If this does turn into a full blown murder investigation I want the MIU briefed and able to hit the ground running.'

Most detectives considered a Major Investigation Unit as an elite, specialist posting, and Rees-Bramley made no secret of the fact that it was where he thought his talents would be best employed. Crosby suspected the high profile status enjoyed by Senior MIU Officers in charge of murder and homicide cases was the real attraction for his DI. In the meantime Rees-Bramley spent a considerable amount of time away from Studwell attending the requisite courses and workshops in readiness for the right opportunity.

'I'll be out and about with you today Frank.' Rees-Bramley had put down the marker pen and returned to his desk. 'I need to get a feel for this one. We'll take a look at the playground site and follow through on PC Stewart's call from last night.'

Crosby groaned inwardly. Being shadowed around by his DI was not how he'd envisaged the day. Rees-Bramley was a skilled co-ordinator, perfectly able to manage staff and resources from an office – he was completely out of his comfort zone handling un-cooperative and hostile elements on the street. Crosby certainly didn't want him glued to his rear-end all day doing everything by the book.

Rees-Bramley swivelled his chair round to Berne and Taylor. 'I'd like swift inroads on this one please. Interim reports by tomorrow morning. If anything major does turn up during the course of today contact DS Crosby or myself immediately.' He waved them towards the door. 'On your way!'

The two younger detectives were quickly out of their chairs. Crosby took his time. He didn't feel the need to impress at this stage of his career.

'With you in ten Frank.' Rees-Bramley flipped up the lid of his laptop again. 'I'm looking forward to getting out and about. I seem to have been driving this desk for months.'

'I'll enjoy the company Sir,' Crosby said, his face expressionless.

By the time he left Rees-Bramley's office, Berne and Taylor were busy on the phones. There was a knock at the far end of the room and PC Stewart's face peered hesitantly around the doorway. Crosby waved him in.

Underneath his yellow tabard Stewart was wearing a lightweight stab vest. It made him far too bulky to navigate the narrow corridor of desks and he dislodged a stack of papers onto the floor as he passed through.

'Prat!' muttered Berne.

Stewart's face flushed as he bent to retrieve the papers.

Taylor mouthed a silent 'It's OK' to him as she continued her conversation on the phone.

Replacing the papers, Stewart carefully edged his way past the remaining desks towards Crosby. Managing to reach the Detective Sergeant without further mishap Stewart lowered his long frame into a nearby chair. 'Did you get my message Sir?' he asked.

Crosby nodded. 'A Mister Broad wasn't it? Wassom Avenue. Number thirty-nine. What did he have to say?'

'Most of it was to do with lack of policing on the estate Sir.'

'You'll get used to it. What about the assault on Sterne and her children?'

'Mister Broad told me that one of his neighbours witnessed it.'

Crosby leant forward. 'Did he now! And how would he know that?'

'Wouldn't say Sir.'

Crosby picked up a pen. 'What's the name of this witness?'

'He wouldn't tell me.'

Crosby put the pen back down. 'Wouldn't tell you?' Stewart hesitated and shuffled his feet. 'Spit it out son!' the detective said.

'He wanted to speak with a more senior officer,' Stewart stammered. 'Told me to come back when I'd got hairs around my dick.'

If Crosby was amused he didn't show it 'We'll sort Mister Broad out later today. Don't take it to heart.'

Stewart got to his feet. 'Thank you Sir. I'll get back then.'

The young PC made his way carefully back down the office, nodding self-consciously at Grace Taylor as he passed her desk.

Rees-Bramley appeared at Crosby's shoulder. 'Ready?'

Crosby got up from his desk. The DI's short, staccato steps had already opened up a gap between them. Crosby followed the fast disappearing back of his DI at a more sedate pace.

CHAPTER 5

Milner allowed the flow of busy shoppers to carry him along the pedestrianised thoroughfare. Occasionally he would pause to look at a window display, but mostly he just drifted with the current, an anonymous face in the crowd. On another day he would have envied the urgency of those about him but this morning was different, he also had important business to focus on, a schedule to maintain. The morality and raw emotion of last night was no longer an issue.

Forgotten job skills had begun to re-surface. Evaluate the risk – calculate percentages – implement a solution. Christ! He could actually hear his brain humming. What was so wrong anyway? They were vermin. It was just waste disposal. If he was successful the local community might even bestow some sort of award on him.

Milner found the idea amusing. Someone nearby laughed out loud. When he looked up to find several passers-by staring at him, his new found confidence stared right back at them. They hurried on.

A powerful adrenalin rush surged through him. Milner embraced it. His ex-wife would be proud of him, and it would show that scheming bitch of a daughter he could still be of some use. Milner's brow furrowed. That didn't sound quite right. Surely it was his ex-wife who was the scheming bitch. He paused to re-arrange the words in his head before continuing along the street.

The shop he'd been looking for came into view on the opposite side of the street. His long, spindly legs carried him across to it in less than half a dozen strides.

Inside the charity shop, long rails of overstuffed second-hand clothes took up most of the available floor space. A frail-looking pensioner was having to use all her strength to prise apart the tightly packed garments in her search for a bargain. Milner made his way past the wall-to-wall shelves of dog-eared paperbacks and obsolete video tapes as he headed for a rack of men's clothing at the far end of the shop.

Scanning the rack Milner pulled out a pair of old jeans, white T-shirt, and a well-worn green fleece. He quickly checked the sizes, anxious to leave – the claustrophobic collection of second-hand jumble had begun to make him edgy. Lined up along the wall was a row of scuffed old trainers. He picked out a pair. Turning one of the shoes over to check its size he found himself staring down at the front cover of a paperback.

Milner spun round. It took him a moment to work out where he was – the trainers were still at the far end of the shop, where he'd been previously standing. He went back to collect them and made his way to the till. An over-friendly, middle-aged charity volunteer stuffed his purchases into a white plastic bag. Her non-stop incessant, chatter irritated him.

Outside the shop, Milner sat on a nearby wooden bench. The episode inside had been unnerving and he dwelt on it. A pale, watery sun broke through thin cloud – it gave him a lift, and Milner convinced himself the disorientation was due to last night's events. He cleared his mind and stood up, before heading back along New Street, towards the Bullring Shopping Centre entrance.

The rendezvous with his daughter was always in the Bullring – Lucy liked to browse its shops. Milner took the opportunity to visit a museum, or the library, joining her later for lunch. They met every Saturday, in the same café, at the same time. His daughter understood the reliance he placed on following a strict routine. She knew how important it was to his stability.

Milner arrived at the café to find the table where they usually sat was already occupied. It annoyed him. He glared at the couple. They looked uncomfortable. Good! It might encourage them to leave. Milner found another table and re-arranged the crooked place mats to his satisfaction before sitting down. He remained bolt upright in his chair, waiting for Lucy to arrive. The café's wall clock clicked round to midday.

Milner couldn't imagine how he would have survived the past few years without his daughter's support. Still at school, when his job and marriage started to crumble around him, it was Lucy who remained in contact throughout the bitter divorce proceedings and some very dark days. Even now she was the only one from his previous life who kept in touch with him.

Always a very bright child, Lucy was currently into her second year of a Business Research and Consultancy course at Aston University. Although she occupied a flat close to the university, Lucy went back home most weekends – where Milner's ex-wife still made sporadic attempts to prise father and daughter apart.

The couple next to Milner still showed no signs of leaving. He checked the time again. She was three minutes late. Milner drummed his fingers against the table-top.

Lucy bounced through the café door at four minutes past twelve o'clock, her jet-black curls framing a heart-shaped face – his colouring – at least it used to be. He waved her over. Carrying several designer carrier bags she threaded her way through the tightly packed tables. Lucy liked her clothes, and thanks to Henry's generous allowance she frequently indulged herself.

Henry was Lucy's step-father, a property broker – not that he needed to work – his inheritance had been substantial. Milner's ex-wife had selected husband number two carefully, a choice that maintained her in the style she both demanded and expected.

Although Milner didn't begrudge the advantages Lucy gained from her step-father's estate, the fact that he wasn't able to provide them still hurt.

Lucy finally made it to the table and dumped her bags. She wrapped both arms around Milner's neck and gave him a hug. 'Kissing your Dad on the cheek is just too formal,' she'd once told him. He appreciated the close contact.

As Lucy sat down Milner jerked his head at the nearby couple. 'They've taken our table.'

Lucy glanced around. 'Bastards! I'll get the manager to throw them out.'

Milner laughed. His daughter's cheerfulness was infectious and he relaxed. They spent the next hour enjoying a familiar ritual of catching up on the previous few days and eating their lunch. As his own weekly routine hardly varied it was usually Lucy who did all the talking, bubbling about life at the university and her busy course schedule. Milner just sat there enjoying the sound of his daughter's voice. She was always very careful to avoid any topic that involved her mother and step-father – Milner still harboured a bitter resentment over the divorce and blamed his ex-wife for the depression and breakdown that followed.

Lucy steered the conversation towards Sixfields. 'You really ought to start thinking about another place to live now Dad. You've made so much progress lately, I'm sure you could cope with moving on.'

Milner shrugged. 'Something I still can't face Lu. You know how important my routines are. If I even begin to think about change and upheaval I start to panic.'

Lucy shook her head. 'You can't enjoy living there.'

'It wouldn't really matter where I lived Lu, the problems would just move with me. At least I'm settled and stable where I am.'

She shrugged and put her hand over his. 'Whatever you're comfortable with Dad.'

Deep down they both knew the move would never happen. There was an awkward pause. 'I take it the invite for a weekend stop over is still on hold then?' Lucy said.

Milner shifted in his seat. He had always discouraged Lucy from visiting his house in Sixfields. 'I have my pride,' was his usual response. It didn't stop her from trying.

The coffee arrived and it was Milner, unusually, who said he had to leave early. 'Some business to attend to.'

Lucy was intrigued. 'What sort of business?'

'More of a favour really.' Milner shifted in his seat again. 'An errand for a neighbour.'

Lucy laughed. 'You don't speak to any of your neighbours. It must be illegal or there's a woman involved.'

Although Milner laughed along with her a tremor in his hand caused the cup he was holding to rattle in its saucer.

They said their goodbyes outside the café. Lucy gave her father an extra hug before heading off to the shops again. After watching his daughter disappear from view Milner re-focused on the blood-stained clothes still in his car boot. He turned towards the exit.

Sixfields Housing Estate: Saturday 20 January 2007: 12 noon

Distinctive yellow and black barrier tape, its colours contrasting sharply with the grey monotone shade of an overcast day, indicated a police crime scene. Crosby looked down into the cordoned-off area from a high, grassy bank.

A row of dilapidated old swings, standing derelict in the far corner, had long since lost their original wooden seats – the loose chains that remained hung down from the framework's crossbar, swinging gently in the breeze.

The playground's single roundabout lay tilted at an angle, most of its side panels either splintered or smashed inwards. Clearly visible on top of the roundabout was a large dark stain, evidence of where the victim's blood had soaked into its dry, bare wood.

Crosby glanced across to where Rees-Bramley was still deep in conversation with Scene-of-Crimes-Officer Ian Brown, a no-nonsense former PC from the Govan area of Glasgow – the SOCO and his assistant were currently involved in a painstaking investigation of the playground and its immediate surrounds. Along with the victim's ripped clothing, a number of blood and fibre samples found at the scene had already been lifted and sent to forensic laboratories for further analysis – but fingerprints lifted from metal bars on top of the roundabout were not of a high enough quality apparently. There had also been very little feedback from a team of PC's who had earlier carried out house-to-house enquiries and a detailed search of Akers Lane.

Raised voices caused Crosby to look up. The discussion taking place alongside him was becoming a little heated – Rees-Bramley had been badgering the senior SOCO about footprints all morning. The DI wanted to know how many were involved in the attack and where they had exited the waste ground. Brown had already told him there looked to be just one pair of bloodied footprints but these had only shown up on the playground's concrete steps.

'There must be blood traces further out than that,' Rees-Bramley persisted.

'How far did you widen the search?'

The SOCO's ruddy colour deepened. 'All exit routes from the wasteland have been examined Sir! We found no evidence of footprints, bloodied or otherwise,' he carefully spaced each word. 'I cannot divert resources to those particular areas again as my assistant and I are still engaged in processing the site itself.'

A muffled ring-tone cut him short. Rees-Bramley retrieved the mobile from his coat pocket and snapped it open. He casually waved Brown away.

The Scot was close to boiling point. 'I know how to do my job Frank,' he muttered to Crosby. 'I don't need some fucking desk jockey on my back giving me advice about it.'

Crosby could only shrug his shoulders, and the unhappy Brown headed back to his crime scene. Rees-Bramley's call was brief – he returned the phone to his pocket. 'That was DC Berne. Sounds as if our hospital patient is going to make it.'

'Can we get a statement?'

Rees-Bramley shook his head. 'Not for a day or so.'

The DI cast an oblique eye towards Ian Brown who was talking with his colleague in the playground below. He eventually turned back to Crosby.

'I think we're just about finished here Frank. We'll try Mister Broad again.' The two detectives had already called at the house in Wassom Avenue earlier that morning but couldn't raise anyone.

Rees-Bramley turned and headed back towards the entrance to Akers

Lane. Crosby fell into step beside him, the pair of them presenting an unlikely looking team. Crosby, tall, slightly overweight, ambled along at a comfortable pace, his jacket stretched across broad shoulders. In contrast, Rees-Bramley's slim, upright bearing would have been better suited to the parade ground, his short, staccato steps executed with military precision.

They drew level with a group of youths who'd been hanging around the crime scene since mid-morning. All of them wore hooded-tops drawn up over their heads. When questioned earlier in the day their attitude had been one of sullen hostility. It had annoyed Crosby more than usual – probably the assault on Janet Sterne's baby still playing on his mind.

The two detectives passed within fifteen yards.

'Oink! Oink!'

The group sniggered, amused by their efforts.

Crosby stopped and looked across at them. 'Not worth it Frank,' Rees-Bramley said without breaking stride. 'Half a day's paperwork and they'll be out of the door with a caution.'

Crosby continued to stare the youths down, until they turned and slouched away in the opposite direction. The detective's temper subsided and he turned to catch up with his DI.

Rees-Bramley hadn't waited. 'There's a lot to get through today Frank. We can do without any diversions.' Crosby didn't reply.

Both detectives headed down the Akers Lane alleyway in silence, taking the first side exit onto Wassom Avenue. Walking along the deserted pavement Crosby felt oddly reassured that two plainclothes policemen, even in today's climate, could still clear a street just by walking down it.

They continued on. Unable to shake off old habits, Crosby noted at least three out of date tax discs among the long line of cars parked nose to tail at the roadside.

The front garden of number thirty-nine Wassom Avenue was just a small patch of concrete – tall, spindly weeds had been allowed to force their way up through gaps in its badly cracked surface. The front door was only half-a-dozen steps from the gate. Crosby thumped its peeling, flaked surface with the butt end of his fist.

'I'm coming! I'm coming!' A broad Midlands accent carried out to the doorstep. It took a moment for the security chain to be engaged before the door cracked open. 'Yes!'

Crosby leant forward. 'Mister Broad?'

'Who is it?'

'Good Morning Sir! I'm Detective Sergeant Crosby from Studwell CID.'

The chain was disengaged and Frederick Broad filled the doorway with his considerable bulk. 'About bloody time! I've been watching your boys running round like headless chickens all morning.'

Broad's large, round face showed two or three days growth of stiff, grey stubble. Crosby put him in his late fifties. The head was completely bald. He wore no shirt, just a grubby vest, traces of his last meal clearly evident down its front. Stretching up and over Broad's large paunch was a frayed pair of braces, barely holding up the rumpled, grey trousers he was wearing.

Crosby nodded towards his DI. 'Detective Inspector Rees-Bramley and I are here regarding the assault that took place in Akers Lane last night.'

'Rees-Bramley!?' Broad repeated the double-barrelled surname with a certain amount of suspicion. He leant forward to take a closer look at the senior detective, who retreated half-a-step – the smell of body odour emanating from Broad almost overpowering.

'Is it possible to talk inside?' Crosby asked.

Broad hesitated. Only after ducking his head outside to look up and down the street did he step back to usher both detectives into a narrow hallway.

There was a clatter of pots and pans coming from the kitchen, cooking smells drifted across from an open doorway – it made Crosby realise he was hungry. It also reminded him that his wife would be eating on her own again today – something else she'd never come to terms with during the course of his career.

Broad showed them into a cold, sparsely furnished lounge. 'I won't disturb the missus, it'll put her behind with me dinner.' He laughed loudly, displaying a row of discoloured teeth. Crosby glanced across at his DI who remained expressionless. Rees-Bramley was not renowned for a sense of humour.

The two detectives were directed towards a pair of large, overstuffed armchairs. Crosby took out his pocketbook. 'We understand from PC Stewart that you may have information for us Mister Broad.'

Broad folded his arms and sat back. 'I may have. What's in it for me?'

'If you mean a reward,' Crosby said, 'there isn't one.'

Broad shrugged his shoulders, 'No harm in trying is there?' He leant forward. 'The boy you sent round last night said it all kicked off just after nine. Right?'

Crosby nodded.

'Well our resident fruit cake lives virtually opposite,' Broad said. 'In Silver Street.'

'Resident fruit cake?' repeated Crosby, sensing Rees-Bramley shifting in his seat.

Broad nodded. 'Bob Milner! Suffered some sort of breakdown a few years back. Left him a bit lightweight in the attic department.'

'And Mister Milner's relevance to our investigation is what?' Crosby asked.

'Well he'd have seen it wouldn't he?' Broad replied.

Crosby made a note. 'You're saying that Mister Milner witnessed the assault?'

'Course he witnessed it! Stands guard duty at the bottom of his garden for an hour every night doesn't he!' Broad tapped the side of his temple.

Rees-Bramley lifted his head. 'Every night?'

Broad frowned and looked across at the Detective Inspector but directed his reply to Crosby. 'Between nine and ten! Regular as clockwork!' he shook his head. 'Not natural is it? And the lanky streak of piss has got these long bloody arms and legs. Looks a bit spooky in the winter when the street lamp lights him up. Gives my missus the willies!'

'Lots of people have routines they follow,' Rees-Bramley said. 'It doesn't mean their behaviour is abnormal.'

Broad snorted. 'Well I don't think it's normal to spend all afternoon going up and down your garden path to check whether or not you've closed the gate.' He leant in towards the two detectives, 'and watching him clean his kitchen window is a good hour's entertainment in itself. Over and over again! It's a bloody miracle there's any glass left. Christ knows what he gets up to indoors.'

'Are you saying this man suffers from an obsessive-compulsive disorder?' Rees-Bramley asked.

Broad paused to look at the DI again and frowned. 'What the bloody hell's that when it's at home? He's not the full ticket is what I'm saying.'

'Mister Milner's evening routine,' Crosby said. 'You seem to be very familiar with it.'

'Wouldn't you be! Seeing him parked out there for the past ten years.'

'You can see him?'

Broad nodded. 'From the bedroom window.'

'And why would you be watching Mister Milner from your bedroom window?'

'I said I could see him!' Broad narrowed his eyes, 'I didn't say I was watching him!'

'It's nothing personal Mister Broad,' Crosby said, 'we're just trying to build a picture.'

Broad didn't look convinced. 'Well it's not me you need to be looking at. I'm one of the few normal ones around here.'

Crosby saw Rees-Bramley's eyebrows lift a fraction.

'You have a good view of the alleyway and gardens from your landing window then?' Crosby prompted.

Broad nodded. 'If I'm upstairs I'll have a quick look outside. See what's going on. More often than not Milner's leant over his gate – looking along the lane.'

'And how many times of an evening would you go upstairs?'

'Varies!' Broad sniffed. 'Depends how often I need to take a piss!'

'Can you recall how many times you saw him last night?' Crosby asked.

'Eh?'

'Mister Milner! How many times did you see him last night?'

Broad shook his head. 'I didn't! There was football on. It didn't finish until after ten.'

'So you can't be certain that he was outside last night?'

'Look!' Broad sounded impatient. 'I've already told you. He's out there between nine and ten. Every bloody night. Has been for the last ten years.'

Is there a particular purpose to it?' Rees-Bramley interrupted. 'This constant monitoring of the alley and gardens?'

Broad struggled into a more upright position. 'Yes there is a particular bloody purpose to it! Those little hooded bastards are always using the lane as a shortcut. If they can't find someone to kick the shit out of on their way home they'll attack your property instead. Roaming all over the garden! Sniffing this! Injecting that! I'm always clearing stuff away. It's a wonder I haven't caught something myself.'

Crosby sat back and allowed Broad to continue his rant. 'And the old toms are always out there as well – backed up against one of the sheds. It's like Piccadilly bloody Circus some nights.'

'A matter for the police surely,' Rees-Bramley said.

'The law!' Broad spluttered. 'The law! I'll tell you where the law is. Sat in a bloody patrol car with a thumb up its ass! They only turned up last night because there was a kid involved.'

Flushed and short of breath, Broad finally ran out of steam. Rees-Bramley made a signal for the interview to be wound up. Crosby ignored it. He flicked back through last night's notes in his pocketbook. 'Robert Milner lives at number sixty-nine Silver Street doesn't he?'

Broad frowned. 'I don't know what the bloody number is! I'm not in the habit of going round there for morning coffee am I.' He struggled to push himself up from his chair. 'Are we about done here? Dinner's almost ready!'

'You wouldn't consider him a close acquaintance then?' Crosby persisted.

The question made Broad laugh. 'No I bloody well wouldn't! It might be catching!' Rees-Bramley was already on his feet. The two detectives followed Broad into the hallway where he opened his front door. Rees-Bramley nodded and stepped outside.

'You've been very helpful Mister Broad,' Crosby said to him. 'I've no doubt we'll be in touch'

'It's not me you need to be in touch with,' Broad called after the two detectives as they set off down the path. 'Get yourself round to Milner's. See what he's got to say for himself.'

Rees-Bramley and Crosby reached the gate. It didn't stop Broad, who raised his voice for the benefit of any onlookers, 'Too many bloody chiefs that's the problem. Get a few of them into uniforms and out onto the beat – that'll bring your crime figures down.'

Broad continued to follow them down the path offering more advice. Crosby closed the gate on him. There was an old Fiesta parked outside and the detective leant forward to peer at the out of date tax disc.

Broad quickly turned and disappeared back into the house.

Rees-Bramley looked across at his Detective Sergeant.

Crosby shrugged. 'He was attracting an audience.'

'We'd better pay this character Milner a visit,' Rees-Bramley said. 'What did you make of Broad's observations?'

'Sounded genuine enough. We'll need to see what the other neighbours have got to say.'

Rees-Bramley shook his head. 'I do find people like Broad very difficult to gauge.'

'That's the general public for you Sir,' Crosby said, his voice non-committal.

Both men set off along the pavement. 'Robert Milner was one of the residents you spoke to last night wasn't he?' Rees-Bramley asked.

Crosby nodded.

'And?'

'Polite and well-spoken,' the DS replied. 'Unusual for these parts. And Broad was right about his physical appearance. It is a surprise initially.'

'And what did our Mister Milner have to say for himself?' the DI asked.

'Claimed he was indoors all evening watching the International.'

'The International what?'

'Football sir! Broad mentioned it earlier. England were playing a European qualifier.'

'Were they!' Crosby was well aware of his DI's view that all sport was a complete waste of time and effort.

The two detectives reached the end of Wassom Avenue. Turning left they followed the road around into Silver Street. 'It is an interesting line of enquiry though,' Rees-Bramley said.

'What is Sir?'

'If Robert Milner really is an obsessive compulsive there's no way he would have missed his nine o'clock routine last night.'

'Which means he must have witnessed the assault on Janet Sterne,' Crosby felt obliged to add.

'Exactly,' Rees-Bramley said. 'I recently attended a Profiling Workshop sponsored by the FBI's Behavioural Sciences Unit. There was a lecture on how OCD affects those unfortunate enough to suffer from it. They're completely addicted to their routines.'

'A useful course Sir!' Crosby managed to keep his voice neutral. 'Unusual in itself.'

'Workshop Frank! Lots of practical hands-on. I think everyone would benefit from it.' Rees-Bramley looked sideways at the Detective Sergeant. 'Including our Senior Officers.'

The two detectives reached number sixty-nine Silver Street. They stopped outside and looked in towards the house. 'If Milner's been less than truthful about witnessing the assault,' Rees-Bramley said, 'he may be hiding something else.' The DI tugged at the cuffs of his thin, black leather gloves. 'Let's see what he's got to say for himself.'

Number sixty-nine's manicured patch of lawn and neat tidy borders were in direct contrast to most of the other gardens in Silver Street. Milner obviously put a lot of time and effort into maintaining it. They reached the front door. 'I'll be leading on this one Frank!' Rees-Bramley said.

'Yes Sir!' Crosby replied.

'He's not in!' someone shouted at them.

They turned in the caller's direction. On the roadside, three doors down, a man with greasy shoulder-length hair, and wearing oil-stained overalls, stood next to the open bonnet of an old Ford Escort. With two of its wheels removed the car had been ramped up on one side by just a single jack, making the whole structure look very unsteady. The two detectives approached it warily, keeping their distance. Turning to face them the man folded his arms and leant back against the vehicle's body.

'Are you a neighbour of Mister Milner's?' Crosby asked.

The man continued leaning against his car. 'Who wants to know?'

Crosby produced his warrant card. The man leant forward to scrutinise the photograph.

'Can I have your name Sir?' the detective asked.

'John Callaghan!'

Crosby took out his pocketbook. 'And your address?'

Callaghan jerked a grimy thumb towards the house adjacent.

'Did you see Mister Milner leave?' Crosby asked.

The man nodded. 'He goes out every Saturday in that old Rover of his. Half eight in the morning until seven in the evening. Never varies.'

'Do you know where he goes?'

Callaghan shook his head. 'Keeps himself to himself. Hasn't spoken a dozen words to me since moving here. And that must be ten years ago.'

Pulling a piece of oily rag from his overall pocket Callaghan began cleaning black grease from in-between his fingers. 'Is this about what happened last night? Couldn't move for all the uniforms round here this morning.'

'Was Mister Milner still at home when the police called earlier?'

'I told you! He's out of the door at half eight on a Saturday. Too early for your lot!' Callaghan blew his nose on the greasy piece of rag. Rees-Bramley's nostrils flared slightly.

'I can pass on a message,' Callaghan volunteered.

'It's only routine Sir,' Crosby replied. 'We'll catch up with him later.'

'If it's only routine,' Callaghan queried, 'why are CID sniffing around?'

Crosby closed the notebook and returned it to his pocket, 'As I said Sir. We'll catch up with him later.'

Callaghan watched the two detectives make their way back along the pavement past Milner's gate before he called out to them again. 'I saw him wandering about outside last night.'

Crosby and Rees-Bramley looked at each other before re-tracing their steps. Callaghan continued to lean against the car.

'Who was wandering where?' Crosby was growing impatient with the man's infantile games.

'Milner!' Callaghan said. 'He was outside.'

'And what time was this?' Rees-Bramley asked.

'Not sure,' Callaghan shrugged, 'just before ten maybe. I heard a noise outside and had a quick look through the curtains. Thought I saw him walking up the path to his front door.'

'You thought!' Rees-Bramley was also losing his patience. 'Well either you saw him or you didn't.'

Callaghan straightened up. 'Someone came through the gate,' he insisted.

Rees-Bramley looked across at the man's house. 'The angle from your window to Milner's garden doesn't give you much of a view does it? And the nearest street light is a good thirty yards away,' he added.

'I can see his path,' Callaghan said obstinately.

'Did you wait to see if anyone came back down the path?'

'No I didn't!' the detective's tone had annoyed Callaghan. 'I don't spend the whole bloody evening looking out of my window.'

'Unlike some of the neighbours,' Crosby muttered to himself.

'If you're not sure who it was,' Rees-Bramley said. 'Why would you identify Robert Milner?'

'Because it's his bloody house!' Callaghan snapped. 'Tell you what! I'm getting a bit pissed off with this. You two bugger off and I'll get on with fixing my car. We'll just forget about me trying to help.' Turning away from both men he ducked back underneath the Escort's bonnet.

'Your input has been appreciated Mister Callaghan,' Crosby said to him. 'We may need to speak again at some point.'

Callaghan didn't reply. The two detectives left, making their way back up towards the alleyway.

'Well?' Rees-Bramley said to Crosby as they neared the Akers Lane entrance, 'Milner's OCD puts him in his back garden between nine and ten. Callaghan's sighting puts him outside his front door around ten o'clock.'

'That's all dependent on whether Broad and Callaghan's observations can be relied on,' Crosby replied. 'I'll call on Milner tonight. Apply some pressure.'

Rees-Bramley shook his head. 'We'll both call on him. Callaghan said he'll be back at seven. One thing about OCD sufferers. You can rely on them to be punctual.' He turned into the alley. 'We'll meet at the station beforehand. Seven o'clock!'

Crosby hung back. 'I'll catch up with you later Sir. Couple of loose ends to tie up with Scene-of-Crimes.'

Rees-Bramley didn't bother to look back. 'Ring me at the office if anything crops up,' he called over his shoulder.

Crosby waited until his DI had disappeared from view before turning in the opposite direction.

Crossing the road, Crosby made his way over a stretch of grassy common in front of Milner's house towards a small bridge in the far distance. On the bridge, a very overweight black Labrador, and his equally overweight owner watched him approach. As he neared them Crosby recognised the facial characteristics of Down's Syndrome.

Donald's weak eyesight caused him to move closer. He peered into the detective's face.

'I'm a policeman,' Crosby said. 'I saw you watching Mister Milner's house earlier. Do you know him?'

Donald nodded. 'Him and Spike are my best friends.'

'We need to speak with Mister Milner. Do you know where he is?'

'He went somewhere in his car.'

Crosby showed his warrant card. 'My name's Frank. What's yours?'

'Donald!'

'And this must be Spike,' Crosby bent to scratch the Labrador's head. 'Where do you both live?'

'Over there!' The boy pointed behind him.

Crosby stood up. 'Is there a building around here Donald? Somewhere the older boys meet?'

Donald nodded. 'I don't go there. They shout at me.'

'Can you tell me where it is?'

'I'll show you!' Donald said. He began to amble awkwardly across the bridge. 'Come on Spike.'

The Labrador struggled to its feet and waddled after his owner. Donald led Crosby and the dog across another stretch of common and up onto a road that ran parallel with it. A street sign indicated they were in Oakdene Way.

Donald stopped at the crest of a high rise that overlooked what seemed to be a disused car park. 'Down there!' he pointed.

A high, sagging, mesh wire fence encircled the whole compound – small bushes and clumps of weed covered a pot holed, rubble strewn surface. Although daylight was gradually fading Crosby could just detect the long, dark outline of a single storey building, tucked away into the far corner.

He turned to the pair waiting alongside him. 'Thanks Donald. I can manage from here. You'd better get Spike home.'

Donald turned obediently and plodded back along Oakdene Way, stopping every so often for the Labrador to catch up with him.

After waiting until they were both out of sight, Crosby made his way towards a single track lane that ran down towards the compound's fenced-in car park.

A nearby sign indicated he was heading towards 'The Oakdene Family Community Centre'.

CHAPTER 6

Treadwell Recycling Centre: Saturday 20 Jan 2007: 2.15 pm

The UK Government's national standard for excellence in customer service is recognised by the award of a Charter Mark. The Charter's distinctive blue and white circular logo was prominently displayed in the lower right corner of a large sign that advised Milner he was about to enter Treadwell's Household Waste Recycling Centre.

Located on an industrial trading-estate, in Birmingham's western suburbs, the recycling-centre was always busy. Vehicles passing through Treadwell's gates at the weekend were always nose to tail – this afternoon was no exception.

Milner eased his car over the speed-humps and through a pair of tall, black, wrought-iron entrance gates. He continued on around the one-way system, familiar with its layout – the depot was on a direct route back to Sixfields and he'd used it before.

An assortment of discarded household items lined the perimeter walls – anything from renovated washing machines to rusty old bicycles – now on offer and general sale to members of the public. His tyres crunched through a carpet of twigs and leaves as he passed a row of skips piled high with garden debris. The untidiness offended Milner's sense of order and neatness. He fought an urge to set about clearing it up.

Pulling up alongside one of the depot's bright yellow land-fill skips, Milner reversed into its unloading bay. Stepping out of the Rover he looked about him for evidence of CCTV camera mountings. Finding none he moved around to the boot of his car, opened it, and lifted out the black, plastic bin liner from inside. After negotiating four metal steps up to the open skip Milner carefully dropped the bag over its side and returned to his car. He knew that waste dumped in the skip would be transferred to a local land-fill site within twenty-four hours.

Milner wound his way out of the industrial estate and back onto the dual carriageway. He was in control again. With the plastic bin-liner and its contents disposed of he could resume his usual Saturday routine. This afternoon would be spent in the anonymity of a half-empty cinema auditorium. Milner felt comfortable in the flickering, dim light, not out of place. It was somewhere he could relax, somewhere that allowed him to concentrate on putting all of his random, unconnected thoughts into neat, orderly slots.

He checked the primary colour in his peripheral vision – a regular routine since his breakdown. Today it was non-threatening, an almost luminous shade of grey. On bad days the encroaching colour would be black – out of which dark shadows would sometimes materialise. Although Milner had managed to resist their advances for the past ten years it was a constant battle, one that had almost worn him to the point of submission. Just recently it had become more and more difficult to deny them.

The signs for Hazel Grove's entertainment and leisure complex loomed up on his left, dragging him back to the present. Milner flicked on the car's indicator as he approached the slip road.

Negotiating the leisure centre's entrance he reversed into a nearby parking space, cut the engine and briefly closed his eyes. Preparation was the key – questions to anticipate, answers to rehearse, operations to plan. Milner smiled. It would be enjoyable. He knew that with his mind fully occupied the shadows would keep their distance.

Another thought suddenly struck him – he'd been forced to leave the garden before ten o'clock last night – breaking one of his routines. Milner wasn't sure what that meant. It was something else he would need to evaluate in the flickering gloom. There'd better not be anyone occupying his usual seat.

Milner opened the car door and made his way towards the brightly lit cinema foyer.

Sixfields Housing Estate: Saturday 20 January 2007: 2.30 pm

At approximately the same time that Milner was entering Hazel Grove's entertainment complex, Crosby was peering through a coarse wire-mesh fence that surrounded the deserted and derelict-looking Oakdene car park. Set into the fence was a tall metal gate, secured by thick-coiled chain and a heavy duty padlock. Adjacent to the gate a jagged opening, large enough for someone to slip through, had been cut into the fence at ground level. From the gaping hole a well-worn path snaked its way towards a long, rectangular, single-storey building, tucked into the compound's far corner.

Crosby flipped open the standard issue communications-radio he'd picked up earlier, switched it on and gave his call sign to the female operator.

'Go ahead Delta-Bravo-Two-Zero-Five,' the operator replied.

Crosby spoke into the radio as he scanned the far building for any sign of movement. 'I require uniformed back-up to assist in the search of a vacated community centre situated off Oakdene Way on the Sixfields estate.'

'Delta-Bravo-Two-Zero-Five. We have two cars currently patrolling in the Sixfields area. Your co-ordinates are being processed to effect the fastest response time.'

A pause as the operator momentarily disengaged. Crosby leant against one of the fence stanchions and waited.

The radio crackled back into life. 'Delta-Bravo-Two-Zero-Five. A patrol car has been diverted to the Oakdene Family Community Centre. Estimated time of arrival is two forty-five pm.'

Crosby glanced again at the far building. 'On their arrival please instruct the officers to site their vehicle in a prominent position outside the perimeter fencing and await further instructions.'

Another pause.

'Delta-Bravo-Two-Zero-Five. Your request has been passed to the patrol car concerned. Do you have any further requirements?'

'Not at this stage,' Crosby answered.

'Thank you Delta-Bravo-Two-Zero-Five,' the operator said. 'This call was terminated at two thirty-five pm.'

Crosby broke the connection, turned off the radio, and dropped it back into his pocket. He'd already decided to have a preliminary look around before the patrol car's arrival and didn't want any distractions.

Moving to his left Crosby ducked underneath the fence, and picked his way slowly across the potholed car park. A thin film of light-grey dust immediately attached itself to the wax polish on his shoes.

He surveyed the building's front. All of the facing windows had been securely boarded-up – fragments of broken roof-tile littered a concrete surround. In red, faded lettering the lop-sided sign that clung precariously to its outside wall spelt out the legend 'OAKDENE FAMILY COMMUNITY CENTRE' – the words barely readable against a flaking, discoloured background.

As there was another padlock and chain securing the double-fronted entrance doors, Crosby moved around to the side of the building – shards of glass and loose gravel crunching under his heavy tread.

There was a narrow gap between the building's sidewall and the perimeter fencing, just wide enough for two people to pass along it. Crosby stood looking down the confined space. It was dark here, the gloom of a winter's day already losing its natural light – large overhanging branches from nearby trees compounded the darkness.

Half-a-dozen steps along the sidewall and it was pitch black, too dark for the detective to see anything in front of him. As he fumbled around in his pocket for the small flashlight Crosby froze. After thirty years out on the street he'd developed a sixth-sense of someone else's presence, and right now the hairs on the back of his neck were standing on end.

The detective swore softly underneath his breath. Although it was only about twelve yards to reach the opposite corner he couldn't get an exact fix on how far ahead of him the danger was. It had to be one of the community hall's temporary residents, making their way from around the back. If they thought Crosby was a rival gang member, encroaching on their territory, there'd be no hesitation in launching an attack on him – and if he shouted 'Police!' at this point it would probably spook whoever was in front of him to lash out anyway. 'Shit!' Crosby slowly swivelled his head to check behind him. Nothing. He thought about edging backwards but that would give his position away. 'Fuck!' 'Fuck!' 'Fuck!' He couldn't just stand there and wait for the squad-car to turn up.

Flattening himself up against the wall Crosby concentrated on trying to penetrate the blackness ahead of him. Still no sign of movement. Was someone there or had his antenna let him down. He waited. Two full minutes passed and his legs began to cramp up. Crosby gritted his teeth, 'Stupid bastard!' Still putting himself into situations at his age.

As he contemplated reaching for his torch again there was the slightest movement ten yards in front of him. It was enough. Crosby concentrated on the exact spot. Another minute passed and his eyes started to lose focus. A shadow finally detached itself from the background darkness and moved forward. A dull gleam briefly punctured the gloom. 'Shit!' Was that a knife? The figure had obviously no idea of Crosby's exact position as it inched slowly forwards, the right arm extended.

The gap closed and Crosby's heart thumped as he felt an adrenalin surge. He held his breath. Only three steps away now and the detective could make out a long-bladed knife being swept from side to side. As the extended arm drew level with him, Crosby smashed both of his fists down on top of the shadow's wrist. There was a startled yelp and the knife fell from its grasp.

In the same movement Crosby took a pace forward and raised his knee sharply towards where he thought the assailant's groin area was. There was a strangled cry as the shadow dropped to its knees. Crosby aimed another kick but didn't connect. Before the detective could recover his balance the shadow was up on its feet and stumbling past him.

Crosby followed, keeping close to the wall. On reaching the corner he edged slowly around it. The slight figure of a young male was already halfway across the car park, picking up speed whilst still managing to avoid all the potholes. Crosby let him go – not that there was anything he could have done about it. He watched the escaping figure duck underneath the perimeter fence and disappear up the exit road, past where the squad car should have been waiting. If the youth was injured in any way it certainly didn't show, and he might return with reinforcements.

Still feeling winded Crosby leant up against the wall, waiting for his breathing to stabilise. After the adrenalin surge he felt slightly nauseous, aware of how fast his heart was pumping. Now would be a sensible time to wait for the backup to arrive – there might be other gang members in the building. The detective in him became restless again. He checked his watch. If there were others inside why had his attacker run off.

Pulling the flashlight from his pocket Crosby focused its beam back down the sidewall. 'Stupid Bastard!' the detective mouthed to himself again as he made his way along the narrow gap towards the rear of the building.

Crosby emerged out into an expanse of open ground. The light was better here and he stepped away from the building to look along the length of its back wall. Sections of old board lay strewn across the grass, where they'd been stripped from all the window openings, a padlock and chain secured the community centre's rear doors.

Crosby moved along to a window opening, its wooden sill smooth and well worn from constant use. He edged forward and looked inside. Just a small ante-room, with cardboard boxes stacked in the far corner. Easing himself over the waist high ledge Crosby dropped through to the other side.

'Bloody Hell!' The interior was like a fridge. It took him just five strides to cross the ante-room's dusty, concrete floor. Reaching the half-open door he carefully nudged it slowly forwards, looking out into what must have been the main hall.

The smell of stale alcohol was familiar enough but the cloying scent of marijuana was almost overpowering. If he was in here long enough there was a good chance of him being able to float out the window rather than climb through it. He flicked a nearby light switch. Nothing! The gloomy half-light from three small skylights allowed Crosby to see part-way into the hall. He stood and listened for noises. Although the room appeared to be deserted he pulled out his flashlight again and played its beam up and down the hall's length. A colourful, kaleidoscope of spray-painted messages and logos reflected back from the walls, most of them incorporating the legend 'SXF Inc'.

Crosby, along with the majority of officers stationed at Studwell, was familiar enough with the gang's name, but he hadn't been aware they were using the abandoned community centre as a base for their activities.

He moved further into the room. A remnant of the original carpet still remained – damp and heavily stained – its surface covered in a layer of fine grit. Dozens of tables and chairs were stacked around all four walls. In the far corner several small armchairs had been formed into a loose circle.

The detective's eyes were drawn to three long handled double-edged knives embedded at right angles into one of the interior doors – Crosby had been involved in enough knife amnesties to recognise them as specialised throwing blades.

He snapped off the flashlight, satisfied that the building was deserted. Re-tracing his steps Crosby pulled open the ante-room door and stared into the thin, white face of a youth wearing an oversized baseball cap. Several metal piercings protruded from his lower lip.

Crosby's appearance took him by surprise. 'Who the fuck is you man?' the youth's attempt to mimic pseudo-street Caribbean with a Midlands accent was more amusing than threatening. 'This is private property!'

'You're the owner are you?' Crosby assessed the gang member's age at no more than sixteen. He didn't feel at risk.

'You'd better do one!' the youth replied, 'I got other bloods inside' – but he was unsure, trying to look over the detective's shoulder.

Crosby moved aside, allowing him a look into the empty hall 'Deserted!' he said. 'Just you and me. Something to do with last night?'

The youth became wary. 'You the law?'

Crosby retrieved his wallet and flipped it open to display the warrant card. When the youth's pinched, white features showed signs of someone who was about to bolt Crosby slipped into his well-practiced, good cop routine. 'Look son, we're not particularly interested in you or this place. I'm here because one of your community day residents ended up in hospital last night. We don't know who he is and I'm making enquiries.'

The gang member still looked unsure but stopped backing away.

'We going to help each other out then?' the detective asked.

'Fuck off!'

Crosby smiled. Not the brightest individual he'd come across. 'Your choice. You can either give me a name or I'll have this place turned over.'

The youth shrugged.

Crosby pulled the radio from his pocket. 'There's a patrol car on its way,' he said. 'Any illicit substances the officers find in here will be redirected to your person. That's overnight bed and breakfast at the station and a visit to the magistrates tomorrow morning.'

The thin white face eyed Crosby's radio, trying to work out the implications.

'And if they can't find anything,' the detective patted his breast pocket, 'I've got something here to fall back on.'

Crosby switched on the radio. 'What's it be then Einstein?'

'It was Steve,' the youth said sullenly.

'Steve who?'

'Steve Roberts.'

Crosby switched off his radio. 'Where does he live?' Instinct told him the youth wasn't lying.

'Dosses down in one of those flats up by the waste-ground.' the youth had dropped his fake English Caribbean slang. 'Past Akers Lane.'

'Any idea who put him in hospital?'

The youth shook his head. 'We're making enquiries.'

Crosby smiled. 'Makes two of us then. Your name?'

The gang member hesitated.

'Not important,' the detective said. 'I know where to find you.'

Crosby brushed past, close enough for the youth to move aside. Inside the ante-room, Crosby eased himself back out through the window opening. Retracing his steps along the sidewall's narrow confines he exited into the car park. 'And now the bloody cavalry's arrived,' Crosby muttered.

A sleek BMW five-series squad car, in distinctive yellow and blue check livery, sat outside the perimeter fencing, headlights blazing. It was now three o'clock in the afternoon and the powerful beams lit up a late afternoon that had lost most of its light. Crosby lifted an arm to shield his eyes against the harsh glare as he crossed to the fence.

PC Jennings was leaning casually against one side of the BMW, smoking a cigarette. Ignoring departmental regulations the policeman had also removed his flat-topped cap and tossed it onto the vehicle's back seat.

Crosby nodded to PC Stewart who had propped himself up on the passenger side, trying to adopt the same casual stance as Jennings. Somewhat self-consciously, the younger PC raised a hand in greeting as Crosby approached.

Jennings threw down the stub end of his cigarette and ground it out under a size-twelve police boot. 'Snooping around on your own again

Frank? I thought the university graduate frowned on any of his harem ploughing a lone furrow.'

Crosby felt obliged to join in the banter. 'You're twenty minutes late Phil. You old pensioners were OK pottering around in a panda car but these high performance machines are far too powerful for you to handle properly.'

'Bollocks!' Jennings said good naturedly. 'When was the last time you waited for any back-up?'

Crosby shrugged.

Jennings held up both hands. 'I'm on your side, Frank. You don't need to convince me.'

The detective shook his head. 'This new breed want to solve cases by sitting in front of a computer screen. I need to be sniffing fresh-air, not desk polish.'

Jennings laughed out loud, slapping the roof of his car. Stewart laughed along with him, nodding in agreement,

'What the bloody hell are you laughing about?' the older man kept his face straight. 'All you do with your spare time is tap around on a bloody keyboard. It's about time you found yourself a woman.' Jennings winked in Crosby's direction. 'I don't want people to start wondering what your preferences are – not with the amount of time we spend together.'

Stewart flushed and slid back into the car's passenger seat. 'I'll close that call,' he said.

Crosby smiled to himself. Stewart might not appreciate it at the moment but he was very fortunate to be learning his trade with Phil Jennings. All that character building would cost him thousands if he had to pay for it – the veteran PC would take good care of his young charge, passing on the wealth of experience he'd gathered during a long career.

Jennings turned to look at the old community centre. 'What did you manage to find then?'

'Only a nest of rats!'

'Do they need flushing out?'

'Not yet. They'll only disappear down another sewer. I need to know where they are just at the moment.'

Jennings pushed himself away from the car. 'We'll be off then. The good citizens of Sixfields require our presence back on their streets. Can we drop you off somewhere?'

'My Hillman's at the far end of Akers Lane.'

'You're not still driving that pile of ancient junk. You'd better get in. I'll show you what a real motor's capable of.'

Crosby opened the rear door. Stewart was still on the radio finishing his call to the comms-centre.

Jennings gunned the accelerator. 'You'll need that seat belt on Frank.'

The BMW's wheels spun viciously on loose gravel as they accelerated up the short incline.

Sixfields Housing Estate: Saturday 20 January 2007: 7.00 pm

Milner's old Rover made its way slowly along Silver Street, pulling into a roadside space outside number sixty-nine. After taking several attempts to manoeuvre the car into a position he was satisfied with, Milner switched off the headlights. He didn't immediately open his door. Fully aware that certain neighbours were familiar with his timetable Milner took a few moments to look up and down the street, half expecting to find a waiting police car. There didn't seem to be anyone in the immediate area. He opened his door.

Compared to last night it was a mild evening, just fine drizzle in the air. It gently wetted Milner's face as he moved around to the back of his car and opened the boot. Three doors down a pair of curtains twitched. Callaghan! Nosy bastard. Always wanting to know everyone's business. Now the man's front door was opening. Milner quickly retrieved two carrier bags and slammed his boot down – the last thing he needed tonight was a nuisance neighbour trying to poke his nose in.

'You've had the law sniffing around today,' Callaghan shouted, as he pushed open his gate and advanced along the pavement. 'Uniformed lot this morning. CID this afternoon. Came to see you especially.'

Milner moved towards the front door. 'They'll be calling again then,' he said, feeling for his key.

Callaghan was already at Milner's gate. 'I expect it was about the trouble we had here last night.'

'Probably.' Milner turned the key in his lock.

'They wouldn't leave a message.' Callaghan made it halfway up Milner's path before the door closed in his face.

Inside the house Milner took his charity shop purchases upstairs to the bedroom and folded them neatly away. They would all have to be laundered twice before he was able to wear them, but it was a job he was comfortable about leaving until tomorrow. As the two white plastic bags didn't bear the charity shop's name he took them downstairs to put with a store of others he'd accumulated – the receipt had already been disposed of. Going through to his lounge Milner switched on the high-wattage light bulb suspended from mid-ceiling – there was no lampshade – nothing to dim the harsh glare. He settled himself into a plain leather armchair, closed his eyes, and waited for the police to return.

Studwell OCU HQ: Saturday 20 January 2007: 7.10 pm

Crosby circled the Studwell HQ car park looking for a suitable space to leave his old Series I Hillman Minx – 'an expensive indulgence' his wife constantly pointed out to him – but then she had always claimed to be the practical half of their marriage.

The vehicle had been an impulse buy, a considerable drain on his resources, but back in the early sixties it was the first car he'd ever owned and five years ago, when the opportunity had arisen to acquire this identical model, common sense played no part in his decision to put in an offer for it. Maybe the purchase had something to do with chasing his lost youth – it was the roomy interior of a Hillman 'Deluxe' where he'd finally managed to achieve one of his early ambitions – breaking down the stubborn resistance of a much sought after Samantha Westbrook.

He only took the old car out occasionally now – it wasn't economical and neither was it reliable – but Crosby still got a kick out of sitting behind the thin, oversized steering wheel – and although the original red leather upholstery had acquired a few more spidery white cracks than when Samantha Westbrook had stretched herself out on it all those years ago, the unique two-tone pearl and green exterior bodywork could still be polished up to a mirror finish.

Finding a suitable parking slot Crosby carefully reversed back into it and cut the engine. After stepping from the car and locking his door he walked around to the vehicle's bonnet and gave the Hillman's 'Wings' motif a quick buff with his sleeve. Having always carried out this little routine whenever he got out of the car it occurred to Crosby that Rees-Bramley would have described it as an obsessive, compulsive gesture. The detective smiled and made his way towards Studwell's CID annex, sited at the rear of the main building.

As he moved smartly along the paved walkway, Crosby checked his watch. Ten minutes late already. Along with all his other disciplines Rees-Bramley was a stickler for punctuality – a lengthy, disapproving glance at the office wall-clock enough to make latecomers feel they had to offer up several excuses.

Crosby's late arrival was due to his lack of sleep from the previous night. Gone were the times when he was able to manage well enough on four hours – if he didn't get a full eight in now it always left him struggling to stay focused the following day.

Earlier that afternoon, Crosby had returned home from Sixfields to a covered dish of unappetising salad left on the kitchen worktop – along with a note from his wife. Having recently acquired a brand new grandson she always seemed to be away visiting the family's new addition.

The note was short and to the point: 'You missed your son growing up and now you're missing out on a beautiful grandchild. I've left you a healthy lunch. Try to get some sleep. Eileen'.

'What no kiss?' Crosby had muttered – but there was a twinge of guilt as he recalled four-year-old Zoe Sterne's small, elfin face from the previous evening. He'd ignored the salad and fixed himself something more substantial before falling asleep in front of the television. The intention had been to call in and see his wife and grandson on the way to HQ but the clock was showing six-thirty when he woke from a fitful sleep. It had taken the whole car journey from home to Studwell for his head to fully clear.

Crosby reached the CID annex and punched a code into the outer security pad. Pushing through a thick glass door, he moved smartly along the windowless passageway.

To his left were a number of small, self-contained offices and interview rooms that ran the length of the corridor. He arrived at a door marked CRIMINAL INVESTIGATION DEPARTMENT. The door was already half-open and Crosby pushed through it.

The main office was unoccupied but at the far end there were lights showing through the frosted glass window of his DI's enclosed cubicle.

He strode through the corridor of desks up to a door marked DETECTIVE INSPECTOR REES-BRAMLEY, rapped once and went straight in. Berne and Taylor were already seated at the far end of the conference table. Rees-Bramley was at his desk. He acknowledged Crosby's arrival. 'Come in Frank. Be with you shortly.'

There was no reference made about timekeeping. Something or someone had put his DI in a good humour. Rees-Bramley waved Crosby to a seat before turning back to the ever-open laptop.

Grace Taylor looked up and smiled at him as he took the chair next to her.

A short, close-fitting, black evening dress obviously meant she was going on somewhere after the briefing. Crosby would have described the plunging neck-line as provocative, but then he was out of touch – as his son constantly pointed out.

The effect of Grace Taylor's exposed cleavage on PC Berne was all too apparent. Sitting across the table from her he was having the greatest of difficulty in looking elsewhere. Every time he managed to drag his eyes away they returned of their own accord. Crosby had a certain amount of sympathy for him.

Rees-Bramley finally closed his laptop. He tapped the lid. 'You might consider these machines advanced now but the next generation of computers will be capable of independent thought processing. Along with ever more sophisticated DNA procedures they'll form the cornerstone of criminal investigation for decades to come.'

'Jesus Christ!' Crosby muttered inwardly. They were investigating a serious crime. If his DI concerned himself more with the present they might all get home before midnight.

'Even our data gathering methods will be radically different,' Rees-Bramley continued. 'A lot of the information we now obtain manually will in the future become direct electronic input from an ever increasing IT literate population. The number of detectives who currently plod aimlessly up and down streets on a door-to-door basis will be drastically reduced.'

Crosby had heard it all before. On another occasion he would have ignored his DI's last remark but tonight it annoyed him. He responded without really intending to. 'Detectives plod up and down the streets to gather meaningful information Sir. They need eye-to-eye contact, whether interviewing suspects or the public. It determines what line of questioning they pursue. How does a remote computer replicate that?'

It was well known within the department that Rees-Bramley didn't take kindly to being challenged. His voice acquired a slight edge. 'Savings in manpower and efficiency will be immeasurable,' the DI said. 'Take today for example. We spent most of it trawling haphazardly around Sixfields without very much to show for it. The methods are antiquated. They belong in the past.'

Crosby was stung and reacted. 'I did some more haphazard trawling around the estate today Sir! – after you returned to the office. Found out that our waste-ground victim goes by the name of Stephen Roberts. Belongs to a gang who call themselves SXF Inc.' It was probably a mistake to make his DI look foolish but Crosby felt as if he'd been personally targeted.

Berne and Taylor suddenly found it necessary to examine the table-top in front of them. Rees-Bramley's demeanour changed immediately. 'And you obtained this information how?'

'One of the locals pointed me towards an old community centre. Told me it was being used by one of the local gangs as a base.'

'You decided to pay it a visit.'

'Yes Sir!'

'Back-up was requested?' the DI's tone was frosty.

'Yes Sir!'

Rees-Bramley didn't look convinced. 'And?'

'I came across one of the gang members.'

'Who presumably volunteered the name of Stephen Roberts during the course of your interview?'

'Yes Sir!'

'All done by the book I hope!'

'Of course!'

'You didn't think the information important enough to pass on?'

'I did try to telephone this afternoon Sir, but you were tied up in the IT department.'

Rees-Bramley looked at Crosby from beneath his eyebrows. 'Did you get an address?'

Crosby nodded. 'I sent someone round. The woman who Roberts shares the flat with confirmed that she hadn't seen him for a week.'

'And this woman hadn't bothered to report him missing?'

'He disappears on a regular basis apparently.'

'Has she identified him?'

'This afternoon, Sir!'

'Does this Stephen Roberts have form?'

'Quite a lot, Sir!'

'I'll leave you to put a report together then.'

Rees-Bramley transferred his annoyance to Paul Berne. 'I believe you were sounding out our paid informants on the Sixfields estate.'

Berne's attention had drifted back to Taylor's cleavage. He quickly re-focused. 'Yes Sir!'

'Do you not find it ironic then,' Rees-Bramley said, 'that Detective-Sergeant Crosby has obtained the name of our victim from a source where you must have paid informants in place.'

'Yes Sir!' Berne said.

'I have no doubt then that you will shortly be carrying out a complete review of all your contacts on the estate with regard to what they're being paid for and the quality of information they supply.'

'I will Sir!'

'And now you can give us the latest news on our hospital patient.'

Berne quickly flipped to the appropriate page in his pocketbook. 'According to the surgeon who operated he's very lucky to be still with us – the back of his head was hit with such force the resulting whiplash would have caused his brain to rebound against the skull.'

Berne flicked to another page. 'Positioning of the wound would suggest he was just on the point of turning when the back of his head was struck.'

'And that's according to whom?' Rees-Bramley asked.

'The surgeon Sir.'

'Qualified in forensic pathology as well is he?' Rees-Bramley grunted 'Anything else?'

'Apart from his facial injuries the kneecap was completely shattered and separated from its connecting tissue and bone.'

'And his condition?'

'I spoke to the hospital again about an hour ago. He's regained consciousness but understandably not taking too much interest in what's going on around him. His condition, however, has been downgraded from critical to serious.' Berne closed his pocketbook and looked up.

'And when can we speak to him?' the DI asked.

'Wednesday at the earliest – if he maintains his current rate of progress.'

Rees-Bramley swivelled his chair around to face Taylor. 'How did you find Janet Sterne today?'

'She's no shrinking violet, Sir.' Taylor's pocketbook was already open at the appropriate page. 'And in the normal course of events she'd be quite capable of standing up for herself.'

'Meaning?'

'She's putting on a brave face, but it's not that convincing. Couldn't get her to open up. Not particularly hostile about my visit but not exactly co-operative either.'

'Is she having second thoughts about identifying Roberts?'

Taylor shrugged. 'Possibly! I think she's worried about the safety of her children.'

'Thank you Grace.' Rees-Bramley glanced at his office wall-clock. 'Robert Milner! Resides in Silver Street. His rear garden backs onto Akers Lane and he's a potential witness to the assault on Janet Sterne. DS Crosby and myself are calling on him this evening, so unless there's anything else, we'll pick this up again tomorrow morning.'

The DI got to his feet, indicating an end to the meeting. 'We'll leave in five minutes, Frank,' he said to Crosby.

Taylor and Berne pushed their chairs back and headed out of the office, keen to get their Saturday evenings under way. Crosby followed them, stopping at his desk to pick up a fresh pocketbook. If his DI was leading the interview with Milner they'd need it.

Crosby continued on down the main office, to where Berne and Taylor were tidying their desks. Berne was the first to close his PC down. 'That's me done. Can I give you a lift anywhere Grace?'

'I'm sorted thanks.'

'Your loss then.' Berne headed towards the door. 'DC Berne is leaving the building. Night Sarge.'

Crosby raised a hand. He watched Berne leave the office before turning to Taylor. 'Does he ever give you any problems?'

'Paul?' she shook her head, looking genuinely surprised. 'Pussycat really, compared to some I've had to fend off. He's just a typical breeding male. Finds it necessary to dangle his reproductive organs in front of me every so often.' Taylor smiled. 'Metaphorically speaking Sarge.'

'OK!' Crosby raised both hands. 'I needed to ask. How was Zoe Sterne today?'

Taylor shrugged. 'Stayed very close to her mother. Didn't say too much. Kids that age usually talk non-stop if you press the right buttons but she hardly opened her mouth. Just kept those big saucer eyes fixed on me all the time I was there.'

Before Crosby could quiz her any further Rees-Bramley emerged from his office. 'I'd disappear before he finds you something else to do,' the DS said.

Taylor picked her coat up from the chair. 'Cheers Sarge! Try not to antagonise him too much.'

Crosby followed her progress as she expertly manoeuvred a pair of very high heels between the narrow corridor of desks. Rees-Bramley appeared at his shoulder. 'Ready Frank?'

The DI made no reference to their minor spat. Crosby regretted it already. Pointless and un-professional! Rees-Bramley would have tucked the incident away for future reference.

'I've had a thought Sir,' Crosby said. 'If we delayed our visit to Milner by an hour we should still be with him at nine o'clock. It'll be interesting to see if he's able to control his OCD and stop himself from disappearing into the garden.'

Rees-Bramley considered it. He checked an expensive-looking Rolex. 'OK! I can kill an hour. Shall we say eight fifteen?'

Crosby nodded.

'Have a look at this while you're waiting. I put it together this afternoon.' Rees-Bramley handed over several foolscap sheets of typed print before heading back to his office. Crosby dropped into the nearest chair and started to read through a detailed list of incidents concerning

Robert Milner.

Set out in chronological date order the number of nine-nine-nine calls and complaints that Milner had lodged over the years must have run into their hundreds. There were calls concerning intruders, damage to property, drug addicts, prostitutes, trespassing, intimidation, disturbances, anti -social behaviour and so the list went on. It also contained a report of an assault carried out on Milner two years ago that had left him with concussion and cracked ribs. He'd been unable to identify his attackers and they were never apprehended.

Crosby hadn't been involved in the investigation of Milner's assault and he couldn't remember calling on him about any of the other incidents, but then most of them would have been swept up by community support officers anyway. The attack on him certainly hadn't stopped Milner's nine-nine-nine calls, which continued immediately after he'd discharged himself from hospital. Crosby tucked the report away in his desk drawer. He used the time remaining to prepare a report on Stephen Roberts. There was a lot of material.

Rees-Bramley was on the dot at eight-fifteen. He outlined how the interview would be handled as they headed for the exit. 'I'll lead Frank. You're on the pocketbook. We'll keep it relaxed. Give him a chance to change his mind about not being there. And I don't want him alerted too early that we're aware of his OCD. Hold it in reserve.'

Crosby bit down on a suggestion that if they'd been living in Rees-Bramley's vision of the future, Milner's interview could have been carried out through some form of remote electronic engagement – but he'd already pushed his luck today.

On exiting the CID annex they separated to their own cars. 'I'll wait for you at the main gate,' Rees-Bramley said.

Crosby opened the door of his Hillman and climbed in. A twist of the ignition key induced no reaction at all, and neither did subsequent attempts. 'Shit!' As his knowledge of the car didn't extend to what was happening underneath the bonnet it would remain at Studwell for the night. Crosby climbed out and locked the door. He could just make out the sleek outline of Rees-Bramley's Jaguar XJK Coupé waiting in the distance. No wife. No kids. Money in the family. What else was he going to spend it on?

Crosby turned up the collar on his coat and headed for the main gate.

CHAPTER 7

Sixfields Housing Estate: Saturday 20 January 2007: 8.35 pm

Light in the windowless, sterile room came from a nest of thin, black candles. Indistinct shadows flickered on dark walls and surfaces. Silent and motionless, a tall, hooded figure waited, head bowed.

In front of him the naked body of a young male had been securely lashed to an upright iron stanchion, cemented into the concrete floor. From the stanchion's base a narrow, red-stained channel ran towards a large, open drain. The victim's hands and ankles had been pulled around behind his back, leaving him completely exposed and defenceless. He was neither gagged nor blindfolded – the cloaked figure's enjoyment came from seeing and hearing the pain he inflicted.

As the young male slowly recovered consciousness he became aware of a long, trestle table covered in crisp white sheeting. On top of the table, spaced out in neat, orderly rows, lay a full set of surgical tools and instruments. When the young male saw what was laid out in front of him he screamed hatred and abuse at the hooded figure – an anger that rapidly turned into fear, as he sobbed and pleaded for his life.

Flat, lifeless eyes watched impassively through slits in the black hood. Thin, long, fingers reached down to pick up a pair of light-blue surgical gloves from the table, stretching them efficiently over delicate, white hands.

The victim instinctively tried to draw his legs together, to protect his exposed genitals, but when he lost control of both his anal and urethra sphincter muscles, the stream of urine ran down his legs and a stench of defecation filled the air.

It only served to bring the hooded eyes to life. The figure selected a small metal hammer, the type that surgeons use to break bones before resetting them. He smacked the hammer several times in the palm of his hand to test its weight and suitability, before smashing it viciously three times onto the table-top.

Milner's eyes snapped open immediately. Someone hammering on the front door. He was instantly awake – aware of who it was and what they'd come for.

At the sound of bolts being withdrawn, Rees-Bramley positioned himself forward of Crosby, waiting for the door to open. If the DI was surprised at Milner's physical characteristics he didn't allow it to show.

'Mister Milner?'

'Yes!'

'Good evening Sir! I am Detective-Inspector Rees-Bramley from Studwell CID. I believe you've already met my colleague Detective-Sergeant Crosby. Is it convenient to speak inside?'

'Come through Inspector. I've been expecting you.' Milner stood to one side.

The two detectives stepped into a narrow hallway. Crosby was immediately struck by its décor. Both the linoleum flooring and interior walls were a uniform light-grey colour, which appeared to continue through the hall and into Milner's kitchen. In the confined space an overhanging light bulb was excessively bright, giving the light-grey colouring an almost luminous tint.

Milner ushered them through to the lounge. Crosby and Rees-Bramley glanced at each other – the walls and flooring were exactly the same shade of grey as his hallway. The lounge furnishings were minimal – two hard, leather armchairs and a settee, neutral in colour – small occasional table – a television in the corner. There were no wall decorations, no photographs, no ornaments of any kind. The room reminded Crosby of a large, bare prison cell. He didn't feel particularly comfortable in it.

Rees-Bramley sat next to Milner on the settee. Crosby took a chair that gave him direct eye-line to both men. Taking out his pocketbook Crosby nodded to Rees-Bramley that he was ready.

'You indicated that we were expected Mister Milner?' the DI opened.

'One of my neighbours felt the need to tell me that you called round earlier.'

'A Mister Callaghan?'

'The very same!'

Crosby got the impression of two combatants circling each other before they started trading punches.

'I believe my colleague spoke to you last night about an assault on a mother and small child in Akers Lane,' the DI said.

'Yes!'

'Virtually opposite your rear garden.'

'So I'm led to believe!'

'Were you also aware that late last night a young male was attacked and seriously injured at the far end of Akers Lane?'

'No I wasn't aware of that Inspector. But then I have just arrived home after being out all day.' Milner appeared very calm, his long spidery legs crossed in relaxed fashion. Crosby thought he detected the hint of a smile on Milner's gaunt features as he responded to Rees-Bramley's questions.

'It is possible that both incidents were connected,' the DI continued. 'You'll appreciate that any information we receive regarding the first assault may assist us with our investigation into the second,' he paused. 'Are you still certain that you saw nothing of the assault outside your house last night?'

Milner glanced across at Crosby. 'I've already told your colleague that I was indoors all evening and didn't see or hear anything.'

'It's important we double-check,' the DI said. 'There's always the possibility you may have remembered something.'

Milner shook his head. 'I'm Sorry Inspector. I really would like to help.'

Rees-Bramley nodded. 'Is it true that you check your garden for intruders every night Mister Milner?'

'Most nights! Not every night!'

'At exactly the same time? Between nine and ten o'clock?'

'Do I?' Milner feigned puzzlement. 'You seem to be far better acquainted with my routines than I am.'

'But last night you remained indoors!'

'Never left the house Inspector. And now I'm beginning to repeat myself.'

'It's just that I have information from a reliable source that places you in your garden at the time of the initial assault.'

'Reliable source?'

'A close neighbour who has become familiar with your evening routine,' Rees-Bramley left the inference hanging.

'And you're implying this close neighbour saw me last night?' Milner enquired.

Rees-Bramley didn't reply.

'Because if Mister Broad did claim to have seen me, then he too must have viewed the assault,' Milner paused, clearly enjoying himself. 'And that would give you two potential witnesses Inspector.'

Milner had anticipated the line of questioning. He was well aware of the neighbour who frequently observed him from a bedroom window opposite, but having run the previous evening through his mind several times he was certain that Broad had not appeared at the window last night.

Crosby looked up from his pocketbook as Rees-Bramley hesitated. The DI recovered quickly enough but Milner's response had thrown him. 'Your evening routine has become familiar to Mister Broad over a number of years,' Rees-Bramley said. 'I didn't infer that he'd seen you last night.'

'You most certainly did Inspector.'

The DI changed tack. 'Are you employed Mister Milner?'

Milner nodded. 'I deliver for a local distribution company. NST Services. They're based on a small industrial trading estate, about three miles from here.'

'Have you always been in that line of work?'

'Difficult to believe Inspector, but I used to be an independent city trader for a global investment bank. Stress levels were incredibly high.' Milner shrugged. 'After suffering a nervous breakdown, and being sidelined for six months, I was never able to pick up the threads again.'

'A young man's game,' Rees-Bramley sympathised. 'How did you end up in Sixfields?'

'Reduced earning capacity! Expensive divorce settlements! Take your pick.' Milner frowned. 'Is all of this really relevant?'

Rees-Bramley looked up from underneath his eyebrows. 'I don't know that yet Sir.' He switched his line of questioning again. 'I understand you remained indoors last night because you were watching football on the television?'

'Yes!'

'Enjoyable match? Lots of goals I'm told.'

Milner's laughter was loud and genuine. 'Shame on you Inspector. Is that the type of subterfuge they teach you on training courses these days?' he shook his head. 'The match was goal-less, but then you would know that.'

Rees-Bramley shrugged. 'I didn't watch it. I'm happy to confess that I know nothing about sport, but that doesn't stop friends trying to convert me. Do you have any close acquaintances Mister Milner?'

'Not anymore!'

'How well do you get on with the neighbours?'

Milner shrugged. 'Why would I want to get on with them?'

'They seem to take more than a passing interest in you,' the detective said. 'Mister Callaghan thought he saw you outside the front door of your house at ten o'clock last night.'

'He doesn't sound too certain about it?' Milner smiled. 'Witnesses like that must really hinder an investigation.'

'You're denying it was you then?'

'Inspector!' some of Milner's geniality disappeared. 'I didn't leave the house last night. What part of that are you having difficulty in understanding?'

Rees-Bramley seemed unperturbed, changing direction yet again. 'I did take the opportunity of reviewing all the calls you've made to us over the past few years, Mister Milner. Would you agree that most of them were of a fairly trivial nature?'

Milner's eyes flashed. He took a moment before answering. 'No! I fucking well wouldn't agree Inspector. Even so, I doubt the police bothered to investigate a single one of them.'

Crosby was taken aback. It was the first reaction that Milner had shown during the interview – he'd looked in complete control of himself. Rees-Bramley glanced across at Crosby. The DI always maintained that if he could get someone to over-react they'd lose concentration – it was all about finding their Achilles heel. Rees-Bramley continued to niggle at Milner. 'We take all of our calls very seriously Sir, and they're always followed up by recommending that the complainant completes one of our incident survey questionnaires.'

Milner stood up. 'I'll fetch you one of your questionnaires Inspector.' He left the room.

Crosby puffed out his cheeks. 'Bloody Hell!' he said to his DI. 'Where did that come from? He was stonewalling everything up until then.'

'All about finding the right buttons to push Frank. If he's hiding something we'll get it now.'

Milner re-appeared. He tossed a form into Rees-Bramley's lap. 'I used to complete these, until I realised that you don't actually do anything with them.'

Rees-Bramley picked the form up. 'Feedback from the public is extremely important to us Mister Milner,' he tapped the questionnaire. 'The information we receive enables us to anticipate future requirements.'

Milner laughed. 'The first question asks whether we've been reassured by what the police did. How much positive feedback do you usually get from that Inspector?'

'You haven't been reassured presumably?'

'No I bloody well haven't.' Milner had recovered himself. 'The police do nothing about anti-social behaviour complaints Inspector. If they bother to turn up at all it's usually in the form of a community support officer, whose preferred method of dealing with the little bastards responsible is to engage them in friendly chit-chat.'

'There is an official complaints procedure to follow if you're not happy with our response to any call-outs,' Rees-Bramley said.

Milner took his time before replying. 'You tend to lose faith in procedures when you're lying in hospital becâuse a group of thugs object to you occupying their space. Stringing the evil little bastards up from a nearby lamp-post would save police time and paperwork, and give most officers a lot more job satisfaction.'

'And that would be your preferred solution,' the DI said.

'There's plenty that would agree with me.'

Crosby was monitoring Milner closely. There was something about the eyes now. Slightly unfocused. The detective sensed he was about to blow again as Rees-Bramley continued to goad him. 'Mister Milner!' the DI said, 'I am aware of the injuries inflicted on you and fully understand your depth of feeling, but unfortunately, that's not why we're here tonight.'

'Isn't it? I understood you were here gathering information about an assault on members of the public by a gang of thugs. I'd say that was relevant!'

Rees-Bramley put the questionnaire aside. 'At no point have we indicated that a gang was responsible for either assault.'

Milner shook his head. 'More of your games Inspector? Of course it was a gang who were involved. All of these hooligans hunt in packs.'

'To be perfectly honest with you Mister Milner, as Janet Sterne and her baby suffered no serious injuries I'm not overly concerned about the first incident.' Rees-Bramley pushed him a little further. 'My priority at the moment has to be the victim who ended up in hospital. It affects my clear up rates if that kind of assault remains outstanding.'

Crosby had to admire his DI's 'coup de grâce'.

Milner took the bait. Any vestige of politeness completely disappeared as he leant forward and thrust his face directly into Rees-Bramley's. Two crimson spots burned high on his cheekbones. 'Fuck your clear up rates Inspector! Fuck you! And fuck the young thug lying in hospital who probably got what he deserved anyway.' The words were spat out in a fine spray.

Crosby stood up, thinking his DI was about to be physically attacked. Breathing heavily, Milner pulled back.

Rees-Bramley looked calm enough. 'My apologies Mister Milner! That was clumsily expressed.'

'I think it was expressed as you intended Inspector.'

The situation passed. Crosby checked his watch. It was nearing nine o'clock.

Milner remained in his chair, clearly agitated, visibly trying to control himself. 'A panic attack Inspector. Fairly frequent since my breakdown. I would appreciate being left alone to deal with it. You'll see yourself out.'

Rees-Bramley stood up. 'Of course! We're just about finished here. Can we help in any way?'

Milner shook his head and turned away.

Crosby followed his DI into the hallway. Rees-Bramley opened Milner's front door, stepped outside, but didn't close the door behind him.

Both men walked to the gate. 'Aggressive and emotional!' Rees-Bramley said. 'Classic OCD symptoms. And you saw him struggling to break his routine. He witnessed the assault on Janet Sterne. And if he's lying about that he could be hiding something else.'

'Priority follow-up?' Crosby asked.

Rees-Bramley nodded and glanced down at his watch. 'I've got a quick call to make. You might want to check that he's OK. I'll see you back at the car.'

Returning along the path, Crosby pushed through Milner's front door and passed through the hallway. A door leading out to the rear garden had been left ajar. Although it was dark outside the single streetlamp allowed Crosby to look down towards Milner's lone figure. Under the gloomy pool of light he looked completely lost. Crosby felt a stab of sympathy for him.

He made his way down the narrow path.

Milner didn't bother to turn around. 'Your Detective Inspector is very good at his job Sergeant. I was angry.'

'He has that effect on a lot of people,' Crosby said. 'Including me.'

Milner smiled. 'What's this Sergeant? The good cop, bad cop routine – one keeps out of the way, while the other softens me up with sympathy and kindness.'

Crosby shook his head. 'That's for television and films Mister Milner. We just routinely plod along until something turns up.'

'Can I suggest then,' Milner said without any malice, 'that you routinely plod your way back up to the house and close the front door behind you this time.'

Crosby nodded. 'Goodnight Mister Milner! We will be in touch.'

Milner had already turned his attention back to the lane. He didn't reply.

Crosby made his way up to the house. He stopped to look back at Milner continuing his vigil, the mass of unruly white hair like a silver halo around his head. The detective glanced across at the houses opposite. There was a dim light and the faintest of shadows at Broad's window.

'Bloody lunatic asylum!' Crosby muttered. He shook his head and went back into the house.

Rees-Bramley was waiting in his car. 'Was he outside?'

Crosby nodded. 'Seems a lot calmer now.'

'I want Mister Milner under the microscope, Frank. Put two officers on it.'

'Yes Sir!'

'And keep away from the office tomorrow. You need some sleep. I'll put the Stephen Roberts report together.'

Crosby didn't argue. Friday and Saturday had wiped him out. He wasn't to know that it would be some time before the luxury of another free day would present itself.

Sixfields Housing Estate: Saturday 20 January 2007: 10.00 pm

After coming in from his garden Milner sat at the kitchen table, his head bowed. The questions had drained him. He had not handled it well. Detective Inspector Rees-Bramley was a skilled interrogator.

Familiar black clouds began to encroach. He tried to push them away, but it was half-hearted, and they persisted. Small, dark shapes began to emerge from the cloud. They edged closer. He was forced to listen. They were very persuasive. Wanted to help.

Milner eventually looked up. A shadow waited in the doorway. It came forward to take his hand.

As they walked from the room, Milner's back door swung silently open to let them out.

CHAPTER 8

Broadwell Trading Estate: Monday 22 January 2007: 4.00 pm

Situated within the confines of Sixfields, at its furthermost westerly point, Broadwell Industrial Trading Estate was a recent new-build, intended to ease the estate's chronic unemployment figures. With just fifty-four thousand square feet of total floor space, Broadwell was small and compact, made up of twelve individual leases. Each unit comprised a simple concrete block construction, with solid floors and a flat, weathered roof.

At no time in its short history had all twelve units been occupied at the same time, and as only three tenants were currently in residence, Broadwell had a neglected, abandoned feel about it. Empty plots had not been looked after or maintained – tufts of vegetation and weed flourished between cracks in the concrete – untended grassed over areas had been left to grow unchecked. At night the area was dark and deserted, its empty buildings creating spaces that echoed.

A wide access road ran in a direct, straight, line through the estate – its entrance identified by a pair of tall, wooden circular poles. There was no boundary fence. Between the two entrance poles, arranged in a vertical row, hung individual wooden slats, displaying the various logos and letterings of companies that had long since vacated the estate.

Unit number twelve was tucked away into a far corner. The 'To-Let' sign hammered into a patch of grass outside its front entrance had tilted sideways over time and was now at an angle where it almost touched the ground. A rectangular, white plastic sign fixed to the unit's wall bore the lettering 'P.D. MOTORS – MOT & REPAIRS'. Lack of customers had forced the garage to close over two years ago – valid MOT certificates being low on the list of priorities for most of Sixfields' car owners.

On this particular afternoon, deep into January, daylight began to disappear from a gloomy, overcast sky quite early. As the afternoon wore on, and it became progressively darker, a light at the corner-facing window of unit twelve became more and more noticeable.

At approximately four o'clock the receptionist for NST Services, a small delivery company situated directly opposite unit twelve, rang Broadwell's leasing agent and left a message about the lights. After making her call the receptionist thought no more about it, presuming that someone had been checking over the premises on Saturday or Sunday and forgotten to turn off the lights.

CHAPTER 9

Studwell OCU HQ: Tuesday 23 January 2007: 10.15 am

Leaning back in his chair to survey the room Crosby stifled a yawn. The usual mix of police and civilian personnel in this morning, all tapping away at keyboards or scratching their way through a pile of paperwork. Not too many empty desks either, the majority of Studwell CID seemed to be in-office, filling up forms and databases. Crosby shook his head. Although the bureaucracy wasn't their fault this was not how a career detective should be spending the day.

He glanced at the pile of buff folders on his own desk – on-going investigations – most of them minor and routine in nature. Top priority at the moment was to identify Stephen Roberts' assailant from the previous Friday, and that was progressing slowly. Although SOCO's team had yet to produce their final report, early findings indicated there would be little in it for detectives to follow up on – and apart from Broad and Callaghan's allegations about Milner there had been little response from the general public either.

Crosby himself wasn't particularly concerned there had been little or no progress – and he was perfectly content for it to remain that way. If Stephen Roberts was responsible for the assault on Janet Sterne's baby then a certain type of justice had been handed out – the detective had no problem with that – and if the police could also nail Roberts through the courts that would be a double result.

They had a problem, however, Sterne was having second thoughts about identifying him. The detective appreciated her position. With two young children she would be extremely vulnerable, exposed to the likelihood of intimidation – but if CID couldn't persuade her to pick out Roberts from an identification line-up, he was going to walk. 'At least it'll be on crutches,' Crosby muttered to himself.

He turned back to the folders. Rees-Bramley had been busy over the weekend. On returning to his desk Monday morning, Crosby had found several e-mails dumped into his post-box – one of the attachments was a detailed report on Stephen Roberts – an offender tagged as violent and dangerous, with little regard for the law. Crosby picked up the report he'd printed off yesterday and flicked through it again.

Roberts had been a consistent serial offender from an early age. By the time he was eleven years old he'd collected several ASBOs. At the age of twelve Roberts had been incarcerated in a Local Authority Secure Unit. During his teenage years there were indictments for breaking and entering, theft, joy riding, vandalism and possession of drugs. Charges against him included burglary, robbery with violence, criminal damages and grievous bodily harm. Not every prosecution had secured a conviction but between the ages of sixteen and nineteen he'd been detained four times in a Young Offenders institution. Twenty-one is the minimum age at which a convicted criminal can be sent to an adult prison and Roberts managed to achieve that distinction in his twenty-first year, when he was sentenced to six months for common assault.

Crosby tossed the report back on his desk – and now Studwell CID were supposed to divert valuable time and resources investigating who was responsible for putting him into hospital. Latest news from the Royal West Midlands indicated a rapidly recovering patient, but his attitude and behaviour, apparently, were already causing problems. Although the woman who lived with Roberts had been able to identify him, the police were currently unable to contact his parents – they were not at their home address and efforts to track them down had so far proved unsuccessful. Doctors at the hospital had indicated that Roberts would be sufficiently recovered to talk with the police on Wednesday. Rees-Bramley, obviously aware of Roberts' CV, found himself otherwise engaged that morning and had delegated the task to Crosby.

Stories of the sensationalist manner in which Roberts had been stripped naked and put on display was already headline news. The interest generated at both local and national level had prompted Rees-Bramley to arrange a press conference – not that he needed much persuading in that direction. Crosby glanced down at his watch. The briefing was scheduled for ten thirty.

He looked up to see Grace Taylor making her way through the office towards him. The DI had requested that both she and Crosby attend the press conference. Mindful of his image Rees-Bramley probably wanted to present the young, dynamic lead-officer flanked by members of his team – the fact that DC Taylor was a woman, and black, would only serve to highlight that equal-opportunity quotients were being met. Crosby shrugged. Rees-Bramley presumably wanted his Detective Sergeant in attendance as the face of experience.

Taylor arrived at his desk. 'Sarge! What exactly does the DI want me to do at this press conference? I've had no briefing from him.'

Crosby leant back in his chair. 'You, Detective Constable Taylor will just need to look switched on and efficient. I on the other hand, will represent my age, looking solid and dependable. We'll be arranged either side of our DI to reinforce who is leading this investigation.'

Taylor didn't look convinced. 'And if I'm asked questions?'

'Our DI will reply on your behalf,' Crosby said. 'You will certainly not assume the responsibility of answering them yourself. He will retain overall control of the briefing.'

Taylor didn't look impressed. 'I'm not a bloody ornament, Sarge.'

The phone on Crosby's desk rang, saving him from having to answer. He anticipated the caller would be his DI so he gave the standard telephone response that Rees-Bramley had laid down for incoming calls. 'Studwell Criminal Investigation Department. Detective-Sergeant Crosby speaking. How may I help?'

He replaced the receiver almost immediately. 'OK Grace. Detective-Inspector Rees-Bramley requires our presence and support. We are summoned to the briefing room.'

They passed an unhappy looking DC Paul Berne on their way out. Berne had already asked Crosby why Taylor was attending the press conference and not him. 'DI's decision Paul. I can query it if you want.' Berne had declined the offer.

Studwell OCU HQ: Tuesday 23 January 2007: 6.30 pm

It had been a long day. After being wrapped in the claustrophobic fug of an efficient central-heating system all afternoon Crosby welcomed the refreshing chill of early evening as he headed for his car. At some point it had rained – the reflected illumination from Studwell's lamp-lights casting dull, orange circular pools onto the car park's wet surface.

The morning press conference had been uneventful. Although fairly well attended the case was yesterday's news, interest already beginning to wane – crime journalists needed the long haul of a serial killer to sustain their newspaper columns – there was only a limited amount of space they could devote to local gangs trying to exterminate each other.

After the morning press conference, Rees-Bramley had briefed everyone involved that as Stephen Roberts was now off the critical list, a Major Investigation Unit would not be formed and the case would remain Studwell CID's responsibility. The DI had then reviewed all relevant information received up to that point, assigned several lines of enquiry, then turned his attention to Crosby. 'The hospital interview with Stephen Roberts tomorrow.'

'Yes Sir?'

'We need something from it. How much time is the doctor letting you have?'

'Very little! It might be difficult. Roberts is not being very cooperative apparently.'

Rees-Bramley thought about it before turning to Taylor. 'Grace! I'd like you to attend the hospital with DS Crosby tomorrow. You might appeal to Roberts' sensitive side.'

Crosby had tried to argue against it. 'I'm not sure that would be a good idea Sir! Roberts has been reported for racial abuse on several occasions and he doesn't appear to have much respect for the opposite sex either. Grace would antagonise the hell out of him.'

'Probably!' was Rees-Bramley's reply. 'Would you feel able to cope with any excesses that Stephen Roberts might throw at you?' he'd asked Taylor.

'I've been dealing with it ever since I joined up Sir,' she'd said.

'Precisely!' The look from Rees-Bramley to his Detective-Sergeant had been final. 'That's settled then.'

Although Crosby still wasn't happy about it Rees-Bramley probably had a point. If they wanted anything from Stephen Roberts he would need throwing off-guard.

Crosby had collared Taylor after the meeting. 'You OK about tomorrow? Roberts is a nasty piece of work.'

'Sarge! It's one of the reasons I joined.' – she'd laid a hand on his arm for longer than was necessary. 'Thanks for worrying about me, but if I can't cope with specimens like that I may as well apply for road traffic duties.' They'd spent the next hour together, preparing questions and agreeing on a general approach.

Earlier that afternoon Crosby had received a call from the consultant who was looking after Stephen Roberts. Initial arrangements had been for the interview to take place at ten o'clock, but Doctor Khani wanted a meeting beforehand. There'd been heavy disapproval in his voice – Roberts living up to his reputation and past history presumably.

Just as Crosby was about to leave for the day, Rees-Bramley had stopped by his desk. 'You'll possibly meet up with the parents of Stephen Roberts tomorrow – we've just made contact. If they do happen to turn up while you're still at the hospital it might be a good idea to have an informal chat with them.'

Crosby finally reached his car – the wife's Fiesta – his old Hillman had opted for another day off. Unlocking the door he shoe-horned his large frame into the driver's seat and pushed the ignition key into its slot.

He shrugged as the engine turned over first time 'So what!' he muttered to himself. Backing out of the parking space Crosby began to relax – once clear of the main gate he'd be able to switch off completely.

CHAPTER 10

Broadwell Trading Estate: Wed 24 January 2007: 10.00 am

On Wednesday morning the leasing agent for Broadwell's Industrial Trading Estate, Derek Johnson, finally responded to the message about lights being left on inside unit twelve.

It had been three months since Johnson's last inspection of the building – enquiries to lease the old 'P.D. MOTORS' property were few and far between. Johnson parked-up next to the unit's front office and cut his engine. After making his way to the frosted-glass door he sorted through a large bunch of keys and inserted one of them into the flimsy looking Yale lock.

Stepping inside Johnson quickly checked the small office before he crossed to a door that opened into the main works-area. Light coming from a far corner of the converted garage space spread a gloomy illumination throughout the interior, casting deep shadows into all of its recesses. A light switch on the wall to Johnson's right was not working. The agent had brought with him a powerful industrial torch and he snapped it on.

Keeping the torch's powerful beam angled downwards Johnson picked his way carefully across the rubbish-strewn floor, towards another light switch in the far corner. Halfway across Johnson sensed a shadow to his immediate right. Something solid bumped against his shoulder and swung gently away from him. Quickly jerking the torch's beam upward he found himself looking directly into a pair of sightless, blood-filled eyes.

It took the agent a split second to realise there was a body hanging upside down in front of him, spinning slowly around on a suspended length of chain.

'Fucking Hell!' Johnson's involuntary response caught in his throat. The black, plastic torch fractured as it hit the floor. Spinning on his heels the agent careered towards the exit. In his blind panic he tripped and sprawled full-length on the floor. It didn't slow him. For a large man he was up on his feet almost immediately, flinging himself at the office door. Wrenching it open he crashed through the front office and out of the building.

CHAPTER 11

Royal West Midlands Hospital: Wednesday 24 January 2007:
9.30 am

The weather opted for light grey cloud and a stiff breeze on Wednesday morning, temperatures gradually nudging their way up into double figures. Crosby and Taylor arrived in the car park at nine-thirty. After securing the car they headed towards the hospital's main entrance.

The Royal West Midlands was one of the first hospitals to be built under Private Finance Initiatives, where rental payments to PFI contractors were already stretching tight budgets in the Health and Education sectors. It was an expensive way to run a business. The general consensus of opinion was that PFI's were not a spectacular success, even though the government's responsibility had been considerably reduced.

Crosby looked up at the hospital's sweeping, architectural lines. Impressive enough, but he'd recently read that the six hundred bed building was pretty much bursting at the seams and there was already talk of a new wing to increase its operating capacity. The detective blamed it on too many people adopting healthy lifestyles – living well past their sell-by date. Little wonder that hospitals were unable to cope.

The two detectives reached a large, revolving glass entrance door and negotiated their way safely through it. At the reception desk they were approached by an elderly woman wearing a 'League of Friends' sticker. Crosby politely declined her offer of assistance and spoke to one of the two receptionists. 'Detectives Crosby and Taylor from Studwell CID. We have a nine forty-five appointment with Doctor Khani of the NeuroSciences Rehabilitation Unit.'

'I'll just check.' The receptionist referred to a lengthy appointments list before pressing numbers on her phone. The call was answered immediately and Crosby's message relayed. 'Certainly Doctor Khani!' The receptionist replaced her receiver. She picked up a pen and crossed Crosby off her list. 'You're to go straight up. Third floor. Doctor Khani has a small office next to the rehabilitation ward.'

Crosby and Taylor headed for the bank of lifts, brushing off another 'League of Friends' representative on the way.

'More volunteers than staff!' Taylor said.

Crosby shrugged. 'Volunteers don't attract salaries.' He punched one of the lift's buttons.

After being deposited on the third floor they followed signs to 'NeuroSciences Rehabilitation'. Housed in the hospital's west wing, it involved navigating their way along a series of interconnecting corridors.

Although the hospital was fairly new, it didn't look particularly clean. Crosby could remember a time when resident hospital cleaners devoted their whole day to making corridors and wards positively shine – that was until the popular innovation of contract cleaning arrived – a concept that usually involved putting the work out to tender before accepting the lowest bid. Crosby was convinced that the money saving policy was responsible for introducing MRSA and other assorted super-bugs into NHS Hospitals.

Conversation between the two detectives was perfunctory. Having agreed on a course of action yesterday, Crosby didn't feel the need to engage in meaningless small talk this morning.

They eventually reached the rehabilitation ward. After applying antibacterial gel from hand-dispensers fixed to the wall Crosby and Taylor pushed their way through a set of double doors. Doctor Khani was waiting just inside. A brief smile revealed very white teeth against an olive skin. His gleaming jet black hair was short and heavily oiled.

After shaking hands with them both Doctor Khani led the way into a small adjacent office. The two detectives weren't asked to take a seat.

'I'm afraid this will have to be brief,' he said in a slightly accented voice. 'An urgent matter has arisen which requires my immediate attention. You will have already seen my report on the patient's injuries. I see no need to repeat them here – suffice to say he is making a rapid recovery.' Doctor Khani paused. 'There are other issues however. I arrived here from Pakistan three years ago, and during that time have experienced a lot of racial prejudice. None of it, however, compares to the level I have been subjected to over the past two days,' he paused again, choosing his words carefully. 'The man Roberts is a bigot, and I am considering an official complaint.'

Crosby nodded. 'We would be happy to pursue that for you Sir.'

Doctor Khani waved a hand. 'Later! I don't have the time at present. Mister Roberts might be sufficiently recovered to answer your questions but procedures dictate that someone should be present to ensure he doesn't tire.' He shrugged. 'Unfortunately I can't spare the staff. You're welcome to go ahead with the interview anyway but I personally think you'll find it a waste of time.'

The doctor glanced at his watch. 'I'm already late. You'll find Mister Roberts in the unit's side ward – second door on the left. We've had to separate him from the other patients. Good Luck!' Picking up a folder from his desk Doctor Khani brushed past both detectives, leaving them alone in the office.

'Better see what all the fuss is about,' Crosby said to Taylor. 'Ready?'

Taylor took off her ankle-length coat and draped it across a nearby chair. Crosby was surprised to see she was wearing a short top, close fitting jeans, and knee-length boots. The look wasn't what Taylor usually adopted for a working day. He hoped that Rees-Bramley hadn't suggested it. Playing mind games with Milner was one thing, agitating Stephen Roberts might result in a very different outcome.

The second door on the left was slightly ajar. Crosby pushed it open.

Roberts was propped up on three pillows. Even though it was badly swollen Crosby could still detect a large, round fleshy face – broad shoulders supporting a thick, squat neck. Most of Roberts' head was wrapped in a layer of bandages – the single sheet, pulled up to his chest appeared to be hiding another layer of bandaging wrapped around his mid-section. There were several fluid-filled, thick, plastic bags hanging from nearby stands – thin tubes ran to both the patient's head and arms. His left leg was raised slightly off the bed, an outline of a plaster-cast clearly defined. Where his right hand lay on top of the white sheet Crosby noted a bracelet of small, black swastikas, tattooed around his wrist.

Although the patient looked completely immobile, a pair of close-set eyes followed Crosby intently as he came through the door. The detective showed his identity card. 'Studwell CID. Are you up to answering a few questions Stephen?'

No reply.

'We're here about the attack carried out on you,' Crosby said.

Still no response.

'Do you remember anything about it?' the detective asked.

Roberts just stared at him.

Crosby shrugged. 'We'll do it your way then.' He nodded at Roberts' injuries. 'You must be losing your touch.'

It drew a response. 'And you can fuck off back to the pigsty!' Even through a damaged mouth the voice was loud and aggressive.

'Must devalue your street cred,' the detective said. 'Getting jumped that easily.'

'Told you to fuck off Frank!'

Crosby didn't let it show, but he was taken by surprise. How the hell did Roberts know his name?

Taylor chose the moment to step out from behind him. Roberts latched onto her. His small close-set eyes roamed over the policewoman's body. He nodded appreciatively. 'This your bitch Frank?'

Taylor looked amused. 'Why is it that men of particularly low intellect feel the need to insult women Stephen? Is it because they feel threatened? Do I threaten you Stephen?'

Roberts tried to push himself upright. 'Watch your mouth bitch!'

'Or what? You'll shut me up? Slap me around? Meet me in a dark alley and assault my kids?'

Roberts' eyes flashed but he didn't reply.

Crosby wondered what the hell Taylor was playing at. This wasn't what they'd discussed yesterday. He glanced across at her. She gave a slight shrug – as if to say 'You weren't getting anywhere.'

Taylor stepped closer to Roberts, invading his personal space. 'A young mother was attacked by a gang of thugs in Akers Lane last night. We have reason to believe that you were responsible for injuring one of her children.'

Roberts didn't reply. Crosby could see he was agitated though.

Taylor continued to pressurise him. 'You were identified!'

'Fucking well charge me then!'

'There's no hurry! It's not as if you're going anywhere.'

'Off you fucking well trot then,' Roberts said to the policewoman. 'Take old Grandfather Plod with you.'

Crosby leant over the bed, keeping his voice low, 'Your existence offends me Roberts. I resent having to spend time investigating this attack.' He prodded the gang-leader's chest with his forefinger. 'Inflicting injuries on babies and small children puts you at the bottom of my evolutionary scale – and I'll be working hard to see that you're put away.'

Roberts pushed his bandaged face forward. 'You don't get it do you Plod! We're fireproof! No-one's going to testify against me. I'd have a word. Get it sorted!' He shrugged. 'That's how it works! And there's fuck all you can do about it.'

Crosby let it go. He pulled a mobile phone from his pocket and snapped a photograph of Roberts lying on the bed. 'Something to pin on our investigation board Stephen. It'll give the team a lift!' Childish! Crosby regretted it.

Roberts struggled to raise his head from the pillow. Even with all the stitching to his face he still managed to screw up his mouth, spitting in

Crosby's direction. The detective made a move towards his bed. Taylor stepped in front of him. There was a rap on the door and it opened inwards. A harassed-looking nurse put her head round. 'Detective Sergeant Crosby?'

'Yes!'

'Urgent phone call for you!' She left immediately.

Crosby headed for the door. Taylor followed him.

'Best keep an eye on that grandchild of yours Frank,' Roberts called after the detective. 'Can't let them out of your sight these days. Not with all these fucking paedophiles around.'

Crosby stopped. Taylor put a hand to his back and eased him through the door. 'We'll need to talk,' he said to her outside. 'We both lost it in there.'

She nodded.

At the nurse's station a telephone receiver had been left off the hook. He picked it up. 'Detective Sergeant Crosby speaking!'

'Sarge! DC Jones here! Urgent message from the DI. You're to get over to Sixfields immediately. The Broadwell Industrial Trading Estate. Just off Bridmore Road.'

'And?' Crosby asked.

'That's all I have,' Jones replied. 'It is priority though.'

'Where's the DI?'

'Already there! So is DC Berne!'

'On my way!' Crosby replaced the receiver. 'Urgent shout in Sixfields!' he said to Taylor. 'Grab your coat!'

As he waited for Taylor to collect her coat Crosby felt a sense of unease, and not just because of how easily he'd lost control of the interview. How did Roberts know his name, and that he had a grandchild.

CHAPTER 12

Broadwell Trading Estate: Wed 24 January 2007: 11.00 am

Broadwell's site entrance was blocked by two squad cars, their emergency warning lights sending out intermittent blue flashes into the grey surround.

Crosby slid his window down. The uniformed PC leant forward to peer at both their warrant cards. 'Probably best if you leave the car outside Sir. It's getting a bit crowded in there.'

Crosby manoeuvred his car onto the grass verge and parked up. Taylor fell into step beside him as they hurried back towards the flashing blue lights. 'Where are we headed?' Crosby said to the PC.

'Unit twelve Sir! Over in the far corner!'

The two detectives made their way to an unmarked white SOCO van and an ambulance, both vehicles parked outside one of the units. Something began to niggle at the back of Crosby's mind. It remained annoyingly out of reach but he didn't have the time to pursue it. They glanced across at a small knot of estate workers gathered outside one of the units opposite. PC Jennings was on crowd control. Crosby raised a hand in acknowledgment.

A narrow ribbon of blue and white warning tape had been stretched across the front entrance of unit twelve. PC Stewart stood guard behind the tape.

'Is it OK to go in?' Crosby asked.

'Yes Sir!' Stewart stood aside to let them through 'The Scene-of-Crimes team are already inside.'

Crosby stooped under the tape and pushed the half-open door. Taylor followed him. Ian Brown was inside taking photographs of the office interior. 'Give me a second Frank and I'll take you through.'

'What have we got?' Crosby asked.

'We've got a dead body!' Brown said without looking up. 'Try not to brush up against anything! It's a tight squeeze in here.'

The SOCO fired off a few more flashes before leading Crosby and

Taylor through into the unit's main service area. Six portable sets of rigged emergency lighting illuminated a grotesque scenario.

'Jesus Christ!' mouthed Crosby.

Suspended above one of the service bays, brightly lit by the powerful arc lamps, hung a man's naked body. Taylor gagged and reached into her coat pocket for a handkerchief. The stench was overpowering.

Crosby had seen enough dead bodies during the course of his career but he still found it difficult to routinely view a life that had been snuffed out by violent means. The two detectives stood motionless for a few seconds, shocked into silence at the scene in front of them.

Concreted into the floor, on either side of the service bay, were two upright metal girders – a short crossbar section bolted across the top. Suspended from the crossbar section was a hoist and pulley device, designed to lift engines from the body of vehicles. Chains from the hoist had been lashed around the ankles of a young, naked male, who'd been hoisted six feet up into the air, to hang upside down over the service bay's pit. A thick rope had been knotted around his neck. Set into the ground below him was a metal hoop, through which the rope had been looped and secured.

'Can't move him yet,' the SOCO said breezily. 'We're waiting for the Home Office Pathologist to arrive.' He walked over towards the suspended body. 'An unusual modus operandi though. I'll give you a guided tour.'

Crosby and Taylor moved reluctantly towards the service bay, familiar with the matter of fact attitude that Ian Brown had to his work. Dead body or not, it was just a crime scene that required processing.

'You don't need to be an expert in forensic pathology to see how he was dispatched,' Brown said as he casually viewed the naked body. 'Neck tied to the floor – chain wrapped around his ankles – motorised hoist used to haul him up into the air by his legs! Poor bastard was literally stretched to breaking point, and then they just kept the motor running. You can see where all the cartilages and joints have been ripped from their sockets.' The SOCO shook his head. 'Hook someone up between a pair of horses running in opposite directions and you'd get the same result.'

Crosby finally managed a question. 'Is that rag stuffed into his mouth?'

'He'd have made a lot of bloody noise otherwise.' Brown pointed to the victim's face. 'Look at his eyes. They've almost been pressurised from their sockets.'

Crosby put a hand over his nose and mouth as he looked down into the service bay's well. The victim's injuries had caused him to bleed profusely, and he'd also voided all his body waste – excrement and urine running down his whole length, before slopping into the blood-covered pit below.

A sour bile rose in Crosby's throat. He forced it back down. 'That's inhumane!'

'Not pretty is it?' the Scot agreed. 'Poor bastard's just been ripped apart. And he's starting to smell a bit ripe now – probably been hanging there for a couple of days. If there's any similarities to the one we had last Friday we've got a very sick individual out there.'

Professional instincts finally kicked in, forcing Crosby to scan the surrounding area. Most of the central floor space was taken up by two service bays – oil-stained wooden workbenches ran around the perimeter walls. In the bay adjacent to where the body was hanging sat a rusting old Ford Escort, its bonnet left raised and open, as if the previous tenants had vacated in a hurry. A SOCO team, clad in their white non-contaminant suits, were busy sweeping the unit's interior.

'We'd better make a start,' Crosby said. 'Is the DI about?'

'Waste of fucking space!' Brown snorted. 'Had an urgent phone call and left. Wanted you to cover the preliminaries.'

Crosby shrugged. 'Doesn't really matter. HQ will be putting a Major Investigation Unit together for this one. Do you know if there's a Senior Investigating Officer on the way?'

The Scot raised his eyebrows. 'Like they're going to tell me!'

'Who else have we got on site?' Crosby asked.

'There's an ambulance crew outside,' Brown replied. 'And we're waiting for a team from the local Fire Station to help cut the body down. Uniformed police are on crowd control and two more squad cars arrived ten minutes ago to check out the other vacant units.'

'Is DC Berne about?'

'He's interviewing the poor sod who discovered our victim.' Brown started to move away. 'Do you need me for anything else Frank? I need to get on.'

'Thanks Ian!' Crosby said. 'I can pick it up from here.'

He turned to Taylor. She'd been very quiet since entering the service area. Crosby took a closer look at her. 'You OK Grace?' She nodded. It didn't look convincing. The handkerchief was still to her mouth.

'Have a nose around the estate,' Crosby said to her. 'See what you can find. There must be some CCTV cameras about. Check out where they're sited.'

'Yes Sarge!' Taylor didn't waste any time in making her way back towards the exit.

Crosby quickly ran through a list of preliminary actions to be put in place before the SIO arrived, but there was still something tugging at his memory. Bloody annoying. He couldn't put a finger on it. Shaking his head, Crosby headed for the fresh air. Ian Brown followed him out leaving his SOCO team to secure the interior. PC Stewart was still stationed in front of the warning tape as both men exited the front office.

A shout of 'Frank!' brought Crosby up short. Rees-Bramley was fifty yards away, striding briskly towards them.

'Halleluiah! We can all sleep safe in our beds now.' Brown murmured. 'Here comes the fucking caped crusader.'

Rees-Bramley's face was unusually flushed. 'A quick word Frank!' He turned to the Scot. 'You as well Ian.' He drew them into a close circle. 'I had to attend an urgent call from HQ. They're about to move in a Major Investigation Unit – the Senior Investigating Officer has already been appointed.' Rees-Bramley paused. 'Due to extenuating circumstances it was not possible to select him from the current standby list.'

Ian Brown continued to look on impatiently, not yet aware of what was coming. Crosby had his suspicions – it didn't give him a particularly warm feeling. Rees-Bramley drew himself up a fraction. 'You may be aware that my name has been on the MIU reserve list for over a year now,' he paused again. 'Twenty minutes ago I was appointed Senior Investigating Officer for this investigation. My promotion to acting Detective Chief Inspector will take place with immediate effect.'

The Scot slowly realised what Rees-Bramley had just said, and what the implications were for him and his team. He muttered an excuse about being busy and headed towards his van.

'We'll need to talk shortly,' Rees-Bramley called after him.

'Aye!' the SOCO responded, 'if you can get your fucking head through the door' – but he made sure Rees-Bramley was well out of earshot when he said it.

'Congratulations Sir!' Crosby said to the new DCI.

'Thank you Frank!' Rees-Bramley shook the detective's extended hand.

'It's a one-off appointment at the moment. I'll need to make an impression.' He took Crosby's arm and steered him to a quiet corner. 'It came with a proviso. HQ have indicated they would like you as my deputy – it would carry an acting rank of Detective Inspector,' Rees-Bramley paused. 'Apparently you've had experience of working in an MIU before.'

Crosby stalled. He might have anticipated Rees-Bramley's appointment but the offer of Deputy SIO had genuinely surprised him – and he wasn't particularly overwhelmed by it.

As a young rookie policeman he'd been involved in two previous MIU investigations, one of them a complete disaster. The initial direction from senior officers had been flawed – and when the killings continued, without any sign of a breakthrough, the press began to crucify them. Morale within the team hit rock bottom – it broke the senior officer in charge and he never recovered his health.

The hours had been long, the pressure intense, and home life was non-existent – at least three marriages within the team hadn't survived. Crosby was single at the time but the experience had scarred him, and he had never actively sought attachment to a Major Investigation Unit again. At his time of life Crosby didn't particularly relish a re-run of those experiences. Rees-Bramley wanted it though. Wanted it badly. Crosby could smell his eagerness.

He looked up. 'Did you support my proposed appointment Sir?'

The DCI hesitated. 'I indicated that your style of investigation might not be suited to the rank of a Detective Inspector'.

Crosby nodded. 'Not your first choice then!'

Rees-Bramley didn't reply.

'An MIU has to be a tightly knit team,' Crosby said. 'If the senior officers aren't compatible it doesn't work.'

Rees-Bramley nodded. 'Absolutely! You may not have been my first choice but we've been working together for over six months now, and I'm confident you can adapt to the role of my deputy. Rees-Bramley shrugged. 'Differences of opinion can also spark a healthy working relationship. If you do decide to accept, I can promise you my full backing and support.'

Crosby hesitated. Rees-Bramley sounded sincere enough but he wasn't entirely convinced. 'I'll need to talk it over with my wife. It'll make a difference at home.'

Rees-Bramley nodded. 'Of course! But I don't anticipate this being a long drawn out investigation. With modern technology and the advances in forensic science we can nail this one early. And if there's a connection with Friday night we can hit the ground running. Preliminary work's already been done.'

Crosby nodded to himself. It was the same kind of rallying cry he'd heard from his DCI all those years back. Three dead bodies later, and no leads, saw senior officers setting up portable camp beds in the MIU office.

'Do we have a serial killer on our hands Frank?' Rees-Bramley asked him.

'Two young males. Both stripped naked! Both exhibited in bizarre circumstances!' Crosby shrugged. 'It's a lot of coincidence! If there is a link you haven't got the luxury of time. It's only been five days since the last attack.'

'Unusual for a serial murderer to target males,' the DCI pursed his lips. 'A possible homosexual link. We'll need to open a line of enquiry.'

Crosby frowned. 'We Sir?'

'Don't pass up the opportunity Frank.' Rees-Bramley said. 'It's the pinnacle of a detective's career to be appointed senior officer in a Major Investigation Unit.'

Crosby had to admit he was tempted. 'I'll ring you with a decision tonight Sir.'

'The greatest privilege a detective can be entrusted with,' Rees-Bramley continued. 'Is to be given responsibility for investigating the murder of a fellow human being.'

'Bloody Hell!' Crosby muttered inwardly. 'I'd save that one for the press conference.'

'The team's already being assembled,' Rees-Bramley began to brief Crosby as if he'd already accepted the post. 'I've requested the incident room be set up at Studwell. It'll be less of a disruption as we are already based there, and it's close to Sixfields. Accommodation won't be a problem,' the newly appointed DCI spoke quickly, running on adrenalin. 'The HOLMES team should be in place and operating by tomorrow morning – I want them inputting everything we've gathered since last Friday. With the statements we take today there should be enough data to initiate some preliminary search patterns.'

'Do you want to run through the checklist for this morning?' Crosby asked.

Rees-Bramley nodded. 'A Home Office pathologist is already on the way. Paramedics have confirmed we have a dead body, so I've cancelled the Police Surgeon.'

'Coroner's Office?'

'They've been informed.'

Crosby realised he was assuming the actions of a Deputy SIO. Perhaps he'd subconsciously accepted the post already. 'Crime scene secure?' he continued.

Rees-Bramley nodded.

'Victim's identity?'

'Not yet established.'

'Evidence?'

'SOCO team are on-site. Investigations on-going.'

'Suspects?'

Rees-Bramley shook his head. 'Not at this stage. We've made a start on taking statements from the estate's workforce. They need to be completed before the day's out. DC Berne is interviewing Broadwell's leasing agent, along with the receptionist from NST Services – she reported the lights being left on in unit twelve last Monday.'

'Shit!' Crosby snapped his fingers. 'NST Services! I must have seen their name when I arrived. It's where Robert Milner said he was employed.'

Rees-Bramley's eyes widened. 'That's a big bloody coincidence!'

'Would he dump a body on his own doorstep?' Crosby asked.

Rees-Bramley shrugged. 'Stephen Roberts was found close to Silver Street. Have a word with Milner's employer later. See if you can get some more background on him.'

'Milner's probably on-site. Do you want to speak with him now?'

The DCI shook his head. 'Not at this stage. Sort out a search warrant for Silver Street. We'll get another interview set up.'

'Yes Sir!' Crosby had given up indicating that he hadn't made a decision about the job yet.

The DCI saw Ian Brown trying to duck back un-noticed into unit twelve. 'I need to see him. I'll catch up with you later Frank.' Rees-Bramley took off, rapidly closing the distance between himself and the Scene of Crimes Officer.

Crosby shook his head. If last Saturday was anything to go by, Ian Brown was about to have his patience tested to the limit.

The detective turned to look across at the NST Services unit.

Robert Milner peered back at him, from a small window in the main storeroom. He had watched the conversation between both detectives and continued to observe as Crosby crossed over the road and headed directly towards him.

After replacing the pair of heavy duty gloves, that he'd removed from the stock cupboard last week, Milner turned and left the room.

CHAPTER 13

The large open plan office, that Rees-Bramley had designated an MIU incident room, looked chaotic and disorganised. Crosby threaded his way through a milling crowd of civilian and uniformed personnel. Members of the team had already claimed individual workspaces, and were busy organising their desks and putting away personal possessions.

Items of British Telecom kit lay scattered throughout the room as two of their engineers busied themselves with connecting telephone lines and communications equipment. It looked as if the IT support group had already moved computers and server units into an area reserved for the HOLMES team. No surprise there. The DCI would have made it a priority request that data input should begin at the earliest opportunity.

Crosby found Rees-Bramley at the far end of the room. His DCI had commandeered one of the partially sectioned-off areas. It gave him a clear, uninterrupted view of the main office. Without a door to knock Crosby peered around the corner. Rees-Bramley's workspace was already tidied and operational, his ever present laptop open and in use. The DCI had removed his jacket and folded his shirtsleeves to just below the elbow.

Crosby got the impression that his DCI was trying to project an image of how a Senior Investigating Officer ought to look on his first day – energetically directing operations at the team's hub.

Rees-Bramley looked-up and waved him in. 'Welcome aboard Detective Inspector! Doesn't get much better than this does it?'

The title had a nice ring to it. Crosby had in fact spent several hours last night deciding whether or not to accept the post. Talking it through with his wife hadn't helped. She said it had to be his decision. Thirty years of marriage told him she wasn't happy though – another level of disruption to deal with.

It had been a long evening. In the end it was probably an excess of single malt that made the decision for him – several generous measures making the rank of Detective Inspector sound very attractive – especially when repeated out loud.

Following on from that it had been very easy to conjure up a picture of Studwell's newly appointed Deputy SIO being solely responsible for bringing the investigation to a speedy and successful conclusion. Crosby had telephoned Rees-Bramley with his decision before the whisky had worn off.

Walking through the incident room this morning had confirmed his decision. The buzz of excitement coming from Rees-Bramley and his assembled team was infectious – and since committing himself there was no denying the frisson of anticipation that had been with him since last night.

'I've sorted you an office next to mine.' The DCI got to his feet and walked through to an adjoining section. Crosby followed him. 'Your telephone and PC have been connected,' Rees-Bramley said. 'You just need to retrieve personal stuff from your old desk.'

Crosby looked over his partition into the main office. 'I see Berne and Taylor have been co-opted.'

'I've had to post them in temporarily.' The DCI shrugged. 'We were short on manpower.'

'Anyone claimed our victim yet?' Crosby asked.

Rees-Bramley shook his head. 'I've arranged a press conference for this afternoon. Someone out there must be missing him.'

'Is there a team brief this morning?'

'Ten o'clock,' the DCI said. 'They've all been made aware of it.'

'Anything specific you need me to be getting on with?'

'I want that search warrant hurried up. It might be tenuous but there's a lot of circumstantial stuff mounting up against Robert Milner. Too many coincidences. We'll need to start looking at motives.'

Crosby made a note in his pocketbook. 'The warrant should be ready for you to sign by this afternoon Sir.'

'Make sure his car is included,' Rees-Bramley said.

Crosby made another note.

'Did you manage to speak with anyone at NST Services about him yesterday?' Rees-Bramley asked.

Crosby shook his head. 'The office manager wasn't there. I'll get someone to follow it up this afternoon.'

'Make sure they have a word with his work colleagues. See what they've got to say about him.' The DCI checked his watch. 'Right! I'll leave you to it. I need some time to make sense of this budget they've allocated me. Team briefing at ten o'clock remember.' He paused just outside the partition's entrance. 'It might be a good idea if both you and DC Taylor accompanied me to the press conference.'

'Again Sir?'

'Continuity DI Crosby!' Rees-Bramley lowered his voice. 'And Frank! Remember what I said. Keep this one tight. By example, eh!'

'Aye Aye Sir!' Crosby muttered under his breath as the DCI turned and left.

On accessing his e-mail Crosby found that Rees-Bramley had sent him a brief résumé and snapshot on each member of the team. He spent half an hour familiarising himself with their details. After tidying away personal possessions and paperwork retrieved from his old office the time had ticked around to ten o'clock. He looked up to find a waiting Rees-Bramley at the partition. 'Ready?' his DCI asked.

The two detectives walked out into the main office. Support staff and communication engineers had completed their work and vacated the room. Members of the MIU team were waiting for them gathered in front of a large white marker-board – the promised electronic briefing screen had not yet materialised. Crosby was surprised to feel a few nerves. He tried to ignore the butterflies as twelve pairs of eyes followed their entrance.

Rees-Bramley had replaced his jacket for the briefing, presenting his usual veneered self to the assembled team. Crosby loosened his collar and tie, standing to one side as the SIO assumed centre stage. 'Ladies and Gentlemen! Good Morning! My name is Detective Chief Inspector Rees-Bramley and I have been appointed Senior Investigating Officer for this enquiry.' He turned to his right. 'This is Detective Inspector Crosby! He is my Deputy SIO and your first reporting officer.'

All eyes swivelled towards Crosby. He hoped his casual nod projected a confident enough air.

Newcomers not familiar with the DCI's style of management were quickly made aware of it. 'You will, during the course of this investigation, become aware of the high standards I expect from my officers. Individuals who do not adhere to those standards can look forward to the privilege of attending a personal one-to-one interview with me.'

Crosby winced inwardly. That was team building covered then. He looked down at his shoes and found an interesting area of carpet to study.

Rees-Bramley moved across to the white briefing-board. Attached to the board were photographs of both Stephen Roberts and yesterday's unidentified victim. 'You are all aware by now that this Major Investigation

Unit has been assembled because of the body found on Broadwell's Trading Estate.' Rees-Bramley tapped the photograph nearest to him. 'Our other victim goes by the name of Stephen Roberts – attacked and left for dead near Akers Lane on Friday night.' The DCI shrugged. 'A possible connection. Roberts remains in a hospital bed but was interviewed yesterday morning.' He turned to Crosby.

The DI took a step forward. 'Roberts is attached to a local gang from the Sixfields estate. A particularly unpleasant individual as DC Taylor will confirm. Refused to answer any questions about the attack on him and was very hostile about us being there.'

Rees-Bramley turned back to the team. 'What I propose this morning is that everyone familiarise themselves with the information gathered thus far. Copies of statements and forensic reports have been forwarded to your e-mail folders. We will re-convene back here at four o'clock. By that time I want each officer to have two separate lines of enquiry which they will present to the team this afternoon.' He scanned the watching faces. 'I'm looking for lateral thinking! Theories! Hunches! Best Guesses!' Rees-Bramley nodded to his DI again.

Crosby had already been briefed about the DCI's brainstorming session and wasn't entirely in agreement with it. 'You might want to take notes,' the DI said. There was a scramble for pocketbooks. 'Areas to be looking at!' he continued. 'Turf warfare! Drug related issues! Straightforward robbery! Unprovoked random attacks! Homosexual revenge killings.'

'Were either of the victims raped Sir?' Taylor asked. 'It wouldn't appear so,' Crosby replied. 'But we are still waiting for a full report on yesterday's victim from the Home Office Pathologist.'

'Will our investigation be focused on the second victim?'

Rees-Bramley interrupted. 'Outwardly yes!' At this stage I don't want rumours circulating about a serial killer roaming the estate. It will create a general panic among the residents.'

Crosby looked across at the office clock and caught Rees-Bramley's eye. The DCI nodded curtly before turning back to the team. 'We'll have to pick this up later. I have another meeting to attend. DI Crosby will be in office for the remainder of this morning should you encounter any problems.'

Nodding to the assembled group, Rees-Bramley picked up his folder and marched back towards his office.

All eyes turned towards Crosby. The Deputy SIO gathered himself. 'My intention is to speak with you all individually this morning. We need to establish the lines of enquiry that you will be responsible for.'

'Sir!' one of the detectives said. 'Will these lines of enquiry be based on the DCI's directives or as a result of this morning's exercise?' – the voice was heavy with sarcasm. Someone obviously trying to create an impression.

Crosby identified the questioner from his snapshot. Brian Jefferies – a thick-set, balding individual, the crumpled suit looking as if it had been slept in overnight. He remained slouched in his chair. Crosby had dealt with dozens of Brian Jefferies' during his career and recognised that he was being tested.

'Brian!' Crosby said, 'I'll warn you now. The DCI doesn't understand irony and will not tolerate being addressed in a casual manner.' The DI paused. 'And neither will I.'

Jefferies eased himself upright.

'To answer your question,' Crosby continued, 'the Senior Investigating Officer will ultimately decide on what lines of enquiry we pursue. This morning's exercise is to ensure that you have all familiarised yourself with the information we have.'

'Sir?' Jefferies again, not yet prepared to give it up. 'As I've been through all of the reports and statements several times, is it still necessary for me to take part in the exercise?'

'Are you able to tell me what Steven Roberts' first conviction was?' Crosby asked.

Jefferies hesitated.

'Do you know what unit number our unknown victim was found in?'

'No Sir!'

Crosby nodded. 'That is the level of detail and typical of the questions that DCI Rees-Bramley will be asking you this afternoon. I suggest that everyone re-reads the statements and reports again. It's that smallest of detail that might provide our all-important breakthrough.' The DI looked at his watch and stood up. 'We're back here in approximately four hours.'

There was a general murmuring and scraping of chairs as the team got to their feet. Crosby made the MIU Exhibits Officer's desk his first port of call. It was to be another hour before he returned to his office with a draft outline of individual assignments for Rees-Bramley to agree and authorise.

In the main office, no-one was leaving for lunch. Sandwiches and coffee were ordered from Studwell's staff canteen as members of the team remained at their desks – working on contributions for the afternoon presentation.

Some of them were getting restless – Paul Berne in particular. Having been sat in front of a computer screen for most of the morning he wasn't impressed with Rees-Bramley's brainstorming session. Detectives followed solid leads – interviewed suspects and witnesses – all this lateral thinking and blue-sky shit didn't sit comfortably with him. He shouted across the office, 'Grace! Is it OK to be thinking outside of your box instead of mine?'

Taylor gave him a warning glance.

Berne pulled a face and turned to Jefferies. 'Lateral bloody thinking! Isn't that what our DCI is paid for?'

'His first major investigation isn't it. Hasn't got a bloody clue.' Jefferies was proving to be as loud and opinionated as Berne. 'Is he married?'

Berne shrugged.

'Jumped up little prick!' Jefferies said. 'Looks like a shirt-lifter to me. You'll need to watch him. Good looking boy like you.' The voice was deliberately pitched to get a reaction. It draw a few sniggers from around the office.

'And what the fuck's that supposed to mean!' Berne didn't like being the butt of jokes and he particularly didn't like being included in references about gays – Berne took his heterosexual reputation very seriously.

Jefferies didn't look too concerned at having annoyed him.

Grace Taylor looked up and shot both detectives another warning glance. The bad language didn't concern her unduly but she felt Berne used it in the office to intimidate other female officers, and he was well aware of Rees-Bramley's code of behaviour.

Berne raised his hand in apology. 'Sorry Grace!'

Taylor knew the apology was insincere but at least others had noted the exchange. She scribbled a short note, tucking it in between a sheaf of papers on top of her desk.

Retrieving an expensive, designer leather handbag, from underneath her chair, Taylor headed for the office door. Several pairs of male eyes followed her progress from the room.

Jefferies turned to Berne. 'I wouldn't say no!'

'In your fucking dreams!' Berne looked genuinely amused. 'You're the wrong shade and in the wrong tax bracket.'

Jefferies shrugged and went back to his screen. Berne got up from his chair and sauntered over to Taylor's workstation. Several sheets of printout had been stacked in a neat pile on her desk. Keeping an eye on the door Berne picked up the printouts and flicked idly through them. 'All my own work Paul!' Taylor's scribbled message said.

He carefully replaced the papers in their original position and wandered casually back to his desk.

Crosby collected DC Taylor from the main office at one thirty pm. Rees-Bramley had arranged a late afternoon press conference in order to catch the morning editions. Passing from the CID Annex into Studwell's central headquarters block, it took Crosby and Taylor several minutes to navigate all of the inter-connecting corridors and stairwells before they arrived at the station's lecture theatre.

Rees-Bramley met them at the door. 'Same procedure as last time,' the DCI said. 'Follow me down to the front. You'll find three chairs set out on the platform. I'll be sitting in the centre. DI Crosby to my right. On the table in front of you will be a copy of the statement being read out. Questions will be dealt with by me. Keep your pocketbooks to hand in case I require you to make notes.'

Crosby raised his eyebrows a fraction as Taylor glanced across at him.

Rees-Bramley opened the door. 'Let's get it done then.'

Crosby bit back an impulse to shout 'Roll cameras!'

The noisy hubbub stopped as they entered the auditorium. Three television units followed their progress down towards centre stage. All of the auditorium seats were occupied today as both local and national media had sent their reporters along – the atmosphere was far more charged than at the Stephen Roberts press conference earlier that week.

After mounting three wooden steps, set into one side of the raised platform, Rees-Bramley strode briskly towards centre stage followed by Crosby and Taylor. Most of the platform was occupied by a long rectangular table, covered in heavy, dark blue cloth. A single microphone sat in front of the DCI's chair. After switching it on Rees-Bramley sat down and reached for the water jug, filling all three glasses on the table. He took a few moments to scrutinise the assembled gathering – he'd told Crosby on more than one occasion that it sent out the all-important first signal to a waiting audience.

The DCI leant in towards his microphone. 'Ladies and Gentlemen. My name is Detective Chief Inspector Rees-Bramley and I have been appointed the Senior Investigating Officer for this enquiry. Two of my team join me this afternoon. Detective Inspector Frank Crosby and Detective Constable Grace Taylor.' Rees-Bramley glanced down at two single sheets of printout in front of him before continuing. 'This press conference has been convened to issue a statement regarding the body of a young, black male discovered on the Broadwell Trading Estate yesterday morning. The statement outlines known facts and includes some of our initial findings.'

As his DCI read out the prepared statement Crosby surveyed their surroundings. The lecture theatre was small, a purpose-built auditorium that accommodated up to fifty people. Five shallow tiers of seating sloped down towards a raised dais at its front. Although Crosby recognised a number of local hacks in the audience most faces were new to him – from the national dailies presumably.

Rees-Bramley was coming to the end of his statement. 'And I would ask that your reports include a request for members of the public to come forward with any information they might have relating to this case.'

The DCI looked up. There was a hubbub of noise as all of the reporters tried to put their questions at the same time.

Rees-Bramley raised a hand. 'I will indicate who has the floor.' He pointed into the front row. 'Your name and who you represent.'

The reporter got to his feet. 'Harry Williams! Wolverhampton Echo! It was only six days ago that another young male was attacked and left for dead on the Sixfields Estate. Are you able to tell us whether the same person is responsible for both attacks?'

If Rees-Bramley had been hoping to suppress rumours about a serial killer he was mistaken. 'The victim of last Friday's incident is currently recovering in hospital' the DCI said. 'That particular case is being dealt with by Studwell's Criminal Investigation Department.'

'At the press conference I attended earlier this week you were actually leading that investigation Chief Inspector.'

'Yes I was!'

'You'd be well placed to judge for similarities between the two attacks then.'

'I've already indicated the two cases are being dealt with as separate incidents,' Rees-Bramley replied. 'Several other lines of enquiry are being currently pursued.'

'Your appointment would be a logical one though,' Williams persisted, 'If there did happen to be a link between the killings.'

Rees-Bramley ignored the question and pointed to another raised hand.

'Bryan Marples! Birmingham Post! You indicated that several lines of enquiry are being pursued. Are you able to tell us what they are?'

'Not at this stage!'

'Might it be a gang related attack?'

'Possibly.'

'Peter Wright! West Midlands Gazette! How close are you to identifying the victim, Chief Inspector?'

'Enquiries are on-going.'

'Has anyone actually been reported missing since the body was found, Chief Inspector?'

'No!'

Rees-Bramley pointed to another raised hand.

'Derek Mahey! Daily Mail! Last Friday night a young mother and her child were assaulted in Akers Way, close to where the first victim was discovered.'

'Unconnected!' Rees-Bramley replied. 'The incident happened some time before Stephen Roberts was discovered and doesn't form part of our investigation.'

Again not strictly true but Crosby could understand Rees-Bramley playing the incident down – Janet Sterne was already under pressure to identify Roberts – If the press discovered that he'd assaulted Sterne's child there'd be reporters permanently camped out on her doorstep.

'Just a coincidence then?' Mahey said.

'Next?' Rees-Bramley was becoming tetchy. Crosby recognised the signs.

'Jon Barton! The Sun! Can I ask DC Taylor what her particular role will be during this investigation?'

Grace Taylor looked across at Rees-Bramley. 'DC Taylor is just one member of the team,' the DCI replied. 'All of our officers are trained to the same exacting high standards – making their individual posts interchangeable.'

Barton was obviously looking for a different slant to his story and addressed Taylor again. 'Can I ask about your experiences in what is essentially a male-dominated environment?'

Rees-Bramley was having none of it 'Mister Barton! This is a murder investigation, not an interview for your general features section. Next!'

Another reporter clambered to his feet. 'Andrew Johnson! Chief Crime Reporter for the Daily Express! Is it true that both victims were found stripped, mutilated, and exhibited in a ritualistic manner?'

A murmur ran round the room. Reporters knew what sold newspapers.

Rees-Bramley shook his head. 'Use of the term ritualistic would be irresponsible and sensationalist.'

'Is it true though?'

The DCI raised his voice slightly. 'You are experienced enough to know that certain crime scene details have to be withheld until further into the investigation.'

There was a muffled comment from the auditorium, and a ripple of laughter ran round the audience. Rees-Bramley sat stony-faced in his chair, waiting for it to die down, but the briefing was already breaking up. Reporters had their story and were already heading for the exit doors.

Crosby and Taylor remained at the table. Rees-Bramley pulled the plug from his microphone.

'They've got newspapers to sell.' Crosby shrugged. 'And a serial killer out on the streets makes better copy than a gang related turf-war being the cause.'

'It still needs playing down,' Rees-Bramley said.

Crosby shook his head. 'They'll run with it now.'

The DCI stood abruptly. 'Lot to get through. And we need to brief the team about what's happened here.'

The three detectives descended into a virtually empty auditorium. Taylor grimaced at Crosby as they followed a briskly striding Rees-Bramley out of the theatre.

Studwell OCU HQ: Thursday 25 January 2007: 8.15 pm

Crosby watched the red-and-white hooped pole rise smoothly upwards, until it pointed into the dark sky. Acknowledging the security guard he nosed his old Hillman out through Studwell's entrance gate and onto the main road. It had been a long day.

After the press conference, Rees-Bramley's mood had continued into the afternoon's brainstorming session – where he'd been less than complimentary about the team's efforts. Paul Berne was again singled out for criticism, concerning the limited amount of feedback coming from his contacts on the estate.

Crosby yawned. His back ached, his eyes felt scratchy, and he was developing a headache. His first full day and the responsibility of higher rank already stretching him. If the breakthroughs didn't come quickly, it wouldn't get any easier.

Tomorrow's press coverage would hopefully generate more response. At the conclusion of their afternoon presentations, although late in the day, Rees-Bramley had sent out six of his team to follow up on earlier telephone calls – Crosby remaining incarcerated in the DCI's office until early evening.

At seven o'clock a messenger had arrived with pathology and forensic reports from the murder site – they had realised very little. Forensics indicated that all the hair, fibre and blood collected from inside unit twelve belonged to the victim. Fingerprints and footprints in and around the pit recess had been of poor quality and unlikely to help.

The Home Office Pathologist's report had more or less confirmed SOCO's interpretation of how the victim was despatched, indicating Saturday night as the probable time of murder.

Crosby blinked in the glare of oncoming headlights. He really was bone-achingly tired. To round off the perfect day his wife had telephoned at six o'clock to tell him she was going away for a couple of days, to look after their grandson.

The detective's eyelids drooped momentarily and he had to wind down the window to let in a blast of cold air. Forcing himself to switch off he concentrated on getting home – where another plate of cold salad was probably waiting for him.

CHAPTER 14

It was a cold, uninviting room – large for a kitchen, and sparsely furnished. The bare, grey walls, devoid of any fixtures or fittings, made it look impersonal, sterile, lacking in any kind of warmth or character. A sink and drainer unit sat in front of the window, their shades of white a welcome relief to the grey decor. Along an adjoining sidewall, between a bulky washing machine and small fridge, two plain, grey storage cupboards had been fitted.

In the middle of the room a small, bare, wooden table looked inadequate and isolated – the only other items of furniture were four straight backed kitchen chairs. In one of them a man sat hunched forward, his head low, looking at a newspaper spread across the table-top's scrubbed surface. The scene was one of intense loneliness, a still life tableau. For several minutes the man didn't move, then he stretched out a hand, his long, thin fingers turning a page of the newspaper.

After Milner had finished reading he carefully folded the newspaper back along its original creases. The article on Sixfields' murder investigation should have given him more satisfaction. Why didn't it?

There was also unfinished business lying in a hospital bed – Milner didn't know why he'd allowed him to survive. His obsessive nature was demanding that he complete the job. It gnawed at him. It needed tidying.

He got up to switch off the kitchen light, plunging the room into darkness. He sat back down. Several black shadows drifted to his side and stood protectively around him. Milner had begun to welcome their presence.

Logic told him the police would call again tonight. How many? Certainly Rees-Bramley and Crosby! Others? He became restless and got up from his chair. The shadows moved aside for him.

Opening a cupboard drawer Milner took out four coasters and placed them carefully on the table. The four plain coffee mugs he took from his cupboard were positioned precisely on top of the coasters.

He looked around the kitchen. Everything tidy and in its place. Milner despised clutter. His mother had always impressed upon him that a tidy mind kept a tidy home, and a tidy home produced a tidy mind. Which one came first though? Sometimes he would stare into space for hours, trying to fathom the logic of his mother's old adage. It was enough to turn sane individuals mad.

Milner laughed out loud. Then the tears welled up in his eyes as he remembered that his mother was no longer with him. One of the shadows gently took his hand and held it. They sat together and waited for the police to arrive.

CHAPTER 15

Studwell HQ: Major Incident Room: Friday 26 January 2007:
5.00 pm

Crosby clicked 'Save' on the word document he'd been drafting, scrolled back to the beginning, and began re-reading it. The investigation had moved on since yesterday and Crosby was putting together a report for his DCI to look through.

By early afternoon the incident room had logged a number of calls, all claiming to know who the murder victim was. Crosby had dispatched detectives to follow up on all of them. One of the calls was from a family whose son had been missing for several days – a common occurrence apparently, which was why it hadn't been initially reported. DC Emma Foulkes, the team's Family Liaison Officer, was currently with the missing person's mother, attending a formal identification at the hospital morgue.

Crosby finished reading through the report for Rees-Bramley and stood up. He looked over his partition into the main office. Virtually deserted today – apart from the HOLMES team at the far end. In addition to detectives following up this morning's telephone calls Grace Taylor was out talking with Janet Sterne again, and Paul Berne was somewhere on the Sixfields estate, hustling his paid contacts.

Officers were also at Broadwell's Industrial Trading Estate. Apart from having to complete statements from employees who'd not been at work on Wednesday, the NST Services Manager was being interviewed about Robert Milner's employment background and recent working patterns. Rees-Bramley wasn't in office either – a meeting with the Assistant Chief Constable. The DCI would be calling at the local magistrates court on his return journey to pick up the search warrant issued for Milner's house in Silver Street.

Crosby returned to his desk. He contemplated ringing his wife. When he'd telephoned her last night she'd told him their daughter-in-law was still not well and she wouldn't be coming home yet. He shrugged. The extended stay was probably due to Crosby's increasing number of late nights. It wasn't about to improve any.

A shrill, persistent ringing cut through his thoughts and he snatched at the receiver. It was DC Foulkes. 'OK Emma,' Crosby said. 'Make sure she gets home. Stay with her! I'll get someone round there to help you out.'

Crosby cut the connection, referred to a list on his desk, and punched in a mobile number. 'Phil? We have a positive ID on the murder victim. Name of Daniel Kwame. Saffron Court! Sixfields! The Families Officer is with the mother now. Get round there. You know what we need but don't push too hard.'

Rees-Bramley appeared just as he was replacing the receiver. 'We have a name and address for our murder victim Sir,' Crosby said. 'I've just sent DC Vickers round there to assist the Families Officer.'

Before Rees-Bramley could reply, the phone rang again. The call was brief, Crosby nodded. 'Yes! Thank you! One of our officers will be there shortly.' He replaced the receiver. 'And that was the hospital. Mister and Mrs Roberts have finally turned up.'

'Right!' Rees-Bramley began pacing the floor. 'Plenty to move on. Do Vickers and Foulkes require assistance?'

Crosby shook his head. 'Too many police. Vickers is experienced enough to get what we need.'

'OK! But tell him I want a full report before tomorrow morning.'

'Are we still interviewing Milner tonight?' Crosby asked.

The DCI nodded. 'Sort out a couple of DC's! Whoever's available! They can carry out the search whilst we talk to Milner. And I want to call in at the hospital on the way. Mister and Mrs Roberts might have something useful to tell us.' He checked his watch. 'We'll leave in ten minutes.'

'Do you need me along Sir?' Crosby asked.

'Yes!'

Rees-Bramley left abruptly – a tightly coiled spring that had been suddenly released. Crosby was decidedly slower out of his chair. He looked over the partitioning to see who was in office. Berne and Jefferies had returned and were at their desks.

'Premises search! Ten minutes!' he shouted down to them.

Two telephone calls later and Rees-Bramley had returned. Collecting Berne and Jefferies en route they headed out of the office.

'Did you ring DC Vickers to tell him I want that report on Kwame as soon as possible?' Rees-Bramley asked as they crossed the car park.

'Yes Sir!'

'What time did Milner finish work?'

'Four o'clock Sir!'

'Did you get any joy from the leasing agent on Broadwell's CCTV cameras?'

'They've not been loaded for the past three years,' Crosby replied.

The DCI nodded. 'Why doesn't that surprise me!'

They reached Rees-Bramley's car. The three passengers opened their doors and eased themselves across the soft leather upholstery. A twist of the key and the Jaguar's 4.2 litre V8 engine coughed into life before subsiding to a throaty growl. Berne and Jefferies sat in the rear, trying not to look impressed. Rees-Bramley manoeuvred the vehicle from its parking space and accelerated smoothly towards the exit barrier.

Out on the road Rees-Bramley switched his attention to Berne. 'You've been in Sixfields today?'

Berne nodded.

'What are your contacts saying?'

'They're telling me it's not down to a turf war Sir.'

'Sure about that are they?'

'Not totally Sir.' Berne leant forward, as if adding weight to his argument. 'But it's a huge estate. There could be as many as twenty gangs out there and most of them are very tight knit. Getting a direct line into them is almost impossible these days. We're having to rely on people at the fringes.'

'No drug conflicts?' Rees-Bramley asked. 'Territorial disputes?'

'It's all quiet Sir.'

'And you're happy with what's being passed to you?'

'I can tell when they're holding anything back Sir. They're as much in the dark as we are.'

The DCI arched his eyebrows. 'You consider we're in the dark then DC Berne?'

Berne started to reply but thought better of it.

Rees-Bramley glanced in his rear-view mirror and caught the smirk on Jefferies face. 'I'm glad you found that amusing DC Jefferies?' Rees-Bramley said. 'A sense of humour might come in useful later on, when you're sitting in the office typing up tonight's report. On my desk first thing tomorrow morning please!'

Crosby smiled to himself. In the current circumstances he found their exchanges a welcome, light relief.

Rees-Bramley looked in the mirror again. 'Have either of you given any thought to what we should be looking for at Milner's house tonight?'

Jefferies and Berne were hesitant to volunteer anything further.

The journey continued in comparative silence.

CHAPTER 16

The continual banging in Milner's head wouldn't go away. He pushed himself up from the table and glanced at his watch. Two hours had passed. He moved across to switch on the kitchen light. A dark shadow drifted away from his side. The persistent knocking continued.

Milner made his way out into the hallway and opened his front door. He surveyed the group in front of him, focusing on Rees-Bramley 'Inspector! Congratulations! Your recent promotion has been well publicised.'

'It's Chief Inspector!' the DCI said. 'There are a number of questions we need to ask if it's convenient Mister Milner.'

'Of course! Come in!' The four detectives followed him through to the kitchen.

Milner sat back down in the same chair. 'This is presumably about the body found near my place of work.'

'And why would you presume that?' Rees-Bramley asked.

'Because at the moment I appear to be the only employee at NST Services not to have been interviewed.'

'A statement will be taken tonight Mister Milner,' the DCI said. 'We also have a warrant to search your premises.'

Milner looked amused. 'Am I considered a suspect then?'

Rees-Bramley gestured at the coffee mugs, 'Are you expecting company?'

'The only visitors I receive these days are the police,' Milner said. 'I can offer you tea or coffee.'

The DCI waved a hand. 'Nothing for me, thank you.'

The other three detectives took their lead from Rees-Bramley and also declined. Milner was immediately on his feet to clear the mugs away, carefully aligning their position in one of his cupboards. Crosby noticed Berne and Jefferies exchanging glances. Both detectives were aware of

Milner's OCD but they still looked a little wary.

When Milner returned to his seat, Rees-Bramley and Crosby sat in two of the other chairs. Berne and Jefferies remained standing.

The DCI leant forward. 'I've just had an interesting conversation at the hospital with your ex-wife Mister Milner.'

'You have?' Milner didn't sound particularly surprised.

'She was visiting Stephen Roberts, the young male who was attacked on waste ground near Akers Lane last Friday and left for dead in the derelict play area.'

'Yes?'

'He is your son I believe.'

Four pairs of eyes focused on Milner to gauge his reaction. He knew the question was coming, and there'd been a whole week to rehearse his answer. 'It doesn't surprise me.' Milner shrugged his shoulders. 'He lost his way some years ago. I no longer have any contact with him.'

Crosby had expected more reaction. Rees-Bramley paused and waited a few seconds. 'You were unaware that the victim of last Friday night's attack was your son?'

'I've already told you!' Milner sounded annoyed. 'We no longer have any contact! Why wasn't I informed about this by the police?'

'According to our records his father is listed as Henry Roberts.' Rees-Bramley replied. 'The address is a flat in Birmingham.'

'That's his step-father! Your records need updating Chief Inspector.'

Crosby glanced across at his DCI. Rees-Bramley didn't look best pleased – "the underlying basis of a successful investigation is the quality of information held about it" – a favourite line he would quote to whoever had his attention.

'During your last visit, Chief Inspector, you inferred there was a connection to the incident in Akers Lane.' Milner folded his arms and leant back. 'Are you saying that my son was involved in the assault on Janet Sterne's baby?'

'Is that why you deny witnessing it?' Rees-Bramley asked.

'My son is a thug Chief Inspector. He wouldn't expect or receive any protection from me.'

Rees-Bramley left it. 'You are currently in the employ of NST Services,' he said. 'On the Broadwell Industrial Trading Estate.'

'Which has already been established.'

Milner sat relaxed in his chair. Crosby knew from their last visit how quickly that could change.

'You're aware that a body was discovered in one of the trading estate's vacant units on Wednesday,' Rees-Bramley said.

Milner nodded. 'Another unfortunate coincidence!'

The DCI looked up at him from underneath his eyebrows. 'I don't believe in them Mister Milner.'

'I suppose a detective's work is mapped out in a sequence of logical, structured steps.' Milner smiled. 'Not dissimilar to someone who suffers from OCD.'

'Unit Twelve!' Rees-Bramley said, a slight irritation in his voice. 'Did you notice anything suspicious in or around the vacated premises prior to last Wednesday?'

'No I didn't!'

'Did you have occasion to visit Broadwell's Trading Estate at any time over the weekend?'

'No!'

The DCI reached inside his jacket pocket to retrieve the search warrant. 'Detective Constables' Berne and Jefferies will be carrying out a detailed search of your house and car. Please check the document's details are in order.' Rees-Bramley placed the search warrant in front of Milner – who looked at it with feigned suspicion before picking it up.

Berne and Jefferies continued to stand rather awkwardly behind Rees-Bramley's chair. Milner had stared at them once or twice – he seemed to be enjoying their discomfort.

Milner took his time reading through the search warrant before handing it back. 'You've not included my garage in the warrant Chief Inspector. I'm no expert but does that mean I can refuse you permission to search it?'

'Fuck!' Crosby swore underneath his breath. DC Stone had been told to check whether there was a garage involved, but it was ultimately the Deputy SIO's responsibility to ensure the details were correct. Rees-Bramley looked distinctly unhappy.

'Our enquiries with the Local Housing Association didn't reveal any garage facilities,' Crosby said.

'The accuracy of their records seem to be on a par with those of the CID.' Milner was clearly enjoying himself. 'And I thought the police always double-checked their enquiries.' He waved a hand. 'It's not a problem. Search where you want. I've nothing to hide.'

Crosby turned to Berne and Jefferies and motioned his head towards the door. They left immediately.

Rees-Bramley waited for the door to close. 'Mister Milner, we would appreciate a brief résumé of your relationship with Stephen, and the background that led to his current circumstances.'

There was a discernable pause. For the first time that evening Milner looked uncomfortable.

The DCI pressed him. 'Mister Milner?'

Leaning forward Milner rested both his elbows on the table. 'I'm originally from London, Knightsbridge,' the voice was less assured. 'I was employed by an International Banking Corporation. When they transferred me to their Birmingham office ten years ago my family came with me. The salary was excessive and the bonuses obscene. Life continued much as before. An apartment in the city, a house in the country and both children at private schools. There was more disposable income than we knew what to do with, although my wife did her best to resolve that particular problem.' He shrugged. 'It couldn't last of course.'

'The recession,' Rees-Bramley said.

Milner nodded. 'The economy works in cycles. Money markets crashed and financial institutions began shedding their staff. I was surplus to requirements. It's frightening how savings can evaporate, especially when you continue living in much the same way as before. That new job offer is always just around the corner and pretty soon it's too late to adjust and down-size. Money and property disappeared, I suffered a long bout of clinical depression, and we eventually ended up in Sixfields.'

'The whole family moved here?' Rees-Bramley asked.

'My wife moved in, and then out.' A shadow passed across Milner's face. 'Taking Stephen and Lucy with her. She managed to last one week.'

'Where did she go?'

'Somewhere she didn't have to concern herself about money.' Milner shrugged. 'I think she must have been cultivating Henry Roberts for some years. A form of backup I suppose. Very astute my wife. After she persuaded the poor sop to take on both her and the kids we eventually divorced. When they married, Stephen and Lucy took the surname of Roberts as well.'

He stopped abruptly and bowed his head. The two detectives glanced at each other, not quite sure what was happening. When Milner eventually looked up there were tears streaming down his long, gaunt face. Crosby felt embarrassed for him. In the short time he'd spent with Milner the man had always come across as completely emotionless, almost robotic. The breakdown was a surprise, and so was the twinge of sympathy that Crosby felt for him – he looked completely lost.

Milner tried to compose himself. 'My apologies gentlemen! It re-surfaces every so often.'

Crosby knew from working with his DCI that sympathy was not an emotion that Rees-Bramley wholeheartedly embraced. He wasn't surprised when the questions continued almost immediately. 'So how did your son end up back here in Sixfields Mister Milner?'

'I blame myself really,' Milner's voice remained low. 'Stephen began staying with me at weekends. It was a mistake. Somebody should have realised that I was in no fit state to look after myself, let alone a growing, hormonal teenager. I let him come and go as he pleased. After being on a tight leash at school all week it was virtually a two day holiday for him, with no restrictions. The inevitable happened and he started running around with one of the local gangs, getting into situations, taking stuff.'

'Did your ex-wife realise what was happening?'

Milner nodded. 'He eventually became a problem at home. Although she stopped him from visiting me, it was too late. They'd lost control, and he just walked out on them.' Milner shook his head. 'How does that happen? One day you're the father of a polite, respectful son, doing well at school, and the next he's running around with a gang of thugs on a problem council estate.'

'It must have been a worry,' Rees-Bramley said unsympathetically. 'Where did Stephen go?'

'Ended up squatting on the estate somewhere.'

'He didn't come back to live with you?'

Milner shook his head. 'We'd drifted apart by then. The drugs had completely changed his personality and I no longer recognised him. My ex-wife still blames me for everything of course.'

'You also have a daughter,' Rees-Bramley said.

Milner nodded. 'Lucy! She somehow came through the separation and divorce unscathed. Because she was that little bit younger Lucy wasn't allowed to stay with me at weekends. Just as well. She might have ended up following in Stephen's footsteps.'

'And where is your daughter currently?'

'Lucy's at university now. We manage to see each other quite regularly, despite my ex-wife's best efforts to drive a wedge between us.' Milner stopped. He looked on the brink of breaking down again.

Rees-Bramley stood up. 'A ten minute break I think.'

The DCI waited until Milner had left the room. He turned to Crosby. 'I want somebody bollocked for that slip-up over the search warrant Frank! It was your responsibility to check it!'

'Yes Sir!' Crosby said. 'We also need to get the records of Stephen Roberts updated. The fact that we haven't got Milner recorded as his biological father could be potentially embarrassing.'

Rees-Bramley didn't reply. They were both aware that it was the DCI who had prepared Roberts' initial report.

'Milner's still playing games,' Rees-Bramley said, 'and enjoying it.'

'He likes the attention Sir,' Crosby replied. 'There's always people like Milner hanging around the fringes of murder investigations. It doesn't make him a suspect.'

The DCI shook his head. 'He's lying about Friday night. He watched his son assault Janet Sterne's baby.'

'Maybe!' Crosby shrugged his shoulders. 'But if Milner did witness the incident then he's probably ashamed of what Stephen did. He'll just continue to deny all knowledge of it.'

Rees-Bramley didn't look convinced. 'Maybe Milner was so ashamed of Stephen's actions that he followed him along Akers Lane.'

'Attacking his own son?'

'It's happened before. And a witness puts Milner in his front garden later that evening.'

'It wasn't a particularly reliable sighting.'

Rees-Bramley wasn't listening. 'And if Milner's able to put his own son into hospital there's no limit to what he's capable of. A recent study into homicide across the USA pointed to clinical depression as a constant and recurring reason for a murderer's actions.'

Crosby didn't want to hear Rees-Bramley quoting from his FBI Behavioural Workshop again. He got to his feet. 'I'll check upstairs. See if Berne and Jefferies have managed to find anything.'

The DCI nodded and took out his mobile.

Upstairs, on the landing, Berne and Jefferies were feeling decidedly chilly – a large old-fashioned radiator fixed to one of the walls was stone cold. Although the rooms up here were even more sparsely furnished than downstairs Milner had at least fitted a flat grey carpet throughout, and his distinct lack of furniture simplified search patterns – the two smaller bedrooms and a bathroom had already been swept.

Using a stepladder he'd found in one of the bedrooms Jefferies was currently accessing the loft space. He'd expected to find the usual junk, dumped haphazardly throughout, but when the attic flap was lifted, and he'd switched on his torch, the powerful beam had revealed just one solitary box, close to the opening.

After man-handling the box to one side Jefferies was able to inspect its contents without coming back down the ladder. There wasn't a great deal to examine – mainly framed photographs of a young looking Milner with his wife and two children – in a variety of happy family poses.

Jefferies completed his search and shoved the box to one side. After playing his beam all around the attic he replaced the flap and started back down.

Milner was standing at the foot of the ladder. 'And what did you manage to find up there officer?' The smile was thin lipped. It didn't reach his eyes. Jefferies ignored him, trying to concentrate on descending the steps – they weren't particularly stable.

'Can I help in any way?' Milner asked.

'No thank you Sir!'

'I'll just leave you to carry on invading my privacy then.'

Milner moved past Jefferies on his way to the bathroom, appearing to deliberately brush the stepladder with his shoulder. Jefferies, who was only halfway down the teetering steps, had to jump off – his substantial bulk landing with a heavy thud. Milner disappeared into his bathroom and closed the door.

Berne appeared on the landing. 'What's all the bloody noise about?'

Jefferies was still staring at the bathroom door. 'That is one serious fucking weirdo! He just tried to knock me off the stepladder.'

Berne smirked. 'We'd better crack on. You've got a report to write up by tomorrow.'

Jefferies shook his head. 'It's not natural. The whole fucking set-up. Did you see how the kitchen cupboard was laid out?'

'Feminine tendencies mate. Just check behind you before bending over.'

'And everywhere's grey. What the fuck's that all about?'

Still muttering to himself Jefferies followed Berne into the main bedroom. Both men pulled on a fresh pair of disposable, protective gloves. There were three items of furniture in the room. A small bedside cupboard, large double wardrobe, and a plain, single bed.

As contents from the bedside cupboard were unceremoniously tipped out onto the bed, Milner's tall, thin frame appeared in the open doorway. He stood watching. The two detectives exchanged glances with each other. Mindful of his presence both men were careful to sort through the personal effects with a certain amount of care. When they'd finished and looked up towards the door Milner had disappeared.

Berne moved across to the wardrobe. Pulling open the two doors he scanned a double rack of clothes inside. It took him a moment to realise how the clothes had been arranged. 'What do you make of this?' he called across to Jefferies.

The other detective walked over to the wardrobe. Berne began shoving items of clothing along the rack. 'Fucking odd!'

Jefferies shrugged. 'What?'

'He's got two of everything! Two shirts! Two suits! Two sweaters! Two pairs of trousers! Two jackets! Two pairs of shoes!' Berne pulled down some items from the top shelf. 'Two ties! Two scarves! Two pairs of gloves! There's even two fucking woolly hats!'

'He's only got one pair of jeans,' Jefferies pointed out.

'What?'

'There's only one pair of jeans.'

Berne checked the rack again.

'What have you found?' The two detectives looked up to find Crosby standing in the doorway.

Jefferies pointed to the rack of clothing. 'We think there's a pair of Milner's jeans missing Sir.'

'I would imagine that's the pair he's currently wearing,' Crosby said impatiently. 'Don't forget there's still got the car and garage left to search.'

The DI turned and went back downstairs.

Berne and Jefferies continued picking their way through the contents of Milner's bedroom in silence.

It was another hour before the two detectives had completed their search of the whole premises and reported back to Rees-Bramley. They'd found nothing suspicious. A further bout of questioning with Milner had also proved unsuccessful. The four detectives left Silver Street just before nine o'clock. A few minutes after their departure Milner left the house to commence his nightly vigil in the rear garden.

When he returned at ten o'clock Milner switched off all the kitchen lights and sat in darkness. It helped him to think. Although Milner had only seen his son occasionally during the last couple of years he'd recognised him immediately last Friday – even with a hood drawn up over his head. The pain that he'd felt as he watched Stephen assault Janet Sterne and her baby still hurt, and as he continued to sit at his kitchen table, the problems and worries spun around and around in his head. They wouldn't go away. Perhaps that was why his blackouts were becoming longer, more frequent – earlier in the week he'd been sitting indoors watching television – his next recollection was three hours later, driving around the estate in his car.

The problems began to spin ever faster, making him dizzy.

They would have to be confronted.

Milner moved another chair around, so that it faced him. Because there was no-one else to share his problems, he was forced to discuss them with himself – a ritual practice he'd assumed over the years. He sat facing the empty chair and spoke directly to it.

'Are the drugs to blame?'

'Partly!'

'I have to stop those responsible.'

'How?'

'I will eliminate them.'

'What about Stephen?'

'Was I wrong to let him live?'

'Yes!'

'Why did I let him survive?'

'Because he's your son.'

'Does he deserve to die?'

'He doesn't deserve to live.'

'Am I to blame?'

'You helped to spawn him.'

'I wasn't to know.'

'It's your responsibility.'

'What should I do?'

'You know what to do.'

'But he's my son.'

'It's your duty!'

Milner ended the conversation abruptly, but continued to sit in darkness. Familiar shadows gathered around him. At least he wouldn't be on his own tonight. Milner got up from his chair, and wandered from the room. He needed to prepare himself.

CHAPTER 17

The lone, male jogger shortened his stride to power up the last of two steep inclines. His warm breath steamed in the cold morning air. Cresting a final plateau of small, scattered rocks and sparse vegetation he finally slowed to a halt, and the whole of Sixfields opened up before him.

At seven hundred feet above sea level Wrexford Hill was high enough for Milner to look down on the entire estate. Thin tendrils of mist drifted above its ugly grey sprawl. Low on the horizon sat a bright, yellow sun – a perfectly formed circle punched into the steel blue, cloudless sky.

Milner was breathing easily now, his pulse already back down to a regular sixty beats per minute. He prided himself on his high level of fitness. The early morning run had been part of a Sunday routine for eight years now and he was convinced it had been instrumental in helping to rebuild his life after the divorce and his illness.

The timetable was precise. He would wake at seven o'clock, pull on the baggy old grey tracksuit, and leave the house fifteen minutes later.

Donald and Spike, more often than not, would be waiting outside on the green. All three of them would walk to the nearby shopping precinct where Milner would buy his two Sunday newspapers. Donald would take them back to Silver Street and post them through number sixty-nine's letterbox leaving Milner to set off for Wrexford Hill.

It took him approximately thirty minutes to reach the outskirts of Sixfields, and then another fifteen minutes to climb the hill. Its steep ascent pushed Milner to his physical limits, and beyond, but it was the part he relished the most, a sensual pain that temporarily numbed the mind.

Milner lingered at the summit today, enjoying a purity of air – it was with some reluctance when he eventually left. Twenty minutes later he was back at ground level, looking neither right nor left as he pounded his way through the drab, featureless streets.

Sixfields had not yet fully stirred itself, there was only a scattering of residents up and about. Every now and then someone might shout a neighbourly 'Good Morning' but his focus was always straight ahead. He ignored them all.

Back at sixty-nine Silver Street Milner prepared himself a breakfast of porridge and weak tea. He read from his newspaper whilst eating. Needing to shower after his run Milner cleared all traces of breakfast away and went through to the hall. There were voices just outside. The intrusion to his Sunday morning routine irritated him and he pulled open the front door with some force.

The woman who spun round to face him looked impatient, annoyed. Milner remembered the look. It had been ten years since he'd last seen his ex-wife, but she didn't seem to have aged at all – the same elfin-shaped face, complementing the high, prominent cheekbones. Milner realised he had never completely erased the features from his memory. There were mixed emotions, including one of bitterness. He didn't let it show. 'Hello Penny!'

His greeting was ignored. 'Do you intend to invite us in Robert, or are we to remain on your doorstep all day?' the voice was manufactured, middle class, pitched a fraction too high to be completely natural. She didn't seem inclined to introduce the man standing behind her. Tall and gangling, with a bald, dome-shaped head, he shifted nervously from one foot to the other. Milner presumed it was Henry, his ex-wife's husband – they'd never met.

Milner stood to one side. Penny Roberts' slim figure brushed past him, a subtle fragrance trailing in her wake 'Henry!' she called, without turning round.

Henry Roberts stepped through the open doorway, his smile uncertain. He extended a hand towards Milner. 'Good to meet you at last old boy. Circumstances could have been better I suppose.' Milner didn't respond. Roberts dropped his hand. 'Quite!' he muttered and followed his wife through to the lounge.

Penny Roberts was sitting stiff backed, on the extreme edge of her chair. She hadn't removed the expensive-looking black winter coat. Her rigid posture and expression suggested she would prefer to be somewhere else. Milner sat down in the chair opposite. Henry Roberts remained standing.

She turned an immaculately made-up face towards her ex-husband.

'I really can't comprehend how you continue to live in this slum Robert. It's nothing more than a zoo. We've just driven past some local inbred who was actually urinating on the pavement.' She shivered involuntarily. 'He didn't even have the decency to turn away. I had to ring the police. Quite apart from obvious health implications he's exposing himself to young children.'

'It was fortunate you called by this morning,' Milner replied. 'You'd have caught him taking a shit there in the afternoon!' The stifled laugh came from Henry. His wife spun round and shot him a venomous look.

She turned back to Milner, her mouth compressed into a thin, tight line 'Gutter humour Robert. Save it for those who find it amusing.'

'What is it you want Penny?' The exchange had stirred old memories. Milner shouldn't have invited them in.

Ignoring the question his ex-wife flicked a disparaging glance around the room. Arching her neck she sniffed. 'No wonder poor Stephen went off the rails. It must have been like living in a prison cell. I'm not surprised he stayed out all hours.'

The remark got to him. He tried not to let it show.

She ran her eyes up and down Milner's sweat-stained jogging-suit, a look of distaste on her face. 'And what are you wearing for God's sake. You're dressed like a tramp. Don't you have any self-respect?'

Milner got to his feet allowing the surge of temper to boil over. 'Are you fucking deaf woman?' he shouted at her. 'I've asked why you're here'.

She blinked hard at the outburst. Henry Roberts, who had remained standing in the doorway, took a hesitant step forward. 'I say! Steady on old chap. I'm sure we can talk this through without having to shout at each other.'

'Sit down and stop hovering Henry,' his wife said sharply. 'I had fifteen years of dealing with this behaviour.' Henry sat. She didn't seem unduly affected by Milner's outburst and turned back to him. 'I'm here because I've just found out that our son is lying at death's door in a hospital bed. As a result Henry and I had to jet back from our winter break in Barbados and I'm totally exhausted.' She bowed her head and pressed manicured fingers to her temple as if to emphasise the point.

Milner recognised the familiar theatrical gesture. 'Don't exaggerate Stephen's condition. The police have told me it's been stabilised.'

'I'm not going to argue with you Robert,' she said. 'The most important thing at the moment is to ensure that Stephen makes a complete recovery – someone should be visiting him on a daily basis.'

'And how does that concern me?'

'Don't be ridiculous. You're his father.'

Milner shook his head. 'We no longer have any contact with each other.'

'For God's sake man! How long is this to continue? He's your own flesh and blood.'

'He's a thug! Even you had to throw him out eventually.'

'Stephen has matured.'

'And what sort of welcome did he give you?' Milner asked.

Penny Roberts didn't reply. Milner nodded. 'Exactly!' He stood up. 'I'd like you both to leave now.'

His ex-wife continued to talk over the top of him. 'Well I intend to organise a visits roster. As his father I will be expecting you to assume a share of the responsibility.'

Milner felt his temper rising again. 'You can organise what you bloody well want. Just don't involve me.'

'Stop being so bloody-minded,' she said to him. 'This is family. It's at times like this that we put our differences behind us.' Penny Roberts pulled a sheet of paper from her handbag and snapped her fingers. 'Henry!' Her husband fumbled inside his jacket pocket and retrieved a pen – clicking the point down for her.

She looked up at Milner. 'You'll need to tell me what days will be convenient for you to visit.'

Milner turned to Penny's husband. 'Henry!' he smiled. 'My ex-wife doesn't appear to understand the fact that I'm not interested in her fucking roster. If I was to stick it on the end of my cock and stuff it up her bony ass do you think she would get the message?'

Penny Roberts stood up, her face a mask. 'How dare you!' her voice rose. 'How dare you speak to me like that!' She wheeled on her husband. 'Are you just going to bloody well sit there and do nothing?'

Henry Roberts had frozen. Only the eyes moved. They darted between Milner and his wife.

She spun back round to her ex-husband, eyes blazing. 'You bastard! Call yourself a man? If you hadn't sat on your ass all these years feigning some imaginary illness you would have moved on. I've managed to.'

'All that you managed to do Penny, was attach yourself to another bankroll.' His ex-wife's loss of self-control was a childish victory but Milner enjoyed it nonetheless.

She feverishly buttoned her coat. 'We're leaving Henry! Now!'

There was a knock at the front door. Milner was not in the mood for another police visit. He barged past Henry Roberts. Still agitated he yanked the door open. 'Lucy!' It was Milner's turn to be taken aback. 'What the hell are you doing here?'

His daughter stood up on tiptoe and kissed him on the cheek. 'I've just been to see Stephen and thought it was about time I visited your bachelor pad. Aren't you going to invite me in?'

Penny Roberts heard Lucy's voice from inside the lounge. Rushing dramatically into the hallway she threw both arms around her daughter.

'I only saw you last night Mum,' Lucy said, trying to prise herself free.

'I'm sorry darling. It's just that your father has been extremely rude to Henry and I. It was very upsetting.'

Lucy frowned at Milner over her mother's shoulder. He shrugged.

Producing a tissue from her coat pocket Penny Roberts dabbed at her eyes, being careful not to smudge the subtle application of black mascara. Milner noted a distinct lack of tears. Penny Roberts grasped her daughter's hand. 'I had no idea you were in the habit of visiting your father darling.'

'I'm not! I've just called in after visiting Stephen.'

Lucy's mother didn't look entirely convinced. 'We're just about to leave. We can give you a lift.'

'No thanks Mum. I have my car. I'll be staying for a while.'

Penny Roberts frowned. 'Are you absolutely sure darling? It's really not safe to be on your own in this god-forsaken place.'

'I'll be fine.' Lucy smiled. 'Dad can give me an armed escort back out to the car.'

'If it's still standing there,' Penny Roberts said. She turned to leave, giving her ex-husband a withering look. Milner smiled and winked back at her.

Pecking Lucy on both cheeks Penny Roberts stalked out of the door. Her husband quickly followed. Milner was pleased to see that Henry didn't warrant a kiss from his step-daughter, just the hint of a smile in passing.

They watched him hurry round to the passenger side of a Bentley Convertible – getting there just in time to open the door for his wife.

Milner closed the front door none too gently on his departing visitors and took Lucy through to the lounge. The atmosphere was a little strained. His daughter was the first to speak. 'Look Dad! I know you're not happy about me being here but I've come to see you. Not to make any judgement about how or where you live.'

Milner had been living in Sixfields for ten years now, with very few visitors during that time. To have both his ex-wife and daughter suddenly turn up on the same day had been a little surreal. It was never his intention that Lucy would see him here though. 'It's embarrassing Lu, compared to where we were before. I get down about it, but the depression stops me from moving on. It's a vicious circle.'

She took his hand. 'Look! I've said before. I'm proud of the way you coped with your breakdown. You came out the other side. Others wouldn't have made it.'

'I'm still not comfortable about you being here Lu,' Milner said.

Lucy didn't push him. 'We'll give it half an hour. See how you feel then.'

It said a lot about their relationship that by the time Sunday morning had progressed into its afternoon Milner had completely relaxed. It felt as if Lucy had been visiting him for years.

They even touched on one of his taboo subjects. Milner, surprisingly, was the one who raised it. 'How did you find Stephen?'

Lucy screwed her face. 'He's not the brother I knew. We were always quite close as children. It's upsetting to see the change in him.'

'We parted on bad terms when I stopped funding him two years ago,' Milner said.

'You knew it was going on drugs?'

Milner nodded. 'The mind was still sharp enough, but his aggression was out of control. I suppose it affects different people in different ways.'

'Maybe there was always a flaw in Stephen's make-up.' Lucy shrugged. 'An accident waiting to happen. It just needed a trigger.'

'And I provided it,' Milner said.

'It's not down to you, Dad. We were all to blame.' Lucy leant forward and rested her hand on Milner's arm. 'I've always told Mum that she has to accept part of the blame. We could have all done more to help.'

'I'm sure she came round to that point of view.'

Lucy smiled. 'I'm still working on it.'

Milner gripped his daughter's hand as she tried to lift it from his arm.

'What?' she said.

He hesitated.

'What is it Dad?' Lucy persisted.

He stood up. 'I get these recurring premonitions Lu. About you and Sixfields.'

Lucy shook her head. 'That's only natural. It's because of the situation Stephen got himself into here.'

Milner didn't look convinced. 'You need to be careful.'

'I will. Stop worrying.'

'Was Stephen OK to you? At the hospital?'

'Not very brotherly. Still just as aggressive.' Lucy shrugged. 'I'll keep on trying, if only for Mum's sake.'

'He didn't mention me?'

Lucy shook her head. 'No! And I thought it best not to.'

Milner nodded. He was tempted to tell his daughter that it was Stephen who put him in hospital two years ago – after his refusal to fund any more money for drugs. They continued to talk. At one point Milner almost told Lucy what his mission was – what he'd been tasked with. But the time wasn't right, not today anyway.

Lucy declined her father's offer of lunch and at one o'clock got up to leave. She gave Milner a hug before holding him at arm's length. 'That was our breakthrough Dad. How do you feel about meeting up here next Saturday, instead of the usual place. I'll bring an overnight bag. Stay for the weekend.' she squeezed his hand. 'For me?'

Milner had always found it difficult to deny his daughter anything and reluctantly agreed. But he wasn't happy. His comfortable, well ordered routines were important to him. The comforting loop of familiar events formed a continuous sequence, and Milner felt agitated about disturbing its natural cycle. He was unsure. There would be consequences.

Lucy had parked her sturdy little Volkswagen Polo just outside. Milner opened the front door for his daughter and walked with her to the gate. Donald and Spike came ambling over the green towards them. 'Sorry Lu. We've got company.'

Milner introduced his daughter. Lucy made a formal show of shaking Donald's hand before bending down to make a fuss of Spike. Because of his poor eyesight Donald had to push in close, so that he could see Lucy's face properly. She didn't seem at all fazed, doing her best to field the barrage of non-stop questions from him. In just a few minutes Milner's daughter had created such an impression that Donald was already pestering her as to when she would be coming back to Sixfields.

'I'm here next week,' Lucy assured him. 'We can take Spike for a walk on Sunday.'

Before she realised what was happening Donald had lunged forward and wrapped her in a huge bear hug. Milner stepped forward to carefully prise his daughter from Donald's embrace. Taking Lucy's arm he walked with her to the car. 'Thanks Lu. He'll be talking about you for days.' Milner kissed her on the cheek. 'I'll see you on Saturday.'

As his daughter was about to unlock the door there was a commotion further up the road. They turned to see a small crowd of youths heading their way, pushing and jostling each other along the pavement. Spotting Donald ahead of them the whole group started to jeer, before breaking into a chorus of grunting noises. Milner ushered Lucy and Donald back into the garden and closed his gate. He'd resisted their intimidation for years now, and if he'd been on his own the group would have had to walk around him, but Milner could see the effect it was having on Lucy and Donald. He moved them back towards the door. They would have to go inside if the situation escalated.

Less boisterous now, with other sport to focus on, the group quickened their pace and drew level with Milner's gate. He could see that three of them were drinking from large, plastic bottles. They stopped and peered over his fence, openly staring into the garden. Milner was surprised to see several black faces among the group – it was a predominantly white area and the cultures didn't usually mix.

Milner had become quite expert at assessing the yobs that roamed his area and although he didn't feel particularly threatened – none of them looked over sixteen – they had been drinking, and were obviously intent on some sort of confrontation. Hands jammed into the side pockets of their hooded-tops, the group continued to shuffle around outside his gate. They were not going to move on.

'Bastards!' Milner muttered involuntarily. He was aware of snarling sounds coming from the back of his throat.

'Dad?' Lucy shook his arm. The noises stopped.

It didn't take long for the ring-leader to identify himself – a rangy, black youth wearing a rainbow-coloured knitted cap over his dreadlocked hair. Hawking a gob of phlegm into the back of his throat he projected it over the fence and into the garden.

Milner waited for the verbal abuse to start. It was Donald who the ring-leader eventually targeted. 'Yo Zombie Boy!' more grunting noises. 'Check it out!' His audience sniggered as the youth held out his arms and imitated Donald's awkward, shuffling walk.

Donald edged further back, holding onto Spike. He was quiet now and eyed the group warily. One of the youths flicked a lit cigarette end over the fence towards them. Milner crushed it under his shoe.

'Fucking scarecrow-man innit?' the ring-leader jeered at Milner. 'You gotta pole stuck up your skinny white ass scarecrow-man?'

Milner continued to stare him down, the youth's insults stoking his temper.

The ring-leader switched his bravado to Lucy. 'Whoa! You is fit girl! You needin' some man-juice?' He cupped his crotch with one hand and turned to the others. More laughter.

The gang was confident now – passers-by had quickly melted away – their intimidation wasn't about to be challenged. A white youth kicked at the gate and it swung open.

Lucy leaned towards her father. 'We need to get inside Dad.'

Milner edged back to the front door. A half-empty cider bottle hit the path with some force. The plastic bottle cracked and split, spewing out its contents. The noise frightened Donald's dog, who suddenly bolted through the gate. Before Milner could react Donald had followed him.

'Fuck!' Milner went after them both without thinking.

Barging his way through the jeering group he could see Donald full length on the ground, being kicked at by three youths. Milner hit all three at once, catching them off balance. Getting to his knees he found the black ring-leader sprawled out next to him. Milner rolled over and wrapped his hands around the youth's throat, digging both thumbs into the delicate bone structure of his Adam's apple. The group quickly surrounded them both, aiming kicks and punches at Milner's head as the two remained locked together, rolling around the pavement. Milner applied more pressure with his thumbs, and the struggling youth continued to choke – his attempts to drag in air growing ever more desperate.

The sound of high pitched sirens sounded close by and a police car skidded to a halt alongside the pavement. Both front doors were flung open and two uniforms jumped out, wading deep into the melee. The group quickly scattered.

Milner felt his thumbs being prised away from the youth's throat.

'Easy Tiger! You can let him go now.' He looked up to find the bulk of a heavy-set policeman dragging the ring-leader to one side and forcing him to lie full length on the ground.

'PC Jennings Sir!' the policeman said to Milner. 'I can take it from here,' Jennings called across to the other officer. 'Cancel that back-up call son. They've all disappeared apart from this one.'

The policeman turned his attention back to the ring-leader. Milner watched as Jennings twisted the youth's arm up and around his back, making him squeal. At the same time a large police boot was placed on the side of his face, pushing it hard into the pavement. The youth squealed again. Milner was surprised at the amount of force being used. Reaching around for his handcuffs the policeman snapped a bracelet around the youth's left wrist. Hauling him over to a nearby fence PC Jennings clipped the other bracelet to a post and snapped the handcuff closed.

The black youth sat back against the gate, a large bruise forming along his cheekbone, angry red weal's around his throat. He looked considerably less arrogant. 'I did fuck all! Bastard jumped me!' the black-rap dialogue was no longer evident. He continued to whine.

'Shut up!' Jennings said. The policeman turned to Milner. 'You OK

Sir?'

'I think so. Just a few cuts and bruises.'

'Don't try to get up for the moment. Do you need medical attention?'

Milner shook his head. 'Is your timing always this good?'

'We had several calls. Seems they've been upsetting other residents along the way.'

'Unusual for you to get here this quickly.'

Jennings let it slide. 'Increased patrols Sir. Due to recent events.' He jerked his head towards number sixty-nine. 'Your house?'

Milner nodded.

'And your name Sir?'

'Robert Milner.'

'And this little runt stopped to pass the time of day with you?'

'Something like that.' Milner felt an arm around his shoulder. 'You OK Dad?' He looked up to find Lucy bent over him.

'I'm fine. Where's Donald?'

'He disappeared across the common with Spike.'

'And you are?' PC Jennings asked.

'My name's Lucy Roberts. Mister Milner's daughter.'

'Well if you're up to it Lucy,' Jennings said. 'I'd like you to give PC Stewart your version of events.'

Squeezing Milner's hand Lucy got up and walked over to the police car.

The black youth began to whine again. 'I want that mother-fucker arrested,' he complained to Jennings. 'White bastard assaulting an innocent black man.'

The policeman went over and knelt down next to him. 'Here's how it is gob-shite,' he whispered softly in the youth's ear, 'you carried out an unprovoked attack on this gentleman. I saw him use the necessary amount of force to defend himself.'

'I know my rights,' the gang-leader didn't sound confident.

'You know bugger all.' Jennings bent to his ear again. 'Now shut the fuck up until I decide what to do with you,' he paused. 'Innit!'

The policeman straightened up and turned to Milner. 'I'll need that statement Sir. I trust you'll be pressing charges.'

Milner knew the intimidation that a prosecution would bring. He wasn't so concerned for himself but it would inevitably involve Donald and Lucy.

He shook his head. 'More trouble than it's worth officer.'

Jennings raised his eyebrows. 'I think that would be a mistake Sir.'

'There's other people to consider.'

'And if the police decide to go ahead and prosecute anyway?'

'Somewhat pointless without my co-operation.'

'Pity!' PC Jennings walked over to the handcuffed youth, whose free hand lay open on the pavement. The policeman deliberately trod on his fingers. Producing a key from his pocket Jennings pushed it into a slot on the handcuffs and twisted the two bracelets apart. He pulled the ring-leader up by his dreadlocks. 'I'd fuck off if I were you,' the policeman said in a low voice, 'while the going's good.'

The ring-leader took Jennings' advice and limped out of sight along the pavement.

Milner got to his feet and went across to the police car, where Lucy had just finished talking to PC Stewart. Lucy thanked the policeman for his help and Milner walked her back to the Volkswagen.

'You OK to drive?' he asked her.

Lucy nodded. 'I'll see you next Saturday,' she said.

Milner wrapped her in a bear hug. 'Are you sure that's a good idea after today?'

'I'll see you next Saturday,' Lucy repeated stubbornly. She pecked him on the cheek and he reluctantly let her go.

Within seconds of closing her car door Lucy had accelerated sharply away from the kerb and disappeared into the distance. Milner gave her a final wave.

He stayed to watch Jennings and Stewart pouring the contents of abandoned cider bottles down a drain before heading back indoors.

It was two o'clock in the afternoon. Henry Roberts and his wife were still en-route to their twelve-bedroom residence in Werlock Falls, a National Trust conservation area deep in the heart of Shropshire. They'd decided against spending the night at their exclusive Edgbaston address in Birmingham. Penny Roberts continued to look straight ahead, her face immobile. Henry Roberts had already given up trying to engage her in conversation – his wife would have to be placated with something expensive before she eventually thawed out.

Stephen Roberts lay in his hospital bed, continuing to upset hospital staff and patients alike. He was making rapid progress however, and impatient to leave. Stephen Roberts had business to attend to.

Daniel Kwame lay in the hospital morgue. He had nothing to be impatient about and no further business to occupy himself with. Locked and filed away in a building basement his whole world had been reduced to the inside of a refrigerated mortuary drawer.

DCI Rees-Bramley was working in his office at Studwell HQ. Both his laptop and personal computer were inevitably lit up as he pored over reports and data stored in the HOLMES database. Buried somewhere amongst all the information was that all-important lead. It just needed identifying.

DC Berne was spending Sunday afternoon in the bedroom of his flat with an eighteen-year old counter assistant from Studwell's police canteen. The pressure of working on a murder investigation hadn't stopped him from successfully concluding what he'd been working on for some two weeks now.

DC Grace Taylor was trying not to let the investigation interfere with her social life either. A restaurant meal in the city centre with her partner of two years would be followed by a late night concert at the Hippodrome Theatre.

PC Jennings and PC Stewart continued their patrol of the Sixfields estate, approximately halfway through a scheduled eight hour shift.

Sunday afternoon found John Callaghan on the road outside his house, still effecting repairs to his ageing Ford Escort, and still keeping an eye on the comings and goings of residents in Silver Street.

DC Brian Jefferies still lived at home with his parents – he was asleep in the lounge of their house on the outskirts of Sixfields, after being cooked Sunday lunch by his mother.

Frederick Broad's wife had spent the whole of Sunday morning at her house in Wassom Avenue cooking a Sunday roast. Her husband had monitored passers-by in Akers Lane from his bedroom window. After finishing his lunch Broad dozed in front of the television while his wife washed the dishes. She was careful not to make a noise. He could turn quite nasty if his nap was disturbed.

Lucy Roberts' Volkswagen Polo continued on its way back to her university lodgings. She tried not to let the incident outside her father's house spoil the day. The visit had gone far better than expected and she was still feeling pleased with herself. Persuading her Dad to change one of his routines had been a real step forward.

Janet Sterne sat watching the cartoon channel with her two small children. She found it difficult to concentrate, due to the recurring flashbacks – last Friday's assault was never far from her mind. Sterne wished the police would stop bothering her about identifying the gang leader. She lit a fresh cigarette from the stub of her old one and drew the two children closer. Someone was following her when she left the house now and it was keeping her awake at night.

Thirty miles south-east of Sixfields DI Crosby was spending Sunday at his son's house. After being run ragged by his three-year-old grandson he was trying to relax in the lounge after lunch. Eileen Crosby sat next to him. It was the first time he'd seen his wife since she'd been staying with their son and the reunion hadn't been a particularly amicable one – probably due to her announcement that she was stopping over for a few more days. The DI sat staring into space, his mind far too preoccupied with the investigation to pay his wife the attention she was looking for. The team's lack of progress was beginning to weigh heavily on him. What they really needed were fresh leads from another murder – and that was not a good mind-set to get into.

Sandra Dredge, an experienced street prostitute of some fifteen years was sitting in front of her bedroom mirror, contemplating a lived in face and another night shift in Sixfields' red light district. Her thirteen-year-old daughter Katy was downstairs finishing weekend homework. Sandra Dredge's pimp, and sometime partner, had disappeared earlier in the day – it didn't look as if he would be coming back to look after the children. Katy was always nervous about being left on her own but it couldn't be helped, she would have to look after the baby tonight. Sandra promised herself an early finish – if trade was brisk she could make her money and be back home by midnight. Pulling back her long platinum-blonde hair into a ponytail she fixed it into place with two lengths of pink ribbon.

CHAPTER 18

Studwell : Major Incident Room: Monday 29 January 2007:
9.15 am

There was very little space left on the white, rectangular briefing board. At its centre was a family snapshot of Daniel Kwame, muted interior colours, softening his light brown, angular features. Pinned next to the photograph, in sharp contrast, was a harshly lit front and profile mug-shot of Stephen Roberts, taken during the summer of last year.

Close-up images from both incident sites depicted how violent the attacks on Roberts and Kwame had been. Although Rees-Bramley had resisted the temptation to include a photograph of Robert Milner on the board, his name featured in several of the highlighted observations. A number written in the board's top right-hand corner indicated how many days the investigation had been running. Rees-Bramley insisted the number was updated each morning in red, using a thick, felt-tip marker.

Crosby stood to one side of the board, appraising the body language of certain individuals. He wasn't encouraged. A lot of energy had been expended, and lines of enquiry pursued, but it was now five days since the body of Daniel Kwame had been discovered, and apart from Rees-Bramley's pre-occupation with Milner they were not even close to identifying a suspect. Crosby had been monitoring the team's mood. Initial enthusiasm had waned and morale was low. This morning's get together was intended to re-energise everyone and kick-start the investigation's next phase.

Rees-Bramley stood directly in front of the board. If he was feeling any pressure from the current lack of progress it didn't show. His legs were firmly planted, the voice loud and confident, 'Ladies and Gentlemen. This morning will be a brief résumé on progress to date and the new initiatives we need to follow up on.' He tapped the central photograph. 'In addition to tracing Derek Kwame's final movements, members of the team have been involved in building up a detailed background on him.' Rees-Bramley motioned Paul Berne forward. 'DC Berne! Your findings please.'

The detective carried a small, plastic cup of vending coffee to the front with him. He read from a set of prepared notes. 'Daniel Kwame! Twenty-one years old. At the time of his murder our victim was living in Stepney Gardens, a block of maisonette apartments in the estate's south-west corner. Kwame's parents have been living there since the mid-eighties – in addition to Daniel they also have a fourteen-year-old son called Samuel.'

Berne sipped at his coffee before continuing. 'Kwame has a fairly busy police record, although most convictions were for gang associated and minor drug misdemeanours during his mid to late-teens. There's no evidence of him being a habitual user.' The detective turned a page of his notes. 'Approximately two years ago Kwame built up an extensive network of local street dealers. Anyone who stepped out of line was efficiently and ruthlessly dealt with. He's been arrested on three separate occasions since his operation was established but there have been no successful prosecutions.'

'Stop you there Paul!' Rees-Bramley held up his hand 'Emma. You've talked to both parents and Kwame's younger brother. Your assessment please?'

Attention focused on Emma Foulkes. The team's Families Liaison Officer got to her feet. 'Mister and Mrs Kwame have been informally interviewed on three separate occasions. Information gathered has been limited. Mister Kwame did not seem unduly affected when informed of his son's death and he has been extremely un-cooperative. Julia Kwame appears to be totally under the influence of her husband and we suspect she's been warned not to say anything about Daniel at all.'

'And his younger brother?' Rees-Bramley asked.

'We have talked to Samuel. He was noticeably more upset by the loss of Daniel than his parents were.'

'Was he able to help?'

'Samuel is a streetwise teenager,' Foulkes said. 'He's obviously been well schooled in the reply of "No Comment" from an early age.'

'Thank You Emma.' Rees-Bramley turned back to DC Berne. 'Paul?'

'Sir!' Berne re-opened his folder. 'I have a history of the family put together by Social Services and the UK's Immigration Agency.'

The DCI nodded for him to continue.

'Derek Kwame!' Berne said. 'Daniel's father! Born in Northern Ghana forty-seven years ago to itinerant land-workers. In the early eighties Derek Kwame was twenty years old and forced to look for work in neighbouring

Nigeria. He was working in their oil fields when the country's economic bubble burst. The Nigerian military government found easy scape-goats for their problems by putting all the blame on its large, migrant workforce – some two million of them were immediately escorted out of the country at gunpoint.' Berne turned another page.

'Derek Kwame was one of the many hundreds that turned up in Britain claiming refugee status. British citizenship would have been Kwame's over-riding priority back then – marrying a UK citizen the most obvious route. Within three months of arriving here he had successfully impregnated Julia Bradfield, a local white girl from Birmingham. They were married twenty-one years ago and moved directly into Stepney Gardens, just before the birth of their first son Daniel Etu Kwame.' Berne looked up. 'Julia Bradfield was twelve years older than Derek Kwame when their paths first crossed. Having met the woman last week I doubt whether she resisted Kwame's master plan for too long, and his proposal of marriage would have been accepted with a certain amount of relief and gratitude.'

Crosby winced. The DCI wouldn't allow that.

'Unnecessary DC Berne!' Rees-Bramley said without turning to look at him. 'Just the facts please.'

'Sir!'

Crosby gave a slight shake of his head. Berne never seemed to get it quite right. Anyone but Rees-Bramley and the young detective might have stood his ground, arguing that his observations were indeed factual, but he continued on, without comment. 'Samuel Kwame!' Berne said, 'Daniel's younger brother. Samuel has been running around with a locally based gang since he was nine years old. DeneValley Comprehensive School have had all manner of problems with him and his attendance record is very sketchy. When Samuel does bother to turn up his behaviour is unruly and aggressive. Last year a member of staff had to take a knife from him. Samuel threatened to come back and get it with the aid of his brother's gun. The teacher thought it highly likely he would do just that, and gave him his knife back.'

'Is he involved in his brother's operation?' Rees-Bramley asked.

'Local sources tell us he's been working as a runner and spotter alongside Daniel Kwame's dealers for the past eighteen months.'

'What do the family's neighbours have to say?'

'The neighbours are intimidated Sir. They won't even say "Good Morning" to us.'

'Did you find anything in the maisonette?'

'Clean!' Berne shrugged. 'Narcotics took the dogs in but there was hardly a trace. Kwame had probably reached the stage where he didn't have to physically handle or store any of his shipments.'

'Stolen goods?'

'Nothing on any of our lists. Neither parents work but their home is kitted out with expensive, luxury items. They did admit to Daniel providing almost everything in the flat but were unable to explain how he managed to fund it all on unemployment benefit.'

'They'd presumably know it was from the sale of narcotics?'

'No question!' Berne replied. 'Having lived most of their married life in the middle of Sixfields drug culture they would be only too aware of what business their son was involved in.'

'Thank you.' Rees-Bramley motioned for Berne to resume his seat 'Graham! You have a timetable of Daniel Kwame's last movements.'

DC Graham Stone climbed to his feet. 'Our victim was found last Wednesday. Pathologist's report puts the time of his death at least three days earlier, which ties in with the last reported sightings we have of him. We've managed to confirm three of those sightings.' Stone continued without the use of notes. 'According to his parents Kwame left Spring Gardens at one o'clock on Saturday afternoon. At two o'clock he was seen talking to one of his dealers in the Edgehill Shopping Precinct – which is about six miles from Stepney Gardens.'

'Do we have a list of his dealers?' Rees-Bramley asked.

'We're in the process of interviewing them Sir.'

The DCI nodded. 'Where does Kwame turn up next?'

'The Sixfields Sports and Leisure-Centre. He was there for two hours and left at five o'clock. There's a gap then until nine o'clock, when he turns up at his local pub – 'The Kings Arms'. A barman remembers him still being there at ten-thirty that night but it's the last confirmed sighting we have.'

'Was he with anyone in particular at the public house?'

'The barman said he was talking to a lot of people Sir. It was his local.'

'Faces out of the ordinary?'

'Plenty apparently. It was a live music night and the place was packed solid.'

'You're still interviewing people from the leisure centre and the public house?'

'Yes Sir!'

'And no-one's responded to Milner's photograph?'

'No Sir!'

The DCI turned to his Families Liaison Officer again. 'Emma! We need to fill in some of these gaps from earlier in the day. His younger brother would seem the most likely source. Apply a little more pressure.'

Rees-Bramley turned back to the briefing board. 'Parallels with Stephen Roberts!' the senior detective said. 'Both of our victims sustained severe head injuries. They were completely stripped and exhibited in a ritualistic manner. Roberts and Kwame have similar police records but there's no indication that Stephen Roberts is a regular dealer.' He looked out to his team again. 'Paul! Remind us of their backgrounds.'

DC Berne was immediately on his feet. 'We know that Roberts is a member of 'SXF Inc!' – predominantly white and based in the estate's eastern sector. Derek Kwame originally ran with a pack known as 'West End Boys' – a background mix of West Indian and African cultures. Kwame retained close links with the gang when he set up his narcotics network. Members provided day to day protection and helped out on the operations side. It's the same gang that Samuel Kwame was co-opted into when he was nine years-old.'

'Anything coming out of these two camps?' Rees-Bramley asked.

'No Sir!'

'Your contacts seem to be permanently tongue-tied.' The DCI turned to his deputy. 'DI Crosby will talk us through the latest batch of reports from forensics.'

Crosby opened a slim, manila folder. 'Footprints! Those left in the dust at unit twelve were too scuffed and indistinct to be of any use. It's not even clear how many pairs were involved.' The DI paused. 'On the plus side a bloody footprint lifted near the waste ground was of a decent quality and can be matched. You will have read the reports and know that Robert Milner continues to be of particular interest to us.' Crosby resisted the temptation to add that it was Rees-Bramley in particular who maintained the interest.

'As a result of the search at Milner's Silver Street address two pairs of trainers were sent for forensic analysis. No matches were identified. Fibre samples have also been collected from Milner's house for comparison testing. Analysis is on-going.'

'Incidentally!' Rees-Bramley interrupted, 'one of our patrol cars had to break up a scuffle between Milner and a gang of youths outside his house yesterday afternoon. I suggest you all access the report.'

'VRP Systems,' Crosby continued. 'We have commissioned the services of a recently developed Voice Recognition Program. The system has been developed to provide a unique 'fingerprint' of an individual's voice through the characteristics of sound and pitch. Comparison tests are still on-going between a recording we have of Milner's voice, and the mobile telephone call that reported Friday's attack on Stephen Roberts.'

Crosby closed his folder and looked across at Rees-Bramley.

The DCI raised his voice slightly, 'Lines of enquiry then. Interviews with customers at the Kings Arms on Saturday night have inevitably produced more names and addresses for us to follow up on. Focus is the key. It only takes one solitary, miniscule piece of information to give us the lead we're looking for.' Rees-Bramley retrieved a note from his jacket pocket and checked a name on it. 'I'm scheduled to meet Professor Hill later this morning on the subject of Criminal Profiling. Professor Hill currently lectures in behavioural psychology at the University of Warwick and is retained by the Home Office to advise on a criminal's personal characteristics and background. Details of our investigation were passed to him three days ago. His observations will be relayed back to you this afternoon.'

The DCI surveyed his audience. 'Questions?'

Computers hummed gently in the background silence.

Rees-Bramley nodded. 'That's all then. Individual interview assignments have been passed to your e-mail folders. You will not need reminding that this is a murder investigation and our progress is being monitored both internally and by the media.'

There was a low murmuring and scraping of chairs as the team returned to their desks.

Rees-Bramley watched them leave. 'Lot of lethargy there Frank. You'll need to keep an eye on that.'

Crosby thought that was exactly what he had been doing, but he didn't pursue it.

'I need a word about Janet Sterne before this Professor arrives,' the DCI said. 'My Office? Ten minutes?' He didn't wait for a reply.

Crosby did a tour of the team before making his way to Rees-Bramley's office.

The DCI waved him to a chair. 'Anything from the telephones?'

'Williams has just taken a call from the hospital. Stephen Roberts walked out this morning. Discharged himself apparently.'

'Oh?' Rees-Bramley looked surprised. 'Is it worth putting someone on him?'

'Berne's arranging it with one of his Sixfields' contacts.'

'We'll need to know who his visitors are.'

Crosby nodded. 'Someone's already been feeding him information at the hospital.'

'What sort of information?'

'When I interviewed him Roberts knew my name and that I had a grandchild.'

Rees-Bramley raised his eyebrows. 'Where would he get that from?'

'I'm presuming my name came from the gang member I crossed swords with at the old community centre.'

'And your grandchild?'

'I hope that was just clever guesswork. Down to my age.'

'It's a concern.' Rees-Bramley looked at Crosby. 'One that I should have been made aware of. Did he make any threats?'

Crosby nodded. 'Only implied. I've got a certain amount of sympathy for Milner though.' The detective shrugged. 'All the problems he had to cope with and then having a son like that. Team of psychiatrists wouldn't be able to sort that relationship out.'

'Especially if the son was put in hospital by his father.' Rees-Bramley leant forward to pick up a folder, tossing it across the desk. 'Just received this report on Milner from uniformed branch. He once belonged to a gun club in the dim and distant past.'

Crosby opened the folder and scanned its contents. 'It was some time ago Sir. Besides, there's nothing in from forensics to suggest a gun was in evidence at either of the two sites.'

'Interesting nonetheless though.' Rees-Bramley took the folder back. 'Doesn't quite fit with his persona does it?'

'You wanted a word about Janet Sterne Sir.' Crosby needed to get on.

Rees-Bramley nodded. 'I'm concerned that DC Taylor still hasn't persuaded her to make this identification of Stephen Roberts yet. Is there a problem?'

'Sterne lives on her own with two young children,' Crosby replied. 'She's had time to think about the implications. Her state of mind isn't likely to improve with the news that Stephen Roberts is back out on the streets.'

Rees-Bramley leant back in his chair. 'Strictly speaking the assault on Janet Sterne isn't really our concern now. Although her identification of Roberts would confirm his movements prior to him being attacked.'

'It would also expose Sterne and her children to a lot of intimidation,' Crosby replied more sharply than he intended.

Rees-Bramley leant forward. 'I'm heading a murder investigation Frank! You are my Deputy SIO. We haven't got the luxury of considering anyone's feelings.'

'Yes Sir!' It was yet another exchange between the two senior officers that morning – the relationship was becoming a little strained.

'You managed to establish some sort of rapport with Sterne last week,' the DCI said. 'It might be worth getting back in touch.'

'Yes Sir.' Crosby didn't really want Sterne coerced into identifying Stephen Roberts – and all the intimidation that would bring. Roberts needed removing from the streets, but not at the expense of putting a mother and two young children at risk.

Rees-Bramley retrieved another printout from the top of his desk. 'You haven't seen this yet. It's just come in.' He held out the sheet of paper. 'There was a patrol car sent round to Sterne's house last night. A report of someone trying to break in.'

As Crosby reached forward to take the report a face appeared from around the partition screen. 'DCI Bramley?'

The DCI looked up, clearly irritated at the shortening of his surname.

'Colin Hill! Warwick University!' A stooped, lanky figure, with shoulder-length, thinning hair stepped around the partition. 'I'm a little early.'

Rees-Bramley stood up. 'Come in Colin. My Deputy Investigating Officer and I were on the point of finishing.' Crosby got to his feet and shook hands with the new arrival, moving aside to let Professor Hill take his vacated chair.

Plonking a scuffed, brown leather briefcase on top of Rees-Bramley's desk the professor sat down and crossed his long, thin legs. Shapeless corduroys, and a sprinkling of dandruff on the shoulders of his faded, tweed jacket fitted the stereotype image of an untidy academic perfectly. Crosby could also smell tobacco – coming from an old briar pipe that protruded from Colin Hill's jacket pocket.

Rees-Bramley looked distinctly unimpressed. Not only was Professor Hill's briefcase cluttering his desk, a smell of stale tobacco was beginning to permeate throughout the office. Crosby left them to it.

Waverley Court: Sixfields Estate: Monday 29 January 2007: 9.45 am

At approximately the same time that Professor Hill was settling himself into Rees-Bramley's office a rusted, old red Fiesta pulled up outside a block of derelict-looking flats in the heart of Sixfields. The woman that emerged wore grey jogging bottoms and a grubby white T-shirt – lank, greasy hair hung from beneath her baseball-styled cap. Clearly visible was the woman's addiction to heroin – scarred needle tracks running up the inside of her thin, bare arms.

As she made her way round to the car's front passenger door, it swung open.

'Well don't just stand there,' Stephen Roberts shouted at her. 'Get the fucking crutches out.'

Opening the car's rear door, she pulled out a pair of crutches from the back seat and held them upright for him. The woman was older than Roberts. She stood and shivered in a biting wind, pinched, white, features, adding to her years.

Stephen Roberts swung a plastered leg out of the car and manoeuvred himself up onto his crutches. A hooded jacket covered his head but the heavily-bruised face was still evident – criss-crossed with lines of black stitching.

When the woman tried to support his elbow as he clumped awkwardly up the path Roberts knocked her hand away. 'Just go and open the fucking door,' he shouted at her.

She dropped her hand and walked on ahead, towards one of the ground floor tenement flats.

Studwell HQ: Major Incident Room: Monday 29 January 2007: 10.00 am

Crosby stabbed his redial button again. The ringtone stretched to over a minute. He was about to replace his receiver when someone picked up.

'Yes?' the voice was terse.

'Janet Sterne?' Crosby asked.

'Who is this?'

'Detective Inspector Frank Crosby. Studwell CID. I interviewed you after the incident in Akers Lane.'

Sterne didn't reply.

'Tracey needed hospital treatment for a cigarette burn,' Crosby persisted.

'What do you want?'

'Would it be convenient to call round and see you?'

'What for?'

'It's a follow up to your emergency telephone call last night.'

'That's been sorted.'

'Just a couple of loose ends to tie up.'

'I'll be out most of this week.'

'You say when,' Crosby said. 'Entirely at your convenience.'

'Is this about the identity parade?'

'Not specifically.'

'Look! I told the black policewoman,' Sterne's voice sounded strained,

'I'm not fucking well identifying anybody. I can't even remember what he looked like.' She put the phone down.

Crosby dropped his receiver back onto its rest. It certainly wasn't the angry, aggressive Sterne from three weeks ago. He picked up the report filed by PC Stewart about Sterne's alleged break-in, and put on a pair of recently purchased metal-framed reading-glasses. They felt uncomfortable, pressing down on the bridge of his nose. 'Bollocks!' he tossed the spectacles back onto his desk and held the report at arm's length.

The call-out looked to be fairly routine. Stewart and Jennings had looked all round the perimeter of Sterne's house but could find no outward signs of an attempted break-in. A similar search of the gardens and surrounding area hadn't revealed anything untoward either. Crosby closed the folder. It wasn't what he was after. There was no reference to Janet Sterne's behaviour or her state of mind.

Crosby picked up his phone again. He pushed one of the internal network buttons. 'John? Frank Crosby! I need a word with PC Stewart before he starts his shift today. Can you send him along to the incident room when he gets in?' The detective nodded. 'Two o'clock's fine. Thanks John.'

Putting the phone down Crosby retrieved another folder from his in-tray and began reading from it. 'Shit!' he said, picking up the reading-glasses again.

Studwell HQ: Major Incident Room: Monday 29 January 2007: 2.00 pm

PC Stewart hovered next to the partition entrance, his slight frame padded out by a bulky stab vest and yellow tabard. Crosby held the phone away from his ear waved him in. Taking off his flat-peaked patrol cap, Stewart edged himself around the partition screen and waited just inside.

Crosby finished his call and replaced the receiver. 'Sit down Peter. I just wanted a quick word about the report you filed on Janet Sterne last night.'

Stewart nodded and wedged his bulk into one of the chairs.

Crosby picked up the folder in front of him. 'She called the police about an attempted break-in?'

'Yes Sir!'

'False alarm?'

'We didn't find anything. Doors and windows were all secure. PC Jennings had a good look around whilst I took her statement.'

'How did she seem to you?'

'Very nervous Sir. She's on medication. Said that someone's been following her during the day.'

'All that should have been included in your report,' Crosby said.

Stewart hesitated. 'Yes Sir!'

'You also attended an incident outside Robert Milner's house yesterday afternoon,' the DI said.

'Just a scuffle really Sir.' Stewart was still smarting from Crosby's observation about the medication. 'A gang of youths drinking and throwing their weight around – Mister Milner refused to press charges.'

'His daughter was visiting at the time.'

Stewart nodded. 'Lucy Roberts Sir. She seemed to have recovered well enough when I saw her this morning.'

Crosby looked up from underneath his eyebrows. 'The incident occurred yesterday afternoon!'

Stewart looked uncomfortable again. 'Yes Sir!'

'So why were you calling on her?'

'It was just a follow-up call really. To see if she was OK.'

'You were off duty!'

'Yes Sir!' Stewart twisted the police cap in his hands.

Crosby allowed the pause to lengthen before speaking. 'You are aware that Lucy's father has been questioned on two separate occasions during the course of this murder investigation.'

'Yes Sir!'

The detective leant forward. 'Do I need to explain the possible consequence of your actions?'

'No Sir!'

'I'll leave you to reflect on it then.' Crosby made a note in his folder.

Stewart half-rose from his chair, unsure as to whether or not he'd been dismissed.

Crosby picked up the phone.

Stewart replaced his cap and backed out of the office.

CHAPTER 19

Sixfields Housing Estate: Tuesday 30 January 2007: 10.30 am

The two nondescript semi-detached houses had been knocked through to form one functional building. Large, colourful lettering, on a white board, identified the site as 'Dots 'n' Tots Day Nursery'. The building conversion, ten years old now, had been basic and economy driven, but it still continued to pass the local authority's annual, fit for purpose inspection – a copy of the current operating licence displayed in a glass-fronted case, attached to the nursery's front wall.

In contrast to its drab exterior the nursery inside was clean and well lit. Brightly coloured paintings and child-like drawings decorated most of the interior walls.

A non-profitmaking enterprise, with subsidised rates for single parents, meant the nursery was always full. A daily average of thirty-five attendees included babies, toddlers and pre-school groups. The children came together from a variety of ethnic and cultural backgrounds, but unlike their adult counterparts, co-existed quite happily on a day-to-day basis.

On this particular morning, problems in the nursery began early and quickly escalated. At eight o'clock there were already several parents outside the front door, waiting to hand over their children – Janet Sterne among them. Three members of staff should have been in place to handle the early morning rush, but only Deputy Manager Ellie Downe had actually arrived.

If safety guidelines had been strictly adhered to Ellie Downe would not have opened the nursery at all, but because of her comparative inexperience, and under pressure from impatient parents, she accepted twenty children into the building. By nine o'clock there were thirty children on the premises, and only two other members of staff had reported for work.

At nine-fifteen the nursery manager telephoned to say she was sick. In quick succession three other members of staff rang to say they would not be coming into work that day. It left only a deputy manager and two nursery assistants in attendance – official guidelines on staff to children ratios indicated there should have been at least six adults on-site. Initial attempts by the deputy manager to arrange emergency cover proved unsuccessful.

Sixfields freezing, overnight temperatures caused the next complication, a burst water pipe in the kitchen that flooded most of the nursery's ground floor.

Under normal circumstances the lack of staff would have meant all children being kept inside for their mid-morning break. However, due to the flooding and lack of space, the nursery's three and four-year-olds were bundled into their coats and ushered out to the garden. Only two members of staff accompanied them. The deputy manager, in addition to telephoning emergency plumbers and parents, took sole responsibility for the babies and toddlers left inside.

Outside, four-year-old Clare Hopkins, who had earlier complained about feeling unwell, succumbed to a spasm of diarrhoea. One of the nursery assistants took Clare inside to wash and change her, which left seventeen-year-old Amy Browne in charge of twenty-one children – who were now running around a double-sized rear garden, virtually unchecked.

Bounded on all sides by a four-foot high, panel fence, the double garden was unusually long, and not particularly well maintained – dense, evergreen bushes grew out of control, covering much of its lower half.

Although individual areas had been created for the nursery's playground apparatus, they were positioned too far apart, and the overgrown nature of the garden made it impossible for Browne to keep all of the children in her eye-line at any one time.

The bottom of the nursery garden backed onto a narrow footpath – sixty yards away from the house – shrubs and bushes were at their densest here, hardy climbing plants growing up and over the wooden fence panels.

A scruffily dressed, middle-aged woman loitered casually on the footpath outside, her arms resting on top of the fence. As the children ran in and out of the bushes, from one play area to the other, she tracked particular individuals. They paid her no attention. Shouting at the tops of their voices two girls ran down the incline to join other children on a mini-roundabout, fifteen yards from the fence. Although it was still freezing outside one of the girls wore neither hat nor gloves, only a thin blue coat. Above the ankle socks her matchstick, thin white legs were bare to the knees. Earlier that morning the woman had watched Janet Sterne dropping the young girl off at 'Dots 'n' Tots' front entrance.

Zoe Sterne quickly tired of the roundabout and jumped off.

'Hello Zoe,' the woman called across to her.

The girl turned. She didn't recognise the woman.

'It's OK Zoe,' the woman said. 'I know your Mum. You live in Wassom Avenue.'

Zoe remained wary. She kept close to the roundabout.

'How's that baby sister of yours?' the woman smiled. 'Tracey isn't it?'

Zoe looked puzzled. The woman obviously knew them.

Retrieving an iPod player from her pocket the woman fussed with its controls, before pushing a small plastic receiver into her ear.

Zoe continued to watch.

The woman pulled a bar of chocolate from her coat pocket, tore off the wrapper, and bit into it. 'Would you like some chocolate Zoe?'

The small, upturned face looked unsure. Although she'd been told many times not to take sweets from strangers the woman seemed to know her Mum, and where they lived. She was confused. Chocolate was a rare treat for Zoe. Her four-year-old mind struggled with the dilemma.

The woman took another bar of chocolate from her pocket and tossed it just inside the fence. Zoe hesitated, but the temptation was too great. Keeping her attention fixed firmly on the woman she moved forward to pick up the chocolate bar. There was no-one else within thirty yards of them – the other children had deserted the roundabout and moved off to another play-area. Amy Browne was nowhere in sight.

Zoe tentatively removed the wrapper. Her small teeth nibbled at the sweet chocolate. She pointed to the woman's ear. 'What's that?'

'It's an earpiece.' The woman smiled. 'You listen to songs through it.'

Zoe didn't have an iPod. She looked curious.

The woman smiled again. 'What's your favourite song?'

'The wheels on the bus go round and round!' Zoe answered immediately.

'I'll put it on.' The woman knew she had her now. 'Would you like to listen?'

Zoe nodded.

The woman leant forward. 'My ear piece doesn't reach that far. If you get closer I can lift you up to it.'

Zoe stepped forward and raised her arms. The woman reached down.

'What are you doing!' the nursery assistant shouted as she hurried down the garden's incline.

'Shit!' the woman swore softly. Standing back she reached into her pocket and pulled out a scrap of folded paper. 'I've got a note for your Mum. Can you see that she gets it?'

Zoe nodded.

The woman held out the note. Zoe reached up and took it.

'You mustn't show anyone else,' the woman said. 'Our secret! OK?'

Zoe nodded again and slipped the square of folded notepaper into her coat pocket, enjoying the conspiracy.

The nursery assistant was almost upon them.

'You won't forget?' the woman said in a low voice.

Zoe shook her head.

Amy Browne reached Zoe and pulled her away from the fence. 'What are you doing?' she said to the woman. Her voice was panicky, and short of breath.

'Zoe and I were just talking,' the woman said.

'You know her?'

'Course we know each other.' The woman looked down at Zoe and winked. 'Don't we?'

The girl nodded.

'You passed her something,' Amy said.

'Only some chocolate.'

Zoe still had the bar in her hand.

'You shouldn't have done that,' Browne said, her voice more authoritative now.

The woman turned away. 'And you should have been looking after her properly. I'll be telling her mother.' She looked back over her shoulder. 'Bye Zoe!'

The girl waved.

The woman continued fifty yards further along the footpath, before emerging onto a side road. Walking up to a parked car she pulled open the driver's door, got in, and slumped behind the steering wheel.

'Where's the fucking kid?' Roberts snapped.

'I was caught! You shouldn't have asked me to do it Steve.'

Roberts curled his lip. 'Fucking useless!'

'It wasn't right.' The woman started crying. 'What were you going to do with her?'

'I fucking well said already!' Roberts shouted. 'It was a warning. We'd have taken her back home. Told the mother she was wandering about outside the nursery.'

'We didn't need to do it,' the woman said. 'Sterne's not going to risk identifying you.'

'I need to make sure! Right! It could screw things up for me.'

'What things!'

'Things that are out of your fucking league. Did you manage to pass on the note?'

'Yes!'

'At least she'll see that we got to the kid.'

'It could have got us into deep shit.' The woman rubbed a sleeve across her eyes.

'Us?' Roberts turned and raised his eyebrows. 'You were the one that tried to fucking well lift her.'

The woman knew he meant it. 'I need some stuff Steve,' she said. 'You promised me. I need it now.'

'Get me the fuck home,' Roberts replied, as he put his head back and closed his eyes. The woman reached forward and twisted the Fiesta's ignition key.

Sixfields Housing Estate: Tuesday 30 January 2007: 3.00 pm

The DI drove slowly by Janet Sterne's house, indistinguishable from all the others in Wassom Avenue. Frederick Broad lived just six doors away. Crosby continued further on down the street before coasting to a halt next to the kerb-side. Picking up his mobile from the passenger seat he scrolled through a list of contact numbers and pressed the call button.

Sterne picked up immediately. 'Yes!'

'Hello Janet. DI Crosby again. I'm in the area. Wondered if it might be convenient to call round?'

'I told you yesterday! Keep away!'

'Janet!' Crosby said quickly before she could put the phone down. 'I'm afraid Stephen Roberts discharged himself from hospital yesterday.'

A long pause as the news was digested.

'I know that you're worried about having to identify him.' Crosby said.

'You haven't got a fucking clue what I'm worried about,' Sterne snapped.

'There are other ways,' Crosby said. 'You don't have to put yourself through the trauma of an identity parade – and we can offer you protection.'

'The fuck you can!'

'Can we talk about it?'

'No!'

The connection was abruptly terminated. Crosby tossed the phone aside and adjusted his rear-view mirror, focusing it on Sterne's front door. He sat back and waited. Five minutes passed. He was aware of youths hanging around one of the street's side entrances. Another five minutes passed. The front door opened and Janet Sterne backed out, pulling a child's buggy behind her. As she closed the garden gate Sterne looked briefly at the group of youths. They didn't appear to be paying her any attention and she hurried away in the opposite direction.

Two youths immediately detached themselves from others in the group. Crosby lowered his head as they passed by. After waiting for Sterne and the two youths to disappear from view he opened his car door and set off after them.

There were a number of people out and about which helped Crosby to keep close – not that concealment from the two youths was necessary – their attention was totally on Sterne. She soon became aware of them following behind her.

After trailing Sterne for ten minutes, satisfying themselves that she'd noticed, the two youths branched off into another street. Crosby hung further back, following Sterne's progress to a large house in Milton Road. Leaving the buggy outside she carried Tracey into the 'Dots 'n' Tots Day Nursery'.

Crosby waited on the opposite side of the road.

Sterne came out of the nursery ten minutes later. Her first reaction was to look round for the two youths that had been following her. She spotted Crosby straightaway and crossed over, pushing Tracey in the buggy. Zoe trailed along behind them.

'I told you to keep out of my fucking way!' But Sterne's aggression was half-hearted, and there were dark circles underneath her eyes. Crosby could see she'd lost weight since last week.

'We can help you Janet,' the detective said. 'I'm aware of what's happening.'

'You can help me by fucking off.' Sterne reached down to strap Tracey into the buggy. 'Just leave me alone.'

Zoe interrupted her. 'I've got a note for you Mummy.'

'I haven't got time to read notes from the fucking nursery,' her mother snapped at the girl. Grabbing the buggy's handle with both hands Sterne set off along the pavement. Zoe followed in her wake, two yards behind.

The four-year-old turned round to look back at Crosby before she turned a corner and disappeared from view.

Studwell OCU HQ: Tuesday 30 January 2007: 9.00 pm

Studwell's overflow car park, at the rear of its HQ building, was fairly deserted. Apart from Rees-Bramley's Jaguar, and Crosby's old Hillman, there were only three other parked cars – another late night for both the Senior Investigating Officers.

The Hillman's engine turned over first time of asking. Crosby was far too tired to be grateful. Not a good day. Earlier that evening his report on Janet Sterne's state of mind hadn't drawn any reaction from Rees-Bramley – too pre-occupied with a detailed profile report from Professor Hill – "Male!" "White!" "Between thirty-five and forty-five years of age!" "Possibly homosexual!" "Separated or Divorced!" "Currently resident on the Sixfields Estate!" "Living alone!" "Likely to exhibit signs of eccentric behaviour!"

Crosby shook his head. The Professor might just as well have typed in Robert Milner's name and saved himself the trouble of having to compile a twenty page report. Rees-Bramley had been literally purring.

The DI flicked on his radio… 'that's Rooney's second yellow card and he's off!' the commentator screeched. Another Euro Qualifier. Crosby glanced at the time showing on his dashboard. After her extended visit away his wife had now returned home – she would not be best pleased about a second late night in a row. 'Bollocks!' he muttered and took a side exit off the dual carriageway – what was one more frosty reception. Committed now, he pushed on towards Sixfields. It was still forty minutes before the final whistle, which would give him plenty of time.

At the entrance to Akers Lane, Crosby's Hillman pulled up behind a dark blue BMW – his headlights picking out a man and woman standing alongside it. The couple hurriedly retreated into their car and closed the doors. Crosby turned off his headlights and radio – the match from Wembley was still in progress.

As he made to get out of his car the BMW accelerated sharply away. Crosby made a note of the car's registration in his pocketbook, along with a brief description of the woman and her companion. The man's nondescript attire had contrasted sharply with the woman's short skirt and thigh-length boots. She'd used a distinctive pink ribbon to fix her long, blonde ponytail into place. Crosby returned the notebook to his pocket – if the woman did bring clients here a regular basis she could have some information about the Akers Lane incident. The only problem might be getting her to talk. There wouldn't be an issue in getting the man to co-operate – they were usually married.

The detective got out of his car and locked the doors. He took a moment to look around. The patch of common opposite Akers Lane stretched away into an inky blackness. There didn't appear to be anyone in the near vicinity – both road and pavement were deserted. It occurred to him that he ought to inform someone at Studwell as to where he was.

'Fuck it!' Pulling up his collar Crosby headed down the alleyway.

Akers Lane seemed darker tonight, just a few hazy smudges of yellow light coming from bedroom windows above the line of fencing. A distant, solitary streetlamp became progressively brighter, the closer that Crosby got to it. His footsteps echoed along the narrow thoroughfare as he approached Milner's garden. The detective slowed. He edged around the protruding garden shed. There was just enough light from the streetlamp to make out a familiar gaunt face and mass of unruly white hair. Although Crosby had anticipated finding Milner in the garden it was still unnerving to actually see him standing there – tucked away in the shadows.

'Good Evening Inspector.'

Crosby inclined his head. 'You don't seem surprised Mister Milner. Was I expected?'

'It's late Inspector.' Milner smiled. 'We only see young thugs, prostitutes and drug addicts at this time of night. You didn't sound like any of those. Process of elimination.'

Crosby turned to look at the house opposite. A head and shoulders silhouette was clearly visible from Frederick Broad's bedroom window. The surreal scenario wasn't lost on Crosby – a police detective and a manic depressive alone in a dark alleyway – both of them being watched over by the neighbourhood's peeping tom.

The DI turned back to Milner. 'Last time England took part in a European qualifier Janet Sterne's child was assaulted – and your son ended up in hospital.'

'A busy night,' Milner agreed.

'And you were indoors watching the football.'

'Yes!'

'But not tonight!'

'No!'

Crosby nodded. 'Mister Milner! Both of us know that you witnessed your son assaulting Janet Sterne's baby. The question is, did you do something about it.'

Milner smiled. 'A dilemma for you Inspector.'

'But it's not just that, is it?' Crosby said. 'Our system software has consistently thrown up your name during the course of this murder investigation.'

'Computers!' Milner's tone was gently mocking. 'However did we manage without them – although I did read somewhere that if you shovel crap in at one end, shit comes out the other.'

Crosby nodded. 'Our shit is telling us that you were in the vicinity when Stephen Roberts was attacked! Our shit advises us that Daniel Kwame was murdered on the estate where you work! Our shit indicates that both attacks were probably carried out by the same person! And our shit suggests that you continue to lie about witnessing the assault on Janet Sterne!'

'That's an awful lot of shit Inspector.' Milner was clearly enjoying himself.

'This is a murder investigation,' Crosby warned him. 'Don't make too light of it. In my experience, if a person is lying about one thing, it usually means they're hiding something else.' The detective paused. 'And we are losing our patience Mister Milner. If you continue to fuck us around, we can make life very uncomfortable for you.'

Milner laughed out loud. 'Make life uncomfortable for me Inspector?' He laughed again. 'My wife managed to achieve that years ago. I doubt you can do better than her.'

Crosby went for Milner's Achilles heel. 'Were you aware that your son discharged himself from hospital yesterday?'

The smile disappeared.

'We've also had reports that Janet Sterne and her two children are being harassed.'

Milner straightened up. 'Stephen?' The detective had hit a nerve.

'Probably!' Crosby shrugged. 'We can't be sure.'

'You'll be putting a stop to it!'

The detective nodded. 'If we can.' He pushed a little further. 'You are his father though! Isn't it about time some responsible parenting was applied?'

It was a mistake. Milner's hands clenched into a pair of fists, his eyes shrunk to the size of small pebbles. Crosby thought he was about to be attacked. The detective held his breath as Milner tried to claw back control of himself.

The moment passed – but the unfocused look in Milner's eyes remained.

It wasn't often that Crosby had felt his life was in danger but he was convinced that only the fence between them had stopped Milner coming for him.

'I'm well aware of my failure as a father Inspector.' Milner was still breathing heavily. 'I don't need reminding of it.'

Crosby said nothing. He still didn't feel completely safe.

Milner turned to his side and gestured. 'I have friends who watch over me now.' He waved a hand around the garden. 'I'm afraid they've interpreted your remarks as a personal slight against me, and they're extremely angry about it.'

The detective was unsure as to whether Milner was playing mind games with him again – but the gentle mocking tone had disappeared, and there was no smile on his face. Whatever line Milner had been treading as a manic depressive, he was very close to crossing over it.

Crosby's instincts told him to leave immediately. Turning on his heel he walked away.

'Goodnight Inspector!' Milner laughed in the darkness behind him. 'You'll need to watch your back. I'm afraid they're beyond my control.'

Crosby retraced his steps along the alley, resisting the urge to look over his shoulder. Although the reception waiting at home might be on the chilly side, it would be a welcome alternative at this moment in time. On reaching the comparative safety of his old Hillman, Crosby puffed out his cheeks and got into the car. 'Shit!' he said to no-one in particular. The detective locked his door. Milner had spooked him.

Tomorrow morning he'd have the issue of trying to convince Rees-Bramley that Milner was openly displaying signs of a mental breakdown.

At precisely ten o'clock Milner left his garden to return indoors. The encounter with Detective Inspector Crosby had only reinforced in his mind what still needed to be done.

CHAPTER 20

CentrePoint: Sixfields: Saturday 3 February 2007: 11.50 pm

In the sixties, as building technology progressed and the country's population expanded, urban planners turned to high-rise tower blocks as the answer to Britain's chronic housing shortage. Dire warnings about social and psychological problems for the thousands of potential residents were summarily brushed aside.

The first high-rise tower block constructed within Sixfields was sited at its geographical centre and named accordingly – local authorities hadn't followed the dictates of other left-wing councils – if they had the building would have been christened with the name of some far off, international, freedom fighter. As it was, the Sixfields tower block was simply identified as CentrePoint.

Fifty years on, time had taken its toll of the building – maintenance was now constant and on-going. The aged, crumbling structure was depressing to look at and unpleasant to live in, but it continued to survive, still providing homes for people to live in.

CentrePoint's original surround had been laid to lawn and flowerbeds – additional landscaping features included the placement of wooden benches and futuristic looking sculptures. Over the years all of CentrePoint's green spaces had been gradually swallowed up as the need for car parking facilities grew. By the late nineties CentrePoint's surrounding landscape had been transformed into a vast expanse of concrete and tarmac. Only a few, small, isolated grassy areas survived the planner's original vision and design.

Day or night the area was never deserted – knots of teenagers hanging around its fringes, residents coming or going, skateboarders making use of the car park's hard-standing surfaces. Strangers were routinely harassed – and if they left their cars unattended there was a high risk of finding them either broken into or hijacked.

Present day access to the site was via its Goodrich Road entrance. Once into the car park CentrePoint's huge tower block dominated the eye-line.

Stretching up from ground level, in rigid, symmetrical lines, the building's only movements came from towels draped over the rails of resident's balconies, as they fluttered in the breeze.

The tower block's entrance hall was built into its south-facing side. Windowless and gloomy it reeked of stale urine. Empty bottles, discarded litter, and evidence of drug taking were the entrance's other permanent features – its actual purpose being to house six separate lift-shafts and a door to the stairs.

Although CentrePoint's lifts were slow they did give passengers plenty of time to admire its wall-to-wall covering of spray-painted graffiti. The smell of urine was even stronger inside the lift's confined space and a handkerchief to your nose was recommended. Visitors were advised not to take the stairs – Centrepoint's stairwells were notoriously popular for the purpose of casual sex and drug taking – those participating did not appreciate being interrupted or having their space invaded.

Michael Damien O'Grady – having crossed CentrePoint's car park – was about to step inside the tower block's entrance hall and take a lift to the tenth floor. It was Saturday night. Precisely three minutes before midnight.

'We need to talk,' a voice said from behind O'Grady.

The twenty-three-year-old full time drug dealer and gang activist was no stranger to people wanting a word, but O'Grady was a thug, and usually relied on his six foot, fifteen stone frame to discuss and sort through any problems that might arise. He spun round, the long-bladed knife already to hand. His eyes reflected a brief moment of confusion before the brain registered a gun pointing directly at him.

'Drop it!' the gun-man's voice was muffled – coming through a thin, black scarf that covered his lower face.

After a slight hesitation O'Grady's knife hit the concrete floor with a metallic ring. 'My people are watching this' he said. 'You're a fucking dead man.' A trace of harsh Belfast in the accent, but his voice sounded uncertain.

There was no response. The gun-barrel waved O'Grady into the entrance hall, towards a far corner. He waited as the gunman summoned a lift.

The lift doors slid open and O'Grady was motioned inside. Following him through the gunman punched an internal lift button. When the dealer realised their destination was the top floor he became agitated. 'What the fuck are we going up there for?'

Still no reply. The gunman's eyes, just visible between the scarf and a loose-fitting black hood, remained expressionless. CentrePoint's lift machinery creaked into action and the doors closed. They began to ascend.

O'Grady wasn't used to being pushed around and the dealer contemplated rushing his abductor. He fixed on the thin, black leather glove wrapped around the gun-butt, but it never wavered, and neither did the short barrel pointing directly at O'Grady's chest. Remaining in opposite corners of the lift both men continued to journey upwards.

Their unbroken ascent to the thirtieth-storey of CentrePoint's tower block took over two minutes. When the lift finally ground to a halt, and the doors opened, O'Grady was ushered into the corridor – towards a nearby flight of steps.

At the top of the steps O'Grady was made to push through an unlocked door. The gunman followed him. Both men emerged out onto the tower block's flat roof. O'Grady was only wearing a short, light-weight jacket and he immediately felt the drop in temperature. It was at least fifteen degrees colder than at ground level and there was a strong headwind.

The tower block's roof space was surprisingly small and uncluttered, its only items of note being two television satellite dishes and a mobile phone-mast, tucked away in the far corner. Surrounded by a four-foot high perimeter wall the roof provided spectacular and breathtaking views of its surrounding area – not that Michael Damien O'Grady was able to take advantage of them – after stepping through the roof's doorway he was expertly rendered unconscious – by a single blow to the back of his head.

Fifteen minutes later O'Grady had recovered consciousness. He found himself sitting back against the perimeter wall, stripped naked, his hands tied securely behind him. Blindfolded and gagged the dealer struggled in his semi-conscious state to recall where he was.

A dull ache to the back of his head became more painful as his senses slowly returned. O'Grady remembered stepping out onto the rooftop, and that there was somebody up there with him – carrying a gun. He knew the firearm was a Walther semi-automatic, because his abductor had told him what it was – and how efficient they were.

Fully conscious now, O'Grady became aware of the icy concrete and rough brickwork biting into his bare skin. Freezing as it was, the dealer's growing fear and panic far outweighed how cold he felt – O'Grady was only too aware the gunman didn't intend for them to just talk.

'I've got money!' he shouted. 'In the flat!' but he couldn't work his mouth behind the gag, his words were muffled, unintelligible.

The seconds ticked by. Silence! O'Grady's fear accelerated. He strained his ears for any sign of noise, or movement, but a gusting wind made it impossible to hear anything. Maybe he'd just been dumped, and left there. O'Grady's hopes lifted. It was short-lived.

'Get up!' a muffled voice instructed.

O'Grady struggled awkwardly to his feet, still pleading, 'I've got ten thousand pounds! In cash!' He pressed himself back into the wall, waiting for the gun to be fired. Nothing. Silence again.

The dealer lost control of his bladder, urinating in short spurts. A gust of wind blew the warm, yellow urine back against him, running down both his legs and forming into a small pool on the concrete below. Bizarrely, the fine line between fear and excitement saw O'Grady begin to display signs of an erection, his penis extending out from a thick bush of curly black pubic hair.

'There's a box next to you,' the gunman instructed. 'Get up on it!'

O'Grady hesitated. He gasped and doubled-up in pain as the gunman punched him hard in the stomach.

'Now!' the voice said.

O'Grady felt for the box with his foot and stepped up onto it.

'Get on the wall!'

The dealer realised what his abductor intended. Half-frozen, unable to move he shook his head. 'No!'

The gun barrel came down with a thud onto the back of his head. O'Grady buckled, the upper-half of his body slumped over the perimeter wall.

Moving forward the gunman pulled a knife from his belt and sliced through the industrial twine that tied O'Grady's hands. Groggy, but still conscious, the dealer started to cry, his tight blindfold stopping the tears from running.

'On the wall!'

Still sobbing, O'Grady hauled himself upright. The top of the perimeter wall was just two feet wide, but with his hands now free the dealer managed to step up onto it. He struggled to keep his balance. Although the blindfold prevented him from looking down O'Grady knew there was a sheer, five-hundred foot drop directly below his feet. The muscle controlling his anus sphincter suddenly gave up on him – a stream of diarrhoea squirted down the back of his legs, slopping onto the top of the narrow ledge. A putrid stench filled the air. Pressing the black scarf to his nose the gunman took a step backwards.

O'Grady's balance wavered again. He braced himself against the wind.

Turn around!' instructed the gunman.

O'Grady shuffled slowly around on the narrow ledge to face outwards. 'And again!'

The gunman made O'Grady turn around several times. Excrement squeezed up between the dealers toes as his bare feet paddled in the flaccid waste. When his feet began to slide around he stopped. Reduced to a childlike state, and knowing he was about to die, O'Grady called out for his mother.

'And now you choose in which direction to jump,' the gunman's muffled voice said. 'Backwards or Forwards!'

O'Grady looked a pitiful sight, his naked, excrement-covered body freezing in the icy wind. He had no idea which way he was facing and he remained rooted to the spot.

Get it right and you walk away.' The gunman laughed. 'Get it wrong and you finish up in the car park.'

Completely disorientated, O'Grady was incapable of making a decision.

'Three seconds! Then I shoot anyway!' The gunman's words were snatched away by the wind. O'Grady's senses were completely scrambled. He had no idea whether the voice was coming from behind, or in front of him.

'Jump!' The Walther's firing mechanism snapped back.

O'Grady tucked his naked body into a ball and screamed as he threw himself forward. Both knees cracked into the concrete floor – four feet beneath him. Blood from his ripped skin mixed with the pool of excrement. O'Grady, still sobbing, lay face down on the concrete floor. He felt no sensation of pain.

The gunman stooped to whisper in O'Grady's ear, 'When you were unconscious I brought you back down in the lift.'

The dealer's eyes darted wildly behind his blindfold.

The gunman chuckled. 'Get up! I'll show you!'

O'Grady struggled to his feet and stood upright, supporting his fractured knee. The gunman ripped away his blindfold and shoved him forward. O'Grady couldn't focus his eyes properly. There were small pinpricks of light in the darkness. They confused him. 'Stars?' he mumbled, shaking his head.

The gunman laughed. 'Street lamps!' he said, moving forward. It required little effort for him to stoop down behind the dealer and ease his body up and over the wall.

It took only ten seconds for O'Grady's fifteen stone bulk to complete the five-hundred foot drop. He screamed all the way down. Smashing into the concrete car park at over one hundred miles-an-hour his body rebounded two foot in the air. The force of a whiplash impact shattered his head, showering brain and shards of skull over a wide area. Most of the bones in his body disintegrated into tiny pieces, some of them pounded to a fine dust.

SOCO's Ian Brown was one of the first to view Michael O'Grady's body the following morning – 'Best of luck Doc!' he greeted the pathologist on his arrival an hour later. 'Bag of jelly you've landed yourself there.'

CHAPTER 21

Crosby braced himself against the wind as it whipped at his thinning, sandy hair. At this height the sheer force of it literally snatched his breath away. He stepped forward and peered tentatively over the perimeter wall, looking down at the busy, individual specks scurrying about below him. Viewed from five-hundred feet their constant movements created a kaleidoscope of changing patterns on the car park's surface. Feeling slightly nauseous Crosby stepped back – the tiny irregular dots had started to blur and run into each other – he'd never been very comfortable with heights.

To the detective's right several strands of blue-and-white chequered tape acted as a barrier in front of the blood and excrement stained wall. Even though SOCO and his team had more or less completed their work here Crosby still edged his way carefully around and back towards the rooftop door. A uniformed PC stood guard outside – another recent recruit who looked about twelve-years-old. The DI took a short flight of stairs down to the lifts and thumbed one of its call buttons.

He ran a list through his mind of what needed to be done this morning and how long it would take to complete on-site investigations. All of the team had been at CentrePoint since daybreak, but the initial routine gathering of information would be a lengthy process – there were hundreds of tower block residents to call on and take statements. Another logistical nightmare were the flights of stairs. Because there was nothing to suggest the murderer had arrived or departed via the lift, every one of the thirty levels and its nine hundred steps had to be searched – and they would have to break the back of it today – most of the extra manpower that Rees-Bramley had been able to call on this morning would not be available tomorrow. At least they were getting feedback from some of the residents. Those groups who would normally turn their backs on a police enquiry were now volunteering information. The estate was becoming unsettled.

Discovery of the body had been made at six o'clock that morning. With Sixfields currently on full alert it had taken only three minutes after the first emergency call for two squad cars to screech into CentrePoint's car park – police then had to disperse a fairly large crowd already gathered around the murder victim. Initial identification hadn't been a problem. Although he was naked, and his face unrecognisable, the name of Michael O'Grady had been quickly volunteered by several of the onlookers.

Preliminary data checks realised a substantial police file on O'Grady, and within one hour of the body being found an initial murder dossier on the victim had been created.

An elevator door finally slid open. Crosby wasn't entirely happy with the lift's reliability, but as nine hundred stairs were not an option he stepped inside. The journey was slow, stopping at several other floors to pick up passengers on the way down. Although residents had been grudgingly co-operative with the on-site investigation this morning, their attitude towards a policeman sharing their limited lift space was still distinctly unfriendly.

The elevator finally reached ground level and Crosby exited the entrance hall into CentrePoint's car park – which looked even more chaotic than when he'd left it to view the rooftop. With residents' cars still parked on-site, hemmed in by vehicles from the three emergency services, everywhere appeared gridlocked. Even around CentrePoint's perimeter the television crews and their vehicles had commandeered whatever space was available to set up their cameras and satellite dishes.

To the detective's right a large, mainly silent, crowd of onlookers watched proceedings from behind rows of hastily erected barriers. Word about the latest murder had spread quickly and Crosby sensed their nervousness. Tears shed for either of the two victims would be few, but the manner of both killings was causing a great deal of local unrest.

Inside the barriers authorised personnel busied around him, intent on their individual tasks. Newspaper and television reporters trailed around the fringes, stopping anyone who looked as if they might provide a quote or comment. The greater public's never ending fascination with murder investigations had to be satiated, and media outlets were only too happy to feed the frenzy.

The DI suppressed a spasm of panic, aware that Senior Officers leading the case would also be under the microscope. Crosby automatically reached inside his jacket pocket for the non-existent pack of cigarettes – three months smoke free, but the strain was obviously getting to him.

Squaring his shoulders Crosby strode briskly past the crowd – heading towards a circle of white screens and the lifeless body of Michel Damien

O'Grady.

'Working on a Sunday Inspector?' The old grey jogging suit was ill-fitting and shapeless. It reeked of stale sweat. Milner's mass of unruly white hair looked windswept and bedraggled as he looked over towards the screens. 'Can't be a suicide. Not with all this manpower on site.'

Crosby tried not to look surprised. 'You're a long way from home Mister Milner?'

'A Sunday morning routine.' The half smile was never far from Milner's lips. 'CentrePoint is on my route. Stopped to see what all the fuss was about.'

Milner's presence on site would have to be followed up but Crosby didn't have time for him or his games this morning. 'You're in a restricted area,' the detective said.

'Am I?' Milner raised his eyebrows in mock surprise and made an exaggerated point of looking around the site. 'I just walked in. No-one stopped me.' He looked around again. 'Bit of a shambles really.'

Milner certainly didn't have the same intense look to his eyes that the detective had witnessed in Akers Lane last Tuesday, but he wasn't convinced of the man's sanity. The incident had shaken Crosby.

'Should I remain on site Inspector?' Milner asked. 'I presume you'll be wanting to interview me at some point during the investigation.'

The detective's response was pure reflex. 'I'm surprised you've managed to retain a sense of humour after all your setbacks Mister Milner. How is your son incidentally? Has he been in touch since leaving hospital?' It had been a long morning. Milner was getting the backlash. Crosby instantly regretted the cheap remark.

'Touché Inspector!' Milner's eyes had clouded. 'Let's hope you too retain a sense of humour over the coming weeks.' He looked back towards the screens again. 'I doubt we've seen the last of those.'

'Just get yourself behind the barriers Mister Milner,' Crosby said brusquely.

The detective watched Milner's long, spindly legs carry him across the car park and into the crowd. He shook his head – Robert Milner was a constant background irritant – and Crosby still had the added complication of unfinished business with his son.

He quickly scanned the site. No sign of his DCI – still conducting operations from the in-situ temporary offices presumably. Crosby grimaced. He'd have to tell Rees-Bramley about Milner's appearance. Yet more ammunition to fuel his DCI's suspicions – 'the perpetrator re-visiting the scene of his crimes,' Crosby could hear him saying.

He made his way towards the circle of white screens. A quick look inside confirmed the pathologist still bent over his work. Not for the first time that morning Crosby forced down a surge of rising bile.

He looked away from the body. Dark red splatterings on the concrete-surround indicated where blood showers from O'Grady's shattered skull had sprayed its surface.

'What's the verdict Doc?'

'Too early to say!'

'Anything unusual?'

'Not yet!'

'Will you manage a preliminary report by this evening?'

'Possibly!'

The pathologist's manner annoyed him. With little to be gained by remaining Crosby ducked out from behind the screens and made his way towards a single-storey annex at the rear of CentrePoint's tower block. The annex contained five decent-sized rooms and served as an on-site administrative and service unit. Rees-Bramley had commandeered the building as temporary offices and interview rooms.

Crosby found his DCI standing outside the annexe's front door pushing buttons on his mobile. 'I was just about to call you Frank,' he dropped the phone back into his pocket. 'I've got a press conference at ten-thirty and a sit-rep with the Chief Constable immediately afterwards. You'll have to take over here.'

'Anything I need to know about?'

'Couple of statements I want you to look at and act on. I've left them inside with Admin Support.' The DCI checked his watch. 'I'm running late. We'll catch up with each other later.' Smoothing down his tie, and fastening the centre button of his jacket, Rees-Bramley took a deep breath before striding away towards the waiting media.

'I'll give the press conference a miss then,' Crosby muttered as he entered the administration annex.

He found admin support's Amy Johnstone in one of the side rooms, sorting through a pile of witness statements. She looked up as Crosby stepped through the doorway. 'Good Morning Sir! You've just missed the DCI.'

'I saw him outside.' He nodded towards the other rooms. 'Are we still interviewing?'

'Yes Sir!' Johnstone gestured towards the files on her desk. 'We've had a lot of feed-back this morning.'

'The DCI left me a couple of statements to look at,' Crosby said.

Johnstone's slim, petite figure got up from the desk, retrieving a folder from the table opposite. Crosby took it to a nearby chair and made himself comfortable.

'Were both of these volunteered?' the detective asked.

'I believe so,' Johnstone said, 'identified themselves as friends of Grady's.'

Crosby quickly scanned the two statements. Pulling out his mobile he selected a number from the contacts list. 'Paul? DI Crosby! Find out where the Red Lion public house is and get yourself down there. I want you to catch the lunchtime drinkers. O'Grady was there for most of last night apparently. Take Jefferies along with you.'

Disconnecting the call Crosby left the room to check on progress in the two interview rooms. Both occupied. Back outside he retraced his steps to the white screens that were shielding O'Grady's body. The solid frame of PC Jennings had taken up sentry duty in front of them.

'Morning Frank.' Jennings jerked his head towards the administration annex. 'Busy in there?'

Crosby nodded. 'Residents are talking.'

'Makes you wonder why everyone's bothering.' Jennings sniffed. 'This lunatic's doing us all a favour.'

'It doesn't look good on my CV,' Crosby replied.

'DI responsibilities weighing a bit heavy then?'

The detective shrugged. 'You know what the press are like. Is young Stewart about today?'

'Called in sick.' Jennings raised his eyebrows. 'Problem?'

'You're aware of the current situation regarding Robert Milner?'

The policeman nodded.

'Stewart's managed to establish some sort of relationship with his daughter.'

Jennings whistled. 'I knew there was something distracting him. Should have realised it would be a woman.'

'I have spoken to him,' Crosby said. 'But I'm not sure he realises the seriousness of the situation – with Milner being investigated it could be embarrassing. Any chance of you having a word?'

'I can try.' Jennings shook his head. 'But you know how it was at that age – he'll be like a dog with two dicks. Won't know what time of bloody day it is.'

Crosby's mobile sounded. The detective pulled it from his pocket and pushed a button. 'Crosby!' The call was brief. 'On my way,' he replied.

'You'll speak to him then,' Crosby said turning back to Jennings.

The policeman shrugged. 'Or take him along to the vets.'

The detective left Jennings and headed towards a Mobile Forensic Unit.

From behind the barriers a face in the crowd followed Crosby's progress across the car park. After watching him disappear into the Mobile Unit, Stephen Roberts turned abruptly, pushing his way aggressively through the crowd, fencing at people with his crutches to clear a path.

The tall figure in front of him stood his ground. Stephen Roberts looked up at his father. They stared at each other. Roberts jerked his head. 'Move!'

Milner remained where he was. 'You've been harassing Janet Sterne and her children, Stephen.'

Roberts waved a crutch at Milner's face. 'Get the fuck out of my way!'

Since talking to Crosby, moments earlier Milner's manner had changed. The face was blank. There was an intenseness to his eyes again. 'We've come to a decision about you Stephen.'

'Fucking barking!' Roberts sneered. 'You should have been put away years ago.'

'I tried to help you.'

'By locking me in the house?'

'I could see what was happening. It was for your own good.'

Roberts shook his head. 'No wonder I needed to get out – I'm lucky not to have ended up like you. Washing your car every day! Rearranging all the tins in your cupboard. Pressing the light switch up and down to make sure it was off! Your mind was fucked then. Christ knows what it's like now.'

'It doesn't matter anymore, Stephen.' Milner shook his head. 'It's too late for you.'

Roberts went to push past him. 'I can't stand here listening to this fucking shite!'

The grey cloud above CentrePoint thinned slightly and a low, pale sun emerged behind Milner's head, silhouetting his white, unruly hair.

Roberts experienced a sudden flashback. The same silhouette outlined itself against a bright full moon. 'Fucking Hell!' realisation slowly dawned on him. 'It was you!'

Milner turned abruptly away, melting into the crowd.

'Freak!' Stephen Roberts shouted after him. 'Fucking freak! When this is all over I'll be coming for you!' – but he sounded more surprised than angry.

Studwell HQ: Major Incident Room : Sunday 4 February 2007: 8.00 pm

DCI Rees-Bramley strode briskly into Crosby's partitioned office at eight o'clock on Sunday evening carrying his lightweight briefcase. The DCI held up a hand in apology. 'Couldn't get away,' he said. 'Shall we make a start?'

Crosby had been waiting at the station for his DCI since seven o'clock and was having difficulty in keeping his eyes open – CentrePoint had been a long day. Rees-Bramley, in a pale grey three-piece suit dropped into the chair opposite, looking refreshed and crisp. Crosby sat at his desk in a rumpled, limp shirt, with the top button of his collar undone. He nodded towards his monitor. 'I saw the press conference earlier.'

'They're looking for scapegoats. We need an arrest.' Rees-Bramley glanced at the pile of folders on Crosby's desk. 'Any progress on the statements?'

Berne and Jefferies went along to the Red Lion at lunchtime.' Crosby picked up one of the files and opened it. 'Several witnesses remember seeing O'Grady leave the pub with a girl shortly before closing time.'

'Has she been traced?'

'We're still checking but it was a live music night. Lots of faces the regulars didn't recognise.'

'Do we have a description of her?'

Crosby referred to the folder. 'Cropped blonde hair. Short red leather skirt. A see through top. Red stiletto shoes. Mid-twenties.'

'Local prostitute?' Rees-Bramley asked.

Crosby shrugged. 'Difficult to tell Sir! Fairly standard outfit for a Saturday night around the pubs.'

'Is it!' the DCI said. 'We need to find her anyway. She'd know if O'Grady was approached outside the pub.'

'We do have another statement that has him walking across the CentrePoint car park around midnight,' Crosby added.

'Alone?'

'Yes Sir! And that's the last sighting we have.'

Rees-Bramley nodded. 'Did forensics turn anything up?'

'They've swept the site and his flat.' Crosby shrugged. 'It doesn't look promising.'

'I suppose we have to consider the possibility of suicide,' Rees-Bramley said.

Crosby shook his head. 'Our pathologist has indicated that O'Grady's body was moved after the event.'

'In what way?'

'It was rearranged,' Crosby paused. 'Similar to how Stephen Roberts was displayed.'

The DCI raised his eyebrows. 'What else did he have to say?'

'We'll have a full report by tomorrow morning!'

Rees-Bramley waved a hand at the statements. 'Anything I need to know about?'

'Robert Milner turned up at the murder site this morning,' Crosby said.

Rees-Bramley's eyes sparked. 'What was he doing there?'

'His early morning run takes him past the CentrePoint Tower Block.'

Rees-Bramley nodded. 'Murderers re-visit the scene of their crimes. That's based on proven research.'

'I anticipated you'd make the connection Sir.' Crosby's face remained impassive.

Rees-Bramley paused and looked obliquely at his deputy before continuing. 'I want a twenty-four hour surveillance operation set up on Milner's home.'

'It'll be stretching resources and expenditure Sir,' Crosby answered.

'Budget for it!' Rees-Bramley said. There was a momentary silence. 'So where do you think today leaves us?' the DCI eventually asked.

'Up the creek without a fucking paddle,' Crosby felt like saying. He shifted in his seat. 'Profiles of the victims still point to it being gang or drug related Sir.'

Rees-Bramley shook his head. 'The bodies wouldn't be displayed in that manner.'

'An individual then.' Crosby shrugged. 'Targeting a specific criminal class.'

The DCI leant back in his chair. 'And the motive?'

Crosby groaned inwardly – Rees-Bramley was obviously in the mood for one of his tedious brain-storming sessions. 'Psychopaths don't require a motive Sir. Just an on-off switch inside their heads.'

'Maybe not even a psychopath.' The DCI leant forward. 'Just someone who objects to the existence of Sixfields' thugs, and wants public attention drawn to what they're doing.'

'A popular Jack the Ripper theory,' Crosby said without enthusiasm.

'Precisely!' Rees-Bramley replied. 'Old Victorian Jack was the original pro-active social reformer. By slitting the throats of local prostitutes in the slums of Whitechapel, and displaying them in bizarre fashion, focused national attention and pricked the government's conscience.' The DCI shrugged. 'Redevelopment of London's East End was probably a direct result of the intense interest he generated.'

'But as he didn't get caught, a motive was never established.'

'Which isn't going to happen with this particular investigation.'

Crosby saved his DCI the trouble. 'Milner?'

'He ticks all the boxes.'

'Apart from there being no concrete evidence against him.'

'All circumstantial,' Rees-Bramley agreed. 'But he's a constant. Whatever line of enquiry we pursue his name comes up again and again. The attack on Stephen Roberts kicked all this off – and Milner's been lying about that since day one.'

Crosby couldn't muster the energy to respond. He stifled a yawn.

Rees-Bramley waved a hand. 'A long day, Frank. Get yourself home. Briefing tomorrow at nine sharp.'

Crosby nodded and hauled himself up.

'Incidentally,' Rees-Bramley said as the DI was pulling his jacket on. 'I was re-reading Milner's file yesterday. There's a report on him being physically assaulted in CentrePoint's car park a few years back. He used to visit someone there apparently.'

Crosby was already at the partition entrance. 'Goodnight Sir!'

Haymoore Country Park: Sunday 4 February 2007: 10.00 pm

Haymoore Country Park lay six miles north-west of Sixfields. The large expanse of wooded parkland was a well frequented, relatively unspoilt beauty spot. It included designated barbecue areas, picnic sites and a signed nature trail for visitors to enjoy during the long summer months.

At ten o'clock, on this particular night, summer had long since departed – outside it was pitch-black, with a howling wind – heavy rain lashed down from the low cloud-base.

Looking lost and out of place in the corner of Haymoore's main car park was a small, red Honda. The car's engine had been left running and an over-efficient heater pumped out waves of hot air towards the driver and his passenger – who had made themselves comfortable on the rear seats.

Lucy disentangled herself from Peter Stewart's awkward embrace. 'You're not concentrating,' she said. 'Is it me?'

'No!' the young PC stuttered in his haste. 'Absolutely not!'

The couple had been seeing each other for nearly two weeks now – Stewart had plucked up the necessary courage to contact Lucy after the incident outside her father's house. The relationship had quickly blossomed.

'I've got a problem,' said Stewart awkwardly.

'Not from where I'm sitting,' Lucy teased, stroking the erection beneath his trousers.

'It's your Dad!'

'What about him!' she laughed, pulling at the zip on his trousers. 'Is he outside?'

'It's difficult!' Stewart's breathing shortened as Lucy tugged his erection free. 'He's being questioned about the two murders in Sixfields.'

'What!' She pulled her hand away. The young PC groaned as he prematurely ejaculated.

Lucy sat up straight and the romantic interlude evaporated. 'What was that about my Dad?'

'He's a suspect.' Stewart was trying to clean himself up. 'Makes it awkward for us. You being his daughter.'

'I don't believe it!' Lucy said. 'There must be some sort of misunderstanding.'

The car fell silent. Stewart waited, his erection a distant memory. He tried to take her hand. 'I don't want it to cause trouble between us,' his voice tailed off.

Lucy shook her head. 'I need to see him. You'd better take me back.'

The young PC looked utterly miserable as he opened the Honda's rear door and got out.

CHAPTER 22

Janet Sterne trudged up the path's slight incline, dragging a push-chair behind. On reaching her back door the young mother dropped two supermarket bags of shopping to the ground and fumbled for a key. She slotted it into the Yale lock. As she stooped to pick up the two bags a wave of nausea swept over her. Struggling to remain upright Sterne slumped back against the wall. Zoe stretched for her mother's hand, the girl's face showing concern at Sterne's chalk-white features.

Sterne snatched her hand away and took several deep breaths 'Don't fuss!' she snapped.

The four-year-old pushed open the door, picked up both carrier bags, and dragged them inside. With some difficulty she manhandled the pushchair containing her sleeping sister into the hallway. Zoe returned to the back door and took her mother's hand again. Leading Sterne through to the lounge she helped her into a nearby chair. The room was a mess. It appeared not to have been cleaned for days, and the smell of stale cigarette smoke permeated throughout. Balanced precariously on the arm of an overstuffed armchair were two plates, bearing the remnants of last night's meal.

Janet Sterne hadn't slept properly for weeks. Prescription tablets from the doctor were not helping, and her mental state was getting progressively worse. The intimidation and harassment had been constant, and showed no sign of letting up – anonymous telephone calls, accosted in the street, doorbell ringing at all hours. Sterne was near to breaking point.

Keeping an eye on her mother, Zoe retrieved a packet of crisps from one of the carrier bags, turned on the television, and settled back in an armchair.

The colour gradually returned to Sterne's face. She got up and made her way slowly into the kitchen.

Arms folded, lounging against the far wall, Stephen Roberts was still wearing the plaster cast on his leg. A thin, weasel-faced looking youth, standing next to him, moved from one foot to the other – he looked agitated and nervous.

Sterne stifled a scream.

Roberts jerked his head towards the lounge. 'Make sure the kid doesn't do a runner.' The youth sidled slowly towards the lounge door. On reaching Sterne he stopped and slid a hand underneath her skirt.

'Leave it!' Roberts raised his voice. 'See to the kid!'

'You said I could fuck her,' the youth whined.

Sterne automatically reached for the self-defence spray she carried around in her coat pocket and held it out towards them – but she looked uncertain, and her hand was shaking.

The youth drew back.

A smell of thin machine oil filled the air as Roberts unwrapped a length of dark cloth he was holding. Retrieving a slim, cylindrical tube from his pocket he proceeded to screw it onto the end of a short-barrelled gun. 'Nine millimetre Makarov semi-automatic,' he said, pulling back the firing mechanism. 'Serbs and Croats bring them in by the shed-load. Goes off like a dud firework with the silencer fitted.' Roberts took aim at the ceiling light bulb. 'Like to hear it?'

Sterne didn't answer.

Roberts turned to the youth. He motioned with the gun. 'See to the fucking kid! Move!'

The youth barged his way past Sterne and went through to the lounge.

Roberts clumped his way awkwardly across to the unmarried mother. Removing the spray from her hand he tossed it onto the kitchen table before pushing his face close to hers. 'You're still getting visitors.' His breath smelt rancid.

Sterne fought another wave of nausea as the bile rose in her throat. She forced it back down. 'I've told them to stay away.'

'That bitch detective was here again yesterday.'

'I keep telling her. I don't want anything to do with it.' Sterne's legs began to tremble. The tremor spread upwards, making her whole body shake.

Roberts raised the gun to her head. She closed her eyes.

'You're lucky!' he pressed the barrel's tip hard against her temple. 'I've been told to back off.' Roberts pushed the barrel more forcefully. 'But if you do fuck this up for me, we'll be having this conversation again.'

He pulled the gun away from her forehead, leaving a small, red, circular indentation in her skin. Sterne's legs gave way and she crumpled to the floor. Retrieving his crutches from the kitchen table, Roberts stepped over the woman's outstretched body and opened the door.

The weasel-faced youth was laughing along at a children's cartoon as Roberts entered the room. Zoe's eyes remained fixed to the screen, an unopened packet of crisps on her lap.

Roberts stumped towards the hallway. 'We're leaving!'

The youth's face turned sullen. 'You said I could screw her.'

'Open the fucking door!'

Roberts stopped at Zoe's chair. He ruffled the girl's hair. 'You need to go and take care of your Mum.'

The youth preceded Roberts out of the lounge. Zoe waited for the front door to close before going into the kitchen to help her mother up from the floor. Sterne lurched unsteadily across the room and threw up into the kitchen sink.

'Go and check Tracey,' she shouted in between retching. 'And put both chains on the fucking door.'

CHAPTER 23

Sixfields Estate: Saturday 10 February 2007: 8.50 pm

With her eyes closed, the woman emitted a series of low moans. Leaning forward she had both arms fully extended, the palms of her hands braced against a window ledge. Standing behind her, Paul Berne's eyes were fully open, most of his attention fixed outside the bedroom window. He pushed hard into the woman as his orgasm approached. A short grunt signalled Berne's abrupt ejaculation. The woman groaned in annoyance as he quickly withdrew from her.

Clearly piqued at not reaching her own climax Detective Constable Hazel Marston snatched up a pile of clothes and marched out of the room. 'Selfish Bastard!' she shouted over her shoulder. Unconcerned at the woman's outburst Berne casually zipped up his trousers and turned his attention back to a tripod-mounted telephoto zoom-lens that had been trained on a house and garden fifty yards along the alleyway. Resuming his chair the detective leant forward and squinted through the digitalised viewfinder. Satisfied the camera's original angle of set-up had not been disturbed he sat back and relaxed.

Berne still couldn't believe his luck. Being teamed up with DC Hazel Marston for surveillance duties had been like manna from heaven. Twenty year-old Marston, who had recently joined the investigation team, appeared to have very few objections when it came to casual sex.

'I suppose it'll help pass the time,' she said to Berne, when he'd made advances on their first night together in the house.

The detective's mind wandered. Already bored with the easy conquest of Marston he wondered what his chances would be if Grace Taylor had to spend the night with him. Berne felt the beginnings of another erection. Perhaps he'd have a word with someone about the surveillance roster.

DC Marston returned fully dressed, the aborted climax still annoying her. 'Is that how you usually screw your women?'

'Somebody had to keep an eye on things,' Berne said, 'and you need to get back and cover the front. We'll get hammered if anything gets missed.'

Marston dropped into the chair opposite. 'Didn't seem to bother you just now. Anyway, Milner's going nowhere at the moment, apart from his back garden.'

'And if he decides to break his routine?' Berne said, his attention still focused outside.

'All sounds a bit desperate to me,' Marston replied. 'Throwing all these resources at one line of enquiry.'

Berne yawned and stretched. 'Investigation's ground to a halt. Milner's the only lead we've got.'

'So what happens if the DCI doesn't get a result soon?'

'Fireproof at the moment isn't he. HQ aren't going to admit his appointment was a cock-up.'

'They'll be squeezing his balls though.'

Berne laughed. 'He might enjoy that – if it's someone tall, dark and handsome.'

Marston raised her eyebrows. 'Is he?'

Berne shrugged. 'Jury's still out.'

The two detectives lapsed into silence as they waited. Images of a rampant Grace Taylor bracing herself against the window ledge filtered through to Berne's subconscious. He put a hand on Marston's knee, moving it up the inside of her thigh. 'Oh fuck off Paul! You're not that irresistible.'

A light flickered in the detective's peripheral vision. He swung round. An oblong of light illuminated the window in Milner's kitchen. 'He's on the move,' Berne muttered.

Milner's back door opened, emitting a strip of light into the garden. A tall, shadowy outline moved quickly down the path. Marston shivered. 'Gives me the creeps. Looks like a fucking ghost with all that white hair blowing around.'

The two detectives watched Milner take up his usual position. He remained barely visible in a dim, reflected light from the overhead streetlamp. A clock next to Berne's surveillance post gradually ticked the minutes away and Milner's stillness eventually merged into the dark background.

At ten o'clock exactly Milner stirred. Emerging from the shadows he made his way back up towards the house.

Marston shook her head. 'That's the weirdest fucking thing.'

'And now what are we going to do,' Berne relaxed back in his chair, 'now that he's safely tucked up inside?'

The woman got to her feet and headed for the door. 'Well I'm going back to the other bedroom, in case he decides to go walk-about through his front door.'

'We shan't get too many more nights here,' Berne called after her. 'Rees-Bramley's applied to have CCTV cameras installed.'

Marston stopped in the doorway and turned to face him. She lifted the front of her skirt to reveal a lack of underwear. 'You'd better make the most of it then Constable.'

'Cheeky fucking mare!' Berne said as she disappeared through the doorway. He looked at his watch and weighed up the odds. 'Bollocks!' he muttered getting to his feet.

'I can give you ten minutes,' Berne shouted through to Marston.

Sixfields Estate: Saturday 10 February 2007: 11.00 pm

Sandra Dredge applied the finishing touches to her make-up before pulling on a pair of scuffed, knee-length, leather boots. She went back to the small oval mirror and fixed her long, blonde ponytail into place with two distinctive pink ribbons. Opening one of the dressing table drawers Dredge retrieved several packs of standard issue condoms and dropped them into a black, plastic handbag. Picking up the bag she went into an adjoining bedroom where her thirteen-year-old daughter lay asleep on a narrow divan. Dredge stooped to kiss the girl lightly on her forehead. 'Back soon,' she whispered, and backed quietly out of the room.

Dredge risked the shortcut through Cedar Gardens – one of several run-down parks dotted throughout the Sixfields Estate. The park's lighting was inadequate – two mature oaks and thick, dense bush, just inside the entrance gates, threw the whole area into dark shadow. Last night, walking through Cedar Gardens to her pitch in Bridge Street, she'd been aware of footsteps on the path behind her. Dredge couldn't see anyone and the footsteps stopped whenever she looked around. It had unnerved her though.

Tonight she was wary. Fifty yards into the park, and just as Dredge was beginning to breathe more easily, footsteps sounded immediately behind her. She spun round to an empty path.

Dredge scrabbled around in the black plastic bag for her mobile. Continuing to glance nervously behind she punched the phone's contact button 'Darren! Where the fuck are you? There's somebody following me through Cedar Gardens.' Dredge shook her head. 'I don't care what you're fucking well doing! I'm not moving until you bring the car. You're supposed to be looking after me when I'm working.'

Throwing the phone back into her bag, Dredge remained where she was, calculating the possibility of retracing her steps back to the park entrance. She certainly didn't feel the blow to the back of her head, and she was already unconscious by the time her face thudded into the tarmac.

A tight-fitting, black leather glove reached into the prostitute's bag and retrieved her phone. The last number she called was reactivated.

Deep in conversation at the Green Man public house a thin, scruffily dressed individual snatched the phone from his pocket. 'What the fuck do you want now?' he shouted into it.

'Darren Shaughnessy?' a muffled voice enquired.

CHAPTER 24

Sixfields Estate: Sunday 11 February 2007: 6.30 am

It was still thirty minutes before sunrise and the room was in complete darkness – Milner sat upright at the kitchen table, both hands flat against its scrubbed, wooden surface. His depression had returned, with a renewed ferocity. Entire days were wiped from his memory. He might be insane. He wasn't sure.

Milner remained at the table, immobile, fighting random, unconnected thoughts. They wouldn't give him any peace. He brought his fist down hard against the table-top. It cleared his mind, allowed him to re-focus. Stephen would be an end to it. Milner was tired. He no longer had the will to fight another debilitating cycle of depression.

There was a polite knock at the kitchen door. They'd become impatient, never far from his side in recent days. Several of them filed into the room, taking their allotted places around the table. Milner closed his eyes, allowing their thoughts to seep into his subconscious.

A series of high-pitched screams ripped through the silence. Milner was quickly to his feet and crossed to the kitchen window. Outside, two cats slowly circled each other, spitting and snarling profanities, ears laid flat to their heads.

Milner turned back into the room. A degree of normality returned and his companions melted away. Picking up two mugs from the drainer a rare smile came to his face – Lucy had insisted on staying the night – she knew he was suffering again. There was no movement from upstairs. The feline spat didn't appear to have woken her.

A premonition suddenly swept across him. A warning? Lucy? Sixfields had already taken Stephen. Milner would have to dissuade her from visiting. She was already getting involved, asking questions about why the police were interested in him. 'It's harassment,' she said. 'I'll sort it for you.' Opening a cupboard door he carefully positioned both mugs inside and left the kitchen.

Out in the hallway, Milner pulled on his battered old trainers. He unlocked the front door and pushed it open. With daylight about to break Milner stepped into the chill air of a crisp, dry Sunday morning.

Donald and Spike were waiting outside the gate. 'Hello Mister Milner.'

'Good morning Donald.'

Spike's tail wagged enthusiastically and Milner bent to pat the dog's head.

'Are you out running today Mister Milner?' Donald asked. 'Can I bring the newspapers back for you?'

'That would be a help,' Milner said, happy to slip into his familiar Sunday morning routine.

The unlikely looking pair set off up the incline towards ParkGate's shopping precinct. Milner glanced back. Last week a large white transit van had pulled up outside number thirty-five and a team of thinly disguised housing sub-contractors had transferred tins of paint, rollers and brushes into the vacant building. 'Idiots!' Milner muttered. He turned back round, resisting the urge to wave into their cameras.

It was a ten minute walk to the precinct and Donald's non-stop chatter lasted the whole way. Spike on the other hand struggled with the uphill slope, finding it difficult to maintain his sedate waddle. They turned into ParkGate just as the busy little Indian shopkeeper was removing two wire mesh shutters from inside the window of his retail unit.

About fifty yards away from them, three shaven-headed yobs appeared from a side entrance, taking Milner by surprise. He immediately knew they were trouble. Unlike the confrontation last week this group was older, all of them bare-chested, stomachs spilling over the tops of their trousers. Still drunk from the night before they shouted and swaggered towards the newsagent's shop, their noise echoing around the deserted precinct. Milner tried to open the shop door but it had already been locked against him. He rapped on the glass. The shopkeeper ignored him, shouting for the police into his mobile.

A bottle hit the ground next to Milner's trainers, the glass smashing into tiny fragments. Contents from the bottle splattered and foamed across several flagstones. Milner turned as the group closed on them. Their abuse was loud and predictable. 'Fuck me! I must still be pissed! It's Snow White and Dopey.' They were close enough for Milner to smell the alcohol. Donald edged away, calling for Spike to follow him. The dog was slow. As it turned one of the group swung a boot, toe-ending the vicious kick into Spike's flank and crushing his rib-cage. The animal's short legs gave way and it slumped onto its side, completely winded. As the dog struggled to draw breath another boot thudded into the side of its head.

There was a huge animal roar from Milner's right. He looked up to see Donald running back towards them, his face an ugly mask.

The shaven-headed yob saw him coming but was either too slow or too drunk to get out of the way. Donald's sixteen-stone bulk hit him hard – at speed – their forward momentum carrying them towards the plate glass window. There was a resounding crack as the force of their combined weight hit the window, shattering it completely. For a split second no-one moved. Milner was the first to react, jumping through the gaping shop-front after them. Inside, the two bodies were rolling around on a carpet of fragmented glass. There was blood everywhere. Donald had both hands clamped around the man's throat, whose face and shaven head had suffused to a deep red as he frantically tried to drag some air into his lungs. The prolonged, hysterical screaming, was coming from the shopkeeper's wife as she cowered behind a row of shelves with her husband.

Milner dropped to the floor and desperately tried to prise Donald's thumbs from the man's windpipe. He couldn't pull them away, they were locked solid, digging deep into the fragile bone structure. A clenched fist punched Donald full in the face – breaking his nose. Bright crimson blood spurted from both nasal passages. Still he wouldn't let go. It took both of the man's companions to eventually haul Donald off. He instinctively tried to curl himself into a protective ball as the two yobs kicked at his head and body.

Milner launched himself at the nearest of Donald's assailants, hitting him hard with his shoulder. The collision sent them both careering across the shop floor, scattering goods and demolishing rows of metal shelving. Unable to regain his balance the man stumbled and pitched forward. In front of him a shelf fitting had been snapped off, exposing four inches of thin steel rod, pointing directly outwards. The man's face ran directly into it, his weight driving the needle sharp sliver of metal deep into the left eye, piercing and bursting his eyeball.

He automatically wrenched his head backwards and dropped to all fours in complete shock, a mixture of blood and watery fluid leaking from his eye-socket.

Milner had already scrambled to his feet, aware of the third man waving a six-inch blade to-and-fro in front of his face. As the knife arced towards him he grabbed a wrist and clamped both hands around it. The attacker, with his free arm, connected several vicious uppercuts to Milner's head and face.

Lowering his head Milner bit into the raised, thick blue veins on the inside of his assailant's wrist. A high-pitched squeal echoed around the shop. The warm blood that spurted into Milner's mouth tasted metallic. He bit deeper, and the knife clattered to the floor.

A bulky uniformed figure shoved Milner to one side. PC Jennings was none too careful as he examined the man's wrist. 'PC Stone!' the policeman shouted over his shoulder. 'More first aid here! And will somebody stop that bloody woman screaming! Get them both in the back and start taking some statements.'

Jennings dropped the man's arm casually to the floor and continued issuing instructions. 'PC Brent! See what you can do for the other one, it looks as if he's convulsing, and hurry that ambulance up. If we're unlucky it might get here in time to save a couple of them.'

The policeman turned back to Milner. 'This is getting to be a habit Sir.' He surveyed the shop. 'Two down and the other one half-strangled. Bloody impressive! I'd be pleased with that myself.'

Milner tried to lift his head. 'Is Donald OK?'

Jennings nodded. 'I'm not sure about his dog though.'

Milner attempted to get up. His legs buckled underneath him and he started to shake. Jennings sat him back down. 'You're in shock. Wait until the medics have checked you over. There's some nasty bruises coming out.' Milner felt his face beginning to swell. He was having difficulty in focusing his right eye.

Jennings turned to PC Stone. 'Finished?'

'Best I can do.' Stone applied a final knot to the tourniquet.

'Right! I'll see to him now. See what's happening outside.'

PC Stone moved away towards the door, glass shards crunching beneath his tread. Jennings walked over to the injured man. 'I'll need to move you Sir. You're lying on a lot of glass.' The man was semi-conscious, he offered little resistance as Jennings pulled him gently behind one of the shop's bulky chest freezers. The policeman stood up to check for the CCTV camera's positioning before stamping the heel of his boot into the man's groin. The prostrate figure was only able to whimper as Jennings stamped on him again. The wail of an ambulance stopped him from bringing his boot down for a third time.

Milner had a vague recollection of Jennings helping him from the shop. He felt dizzy and nauseous, his right eye completely closed. As medics assisted him into the ambulance he had a fleeting glimpse of Donald sitting on the pavement, cradling Spike in his lap.

CHAPTER 25

Crosby sat across from his DCI. This morning's briefing had been depressing and downbeat. In a worrying development for the investigation a local prostitute by the name of Sandra Dredge had gone missing over the weekend – and she didn't fit the previous victim's profiles. If her disappearance was a continuation of the recent murders, it meant their killer was now striking at random.

Dredge's thirteen-year-old daughter Elaine had raised the alarm yesterday morning, after her mother had failed to return home. This was quickly followed by calls reporting an incident in Cedar Gardens. There was plenty of evidence to suggest the prostitute had been attacked there, not least a pool of congealed blood spread across the park's tarmac path. A subsequent search found Dredge's handbag hanging from nearby branches. Her bright, red lipstick had been used to crudely sketch 'No 4 – R.I.P.' on its black, shiny plastic.

They'd initially hoped the killing was domestic – Sandra Dredge's partner Darren Shaughnessy had also disappeared – but the message on Dredge's handbag appeared to rule that out.

For the first time during their investigation Crosby thought Rees-Bramley was beginning to doubt himself. Publicly he maintained his professional façade, but within the team he'd become terse and short-tempered. Their Chief Constable, along with the Regional Independent Police Authority, wanted progress, and an increasingly impatient media were mounting ever more criticism at press conferences, slowly picking at Rees-Bramley's calm exterior. Pressure was being applied and his DCI was showing signs of stress.

Crosby wasn't immune to it. As Rees-Bramley's second-in-command his position of Deputy Investigating Officer was also attracting attention.

He was finding it difficult to switch off – unable to sleep properly – whenever Crosby closed his eyes details of the case would nag at his subconscious. He'd also taken to snapping at his wife. She'd so far resisted the opportunity to say I told you so, but her inference about accepting the job was always there.

The DCI's telephone rang. He snatched at it. 'Rees-Bramley!' a pause. 'I'll send him over now.' He replaced the receiver. 'That was DC Taylor. A development at Janet Sterne's house. You'd better get over there.'

Crosby was already on his feet and heading for the door.

Sixfields Estate: Monday 12 February 2007: 10.30 am.

Turning into Wassom Avenue Crosby saw both ambulances immediately. 'Fuck!' Four-year-old Zoe Sterne's face flashed across his subconscious. He parked halfway down the street and walked towards a knot of people gathered outside Janet Sterne's house. Crosby held up his warrant card and the PC on duty pushed open a small gate for him. The detective walked up to the front door where he found Grace Taylor standing outside. She looked upset. 'Fuck!' he muttered again.

'Paramedics are bringing them out now Sir,' Taylor said.

'Well?' Crosby asked brusquely. 'What happened?'

'Janet Sterne and Zoe are both unconscious. The baby might already be dead.'

'How?'

'There were some empty prescription bottles scattered around,' Taylor said. 'I'm guessing she forced tablets into the children, then swallowed what was left herself. I'll go back in and have another look when the house is clear.'

'Everyone been notified?'

'Yes Sir!'

They waited in silence.

The first stretcher emerged. Janet Sterne's chalk-white features were partially obscured by an oxygen mask. Zoe followed, also wearing a mask, her face dwarfed by the large pillow cushioning her head. A third stretcher emerged. Underneath the thin, grey ambulance blanket Tracey Sterne's small outline lay very still. The watching crowd remained respectfully quiet.

Crosby and Taylor waited as all three stretchers were carefully lifted into the waiting ambulances. Only a far off, distant rumble of traffic disturbed the street's silence.

As both emergency vehicles pulled away Crosby's anger returned –

anger at the baby's death – anger at not being able to give Janet Sterne the support she needed – anger that Stephen Roberts was still walking the streets – anger at the whole fucking mess. He suppressed it, turning back to Taylor. 'Any particular reason for you being here?'

'Sterne called me on my mobile. She was rambling. When the line went dead I alerted the medics and got over here.' The policewoman handed Crosby a clear plastic wallet. 'She left us a note,' Taylor paused. 'It says that Stephen Roberts broke into the house and threatened her with a gun.'

Crosby scanned Sterne's child-like scrawl before handing the wallet back. 'Can you pick it up from here Grace? I've an appointment at the hospital.'

Taylor looked surprised at the timing. 'Nothing serious Sir?'

'Serious enough!'

Crosby left the policewoman and walked back down the street. His overriding priority now was to make Milner aware of what Stephen Roberts had caused. He knew full well what the outcome would be, but his conscience was clear. It was personal now – last night his wife had received an anonymous phone call enquiring about the health of their grandson.

There might be consequences however – at some stage Rees-Bramley would work out what Crosby was about to set in motion. The detective shrugged.

On reaching his car Crosby got inside and slammed the door shut – the detective couldn't be aware that he was about to spark a chain of events that would not only turn the investigation upside down, but have a devastating effect on Sixfields itself.

Royal West Midlands Hospital: Monday 12 February 2007: 11.30 am.

It took about thirty minutes for Crosby to reach the Royal West Midlands. Images of Tracey Sterne's small body being stretchered into the ambulance blotted out most of his journey. Stephen Roberts had got to him, compromising and overriding all his years of detached professionalism.

Crosby drove twice around the hospital car park. No spaces! It pissed him off. He had neither the time nor patience this morning. Strictly speaking, his visit was neither scheduled nor official, but he parked in a restricted area anyway. Once through the hospital's large revolving entrance doors he headed straight for a bank of lifts, bypassing the enquiry desk and volunteer guides. He knew the ward that Milner had been assigned to.

The lift deposited Crosby at level five where he followed the arrows to Falconhurst Ward. Ignoring the recommended times for visitors he went straight to Milner's bed, tucked away in a far corner of the ward.

Milner was lying on top of his bed, fully dressed, a rash of ugly purple bruising to his face still prominent. Crosby thought he'd lost even more weight since seeing him last.

The detective pulled up a bedside chair. 'How are you feeling today Mister Milner?'

Crosby's arrival hadn't been acknowledged. Milner's gaunt features continued to stare at the ceiling.

The detective nodded at his clothes. 'You're going home shortly?'

No response.

'A nasty incident!'

No reply.

'PC Jennings was surprised there were no fatalities.'

It got a reaction. 'You wouldn't term kicking a family pet to death as a fatality then?'

'I can appreciate the upset that must have caused.'

'Can you really Inspector?' Milner raised himself up on one elbow. 'And will these yobs be charged for it?'

Crosby spread his hands. 'I'm sure it will be investigated.'

'And I'm sure it fucking well won't!' Milner returned to staring at the ceiling. 'But the police are, however, considering whether Donald and I should be charged with causing grievous bodily harm.'

'Due process of the law will determine who the guilty parties are,' Crosby said, but even he was aware of how his response sounded.

'The law will do fuck all! As usual!' Milner replied, turning his head towards the detective. 'Do you not have an opinion Inspector?'

'We aren't allowed personal views Sir.'

Milner nodded. 'Let the bastards keep knocking us senseless then. If they happen to injure themselves in the process you can always offer them some decent compensation and prosecute those responsible.'

Crosby didn't have the luxury of time. He had to gamble on telling him now. 'There was another incident this morning Mister Milner. Janet Sterne's been rushed into hospital after taking a suspected overdose,' the detective left it hanging for a few seconds. 'It looks as though she forced tablets into the children as well.'

Crosby waited.

Milner propped himself up.

'Zoe Sterne is in a coma.' Crosby said. 'The baby's dead. Sterne left a note to say that your son had broken into the house and threatened her with a gun.'

Milner received the news with a flicker of his eyelids. He swung his legs off the bed. 'And as that was the sole purpose of your visit Inspector, I would appreciate it if you left now.'

Crosby immediately got to his feet. 'Good luck Mister Milner.'

'Good luck to both of us Inspector!'

As Crosby disappeared through the exit doors Milner lashed out at a jug of water on his bedside cabinet, scattering its contents to the floor. Other patients in the ward looked across in alarm. The wave of anger passed. Milner would settle his affairs today and find Stephen tomorrow. He knew where to look.

Gathering up the few items that his daughter had brought to the hospital for him, Milner proceeded to stuff them into an old sports bag. Lucy had wanted to stay, but he'd managed to assure her that his injuries were not serious, and insisted she return to the university.

Milner walked towards the exit aware that his companions were following him. 'I don't need help with this.' he said out loud, and the shadows fell back. Other patients in the ward looked the other way as Milner strode past their beds.

He passed a young staff nurse at her workstation. She got to her feet. 'We're still waiting for the doctor to discharge you Mister Milner.'

He carried on out into the corridor.

'Mister Milner!' the nurse called after him. She shrugged and made a brief telephone call before returning to the screen in front of her.

Three floors below, outside the intensive care unit, Grace Taylor was waiting for news of Janet Sterne and her daughter. Although both of them had been pumped free of the drugs their conditions were being closely monitored, and they remained on the critical list. Crosby stood alongside Taylor, viewing the four-year-old through an observation window. Zoe lay underneath a single, white hospital sheet, showing no sign of movement. Tubes and wires trailed from her small body into the various monitoring devices positioned around her bed.

Crosby and Taylor went back to the seating area.

'How's Sterne going to live with this?' Taylor remarked.

'She won't!' Crosby replied.

'What'll happen to her?'

'If she survives?' Crosby shrugged. 'Prison? And her daughter put into care.'

The two detectives sat in silence. There was a commotion from outside and Janet Sterne's mother burst into the room.

Taylor got to her feet.

'I'll speak to her,' Crosby said, putting a hand on the policewoman's arm. 'See if you can get the Families Liaison Officer over here.'

CHAPTER 26

Sixfields Estate: Tuesday 13 February 2007: 7.00 am

Milner awoke later than usual. He'd slept well. A huge burden of responsibility had lifted from his shoulders and the release was almost physical. He felt no stress. There was no agitation. Last night he'd been able to resist routines and drills that had ruled his life for the past ten years, It was a sign. He could soon let go completely. Just one more task.

By seven thirty he was fully dressed and downstairs – the plain, white envelope still lay on his kitchen table. Although writing to Lucy had been difficult it was the right decision. Had he spoken to her personally of his plans she would have tried to stop him, talk him around.

Milner busied himself with breakfast, it was necessary. He would need all of his physical and mental energy today. After finishing the meal Milner was able to leave his plate and mug on the kitchen table – he didn't find it essential to immediately clear them away. It was further confirmation. He felt an inner calm. Fully committed to what had to be done.

Milner left his house at nine o'clock. It was cold outside, the remains of a ground frost still visible. He looked out across the common, towards a lone, solitary figure standing on the small bridge. Even from this distance Donald looked lost without Spike at his side. Milner waited. After the briefest of glances Donald turned his back and walked in the opposite direction. Milner recognised the grieving. It would be pointless to go after him.

He continued along the street, police surveillance equipment in the bedroom of number thirty-five recording his progress towards the garage block.

Inside his garage Milner started the old Rover's engine for what he envisaged would be the last time. After reversing out onto the hard-standing he returned to the garage and pulled out a loose brick from one of its interior walls. Retrieving a long-bladed knife from the recess Milner wrapped it in an old yellow duster. He slid the knife into his coat pocket and replaced the loose brick. A length of garden hose that he took down from a supporting nail had already been adjusted to fit the Rover's exhaust.

His journey to Shurville Gardens took approximately fifteen minutes – the cul-de-sac of ten, boarded-up, derelict houses had been vacated and abandoned some time ago. As one of the first plots to be developed in Sixfields the buildings were considered beyond economic repair, and had been ear-marked for the bulldozers some eighteen months ago. Neighbouring sites had already been razed to the ground, leaving the cul-de-sac in crumbling isolation, surrounded by mounds of brick and rubble.

Milner left his car hidden among the huge piles of debris. Taking up a position nearby he stood for ten minutes watching one of the houses. After satisfying himself the building wasn't occupied, Milner walked towards a bare, weathered front door. It swung open to his touch and he stepped into the gloom of a narrow hallway. There were no lights. All utilities had been disconnected when the building was previously vacated.

Milner sniffed at the dank smell – crumbling slabs of damp plaster littered the floor, a film of fine powder coating its surface. His progress through the hall caused tiny clouds of dust particles to eddy and swirl, before they settled on the surface of his shoes. Reaching the lounge door he pushed it open – a little daylight filtered through from the damaged, boarded-up front window. Apart from a pair of dust covered, thread-bare looking armchairs the room was completely gutted – fixtures and fittings long since stripped and spirited away.

He moved on through to the kitchen, his arrival causing a commotion of frantic scraping and scrabbling. It was pitch-black in here, the window securely boarded. Milner pulled a torch from his pocket and switched it on. The beam lit up a floor covered in black, spindle-shaped droppings and tiny clawed footprints, imprinted in the dust. Several upturned packing crates had been left in the room, surrounded by shoeprints – the scuff marks indicating there'd been further activity since Milner's last visit.

After emptying his bladder in the corner he switched off his torch, and eased himself into a small recess behind the door. Perched on top of the bricks and debris, Milner hunched into himself and waited for his son to arrive. As the afternoon wore on it became very cold, the type of cold that numbs the bones. Milner didn't feel it. And when the rats ventured back from the security of their nests, to sniff at his urine, he didn't notice them either.

Finding time to follow Stephen, who was travelling to the house in Shurville Gardens on a daily basis, hadn't been a problem. When there was a need to be away from work Milner went to the doctor. Once his past medical history was flashed to their screens all the necessary sick certificates would be signed and dated before he'd finished describing his symptoms.

Milner hadn't been into work for a week now but he doubted whether the police were even aware of it. Apart from his overnight stay in hospital their surveillance equipment would have logged him leaving in the morning and arriving back at his usual time.

Milner had been tracking his son since the previous week. Stephen was driving again now, and although limping badly, the plaster-cast and crutches had disappeared. On the fifth day, after waiting for Stephen to leave the cul-de-sac, Milner had taken a heavy-duty torch and entered the house. It hadn't been locked and there'd been no-one else inside. Apart from signs of recent activity in the kitchen area he'd found nothing untoward in any of the rooms.

Milner's right leg began to cramp up, dragging him back to the present. He stretched it out in front of him, disturbing some loose rubble. It caused the rats to sit upright on their haunches. Tiny slits of light pierced the darkness as their heads swivelled in his direction. Milner switched on the torch to check his watch, causing them to squeak and scurry into the dark corners.

He just wanted it over now. If Stephen was following the same timetable as in previous days he'd be here soon. Milner switched off the torch and prepared himself.

Ten minutes elapsed and a door scraped open. The sound of it echoed through to his recess. Milner stood up and slid a hand into his pocket – feeling for the knife. He waited. There were several muffled noises and movements before the house lapsed back into silence again. Milner leant forward, straining his ears. Wherever Stephen had gone it wasn't into the kitchen. He continued waiting. More silence.

Easing himself out of his recess Milner moved slowly across the room – impossible to be quiet. He reached the hallway. Milner held his knife low, waiting for Stephen to come at him through the open lounge door. It was difficult to see anything. He inched his head slowly around the doorframe. There was just enough light for him to take in the whole room. Stephen sat facing him in one of the armchairs, as if he'd been waiting. They stared at each other. Milner tightened the grip on his knife. It had to be quick. Just an animal being put to sleep. His long stride took him quickly across the room. Knife raised, Milner stood directly in front of his son. He didn't complete the strike.

Blood trickled from a neat, round hole in the middle of Stephen's forehead. The look on his face was one of surprise. He stared up at Milner, his eyes wide open. The lounge door creaked and Milner spun round.

A man stepped out from the shadows, dressed completely in black. His face was angular, lightly tanned. He looked foreign. The gun pointing directly at Milner's chest had an elongated silencer screwed into its short barrel.

A woman with short, cropped blonde hair appeared next to the gunman. 'Don't just stand there!' she instructed. 'Take the fucking knife off him!'

The man moved slowly across the room, his gun extended out in front of him. Remaining at arm's length he carefully eased the knife from Milner's grasp.

Lucy ripped the blonde wig from her head. She motioned Milner to the other chair. 'Sit! I need to think this through.'

Milner was rooted to the spot, unable to take it in. 'Lucy?' he kept repeating.

'Sit the fuck down!' his daughter shouted at him.

CHAPTER 27

Studwell : Major Incident Room: Wednesday 14 February 2007: 5.00 pm

Crosby tossed his reading glasses onto the desk. He was currently ploughing through several screens of vehicle registration numbers caught on ANPR CCTV cameras within the Sixfields estate – resulting interviews were stretching MIU resources to the limit.

An afternoon in front of the VDU screen had made Crosby's eyes tired and scratchy. He fought the urge for a cigarette and got up from his desk to look over the partition screens surrounding his office area. The main office was virtually deserted, most detectives out on the street. Crosby missed it – the administrative tasks of a DI were repetitive and time-consuming – a report he was compiling for his DCI on the investigation's soaring overtime budget lay incomplete on his desk.

Rees-Bramley's telephone rang in the next office. Crosby instinctively knew it was trouble. His DCI slammed the phone back down. 'Frank!'

Crosby walked across. Rees-Bramley's face was flushed and angry. 'They've fucking well lost Milner!'

'Lost him?'

'I've just had a call from the Central Observation Unit.' Rees-Bramley was seething. 'He left the house at his usual time yesterday morning. Never came back.'

'Why the hell weren't we told before?' Crosby was stalling. His hospital visit to Milner on Monday morning had to be a factor.

'The monitoring supervisor told me that her brief was to only raise an alarm if Milner left the house at night,' Rees-Bramley was having difficulty in containing himself.

Crosby shook his head. 'They were also given Milner's usual departure and arrival times. We should have been informed immediately of any changes to his routine.'

'Well somebody's made a bloody cock of it.' The DCI drummed his fingers on the desk. 'Who's the liaison contact at this end?'

'I am Sir!'

'What was the last update we had?'

'CCTV footage shows him returning to the house on Monday afternoon, after he'd discharged himself from hospital.'

'What time was that?'

'About twelve o'clock Sir. Just after I'd left him.' It was sooner than Crosby intended, but he knew that his DCI had to be told about the visit at some point.

Rees-Bramley stopped drumming his fingers and looked up. 'You went to see him in hospital?'

'Yes Sir!'

'Any particular reason?'

'I was there with DC Taylor.' Crosby shrugged casually. 'She was waiting for a report on Janet Sterne's condition.'

'Milner's already been questioned about the shopping centre incident.' Rees-Bramley said. 'Why would you visit him?'

'He is still under investigation Sir!' Crosby said pointedly.

'You didn't submit a report,' the DCI said.

'Nothing to report Sir. He wasn't very talkative.' Crosby reached into his pocket. 'I did make an entry in my notebook.'

'Did you tell Milner about the events at Sterne's house?'

'No Sir!'

'About his son allegedly pulling a gun on her?'

'No Sir!'

Rees-Bramley didn't look convinced, but let it go. 'Milner's been missing for over twenty hours now.' he said. 'Get his details circulated to uniformed branch. Put out an APW. Priority! If anything happens as a result of his surveillance mismanagement we'll get roasted.' The DCI got up from his chair. 'I'm going over to the Monitoring Unit. See if I can get any sense out of this supervisor.' He looked over his partition screen. 'Anybody in office?'

'One or two Sir.'

'Get over to Milner's place and have a look around. Take some backup.'

'Yes Sir!' Crosby was on his feet immediately, impatient to leave the office.

'We'll discuss your hospital visit at a later date,' Rees-Bramley called after him.

Every instinct told Crosby that Milner was missing because he'd gone after his son. He needed to check on whether Stephen Roberts had also disappeared.

Crosby headed into the main office. 'Brian!'

DC Jefferies stood up from his desk.

'We're off to Sixfields,' Crosby said to him.

Jefferies grimaced. 'I did have something planned for tonight Sir.'

'Cancel it,' Rees-Bramley said as he swept past them both, towards the door.

Crosby picked up Jefferies' coat and handed it to him. 'I'll brief you on the way.'

The two detectives followed their DCI out of the office.

Sixfields Estate: Wednesday 14 February 2007: 6.00 pm

Heavy rain lashed continuously at the windscreen. With Crosby sitting alongside him DC Jefferies paid careful attention to his speed, making the journey to Sixfields slightly longer than usual. They parked near the Akers Lane alleyway. 'See what's happening around the front,' Crosby said to Jefferies. 'I'll check the back.'

Opening his car door Crosby stepped outside. It was still raining. He pulled up the collar on his coat and set off down what was becoming a familiar route. Milner's house was in darkness. CCTV equipment monitored Crosby's progress up the narrow path and recorded him trying to open the back door. It was locked. Moving across to Milner's kitchen window Crosby shone his torch inside.

He turned at the sound of DC Jefferies trying to hurry his heavyweight frame up the path. Not accustomed to moving at any great speed the detective struggled to get his breathing under control.

'Anything?' Crosby asked unsympathetically.

'There's no lights.' Jefferies was wheezing, his large, round face wet from the rain, 'and the door's locked.'

'So is this one,' Crosby said, 'we'll need to force an entry.'

'Do we have the grounds Sir?'

'I detected some movement in the kitchen,' Crosby replied. 'We're concerned about Milner's welfare.'

Jefferies had been warned about his DI's shortcuts. He shrugged and tested the door with his shoulder. 'It doesn't look particularly solid Sir.'

'Get on with it then!'

Taking a step back Jefferies launched his considerable bulk at the door.

Its flimsy structure cracked and splintered, ripping two bolts and a lock from their moorings. Jefferies kicked the door off its remaining hinge and stepped inside. His DI followed him through. Both men moved into the kitchen where Crosby turned on the lights. Jefferies blinked in the harsh glare. 'No-one about Sir. You must have been mistaken.'

The DI shook his head. 'You're not in a bloody amateur dramatics production. Save it for when you're asked why Milner's door was kicked in.'

'Me Sir?'

Crosby pulled a pair of blue, forensic gloves from his pocket. 'I'll take the ground floor. See what you can find upstairs.'

'No-one ever wants to look in the bedroom,' complained Jefferies as he disappeared along the hallway.

Crosby wasn't listening. He was more concerned about breakfast remains left on the kitchen table, a scenario that didn't fit with the man they'd been investigating. The detective picked up a sealed, white envelope, simply addressed to "Lucy". Unfolding a plastic, transparent wallet Crosby dropped the envelope into it.

Both detectives spent the next hour carrying out a systematic search of the house, finding nothing of any significance.

At eight o'clock Crosby rang his wife to explain away another late night. The conversation lasted less than two minutes before she hung up on him. He shrugged and turned to Jefferies. 'I'm going back to the office. You'll have to wait here until we can get someone out to board the door up.'

Jefferies looked distinctly unhappy. 'And if Milner turns up, I'll be here to explain the gaping hole where his back door should be.'

Crosby merely nodded – he wasn't feeling particularly sympathetic after the conversation with his wife. The DI tossed Jefferies a key. 'It's a spare to Milner's garage. Take a look. He might be sitting in there with a hose running from his exhaust.'

'Thank you Sir.' Jefferies left for Milner's garage – the last chance of resurrecting his evening now gone.

Crosby activated his phone again and rang Rees-Bramley's number.

'May as well piss somebody else off,' he muttered to himself.

Studwell : Major Incident Room: Wednesday 14 February 2007: 9.00 pm

Rees-Bramley was already behind his desk when Crosby arrived back at the office.

The DCI snapped his fingers. 'Let's see it?'

Crosby tossed the plastic wallet onto his desk.

Rees-Bramley shook the envelope out and slit it open. 'You can justify the forced entry to Milner's house?' he asked.

'Yes Sir!'

'The DCI lifted out a single sheet of notepaper. Holding the top corner between his thumb and forefinger he scanned its contents. 'Suicide note!' Rees-Bramley laid it on the desk for his DI to read.

'Just a matter of time I suppose,' Crosby said. 'Given his state of mind.'

Rees-Bramley didn't look convinced. 'He's coped with this depression for years. Why now?'

Crosby shrugged. 'Getting laid up in hospital again?'

His DCI looked up. 'Or maybe he found out that his son was responsible for Janet Sterne killing her child.'

Crosby didn't reply.

'You'd better check on the son's whereabouts,' Rees-Bramley said.

'Yes Sir!'

'What about Milner's car?'

'DC Jefferies confirmed the garage was empty.'

'Make sure his number plate gets added to the ANPR database.' Rees-Bramley said. 'Anything else?'

'There's evidence at the house that Milner's abandoned his routines.'

'I'm aware of it.' Rees-Bramley pointed to a surveillance log on his desk. 'CCTV footage from Monday night. He didn't leave the house between nine and ten o'clock.'

'Which leaves us where Sir?'

'Something's spooked him,' Rees-Bramley said. 'Milner's behaviour patterns were essential in keeping his life on an even keel. He's obviously gone looking for something.'

'You're not convinced about his suicide then?'

Rees-Bramley shook his head. 'Milner's crossed over into some kind of parallel existence – it's why he left a suicide note.' The DCI tapped a folder on his desk. 'It's all in Professor Hill's extensive summary.'

Crosby had been forced to endure a lot of pretentious claptrap and bollocks during his long career, but Professor Hill's observations were up there with the best of them. The detective was tempted to tell his DCI that Robert Milner's simple intention was to kill his son, and then commit suicide – but instead he just shook his head. 'It's all too deep for me Sir. These experts operate at a far higher level than I'm capable of reaching.'

Rees-Bramley checked his watch. 'I'll leave you to get in touch with Milner's ex-wife and his children. They'll need informing tonight.'

Crosby got up to leave.

'Incidentally,' his DCI added, 'Lucy was at Milner's over the weekend. CCTV showed her leaving the house on Saturday night and not returning until two o'clock in the morning. Put somebody on it.' Rees-Bramley returned to his laptop. Crosby took it as a sign he was dismissed.

Back in his office the phone rang. DC Jefferies' voice was very faint. 'I'm still at Silver Street Sir. Any chance of hurrying up the maintenance contractor. This place is giving me the bloody creeps.'

'Would you like a patrol car sent round to babysit you?' Crosby asked, but his sarcasm didn't translate over the airwaves.

'It might be my imagination Sir,' Jefferies said, 'but I think there's someone been watching the house.' His voice began to fade. 'Hang on! This must be the contractor now. Someone's just come through the gate.'

'I'm losing you,' Crosby shouted. 'You'll have to speak up.'

'I'll just go and...' Jefferies started to say before the signal cut out completely.

CHAPTER 28

The dog's owner was unshaven, scruffily dressed. Shoulders hunched, he picked his way through scattered debris, hands shoved deep into the pockets of his shabby anorak. The young spaniel cross was just excited to be out, zigzagging the derelict waste land at breakneck speed, his nose never more than an inch from the ground. No sooner had the dog picked up a particular scent trail then another one would cross its path, and he'd veer away in the opposite direction.

Every so often the dog's perpetual motion came to a halt, the upright stump of a tail would cease wagging, and he'd look up to check on the whereabouts of his owner. The interruption would only last for a few seconds, before the spaniel's all important work of pursuing yet another dead-end was resumed.

Approaching Shurville Gardens the dog suddenly froze and sniffed the air, cocking its head to one side. His owner continued walking. Emitting a low growl the spaniel instinctively sank to its haunches and belly-crawled towards one of the houses, his attention fixed on a small, concrete-latticed air vent. On reaching the house it became even more excited, pawing and scratching at the open vent. Even when called to heel the dog continued to scratch at the latticework. 'Stupid fucking animal!' his owner shouted at him. 'It's only rats.' Roaming packs of grey rats were a familiar sight in this particular area. The dog's owner would often watch them moving from house to house, their greasy coats scraping the rough brickwork as they instinctively hugged the building's walls.

When the dog still wouldn't come to heel his owner became impatient, and went back for him. Even then, it was only after a dog chain had been whipped hard across his back did the young spaniel finally edge to one side. An over-powering smell, coming from the open vent, stopped the dog's owner from moving off. Hesitating momentarily he pushed his heel through the vent's crumbling latticework, sending a shower of masonry down to the cellar floor below.

Covering his mouth and nose the man stooped down and tried to peer into the cellar. It was pitch-black. When the young spaniel started to bark and paw at the open vent again his owner had to clip on the chain and forcibly drag him away.

Later that day, when he walked his dog again, the man took a torch with him. He was curious. It was unusual for the spaniel to get over-excited about rats. They approached Shurville Gardens in semi-darkness, the late-afternoon sun hidden behind dark cloud. Once again the spaniel showed signs of agitation as it reached the house.

Dropping to his knees the man crouched down in front of the open vent and switched on his torch, directing its beam into the cellar below. In the basement's confined space dozens of scurrying rodents frantically sought a dark corner, away from the harsh glare.

The beam of light swung round to the cellar's far wall and lingered for several moments, as if trying to decipher what it had found. Quite abruptly the man twisted to one side. He stayed down on all fours as the stream of vomit came in a rush, splattering both his hands and the ground around him.

When the man finally stumbled away, retching on an empty stomach, his dog remained behind, whining into the open vent.

Sixfields: Waverley Court: Friday 16 February 2007: 4.00 pm

At approximately the same time that events were unfolding in Shurville Gardens, Detective Inspector Crosby was sitting in the front passenger seat of PC Britten's patrol car, watching a ground floor tenement flat in Waverley Court.

With Rees-Bramley summoned to HQ that morning, most of Crosby's day had been spent at his desk, co-ordinating the team's response into Milner's disappearance. Feedback had been disappointing. By late afternoon one particular task remained – a follow-up call to the home of Stephen Roberts. Crosby had kept it back for himself.

In the past twenty-four hours two uniformed patrol calls had reported no-one at the flat in response to their calls. Crosby's instinct was still telling him it was no coincidence that both Milner and his son were now missing. Of more concern was the fact that Milner's daughter Lucy couldn't be located either.

Crosby and Britten continued to sit in silence. The detective had requested uniformed back-up because of the neighbourhood – a particularly notorious area within the Sixfields estate. The tenement block they were parked in front of was a grey, concrete rectangle, five levels high. Two flights of well-worn steps at either end provided access to all floors. Crosby couldn't detect a lift. The tenement's depressing façade was only partially alleviated by a number of spray-painted logos, warning visitors of their encroachment into 'Network Z' territory.

The squad car's arrival ten minutes ago had immediately attracted the attention of hooded youths congregated around Waverley Court's stairwells. Every so often a small clique would detach themselves from the main group and saunter arrogantly past the car.

As evening began to fall a faint light appeared in the flat window. It was quickly extinguished. Crosby opened his passenger-side door. 'You'd better wait here,' he said to Britten. 'PC's are expendable. The car isn't.'

If PC Britten intended to voice concerns about remaining on his own he was too late, Crosby had already shut the car door. From their vantage point on the stairwells an ever-increasing crowd watched his progress towards the ground floor flat.

Crosby reached the front door and thumped it with the heel of his fist. 'Police!' he shouted. No response.

Crosby sensed someone behind the door. He leant forward. 'We've just seen the light being switched off. I've got police officers in the car with specialist door-breaking equipment. You've got ten seconds.'

Two security chains were engaged before the door cracked open. 'What?' A woman's thin, white face pushed up against the opening – bruising around both her eyes.

'Trudy Watkins?'

'Who wants to know?' the gravel tones of a heavy smoker.

'Just open the door Trudy,' Crosby held up his warrant card. 'This is our third visit.'

'Steve's not here.'

'We'll talk about it inside,' the detective said.

'It's not convenient!'

'Neither are my working hours,' Crosby said, pushing at the door. 'And if you continue to piss me around I'll have the door broken down and we'll continue this at the station.'

A rattle of chain preceded the door being pulled open. The woman wore only a long, shapeless woollen jumper, which couldn't disguise how painfully thin she was. Her legs were mottled and bare – lank, unwashed hair hung down in greasy clumps to her shoulders. She didn't wait for him. Crosby followed her down a hall and into the living room. It was a mess.

The small, coffee table was stacked with fast food cartons and empty bottles – cigarette-ends had been routinely ground into the heavily stained, beige carpet.

Although Crosby thought he detected the acrid whiff of marijuana, a stench of unattended, ripe animal faeces over-powered it – the culprit was chained to a radiator pipe in the far corner. Crosby took in the dog's large head and powerful neck 'Is that a pit bull?'

'No!' Watkins crossed to an old settee smothered in long, black dog hairs. She slumped down on it, tucking a pair of thin, white legs underneath her. Crosby thought he detected tiny movements in the settee's greasy fabric and remained standing. On the couch, next to Watkins, was a teenage boy, his head tilted backwards, eyes closed. He had a grey, unhealthy pallor and his breathing was shallow. The detective walked over to him and picked up his wrist.

'Who's this?' Crosby asked.

'Dunno,' Watkins answered sullenly, 'it's somebody that Steve knows.'

'What's he been taking?' Crosby dropped the boy's wrist. His pulse seemed healthy enough.

The woman shrugged. 'Dunno!'

'You don't seem to know very much,' the detective said. 'Do you know where Stephen Roberts has disappeared to?'

She shook her head. 'He went out last Tuesday morning. Haven't seen him since.'

'Time?'

'About eleven.' The woman's hand shook as she opened a battered old tin, and started to roll tobacco from it.

'Where was he going?'

'Steve never tells me where he's going.'

'Would it be unusual for him not to come home for three days?'

Watkins thought about it. 'Suppose so.' She flicked a lighter and sucked at the thin cigarette.

'But you didn't report him missing,' Crosby persisted.

The woman frowned. 'Why the fuck would I do that?'

'Does he have a car?'

The woman nodded.

'Did he leave in it?'

'Yes!'

'Registration?'

Watkins looked blank.

'Was there anyone with him?'

'No!'

'Did Stephen mention his father before he left?'

The woman looked genuinely surprised. 'He never knew who his father was.'

'Stephen was attacked recently and badly beaten,' Crosby continued. 'Did he ever talk about who might have done it?'

Watkins shook her head. 'No!'

A shadow passed across the lounge window as someone walked by. There was a low growl from the corner. 'Is that animal secure?' Crosby asked.

Before Watkins could reply a piercing, high-pitched wail filled the room. It spooked the dog. Baring his teeth the animal strained against its leash, threatening to wrench the radiator from its wall. Crosby moved across to the window. Lifting a curtain to one side he found the squad car's revolving blue warning lights flashing into the darkness.

Crosby hurried to the front door and pulled it open. Both the siren and lights were abruptly extinguished. 'Sorry about that Sir.' Britten was standing by the car's open door. 'I was trying to frighten them off. Someone just bounced a brick off the windscreen.'

The detective made his way back along the path.

'We finished here Sir?' the PC enquired hopefully.

Crosby nodded. 'Just about.'

'Back to the station?'

The detective turned to find Trudy Watkins framed in the doorway. 'Call drugs enforcement first,' he said to Britten, 'get them to search Stephen Roberts flat. And you can tell them there's an illegal breed of dog on the premises.'

The detective's mobile sounded. He pulled it from his pocket and stabbed a button. 'Yes?' DC Berne's over-excited voice was shrill in his ear.

'Major development Sir! Shurville Gardens on the Sixfields Estate. Do you know where it is?'

'We'll find it.' Crosby cut the connection and turned to Britten. 'Shurville Gardens.' He opened his door. 'And let's have the sirens back on.'

Sixfields: Shurville Gardens: Friday 16 February 2007: 5.00 pm

Shurville Gardens without street lighting was a very dark corner. That evening however, when Crosby arrived at its entrance, the cul-de-sac was a sea of blazing headlights and flashing blue lamps. The detective terminated his call to Rees-Bramley and quickly exited PC Britten's squad car.

DC Taylor emerged from a crowd of people to meet him. 'Three bodies Sir!' she rushed her words. 'In one of the cellars!'

'Jesus Christ!' Crosby swore.

'Scene of Crimes is waiting to see you,' Taylor indicated a figure clad in white protective coveralls, standing outside one of the houses.

Crosby signalled to Ian Brown that he was on his way before turning back to Taylor. 'Round up some personnel Grace. Get them to check out the surrounding area.'

'Yes Sir!'

Crosby ducked between two strips of plastic barrier tape and hurried up towards the house. Ian Brown came forward to meet him. A small generator chugged away outside the front door, leaving a smell of petrol in the air, lines of electric cabling snaked their way from the machine into the house.

'You were quick off the mark,' Crosby said to Brown.

'We're anticipating them now,' the Scot said in his broad Glaswegian. 'He is taking the piss though. Knocking off three at the same time.'

'DC Taylor said they're all down in the cellar. You've seen them?'

The SOCO nodded. 'Aye! I have!'

Crosby grimaced. 'How bad is it?'

'Your worst fucking nightmare laddie. Shall we get it over with?' He turned and stepped through the doorway. 'Where's Sherlock Holmes tonight?'

'On his way.' Crosby followed Brown through to the hall.

'Can you keep him occupied?' the Scot shook his head. 'I don't want his prick up my arse all night, following me around.'

Brown stopped in front of an open door. Crumbling concrete steps led down into a solid wall of white light. 'Basement cellar!' he said. 'We've set up two arc lamps. You'll need a handkerchief.'

Crosby shielded his eyes from the harsh glare and followed Brown down the steps. He instinctively covered his mouth and nose as the smell hit him.

On reaching the cellar floor Brown stood aside, opening up the far wall to Crosby's line of sight. 'Fucking Hell!' the detective turned his head away.

'I'd appreciate you not throwing up,' Brown said, 'we haven't started processing down here yet.' He waited patiently. Crosby forced himself to look at the three, white, naked bodies again.

The blinding glare from two powerful arc lamps made the lifeless bodies look almost translucent. Symmetrically aligned in a neat row all three victims sat upright on the bare, concrete floor, their backs against the wall. Each body had been identically arranged, three heads positioned at exactly the same angle, all of them facing the cellar steps for maximum effect. Three pairs of empty eye sockets stared lifelessly across the intervening space in Crosby's direction. He could only stare back at them.

'Rattus Norvegicus!' the Scot pronounced.

'What!' The detective couldn't drag his eyes away.

'Rattus Norvegicus! From the Latin!' Brown folded his arms. 'The most enterprising mammal on planet earth, apart from humans.'

Crosby was still transfixed.

'More bloody rats here than you can shake a stick at!' SOCO looked across at the dead bodies. 'Ravenous little bastards, aren't they? Teeth like bloody needles. And the nearest McDonalds is miles away – they must have thought all their birthdays had come at once.'

The detective felt an acrid bile rise in his throat. He forced it back down.

Brown inclined his head towards the wall again. 'Recognise any of them?'

Crosby's attention fixed on Stephen Roberts. 'The one with a bullet hole through his forehead looks like Milner's son,' he couldn't stop the tremor in his voice. 'I'm guessing that our missing prostitute is the one with pink ribbon in her hair.'

The Scot motioned him towards the other victim.

'Could be Darren Shaughnessy.' Crosby leant forward. 'Looks like a glass bottle's been forced into his mouth.'

Brown nodded. 'Half a bottle. The broken end has been shoved so far into his mouth both jaws have locked around it.'

Crosby shook his head. 'To gag him?'

'Possibly!' Brown stooped down to the victim. 'I do have another theory.'

Crosby wasn't sure he wanted to hear it but the Scot continued anyway. 'Have a look at all these dark hairs inside the bottle.'

The detective shrugged. 'And?'

'Medieval torture routines!' the Scot said. 'They used to be an interest of mine.' He stood back up. 'One of the most popular involved rats being dropped into an open container. Usually a metal one. The container would be turned upside down and strapped onto a victim's bare midriff,' Brown warmed to his theme. 'Trapped in a confined space the rats would have gone fucking spare. And as there was no escape up through the metal container they'd eat their way down through the bare stomach until they found a way out.'

'You're telling me there was a rat inside that bottle!'

Brown nodded enthusiastically. 'Wouldn't need to be a particularly large one. When the pathologist gets to open our victim up I reckon he'll find a specimen of rattus inside – still looking for the exit and twice its normal size.'

'That's obscene!'

'Bloody enterprising though!' The Scot shrugged. 'Our ancestors spent years devising these routines. Another of their favourites was to heat up a thin, steel rod and insert it up the victim's rear end. They reserved that one for convicted homosexuals.'

Brown's knowledge of the subject was obviously extensive but Crosby cut him off. He pointed at the victim's arms, tied behind his back to a vertical heating pipe. 'Would he have been alive when all this was carried out?'

'Possibly!' Brown replied. 'You'd hope he was a bad person to have suffered that sort of ending.'

'Our university professor will have a field day with all of this,' Crosby said.

'Who?'

'Rees-Bramley's got a criminal psychologist on board.'

The Scot snorted. 'Bloody amazing they are! Spend all those years studying at university to tell us that we're dealing with fucking lunatics.'

'How long do you think the bodies have been down here?' Crosby asked.

Brown turned to look them. 'Three days? Those two on the left were certainly in residence first – they're right down to the bone in places.' He nudged the scattered rat droppings with his shoe. 'Not surprising really. There must be hundreds of the little bastards nesting around here. Did you know that rats start screwing each other at three months old and the female bangs out a litter twenty-two days later? No wonder they're over-running us.'

'Another of your interests?'

Brown shrugged. 'It's all useful background in this job. Rats live alongside us because they eat all the stuff we throw away. Occasionally, if circumstances are favourable, they'll eat us as well. Nothing personal. It's just fuel to them.'

Crosby dragged the SOCO back again. 'Did you find any items of clothing or personal effects?'

The Scot shook his head. 'No! Our man removed everything off site.'

'You're ruling out a woman then?' the detective asked.

'Women aren't that cruel to animals,' Brown said in all seriousness. 'Not even rats.'

'Is that it for the moment?' the detective was desperate for some fresh air.

Brown nodded.

'I'll catch you later.' Crosby left the Scot to his work and climbed back up the cellar steps. DC Taylor was waiting outside the front door. 'We've found Milner's car Sir. About half a mile away.'

'Was he in it?' the detective asked too quickly.

'No Sir!'

Crosby kept the disappointment from his voice. 'Put someone on sentry duty, until we can get forensics there.'

'Already done Sir.'

'Who found the bodies?'

'Local man. Out walking his dog.'

'Who's processing him?'

'DC Berne Sir.'

A high-powered Jaguar XJ6 squad car screeched into the cul-de-sac, its blue light flashing. Crosby watched an expensive tailored, black overcoat exit the car's passenger-door. Rees-Bramley spotted his DI up by the house and strode briskly towards him.

Crosby turned back to Taylor. 'See if our dog walker has volunteered anything that we need to follow-up on.'

'Sir!' Taylor left immediately.

The detective took a deep breath. From a personal point of view he felt vindicated that Stephen Roberts was sitting in the cellar basement below – it was what he'd intended – but in light of the note left at Silver Street, he had anticipated that Milner would commit suicide, immediately after killing his son. So where the hell was he!

Rees-Bramley reached the house. 'What have we got Frank?'

'Three bodies in the basement cellar Sir.'

'Recognise any of them?'

'Stephen Roberts and Sandra Dredge Sir. The other one is probably Darren Shaughnessy.'

'Any sign of Milner?'

'No Sir! But we have found his car half a mile away.'

Rees-Bramley raised his eyebrows. 'Have we! Let's see about getting him picked up then.' He turned towards the house. 'Who's the SOCO on

214

duty?'

'Ian Brown Sir. He's waiting for you inside.'

'Right!' Rees-Bramley said. 'I need to point him in the right direction. Make sure the search for Milner is escalated. Top priority!'

'Yes Sir!'

Rees-Bramley disappeared through the front door, his body language understandably buoyant. Finding Milner's car on the same site as three more victims was probably stretching coincidence too far.

Crosby wasn't comfortable with it though. Certain pieces didn't fit the overall jigsaw he'd been putting together – and Milner's continuing disappearance posed more questions than answers.

CHAPTER 29

From his chair opposite the window Crosby watched a dull, orange sun haul itself up and over the horizon. The standard issue office wall clock ticked around to fifteen minutes past seven o'clock. Rees-Bramley stood up to take off his jacket. Shaking out the creases he crossed to a nearby coat-stand and draped the jacket over a wooden hanger. Both men were sitting in the main office, alongside a busy and detailed briefing board. They'd been at work for over an hour.

Rees-Bramley returned to his open laptop. With a press conference and committee briefings arranged for later that day the DCI was on a tight schedule – fresh developments had arisen since last Friday and he needed to be familiar with all of them. Crosby meanwhile, was poring over the team's rescheduling lists. As a result of the discovery at Shurville Gardens several new lines of enquiry had to be prioritised and investigated, the whereabouts of Robert Milner being top of their agenda.

The weekend had also seen unrest on the Sixfields estate escalate to another level. A stream of anonymous messages, posted on websites immediately prior to Shurville Gardens, had promised further executions of local gang members. The reaction was disorder and unrest on the streets. Packs of youths took to patrolling their territories at night, some of them firing handguns indiscriminately into the air as they went looking for rival gangs. Terrified residents barricaded themselves behind locked doors, swamping the emergency services with non-stop telephone calls.

When news swept across Sixfields that a woman had also become victim to the killings, panic turned to near hysteria – in their midst a serial assassin, now selecting targets at random. Police were finding it difficult to keep a volatile situation contained, extra officers having to be drafted in from adjoining regions. Crosby sensed the whole estate was teetering on the brink.

In the hope that it would ease mounting tension, Rees-Bramley had announced Robert Milner was being sought in connection with the discovery at Shurville Gardens. A recent work's photograph was released. It showed Milner's gaunt, unsmiling features staring uncomfortably into a camera lens, his mop of untidy white hair dominating the head and shoulders shot. Going public was a miscalculation.

When newspapers were tipped off that Milner's son was one of the victims found at Shurville Gardens it presented reporters with material that comes along once in a lifetime. Crosby didn't want to contemplate the headlines they would generate when it was discovered that Milner had a daughter – who the police were also unable to locate.

Lucy's disappearance had to be addressed. It was too much of a coincidence. After the discovery of Milner's suicide note, initial attempts to locate Lucy had been unsuccessful. There was no-one at her Birmingham student address, and the family home in Oswestry had been unoccupied for two weeks – Henry and Penny Roberts resuming their midwinter break somewhere in the West Indies.

After the events of Friday evening Crosby had immediately despatched one of his team to question university staff and students with regard to Lucy's whereabouts. Late on Saturday night DC Bowers had e-mailed the transcript of an interview he'd just completed with the university's Vice Chancellor. Its contents took Crosby by surprise. Despite an exemplary university record, and previous excellent character, Milner's daughter had been suspended from campus two weeks earlier for suspected drug dealing. The university's disciplinary sub-committee, who were deciding what action to take, had since lost all contact with Lucy.

Her disappearance was an added complication that Rees-Bramley had to factor in.

Lucy's uncharacteristic behaviour had continued to nag at Crosby. As a consequence he'd arranged a meeting with the regional drugs enforcement agency – a department notorious for not sharing their information if they thought it might compromise on-going investigations.

Rees-Bramley snapped shut the lid of his laptop, cutting across Crosby's thoughts. 'We'll have to pick this up later Frank,' his DCI said. 'My first briefing is at eight o'clock. Don't forget that forensics promised us their findings this morning. Chase them up if they're late.'

'Yes Sir!' Crosby made a note. Individual reports on each of the three victims found at Shurville Gardens had already been submitted by the department's Home Office Pathologist. In his reports, Doctor Michael

Grainger attributed the extensive mutilation of all three bodies to what he described as a feeding frenzy from the high level of in-situ rat infestation. Stephen Roberts and Sandra Dredge were killed by single gunshot wounds to the head – two bullets had been recovered from the murder site. Crosby was present at the autopsy of Darren Shaughnessy when Doctor Grainger removed half a bottle from the dead man's mouth.

Later into his examination Grainger also pulled the body of a bloated, suffocated rat from the drug dealer's half-eaten internal organs. 'It looks a bit pissed off,' the pathologist had commented as he held the creature up by its tail, 'maybe it was expecting dessert.'

Crosby half-smiled as he recalled the pathologist's remarks.

'Something amusing you Frank?' Rees-Bramley was on his feet, ready to leave.

'Just a touch of black humour Sir.'

'Something I've never really seen the point of.'

'It can be difficult to appreciate,' Crosby replied.

Rees-Bramley pulled a file from his briefcase. 'Professor Hill has updated our suspect's psychological profile. He's incorporated the additional behavioural evidence gleaned from Shurville Gardens.'

'Oh Yes!' Crosby was unable to inject a great deal of enthusiasm into his voice.

'It's Professor Hill's opinion that our subject is suffering some kind of meltdown.'

'Meltdown?' Crosby repeated.

'He's lost touch with reality.' Rees-Bramley dropped the folder in Crosby's lap. 'Aligning all three bodies in the cellar suggests he's looking for different ways to exhibit his work.' The DCI shook his head. 'And the foraging rodent indicates a blood lust that's out of control. He's extremely dangerous.'

Does Professor Hill still maintain that one person is responsible for all of the murders?' Crosby asked.

'Yes he does!' Rees-Bramley crossed the room to retrieve his jacket.

'Even though there's no evidence of a gun being used previously?' Crosby queried.

'It's all in the report,' Rees-Bramley replied.

'I'll look through it this morning Sir.' Crosby picked up the folder. 'I'm guessing that Robert Milner still fits the new profile?'

'The profile is not new!' Rees-Bramley's response was curt. 'It's been updated.'

As the DCI finished buttoning his jacket he hesitated – there was obviously something else on his mind. Crosby second-guessed what it would be about.

'Professor Hill's report also makes reference to a trigger,' Rees-Bramley said, 'one that would have caused Milner to abruptly abandon his routines.'

'A trigger Sir?' Crosby knew his DCI wouldn't let it drop.

Rees-Bramley nodded. 'If I find out that one of my officers has compromised the outcome of this investigation by following their own personal agenda, I'll have no hesitation about initiating immediate disciplinary procedures.'

'With every justification Sir,' Crosby replied.

Rees-Bramley looked across at him. 'It was for precisely this reason that I had reservations about your appointment in the first place Detective Inspector.'

A telephone rang in the DCI's office. He left to answer it.

Crosby exhaled. At least it was out in the open now, and he still had no regrets about engineering Roberts' death. Milner was a problem though. If he was still alive, their hospital conversation might eventually come to light – and Crosby had already lied to his DCI about that. The detective experienced a spasm of unease. If found culpable, there was every possibility he could be dismissed from the force, losing his pension and a substantial retirement pay-out. Allowing Milner to make the allegation was not an option.

'And you're absolutely sure about that?' Rees-Bramley's voice sounded from the direction of his office. 'Excellent work! I'll send someone over to pick up the report.'

Crosby heard the receiver being slammed back onto its base. His DCI emerged from around the partition screens. 'Got the bastard!' he shouted. 'That was forensics. They've had a result.' Rees-Bramley strode back down through the main office.

'Microscopy tests have confirmed a match against some grey carpet fibres found on the ribbon left in Sandra Dredge's hair.'

'Milner's bedroom?' Crosby asked.

Rees-Bramley nodded. 'Scene of Crimes took samples last week.'

'Any margin of error?'

'A perfect match,' the DCI replied. 'Unusual shading and texture apparently.'

'It certainly narrows down the possibilities,' Crosby said.

'Narrows it down!' Rees-Bramley sounded annoyed.

Crosby shrugged. 'We know that Sandra Dredge worked the area. She could have picked up the fibres direct from Milner's bedroom – not necessarily from him.'

Rees-Bramley shook his head. 'There's nothing in his records, or on CCTV, to suggest that he entertained prostitutes at the house – and apart from his daughter, he didn't get visitors.'

Crosby pursed his lips. 'There is another possibility.'

'Yes?'

'The initial search of Milner's house was carried out by detectives from this team, who may have picked up fibres from the carpets.' Crosby pulled out his pocketbook and made a note. 'They'll have to be eliminated. I'll start procedures.'

Rees-Bramley looked up. 'Were you involved in the initial search?'

'Yes Sir!'

'Did you enter Milner's bedroom at any stage?'

'I did!'

Rees-Bramley nodded. 'I'll deal with your clearance. You obviously can't eliminate yourself.'

'Yes Sir!' It was Crosby's turn to be annoyed. His DCI didn't have to personally involve himself in checking out one of his teams' movements.

Rees-Bramley looked at his watch. 'I'm back in office about twelve o'clock. You'll need to brief the team on this morning's forensic report.'

The far door opened. Both detectives turned towards a tall, immaculately dressed figure striding briskly towards them. Superintendent John Bairstow's dark blue police uniform, with appropriate badges of rank, sat comfortably on his slim frame, the neatly trimmed grey hair just visible, beneath a blue and white peaked cap. Crosby and the Superintendent had been acquainted for over forty years, pounding Birmingham's streets together as rookie PC's in the early seventies. An encyclopaedic memory for the minutia of police regulations, and his unflappable temperament, had seen Bairstow rise steadily through the ranks. He'd been elevated to his current position as Studwell's uniformed head of station just over a year ago.

The Superintendent dropped a weighty briefcase to the floor. Crosby's antenna told him their day was about to take a turn for the worse.

Bairstow nodded briefly in Crosby's direction before turning to Rees-Bramley. 'Good morning Oliver.'

'It'll have to be quick John,' Rees-Bramley replied. 'I'm briefing the Chief Constable about Shurville Gardens at eight o'clock.'

Bairstow nodded. 'I thought we could travel there together,' he said. 'I've been invited along as well.'

The DCI raised his eyebrows.

The Superintendent leant nonchalantly against a nearby filing cabinet. 'Chief Constable's concerned about the recent increase in Sixfields' gang activity. This string of killings appear to be manoeuvring the estate's thug culture towards some sort of confrontation. The Chief doesn't want a war zone on his hands.'

'It's not this bloody website traffic again is it? About Sixfields' gangs targeting each other?' Rees-Bramley sounded exasperated. 'Apart from Stephen Roberts, none of our victims were active members at the time of their deaths.'

Bairstow shrugged. 'The website seems to be well informed – it's got all of the gangs looking over their shoulders at the moment.'

'For Christ's Sake John!' Rees-Bramley gestured towards Sandra Dredge's photograph. 'One of the victims was a woman – which you're very well aware of. This internet traffic is someone working to a different agenda. Out to cause trouble.'

'And succeeding! Have you made any attempt to trace these web sources?' the Superintendent asked.

'It's not that simple!' Rees-Bramley answered tersely. 'The operators can shut a portable server down in minutes, and just move it to another location.'

The Superintendent persisted. 'It's not a line of enquiry you're actively pursuing then?'

'No! It bloody well isn't. We don't have the time or resources to waste on something that doesn't have any bearing on this investigation,' the DCI deliberately spaced his words. 'Our major line of enquiry indicates a single person acting alone. We've just had confirmation of that this morning. Our suspect certainly doesn't possess the necessary IT equipment to build internet sites. It's an irrelevance! Not my concern!'

'It is a concern to the Chief Constable unfortunately.' Bairstow seemed unperturbed at Rees-Bramley's irritation.

'In what way?'

'Intelligence sources are telling him about weapons being stock-piled throughout Sixfields.' The Superintendent shrugged. 'It's possible that these rogue websites are using the murders to engineer another Draywood Manor situation. Our Chief still bears the scars from that one.'

'He was involved at Draywood Manor?' the DCI sounded surprised, his annoyance temporarily shelved.

Bairstow nodded. 'Full scale riot! He was acting Assistant Chief Constable at the time.'

'I remember it,' Rees-Bramley said. 'The police were totally overrun. Media coverage about strategy and tactics were scathing.'

'It's why he's twitchy about the Sixfields situation.' Bairstow indicated his briefcase. 'I've just been informed that the contingency plans for managing a major incident have been dusted off and will shortly be raised to stand-by level.'

Rees-Bramley shook his head. 'Sounds like an over-reaction. I wouldn't have thought we were at that stage yet.'

The Superintendent raised his eyebrows. 'Not a point of view I'd risk putting forward this morning. There were three fatalities at Draywood Manor. The Chief doesn't want to be accused of acting after the event.'

'What happens to my on-site investigations if the situation does deteriorate?' Crosby asked.

'Non-essential personnel will be withdrawn from the estate immediately,' Bairstow said. 'All on-site operations suspended.'

Rees-Bramley looked distinctly unhappy. 'Scene of Crimes haven't finished processing Shurville Gardens yet, and we believe our suspect is still holed up in Sixfields somewhere.'

The Superintendent shrugged. He glanced at his watch. 'We'd better make a move. See what they've got planned for us.'

Both men left the office without a backward glance. Crosby dismissed the snub. It didn't bother him unduly that the discussion had taken place as if he wasn't there. His mind was too preoccupied with Milner's non-suicide, and the threat to early retirement plans.

Picking up Professor Hill's report Crosby returned to his office.

After completing two telephone calls he quickly skimmed through the professor's deliberations before tossing the buff folder into an out tray. 'Fucking academics!' but there wasn't a great deal of venom in his remark.

The hubbub of voices from next door grew in volume as murder squad detectives arrived at their desks. One consolation was that it wouldn't feel much like a Monday morning – most of them had been working until late yesterday – pushing an overtime budget to its limit.

Crosby looked up to find Peter Stewart hovering in the doorway. 'You wanted to see me Sir!' the PC said.

Crosby ignored him. The detective eventually got up from his chair and walked into the main office. DC Berne was at his desk. 'Let me know when everyone's arrived Paul,' Crosby said to him. 'I'm giving a briefing. There's a positive result in from forensics.'

'We could do with one,' Berne said. 'Is it Milner?'

'You'll have to wait until we're all here.'

Crosby returned to his office. Stewart had remained in the partition entrance. He looked uncomfortable, transferring his police cap from one hand to the other. The detective didn't particularly want to use bullying tactics but his sympathetic approaches had been largely ignored.

The young policeman remained stiffly to attention. There were dark circles under both eyes, his face a white, pasty colour. Even through the bulky uniform Crosby could see he'd lost weight.

The detective pulled a folder from his desk drawer. Stewart had already been questioned by the team about Lucy's disappearance. It was for reasons of his own that Crosby had called him in again. He motioned the PC forward, but didn't invite him to sit down. 'You're aware that Milner and his daughter are still missing.'

Stewart's Adam's apple bobbed in his throat. 'Yes Sir!'

'Remind me of when you first heard about that?'

'We were briefed to look out for them last week Sir.'

'And when was the last time you saw Lucy?'

'Approximately two weeks ago Sir.' Stewart looked nervous.

'Not approximately!' Crosby's tone was terse. 'Exactly!'

Stewart flinched. Noiselessly working his lips he calculated the date. 'It was the fourth of February Sir. Sunday night.'

'You're sure of that?'

Stewart nodded.

The detective had already viewed CCTV footage of Lucy leaving her father's house in Sixfields on Sunday the eleventh of February. It was the last known sighting they had of her.

Crosby read from the open folder on his desk. 'I advised you on Monday the twenty-ninth of January that it would be inadvisable to continue your relationship with Robert Milner's daughter.'

'Yes Sir.' Stewart swallowed.

'But you were still seeing her six days later.'

The PC didn't reply.

Crosby looked up. 'I repeat, you were still seeing Milner's daughter six days later.'

'I couldn't find a way to tell her Sir,' Stewart mumbled. 'It was difficult.'

'But you did end the relationship at that time?'

Stewart hesitated. 'Not exactly. Lucy rang the next day to say it was better we didn't continue seeing each other.'

'She ended the relationship?' Crosby's tone was sharp.

'Yes!' The PC shuffled his feet. 'I have already volunteered this information Sir.'

The detective looked up at him. 'And now you're volunteering it again. Have you tried to get in touch with Lucy since?'

Stewart hesitated again. Crosby waited. They had records of Lucy's recent mobile calls from her network provider. Robert Milner possessed mobile and landline telephones but he didn't appear to use either of them.

'I tried to contact her again at the weekend.' Stewart looked even more uncomfortable. 'She wasn't answering.'

Crosby knew that Lucy's mobile signal had disappeared at some point during the evening of February the thirteenth. Milner had gone missing on the same day. 'Did Lucy ever mention names of friends or acquaintances?' the detective asked.

'No Sir!'

'Places she used to visit? Holiday destinations?'

'No Sir!'

'And you have absolutely no idea of where she might be at this moment?'

Stewart shook his head.

'How did you and Lucy spend your evenings?'

'We drove around Sixfields quite a lot Sir.'

'Strange place for a young couple to spend their time. Not the most romantic of locations.'

Stewart cleared his throat. 'Lucy was writing a thesis as part of her degree. She was collecting background material on social and community development within large housing estates.'

Crosby arched his eyebrows. 'Is that what she told you? An odd subject for someone studying Business Consultancy.'

Stewart blinked. He didn't reply. Crosby could only guess that Lucy's tours around the estate were something to do with her drug dealing activities. The detective found it difficult to believe that Stewart would be involved. Probably just being used.

'Did you ever meet anyone on these nocturnal jaunts?'

'No Sir! We drove around in the car while she made notes.'

'Your relationship with Lucy? Was it a physical one?'

'Yes!' Stewart's reply was barely audible.

'Were you ever invited back to Milner's house?' Crosby asked.

'No Sir!' Stewart shook his head. 'She said her father felt awkward about meeting other people.'

'You've never been in Lucy's bedroom at sixty-nine Silver Street?'

'No Sir!' the policeman said.

'Did Lucy ever talk about her father to you?' Crosby asked.

'Hardly at all Sir.'

'About his life before Sixfields?'

Stewart shook his head.

'What about places that he might go to on holiday? Or for a short break?'

'I don't think he went away very much Sir.'

The detective sat back. Stewart wasn't telling him anything new. He jerked his head towards the partition exit. 'You're a disappointment Constable! Get out!'

Stewart hesitated, as if he wanted to add something. The young PC eventually replaced his cap and left the office.

Crosby remained at his desk, well aware that he wasn't exactly leading by example. Flicking through Stewart's notes, he added the PC's name to a list of officers that might have picked up carpet fibres from Milner's house.

At ten o'clock Crosby went through to brief the main office.

If he'd been aware, the detective could have warned his team that a shed load of shit was about to hit a very large fan.

CHAPTER 30

WEST MIDLANDS GAZETTE: Monday 26 February 2007:

SIXFIELDS RIOT LATEST:
DEATH TOLL REACHES DOUBLE FIGURES.

Gazette reporters have compiled the following timetable of events:

Sat 10.30am: Police HQ: Officers monitoring mobile telephone traffic in the Sixfields area report a simultaneous release of coded messages. Police believe the messages signal an imminent turf war offensive between local gangs.

Sat 11.30am: Dreede's Square: Security staff at a shopping precinct adjacent to the estate's West Indian quarter report a large gathering of hooded youths inside the square's pedestrianised centre.

Sat 11.50am: Loddeston District: One mile south-west of Dreede's Square, members of 'Loddeston Old Boys' congregate in and around the 'Creswell Arms' public house – an established focal point for the gang's activities.

Sat 12 noon: Police HQ: Contingency plans for managing a major incident in the West Midlands are raised to alert status by the Chief Constable.

Sat 12.10pm: Police HQ: Police continue to monitor both Loddeston and Dreede's Square. Movements are reported in other parts of the estate.

Sat 12.30pm: Police HQ: Alcohol related incidents and unruly behaviour reported at both sites.

Sat 12.40pm: Police HQ: West Midlands major incident plan raised to operational status. Chief Constable briefs the three officers assigned to Gold, Silver and Bronze levels of command.

Sat 1.00pm: Police HQ: Control of resources and overall strategy assumed by Chief Superintendent Ewart inside the Gold Suite. Loddeston and Dreede's Square groups have now been massed together on their respective sites for over two hours.

Sat 1.05pm: Police HQ: Superintendent Ewart's first directive is to order clearance of the immediate area at both sites. Riot police units are mobilised and moved forward to operational positions. Police helicopter launched to provide Command Centre with live video feed from the air.

Sat 1.10pm: Sixfields Estate: The build-up of gang activity at Loddeston and Dreede's Square diverts attention away from vehicles carrying several groups of left-wing activists into Sixfields.

Sat 1.20pm: Sixfields Estate: Temporary barricades belatedly erected on major routes into the estate.

Sat 1.30pm: Sixfields Estate: Activists already inside Sixfields re-group and congregate close to Dreede's Square. Three potential flashpoints now exist, all within an area of one square mile.

Sat 1.35pm: Loddeston District: Rumour sweeps through the 'Creswell Arms' public house that a white youth has been attacked in Dreede's Square. Mob of eighty hooded youths stampede from the area en masse.

Sat 1.40pm: Loddeston District: One hundred police in full riot gear confront the hostile mob who scatter and run into adjoining side streets, smashing windows of nearby houses and cars.

'I'd been calling the police all morning,' landlord Bill Trevis said. 'But they kept stalling me. Then everyone in the pub started shouting and they all charged outside.'

Sat 1.45pm: Dreede's Square: Mobile telephone calls warn of the rival gang heading from Loddeston towards Dreede's Square. Precinct fills with angry mob as both public houses empty into the Square. Shop windows smashed and bottles thrown as riot squad police confront them. Batons, tear gas and police dogs used to drive rioters back in violent, close quarter clashes.

Sat 1.55pm: Avondale House Complex: Police pursue mob through car park into grounds of 'Avondale House' residential home. Rioters break into resident's day room and drag occupants from their chairs.

Sat 2.00pm: Avondale House Complex: HQ Gold Command instructs riot-squad to draw back as hostages forced outside at knife-point to face advancing police line. Mob kick through a perimeter garden wall to hurl bricks and masonry at police shields.

Sat 2.05pm: Loddeston District: Riot squad police at Loddeston are moved across the estate to Dreede's Square.

Sat 2.05pm: Avondale House Complex: Police mobile unit unsuccessful in trying to stop a group of eighty external activists advancing towards 'Avondale House'.

Sat 2.15pm: Avondale House Complex: Rioters continue to shelter behind their human shield of elderly hostages. Large, hostile crowd gathers behind police lines as Sixfields residents join Loddeston gang members and external activists congregating outside the 'Avondale House' complex.

Sat 2.20pm: Sixfields Estate: News of 'Avondale House' confrontation spreads to other parts of the estate. Hooded youths rampage through streets towards Dreede's Square.

Sat 2.25pm: Avondale House Complex: The mob behind police lines swell to over five hundred.

Sat 2.30pm: Avondale House Complex: Armed Response Units called forward as random shots heard from nearby buildings. Chief Superintendent Ewart in the Gold-Suite comes under severe pressure as situation continues to deteriorate.

Sat 2.40pm: Avondale House Complex: Petrol bomb thrown from crowd signal a sudden mob-surge towards police lines. Rioters in grounds of 'Avondale House' abandon hostages to join in the attack. Police forced to make a tactical withdrawal back into Dreede's Square.

Sat 2.45pm: Dreede's Square: Riot now at its height. Shields, batons and stun guns used to ward off mob armed with baseball bats wrapped in barbed wire.

Sat 2.55pm: Dreedes Square: Mounted police and riot-squad reserves sent in to break-up and manoeuvre rioters into small, isolated groups.

Sat 3.10pm: Dreedes Square: Mob eventually break ranks and fall away as police riot-squads gradually take control.

Sat 3.20pm: Dreedes Square: Dreede's Square and surrounding area secured by riot-squad. Precinct resembles a battleground. Shop fronts pushed through. Broken glass, weapons and debris litter the whole area. Six rioters and one policeman dead. Over one hundred injured.

Sat 4.00pm – 12.00pm: Sixfields Estate: Mobile riot-squads engage in sporadic running skirmishes with breakaway groups of rioters as arson attacks continue throughout the estate. Firefighters on permanent call-out during the night attending to burnt-out cars and buildings. Armed response units also engaged in overnight shooting incidents. Death toll rises to ten.

Sun 7.00am: Sixfields Estate: Sunday morning. Residents venture out into street scenes reminiscent of sectarian violence experienced by Belfast in the late sixties. A pall of grey smoke hangs over the estate as burnt-out cars and buildings smoulder in the early morning light. Manned barricades remain in place on major routes in and out of Sixfields and armed police units continue to patrol the estate.

Sun 10.00am: Police HQ: Part of a statement issued by Chief Superintendent Ewart at a press conference held on Sunday morning:
'External influences were directing activities from the very outset. Storage and distribution of stockpiled weapons and petrol bombs indicated a high degree of organisation and pre-planning.'

CHAPTER 31

Tuesday 27 February 2007: 10.30 am

Checking her rear-view mirror DC Grace Taylor switched lanes with nonchalant ease, manoeuvring the dark blue Mondeo Zetec past a slow moving goods lorry. From his front passenger seat Crosby glanced across at Taylor's sharply defined profile, but her concentration was focused totally on the traffic in front of them. Discussion about last night's development would have to wait.

Since joining the motorway twenty minutes ago conversation between the two detectives had been limited, both of them lost in their own thoughts. Not surprising really, last weekend's events would remain long in the memory. Staff based at Studwell's regional headquarters were particularly hard hit – Phil Jennings had been a police constable there for over thirty-five years and the manner of his death had affected everyone.

Crosby, having been closely acquainted with Jennings for most of those thirty-five years, had been unable to watch CCTV footage of the PC's final moments.

At the riot's height Jennings had somehow found himself isolated and adrift from police lines. Surrounded by a gang of hooded youths he'd been quickly hacked down, disappearing from view as the riot helmet was ripped from his head. By the time reinforcements got through to him, Jennings had been kicked into a state of unconsciousness. He died in an ambulance on the way to hospital.

It was not a fitting end to thirty-five years of dedicated service. Phil Jennings was a policeman whose sympathies erred on the side of victims – and Crosby still couldn't put into words the anger he felt.

Six rioters had also lost their lives that afternoon, but Crosby didn't feel anything for them or their families. If someone saw fit to identify that as a basic flaw in his character he didn't have a problem with that either.

It still wasn't clear who had been responsible for the rioters' deaths.

Investigators were still gathering evidence to establish where, and at what point, the six were killed. Amidst the mayhem and confusion, CCTV footage was inconclusive, and so were unsubstantiated reports that individual gang members had been targeted and attacked during the riot.

Crosby was surprised that only ten deaths in total had emerged from the clashes, such was the savagery and violence meted out by both sides. The weekend's raw emotions would take years to heal.

Another casualty of the riot had been Peter Stewart. He'd reacted badly to the news of his partner's death. Phil Jennings had been mentoring the young PC for over a year now and the two had developed a close working relationship. Stewart had been given immediate leave and referred to the department's counselling service, a facility that was still alien to Crosby and the era he'd first served in.

Sixfields riots, in the meanwhile, would become a short term agenda item for politicians and the chattering classes – who'd be keen to offer their solutions and apportion blame. Only after another high profile tragedy had taken its place would the estate revert back to its previous life.

In the riot's immediate aftermath Rees-Bramley had refocused his team, reminding them they were all professionals, and there was still a job of work to do. It rang a little hollow. His brief ended with a reminder that Milner had now been missing for ten days.

Crosby yawned and checked his watch. If the Mondeo had a clear run they would reach Oswestry in under an hour – Penny Roberts had agreed to speak with the two detectives that afternoon.

Lucy's mother and her step-father had returned to the UK yesterday evening – police eventually making contact with their private yacht two days ago. After intercepting them both at Birmingham's International Airport, it was Families Liaison Officer DC Emma Foulkes who broke the news of Stephen's murder and Lucy's disappearance. Although Penny Roberts hadn't broken down completely, her husband insisted she was examined by a duty doctor before they both left the airport.

Charged with the delicate task of support counselling, whilst also trying to elicit information, DC Foulkes had accompanied them back to the family home in Oswestry. After recovering from her initial shock, Penny Roberts subsequent behaviour towards the Families Officer had been offensive and ill-mannered. Rees-Bramley's directive that a senior ranking officer should assume control saw Crosby and Taylor en-route to Shropshire and the Welsh borders. Crosby wasn't totally surprised that Rees-Bramley had another engagement that morning – the DCI having previously encountered Penny Roberts at the Royal West Midlands hospital, where she was visiting her son.

Making the woman's acquaintance again wasn't top of Crosby's wish list either, but their investigation had stalled, it was in dire need of some forward momentum. Any light that Penny Roberts could throw on the whereabouts of her ex-husband or Lucy, would be more information than they had currently.

Alongside him Taylor shifted her position slightly, as if she had something on her mind. 'Sarge?'

'Yes Grace!'

'Word around the station is that you've developed a bit of a sixth sense over the years.'

'Inspired hunches!' Crosby shrugged. 'Comes with experience and old age.'

'A few successes though.'

'I get lucky now and again.' Crosby played it down. The murder squad needed to focus on their chief suspect, he didn't want to influence a team member with what his antenna was telling him. 'I don't have second sight if that's what the story is,' Crosby added.

Taylor persisted. 'So what are your hunches telling you about the investigation now?'

'They're not!'

'It's still down to Milner then?'

The senior detective nodded. 'That's what forensics are telling us.'

'And the suicide note?'

'The experts say it's his handwriting.'

Taylor didn't look convinced. 'But still no sign of a body.'

'No sign of his daughter either.' Crosby diverted the focus away from Milner. 'Where do you think Lucy fits into all this?'

'I don't think she does,' the policewoman replied.

'No?'

Taylor shook her head. 'Lucy took off because of the drugs investigation.'

Crosby nodded. 'Possibly!'

'How did her mother react to the fact that Lucy was caught dealing in drugs at the university?' Taylor asked.

'She doesn't know yet!'

The policewoman raised her eyebrows. 'I thought our Families Liaison Officer was in Oswestry preparing the ground for us.'

'That was the intention,' Crosby said. 'Until Mrs Roberts told her she wasn't about to be patronised by a glorified bloody social worker who looked as if she'd just left school.'

Taylor winced. 'DC Foulkes is no longer at the house then?'

'Thrown out last night.'

'Is the husband any more agreeable?'

'Keeps a low profile most of the time,' Crosby replied. 'Doesn't contribute anything without his wife's approval.'

'I could have a few words with him on his own,' Taylor suggested. 'While you're interviewing Mrs Roberts.'

'Maybe! We'll play it by ear. I don't want to antagonise her unnecessarily.' Crosby paused. 'As she's been out of the country Penny Roberts might also be unaware that her ex-husband is a murder suspect.'

'Bloody Hell! Didn't DC Foulkes tell her anything?'

'She didn't get the chance,' Crosby said. 'And I've no doubt that Mrs Roberts will be looking around for more easy targets this morning.'

'That'll be us then!'

The detective nodded. 'Enter PC Plod. Stage left.'

Their conversation was halted briefly as Grace Taylor negotiated the Mondeo's exit from a busy M6 onto the relatively quieter M54. 'Fifteen miles to Telford Services Sarge. Are we taking a break?'

The senior detective shook his head. 'We'll crack on. I half-promised the wife we'd be eating out tonight.'

Taylor glanced across. 'Half-promised?'

'It's her birthday!' Crosby answered.

'Oh!' Taylor didn't pursue it and the car lapsed into silence again.

Continuing along the motorway for another thirty minutes they exited Mile End roundabout onto the Oswestry road. Taylor leant forward to activate a small, unobtrusive satellite navigation unit, perched above the Mondeo's dashboard. A monotonous, disembodied voice began to issue instructions. Taylor had obviously pre-programmed the sat-nav to assist them with the final few miles of their journey.

Crosby viewed the screen's colourful road map with suspicion. 'You find these things reliable?' he asked.

'Most of the time,' Taylor replied. 'Have they caused you problems?'

The senior detective sniffed. 'Not really! I manage well enough without them.'

'That's a man thing,' Taylor said.

'Is it!'

Taylor nodded. 'Male drivers seem to think they're the equivalent of stopping and asking for directions. My partner's exactly the same.'

'Is he!' Crosby replied.

Arriving in Oswestry the sat-nav's disembodied voice guided them efficiently through the small, bustling market town without incident. Two miles further on it instructed Taylor to take a sharp right. Allowing the steering wheel to expertly spin back through her hands she straightened the car up as it swept through a pair of ornate, wrought iron gates. The policewoman made a point of leaning forward to switch off the sat-nav unit. 'I think we can find our own way from here Sir.'

Crosby glanced across at her but didn't reply. He turned his attention outside to an avenue of evenly-spaced mature conifers, flashing past his window – intermittent glimpses of manicured lawns and well-tended shrubberies showing through gaps in the trees.

The single-track, tarmac road took them on for another half mile, where they emerged from a tunnel of foliage into view of the house itself. Grace Taylor whistled in appreciation.

Crosby leant forward to get a better view. 'Grade Two listed!' he said. 'Eighteenth century Georgian, with Regency and Victorian additions. Two walled gardens and a private lake. Been in the family for generations apparently.'

Taylor nodded. 'Not forgetting a cantilevered mahogany staircase inside the house, leading to a twelve bedroom galleried landing.'

The senior detective raised his eyebrows.

Taylor shrugged and smiled. 'I looked it up as well.'

The Mondeo's tyres crunched through a wide expanse of white chipped gravel in front of the house. Taylor reversed the car into space between a BMW Convertible and Freelander station wagon. Pulling on the handbrake she cut the car's engine and removed its ignition keys.

An elderly gardener looked across at them from a nearby flowerbed. He straightened up and touched his cap as they got out of the car.

'Bloody Hell!' Taylor laughed. 'I didn't know they still did that. Do you think I ought to acknowledge him?'

Crosby nodded towards a small, raised terrace. 'You could always curtsy to the owner instead.'

Henry Roberts' tall gangling figure was already halfway down a flight of stone steps, heading directly towards them. He wore crumpled brown corduroys and a tweed jacket – his balding, domed-head gleamed palely under a weak morning sun.

The handshake he offered Crosby and Taylor was both limp and brief, his voice apologetic. 'I'm sorry to intercept you Inspector but my wife is feeling particularly fragile this morning. I thought it best to advise you beforehand.'

Crosby feigned a look of concern. 'I'm sorry to hear that Sir.'

'Understandable I suppose.' Roberts nervously rubbed the palms of his hands together. 'I'm assuming the interview will not be too intense.'

'Very low-key given the circumstances,' Crosby glibly assured him.

'I'm afraid the dreadful news about Stephen has been extremely traumatic for both of us.' Roberts looked towards the house. 'And then to be told that Lucy had suddenly disappeared as well.'

'Would Mrs Roberts be more comfortable if I spoke to her?' Taylor asked.

Roberts raised his eyebrows. 'No disrespect DC Taylor but my wife specifically requested the interview be conducted by a senior ranked officer.'

'That's fine Sir,' Taylor said. 'Would you mind if we talked informally – whilst Inspector Crosby interviews your wife.'

Roberts frowned. 'Why would you want to do that?'

'It was merely a way of minimising the time we were here,' the policewoman replied. 'I was just thinking of Mrs Roberts.'

'I'm sure my wife would prefer we did this together.' He turned to the house. 'If you're ready? She is waiting for us.'

The two detectives exchanged glances as they followed Roberts towards the terracing. Crosby nodded at the grounds. 'A lot of real estate Sir.'

'Sixty acres altogether.' Roberts nodded to the elderly gardener who touched his cap again as they passed. 'It requires a deal of upkeep and attention.'

'And the house?'

'It's listed unfortunately. A privilege to call it home of course, but the next expensive problem is always just around the corner.'

Crosby continued to small talk. 'Are you open to the public?'

'Only the gardens,' Roberts replied. 'But we do run a number of corporate events throughout the year.' He led them up a shallow flight of stone steps to the raised area of paved terracing. Access into the house was through a pair of discreet, tinted French-windows. Roberts slid one of the windows noiselessly open and ushered both detectives into a high-ceilinged reception room. Crosby was no expert but the influence of exclusive, interior design was clearly evident.

The lady of the house sat facing them, her face immobile, a pair of slim, tanned legs, crossed, and angled to one side. She didn't get up. The stiff backed posture signalled a warning.

'Shit!' Crosby muttered to himself. He recognised the body language.

Trauma affects people in different ways. Some collapse inwardly, others look for someone on which to vent their anger. It wasn't difficult to gauge in which direction Penny Roberts was about to launch herself.

Quickly crossing the room, Henry Roberts bent to kiss his wife on the cheek. She shrugged him away, keeping her attention fixed on the two detectives. He stepped to one side and took up a position behind her chair.

However much she was suffering, Penny Roberts had obviously spent time on her personal appearance. A light foundation and pale lipstick had been perfectly applied, to complement the short, cropped, black hair. Dressed in a pencil-slim skirt and three-quarter length cashmere cardigan, she wore a delicate chain of white gold around her slender neck.

Milner's ex-wife slid on a pair of dark glasses – from where he was standing Crosby could see she'd been crying. The detectives waited inside the door. Penny Roberts remained in her chair.

'Now what?' Taylor murmured.

Crosby waited a few moments before stepping forward. 'Mrs Roberts. My name is Detective Inspector Crosby.'

She cut him off. 'I know perfectly well who you are Inspector. We met at the hospital.'

Crosby turned to the policewoman next to him. 'Detective Constable Taylor is a member of our investigation team.'

Milner's ex-wife flicked a glance at the female detective – her look of disdain was barely disguised. Crosby filed it away for future use. Did Penny Roberts have a problem with policewomen? Was colour an issue? Grace Taylor must have noticed the look as well.

'Do you intend joining us Inspector?' Penny Roberts called across the room. 'Or will you be conducting the interview at long distance?'

'That would be preferable!' Crosby muttered to himself. The woman's high-pitched, nasal drone was already beginning to grate on his hearing.

She waved the detectives towards two vacant chairs.

'Mrs Roberts!' Crosby said as he sat down. 'We fully sympathise with your loss and appreciate how you must be feeling but it was important we spoke at the earliest opportunity.'

Penny Roberts gave no indication that she'd heard him. 'Inspector! Please be aware that a formal complaint has been lodged against your department. The officer junior sent to meet us at the airport yesterday was totally unsuitable and under-prepared.'

'Mrs Roberts!' Crosby replied. 'I can assure you that DC Foulkes is an experienced, fully trained Families Liaison Officer.'

'I don't care what she's been trained in,' Penny Roberts said icily.

'Your department will not fob me off with some slip of a schoolgirl who seemed to have very little knowledge of what stage your investigation has reached.'

Crosby's voice remained polite. 'DC Foulkes role as Family Liaison Officer was to offer you help and support after the immediate loss of your son.'

'Inspector!' Penny Roberts clenched both hands together. 'I lost Stephen some years ago, but I'm still close to my daughter. She's very precious to me. What I needed was someone in authority to assure me that Lucy hasn't become another victim of this psychopath who's currently roaming around Sixfields.'

'Was there a reason for your concern?' Crosby asked.

'Lucy's been staying with my ex-husband in Sixfields recently.' She made a dismissive gesture with her hand. 'Why anyone would want to visit such a god-forsaken place is beyond my comprehension.'

'Mrs Roberts!' the detective took a deep breath. 'The likelihood is that Lucy has disappeared of her own accord.'

Penny Roberts looked more puzzled than annoyed. 'You're not making sense man! Explain yourself.'

'Your daughter was recently suspended from her university.' Crosby said. 'An investigation is being carried out into her alleged dealing of narcotics within campus grounds. We believe that is the reason for her sudden disappearance.'

It took a few moments for the news to sink in. Both Penny Roberts and her husband straightened in surprise.

'Narcotics?' she repeated.

'Heroin to be precise.'

Penny Roberts' nostrils flared. 'Don't be so bloody ridiculous!' she said, her voice raised. 'Lucy doesn't have anything to do with drugs. It's a nonsense!'

'Penny!' Grace Taylor reached forward to lay a sympathetic hand on the other woman's arm. 'I'm afraid the university does have evidence to the contrary.'

Penny Roberts spun round to face the policewoman, her face white with anger. 'You are not on first name terms with me,' she hissed, 'and you will not presume to know my daughter better than I!'

Henry Roberts made an attempt to take his wife's hand. Penny Roberts snatched it away and wheeled on Crosby. 'Yet another example of your department's bungling incompetence Inspector. Any detective with half a brain would be able to disprove such absurd claims.'

'You mustn't upset yourself darling.' Henry Roberts hovered beside his wife's chair. 'I'm sure there's a perfectly simple explanation.'

She ignored him. Her attention remained on the senior detective. 'Your Chief Constable is a regular dinner guest at my table Inspector. He will be appraised of your conduct.'

Crosby interrupted before she could launch any more threats. 'Have you been in touch with your ex-husband recently?'

'What the bloody hell for!' Penny Roberts snapped back at him. 'I've just lost my son. My daughter is missing. My ex-husband's existence is of no concern to me whatsoever. Why would I want to get in touch with him?'

'While you were abroad Robert Milner disappeared.' The detective paused. 'He left a suicide note.'

Penny Roberts shrugged dismissively. 'Not my concern! He should have disposed of himself years ago.'

Crosby leant forward. 'And you're presumably not aware that a warrant has been issued for his arrest in connection with the recent murders in Sixfields.'

There was a short silence. Henry Roberts broke it. 'Are you alleging that Penny's ex-husband has been involved in these murders?'

The detective nodded. 'He is wanted for questioning.'

Roberts considered the implications. He shook his head. 'But his son is one of the victims.'

'Yes!'

A longer silence this time. Penny Roberts suddenly stood up. 'Jesus Christ!' There was panic, verging on hysteria in her voice. 'Lucy's been staying with him! That's why you're here! The bloody maniac's done something to her!'

Crosby tried to calm her. 'Mrs Roberts! I said earlier. We do not believe Lucy's disappearance is in any way connected to our investigation. Tracing your ex-husband's current whereabouts is the reason for us being here.'

The news about Milner had shaken Penny Roberts. A manicured hand remained at the base of her throat.

'Do you have any thoughts as to where your ex-husband might have disappeared to?' Crosby asked.

There was no response.

The detective looked up at Henry Roberts, who shook his head. 'I know very little about the man Inspector. We've only met on one previous occasion.'

'What about Lucy?' Crosby asked him. 'Do you know where she might be?'

'We've tried all of her friends and acquaintances,' Roberts replied. 'She's not been in touch with any of them.'

'Is there anywhere she'd go for a short break?'

It sparked something in Penny Roberts. Her head suddenly came up. 'We didn't try Dryffed's Farm.'

Crosby's antenna twitched. 'Dryffed's Farm?'

'We bought it five years ago,' Henry Roberts said. 'Converted the old farmhouse into a holiday letting.'

'And where exactly is this farm?' A familiar tingle spread to the base of Crosby's neck.

'It's in Wales!' Penny Roberts was recovering quickly. 'Just over the border! We should have thought of it before. Lucy occasionally goes there for a weekend.'

'By herself?'

'It depends on her mood,' Penny Roberts said. 'She might take friends from the university. They go there to study, or unwind for a few days.'

'Does your ex-husband know of it?'

'Why the hell would he!'

'Is there a telephone?'

Henry Roberts shook his head. 'The whole area's a mountain range Inspector. You can't even get a mobile signal.'

'We'll need to get it checked out.'

'It's very remote,' Roberts replied. 'Appeals to those clients who enjoy being completely cut off and isolated. The single-track roads make precise directions almost impossible. It even defeats the sat-nav aids.'

'So how do your clients find this place?' Crosby asked.

'They're usually escorted. We employ an agent who lives in a village about fifteen miles from the farm.'

'Couldn't you get him to run up there?'

Roberts shook his head. 'Unfortunately not! He's had to leave the village for a few weeks. Family illness.'

'We'll drive there!' Penny Roberts began to gather up items from a nearby table. 'Standing here talking won't get it done!'

Her husband looked unsure. 'I'm not sure you're well enough to travel just yet darling. And it's most unlikely that Lucy would be at Dryffed's in the middle of winter anyway.'

'She has this absurd accusation hanging over her.' Penny Roberts was already crossing the room. 'We don't know how it might have affected her.'

'It's a difficult journey darling,' her husband persisted. 'Let me go. You can stay here and rest.'

She opened the door. 'I'll be ready to leave in five minutes.'

Henry Roberts offered no further argument as his wife left the room. He raised his eyebrows at the two detectives. 'She can be very headstrong on occasions.'

'If it's not inconvenient Sir,' Crosby said as he got up from his chair, 'we'd like to accompany you.'

Roberts nodded. 'Of course! We'll have to take our four-wheel drive. The access lanes are fairly well maintained but it does get rather steep in places.' He checked his watch. 'There's not much daylight left either. I'll need to rustle up some torches.'

'We'll wait outside,' Crosby said.

Roberts headed for the door. 'I suggest you retrieve your coats from the car. We'll be fifteen-hundred feet above sea level and it's a different weather system at that height.'

The two detectives made their way out onto the terracing. Negotiating the flight of stone steps they headed back towards the parked cars. Taylor switched her mobile on. 'If we're being transported halfway up a mountain, I'd better ring home and leave a message.' She looked across at Crosby. 'Didn't you ought to call your wife? I thought you were taking her out tonight.'

The senior detective looked up to see Henry and Penny Roberts coming towards them. 'It'll keep,' he said, springing open the Mondeo's boot. 'Don't forget your coat.'

Milner's ex-wife was wrapped in a thickly quilted waist length anorak. The backless, heeled sandals had been exchanged for a pair of sturdy leather walking boots. Without acknowledging either of the two detectives she waited for her husband to open the Freelander's front passenger door before climbing in.

Grace Taylor looked more than a little surprised when Henry Roberts turned to also open the rear passenger door for her, placing his hand lightly under her elbow as she stepped inside. Crosby smiled and made his way around to the other side. Roberts waited for the detective to clip his seat belt into place before firing-up the Freelander's powerful V6 engine.

Driving back down through the estate's avenue of conifers Penny Roberts stared into the distance, making no attempt at conversation. 'We'll have the heating up,' were the only words she spoke to her husband as he turned left out of the gates.

Heading due west they passed road signs to Offa's Dyke and Racecourse Common. A larger sign, in both Welsh and English, flashed past Crosby's window, telling him they'd just crossed over into Wales. The border plaque included a small, red dragon. It didn't look particularly friendly. An advertising hoarding for Clun Castle's Marcher Fortress loomed up ahead of them.

Taylor leant towards her DI. 'What's a Marcher Fortress?' she asked, keeping her voice low.

'Medieval police stations,' Crosby answered. 'We built a whole string of them along the Welsh Marches.'

'Marches?'

'The original no-man's land between England and Wales,' Crosby said. 'William the Conqueror established Marcher Lords after the Norman Conquest to subdue the Celtic hordes and control its border regions.'

Taylor looked impressed. 'And they did that by throwing up a few castles?'

'A few hundred castles,' Crosby replied. 'Keeping the Welsh out has never been easy. Look at how they invaded us after the Severn Bridge was built.'

Taylor didn't seem particularly amused and went back to looking out of the window.

The senior detective turned his attention to Penny Roberts. She'd withdrawn into herself, hiding behind a pair of over-sized dark glasses.

He leant forward. 'Mrs Roberts! We do appreciate that your main concern is for Lucy but locating your ex-husband is critical to our investigation. Is there anything you can recall from the time of your marriage that might indicate his current whereabouts?'

The dark glasses remained fixed on the road ahead.

'However insignificant that might appear to be,' Crosby added.

No reply.

Crosby persisted. 'I understand you had occasion to visit your ex-husband recently. Is it possible he said something at the time about going away?'

'Inspector!' She removed her glasses but didn't bother to turn around. 'Once and for all! Robert is no longer part of my life. I don't know where he is! I don't care where he is! I don't want to know where he is!'

'Even though there's a likelihood he's been involved in your son's murder?' Crosby risked.

Penny Roberts slowly and deliberately adjusted her rear-view mirror to look back at the detective. 'Inspector! You know full well the history between my ex-husband and Stephen. It was an accident waiting to happen. Robert's mental health was probably a factor, and I can't imagine the situation has improved in that respect – considering his deterioration

241

towards the end of our marriage.'

'I understood that Mister Milner's problems were as a direct consequence of his chronic depression,' Crosby paused. 'Brought on by your divorce ten years ago.'

Now the detective had her attention. She unclipped her seat belt and turned to face him. 'Don't try to play emotional fucking mind games with me Inspector. You'll be wasting your time. Understand this! I feel no moral responsibility for my ex-husband and I'm certainly not interested in discussing anything about your sordid little investigation. My only concern is the current whereabouts and welfare of my daughter.'

Penny Roberts turned back to the front and re-clipped her seat belt.

Apart from humming nervously to himself Henry Roberts offered no comment – his attention remaining on the road. Another strained atmosphere settled inside the station wagon.

'I always find witnesses more responsive if you don't upset them Sir,' Taylor whispered to her DI.

Crosby grunted, his sense of humour temporarily deserting him. He leant back. Penny Roberts would have to wait until after they'd checked out Dryffed's Farm. Although his hunches were not always a hundred percent reliable, something about the farm's name had tweaked his interest.

The Freelander continued on, passing signs for Pistyll Rhaeadr Waterfalls and the Berwyn Mountain Range.

After swinging the station wagon off its main route, Roberts took them up a succession of inclines and single-track roads – bounded by tight hedgerows and high, grassy banks. It was rolling sheep country, and the lush, surrounding meadowland would soon be alive with thousands of newly-born lambs, ushering in another season. They continued to climb.

At seven hundred feet the rural lowlands gave way to bleak areas of scrub moorland. Henry Roberts barrelled his Freelander along the lane's narrow confines, seemingly unconcerned about the possibility of vehicles approaching from the opposite direction. Crosby hoped his reflexes were sharper than his personality.

Occasionally they would pass a thin wooden finger of weathered signpost, pointing in the direction of Dryffed's Farm. Not that it helped. Crosby was completely disorientated now, hypnotised by the maze of narrow lanes that had got them this far – and even though his ears had popped under altitude some time ago, the station wagon was still climbing. He'd given up trying to look for indications that other vehicles had recently passed this way.

After one particularly steep incline they were suddenly enveloped by thick mist. Roberts immediately flicked on his station wagon's powerful headlights, but the solid, grey wall in front of them was virtually impenetrable, slowing the Freelander to a virtual crawl. Henry Roberts spoke over his shoulder to the two detectives behind. 'There's always the possibility of a low cloud-base at this height – we're currently nine-hundred feet above sea level.'

'Can you focus on what's in front of us!' Penny Roberts snapped at her husband. 'We're not geography students on a bloody field trip.' Silence descended again. Henry Roberts turned on his windscreen wipers as they continued to climb up through the curtain of damp, grey cloud.

Crosby's head began to gradually droop, his eyelids fighting a losing battle against the station wagon's powerful heating system. Taylor nudged him with her elbow. He opened his eyes to see Dryffed's Farm materialising out of the mist. Two beams of light from the Freelander's headlamps projected across a large, open yard, picking out the bleak-looking farmhouse tucked away in a far corner. It was now mid to late afternoon.

Scattered haphazardly around the farmyard's perimeter were a number of weathered outbuildings, most of them constructed of local stone and slate roofs. All of the buildings showed various states of disrepair – along with the several items of rusting, abandoned, agricultural machinery. Maintenance of the site was obviously kept to a bare minimum, deliberately cultivating a disused, slightly neglected look.

It didn't look much like holiday accommodation to Crosby, but Roberts had told them Dryffed's was popular with clientele who wanted to experience the living conditions of eighteenth century hill farmers. First impressions wouldn't have disappointed them.

'Doesn't appear to be any lights on,' Roberts said, as he coasted the station wagon down a slight incline towards the farmhouse. 'No sign of Lucy's car either.' He stopped outside the front door and cut his engine. 'I'll check inside.'

Penny Roberts zipped her padded jacket together. 'I'm coming with you!'

Crosby peered out of the window. 'Place looks deserted,' he murmured to Taylor. 'Keep an eye on them. I'll have a look around outside.'

Opening his rear-passenger door Crosby immediately felt the drop in temperature. It was bitterly cold, a light wind causing the mist to eddy and shift in front of him. Visibility was down to about fifty yards.

A movement across the yard triggered Crosby's peripheral vision. Swivelling around he picked out a shadowy, indistinct figure, standing next to one of the outbuildings.

'We've got company,' he called out to the others.

They stopped and turned. The detective strained his eyes, trying to re-focus. A swirl of mist and the figure was gone. Crosby blinked. Did he imagine it?

'I should have warned you about him Inspector.' Henry Roberts had walked back to the car. 'It may have been our resident house guest.'

'House guest?'

'Davydd Remlin! Back in the late eighteenth century he was a tenant farmer here – returned from the fields one day to find his wife hanging from a rafter in the old lambing shed.' Roberts indicated the building Crosby had been looking towards. 'They had two young children. Neither of them were ever found.'

The detective nodded. 'And no doubt Remlin's restless soul wanders around the farm in a never ending search for his lost children.'

Roberts shrugged. 'It wouldn't be good for business if he found them. Our clients look on sightings of old Davydd as an added attraction.'

'We'll do our best not to frighten him off then,' Crosby said, turning back to look at the old lambing shed again.

Penny Roberts interrupted them. 'Will you get this door unlocked!' she was standing impatiently outside the farmhouse. 'Not everyone's interested in the bloody nonsense you peddle to your inbred holidaymakers.'

'On my way darling.' Henry Roberts left Crosby standing by the station wagon.

Grace Taylor walked over to join her DI. He slipped his coat on. 'I'm going across to check this old outhouse.'

'You'll need to take care Sir,' Taylor said. 'It is rather a spooky coincidence.'

Crosby frowned. 'What is?'

'Davydd Remlin!' Taylor's face remained expressionless. 'Didn't you notice that his surname is an anagram of Milner?'

The senior detective looked at her from underneath his eyebrows but didn't rise to it.

Taylor smiled. 'At least you won't need a satnav if you get lost – old Davydd will be able to give you directions.'

She turned back towards the farmhouse, ignoring Crosby's muttered reply. Although the detective in him could justify sixth-sense hunches, tormented spirits were a nonsense too far.

He set off towards the old lambing shed – if there was someone hanging around it needed checking out. Crosby quickly found that his footwear was completely unsuitable for crossing farmyards – the loose shale and grit scattered on top of damp, greasy concrete was an accident waiting to happen.

Halfway across he stopped to look back at the house. Even from this distance the three figures standing outside had become indistinct, their sounds muffled. Crosby waited for them to disappear through the heavily studded front door. Another movement caught his eye. Further along this time. The detective changed direction and made his way towards it.

In the distance a hazy figure stood next to what looked like an old barn, but again it disappeared as yet more cloud rolled in.

The barn's dilapidated state became more apparent as Crosby neared it. Constructed from huge sheets of corrugated tin, the building's whole exterior seemed to be covered in a thick layer of brown rust. On reaching its front entrance Crosby found reinforced steel double doors secured with padlock and chain. A sudden gust of wind picked up the heavy chain and dropped it back against the steel doors, causing a series of echoes to rattle around the empty yard.

The detective moved across, to where he could look down the whole length of the barn. Visibility was down to thirty yards here. Crosby glanced back towards the farmhouse – there were lights on at all of the windows now – and everyone was inside. He should have waited for Taylor's assistance, but found himself walking cautiously along the side of the barn, a layer of loose shale crunching under his tread. He no longer had a direct eye-line with either the farmhouse or the yard.

Halfway along he came to a narrow swing door, cut into the corrugated tin. Crosby stopped, listening for any sign of movement inside. He waited. An owl hooted in the distance. He waited some more. Nudging the door slowly inwards he took a telescopic steel baton from his pocket and flicked the weapon out to its full length, before peering cautiously through the door's opening. His antenna was telling him nothing. He stepped inside.

Most of the barn's interior was in deep shadow, its light coming through a high ceiling roof of transparent perspex. Beneath his shoes, wisps of straw and hay lay scattered across a ridged, concrete floor.

Sometime previously the barn must have been converted into a shelter for cattle or sheep – two long rows of individual stalls running along both sides of a wide, central walkway.

Although all of its livestock had long since disappeared the building's interior still carried an acrid reek of animal excrement and urine, permanently ingrained into its walls and flooring.

As the detective felt for his small pocket-torch, a thin, white face materialised out of the shadows in front of him. He instinctively raised his baton.

'Stewart!' Crosby was aware of the surprise in his voice.

Peter Stewart edged forward. 'I'm sorry Sir.'

Crosby became aware of a handgun pointing at his midriff.

'I was only trying to help Sir,' the young PC looked very pale.

Crosby didn't move. His attention remained on the gun.

Someone pushed Stewart forward. The gun remained pointing at Crosby's midriff. Milner stepped into the open.

Crosby had last seen him at the hospital several days ago. From his appearance it looked as if he'd been sleeping rough – he didn't look a well man. With several days' growth of grey beard covering his face, and hair almost down to his shoulders, Milner cut a desperate looking figure, the only colour in his face were the eyes – black, like small marbles. They looked abnormally bright, slightly unfocused.

Although Crosby wasn't qualified to assess levels of insanity, it looked to his untrained eye as if Milner was on the other side of whatever line you had to cross. The detective did know it was vital to engage with him immediately.

'There's been a lot of people looking for you Mister Milner.'

'Drop the baton!'

Crosby let it fall to the floor. Milner waved both men into an adjacent stall, his thin fingers wrapped tightly around the gun's handle.

'The note you left at Silver Street caused everyone a lot of concern,' Crosby persisted.

Milner motioned towards the detective's pockets. 'Empty them!'

Crosby placed the contents of his coat pocket on top of the stall's ledge.

'All of them!' Milner instructed.

The detective emptied jacket and trouser pockets. Milner waited for Crosby to finish before waving both men to the back of the stall.

He picked up one of the thin, plastic restraining strips that Crosby had placed on the ledge and tossed it towards Stewart. 'Turn him around and tie his hands!'

Crosby turned to face the back wall and Stewart stepped up behind him, trying to loop the thin strip of plastic around his wrists. He fumbled with the fastener.

Crosby twisted around to look over his shoulder, desperate to keep Milner talking. 'Your daughter's been extremely worried about you.'

'You haven't seen my daughter,' Milner's voice was flat, detached. There was no hint of the earlier mind games he'd played with Crosby. He was talking though.

'You're not well Mister Milner,' the detective said. 'You need help.'

'Like the help you gave me during your hospital visit Inspector.'

'The incident room is aware of our current location,' Crosby said.

'It's of no consequence.' Milner waved the gun. 'I'll be finished here long before anyone comes looking for you.'

Crosby winced as Stewart pulled hard to secure the plastic strip.

'Face down!' Milner said to the young PC. 'Hands behind your back.'

The policeman spread himself full length on the ground.

Laying his gun on top of the ledge Milner retrieved another length of plastic restraint and quickly tied Stewart's hands together. He hauled the policeman to his feet and pushed him in the direction of Crosby.

'Back against the wall,' Milner said to both of them. 'Sit!'

The two men lowered themselves awkwardly to the ground.

Crosby tried to ease himself into a more comfortable position – the ridged, concrete flooring hard and uncomfortable through his thin trousers. The detective's stomach spasmed. 'Fuck!' An image of the cellar in Shurville Gardens, with three bodies sitting propped against its back wall, flashed into his mind.

Milner picked up his gun and left the stall, walking out onto the wide, central walkway. Crosby watched him disappear through deep shadow into one of the stalls opposite.

Several minutes passed. A near freezing ground began to numb Crosby's buttocks, and the plastic restraining strips were biting deep into his wrists. He was angry with himself. Taylor could have provided back-up.

The young PC shifted his position. Crosby turned on him. 'What the hell are you doing here Stewart?'

'I was looking for Lucy Sir.' Stewart's voice caught in his throat. He looked scared.

'So how would you know about this place?'

Stewart started to shiver with the cold. 'Lucy had business cards about the farm in her car. I picked one up. She was going to bring me here for a weekend.'

'And just how the hell did you manage to find your own way here?'

'There were directions on the card Sir.'

'I've just made the same journey. I wouldn't have found it from a few printed directions.'

'I was lucky Sir.'

'Not so bloody lucky now are you?'

'No Sir!'

'And you had this information to hand when I spoke to you last about

Lucy's disappearance?'

'Yes Sir!'

'But you chose not to share it with me.'

Stewart didn't reply.

'How long have you been here?' Crosby asked.

'Just before you arrived Sir.'

'And where's your car?'

'Milner made me put it round the back.'

'Is Lucy here?'

'I haven't seen her.'

'Is there anyone else around?'

'I don't think so.'

Crosby shook his head. 'Bloody Hell Stewart! If we get to walk away from this you are in deep shit!'

'What will he do Sir?'

'How the fuck do I know what he'll do! The man's unbalanced. Insane probably.' Crosby was angry, and a little too scared himself to offer any words of comfort.

'They were all sitting like this in the cellar Sir.' Stewart started to shake. 'We need to call the others.'

Crosby turned on him, feeling little sympathy for the young policeman. 'You'll sit there and keep your mouth shut.'

Stewart subsided back against the wall and lapsed into silence.

Minutes ticked by. As daylight started to fade it became progressively darker inside the barn, a heavy rain began to pound against the building's roof.

Crosby's head lifted at the sound of someone shouting his name. He could just make out Grace Taylor's voice above the rain. She sounded some distance way. Milner materialised out of the shadows and pressed the barrel of his gun against Crosby's temple. 'How many came up with you?'

'Three!' the detective answered. There seemed little point in not telling him.

'Who are they?'

Before Crosby could answer, the shrill tone of Penny Roberts' voice sounded outside the barn's entrance doors. 'What the hell was he thinking of anyway! Wandering around this pigsty on his own!' Milner's head snapped towards the barn doors as he recognised the sound of his ex-wife's voice.

Taylor called out again 'Inspector Crosby! Are you in there?'

Crosby was acutely aware of the gun at his head as he sat and waited.

Stewart shrunk further back against the wall, his eyes darting between the gun and Milner's face. There was an urgent mumbled discussion outside the barn door. Penny Roberts' voice again. 'Do what you bloody well like! I'm going back to the car.'

The sound of footsteps retreated into the distance. Silence again.

Milner stood abruptly, moving across to the front of the stall. He waited there, looking up and down the barn's central walkway. His ex-wife's presence had agitated him. He was talking to himself. When Milner eventually decided to move, his thin, spindly legs carried him quickly into the stall opposite again.

'Are they coming back for us Sir?' Stewart asked. Crosby looked across at him. A large wet patch had spread slowly out from the PC's groin, showing dark against his light-coloured trousers.

'They know I'm here somewhere,' the detective replied with more confidence than he felt. Crosby's mobile phone suddenly burst into life on top of the stall's ledge, its small reflective screen pulsing flashes of blue light into the semi-darkness.

'Roberts told me there was a problem with signals up here.' Crosby said to Stewart.

The PC's attention fixed on the flashing square of light. 'It must be DC Taylor Sir.' Some of the tension lifted from his face. 'She's trying to ring you on a direct connection.'

Crosby vaguely remembered the new technology being explained to him when they took possession of their new mobiles. The telephone's persistent ringtone continued to jar the silence.

Milner appeared from the opposite stall again. He picked up Crosby's phone and pushed the receive button, muffling his voice and cutting across the caller. 'I've locked myself into one of the barn's store rooms,' he said. 'You'll have to use the side entrance to get in.' Milner dropped Crosby's phone to the concrete floor and put a heel through it. Moving across to the stall's opening, he covered the side entrance door with his gun and waited.

Crosby listened for signs of movement outside. He didn't know whether to warn Taylor. It might panic Milner into using the gun. Alongside him Stewart began to shake again.

'I can turn the lights on from here.' Henry Roberts' voice sounded from outside the barn's double doors. 'There's an exterior switch.'

Milner swivelled towards the doors.

A series of flickering lights from the ceiling caused Crosby to look up. Several rows of hanging fluorescent tubes, suspended from metal struts suddenly flashed into life – filling the barn's interior with a blinding white light. Crosby closed his eyes against the brightness.

He opened them to the sight of Lucy Milner lying full length in the stall opposite, chained to an upright wooden post.

Even under the harsh, fluorescent glare, Lucy's face looked grey. She lay very still, almost comatose. The greasy, matted hair was covered in wisps of straw, her heavily soiled clothes caked in dust and excrement. Crosby gagged. It looked as if she'd been chained to the same spot for days, rolling around in her own waste.

Peter Stewart was staring at the scene opposite in complete shock. Crosby elbowed him hard in the ribs. 'Keep a fucking grip! We both need to stay on top of this.' Stewart wasn't listening.

Crosby looked across towards Milner, who was now standing out in the central walkway. It didn't seem to concern him that his daughter lay in full view of the two policemen.

Milner's head turned towards the sound of chains being withdrawn. Metal scraping against concrete screeched through the barn's interior. Crosby couldn't see the entrance from where he sat but clearly both of its large steel doors were being slowly opened.

Milner ducked back inside the stall. There was a short pause. Hesitant footsteps echoed along the walkway towards them. Milner waited for the footsteps to draw level before stepping out. Grace Taylor's momentary look of surprise changed when she saw the gun. Milner grabbed her arm and shoved the policewoman back towards Crosby and Stewart. 'Sit down!' Taylor lowered herself cautiously to the floor, frowning at Crosby as she recognised Peter Stewart. The senior detective indicated with his head towards the stall opposite. Taylor's eyes widened at the sight of Lucy's outstretched body.

Milner ignored them, continuing to watch the barn's entrance doors.

Crosby leant in towards Taylor, keeping his voice low. 'Where are the other two?'

'Penny Roberts went back to the car.'

'What about her husband?'

'He picked up a set of keys from the farmhouse,' Taylor whispered. 'To open this place up.'

'So where is he now?' Crosby asked.

'I left him securing the doors. He said he'd follow me in.'

'Probably saw what happened to you and dived into one of the other stalls,' Crosby said.

'Will he go for help?'

The detective glanced across at Milner, who was still looking towards the entrance doors. 'I doubt he'll risk making a run for it, especially if he's seen the gun.'

'Penny Roberts isn't going to wait in the car all afternoon.' Taylor said, 'And she could be in danger. What if Milner intends to wipe out the whole family. She would be the next target.'

Alongside them Stewart shifted slightly, his attention still fixed on Lucy in the stall opposite.

'What's he doing here?' Taylor asked.

'Nothing!' Crosby replied. 'Apart from being a bloody liability. He came looking for Lucy.'

'Is he hurt?' Taylor asked.

Crosby shook his head. 'He's frightened.'

Taylor looked across to the stall opposite. 'Is Lucy still alive?'

'I've only just found out she was here.' Crosby said. He leant forward. 'Mister Milner! Your daughter is in urgent need of medical attention.'

No response.

'I can make her comfortable,' Taylor called across to him.

'My daughter is being punished,' Milner said.

'Punished for what?' Taylor asked.

'She killed her brother!'

The two detectives exchanged glances. Crosby's face registered less surprise than Taylor's. The revelation supported information Crosby had received earlier that morning – it reinforced his hunch that Milner hadn't been involved in the estate's murders.

Crosby would have to back his instincts. Milner had to be pressured. The unpredictable state of his mind made it dangerous, but their options were limited.

'Are you saying that Lucy was responsible for what happened at Shurville Gardens?' the detective asked.

'Bad genes Inspector!' Milner remained at the stall's entrance. 'I have to eliminate them. My responsibility!'

Crosby needed to drag him back, the man was unstable enough, he didn't want him becoming emotional. 'You need to be aware of what's happened over recent weeks Mister Milner,' the detective said.

'I know what happened!' The tears came freely, running down his heavily creased cheeks. 'Lucy turned on me. As Stephen did.'

Crosby shook his head. 'I'm talking about the murders in Sixfields.'

'That was just removing vermin.' Milner's eyes glittered from the tears. 'I've been putting bad people to sleep'.

'It's all been inside your head Mister Milner.' Crosby had committed himself now. 'You need help. You're not a well man.'

'I was tasked'

'You've been used,' the detective said. 'To divert attention.'

Milner shook his head. He waved an arm behind him. 'Ask them! They've been helping me!'

'There's no one else here,' Crosby said.

Grace Taylor whispered in Crosby's ear, 'I'm not sure this is a good idea Sir.'

The detective ignored her. 'Why did you allow your son to survive Mister Milner?'

'I left him to die.'

'You called the emergency services.'

'It wasn't his time.'

'You had further opportunities,' Crosby said. 'The truth is Mister Milner you're incapable of killing anyone. Including your son. I doubt my hospital visit had any influence at all.'

Milner didn't reply. Clearly agitated he left the stall and began to pace up and down the central walkway.

Taylor leant in towards Crosby, her voice more urgent. 'This isn't working Sir. You're pushing him too hard.'

PC Stewart had been following the exchanges. His eyes darted between the two detectives. Crosby kept his attention on Milner, hoping he hadn't miscalculated. They sat and waited.

When Milner acted it was sudden and abrupt. He swung round, pointing the gun directly at his daughter. 'My responsibility!' he shouted. The single shot was deafening.

Turning back towards the three hostages Milner pointed his gun directly at them. Sparks flew in the darkness as a bullet struck three feet above Crosby's head, ricocheting off the corrugated tin sheeting.

In the ensuing silence Stewart started whimpering. A smell of cordite and gun-smoke hung in the air. Out on the walkway Milner hadn't moved, the gun hanging loosely from his hand.

Taylor expelled her breath. 'Fucking Hell!'

Crosby's heart was thumping, his ears still ringing. 'That was deliberately over our heads,' the detective said. 'Lucy's as well.' He tried to sound more confident than he felt.

Taylor was struggling to get her breathing under control. She shot him a look.

'It was a calculated risk,' Crosby said. 'We have to jolt him out of his current state.'

'What now?'

'Don't know!' Crosby leant forward. 'Mister Milner! We need to talk about a telephone call I received earlier this morning.'

No response!

Crosby's hand was forced. 'The call was from our regional drugs enforcement agency. They rarely discuss any of their cases, but last weekend's riots have forced them to disclose information about an investigation they're currently working on.'

'He's not listening Sir,' Taylor said.

'Mister Milner!' the detective raised his voice. 'You may be familiar with the phrase 'Out Of Chaos Comes Order'. We believe it formed the basis of a plan to disrupt Sixfields and gain control of all narcotics operations within the estate. Stephen and Lucy were involved.'

Milner remained where he was but lifted his head. 'ordo ab chao,' he said, 'from the Latin – Create the problem. Incite a reaction. Offer your solution.'

Crosby had his attention. He talked quickly. 'Sixfields drug turnover is a multi-million pound industry. Minimal policing on the estate provides a reasonably safe and convenient place for the area's connections to conduct their business. It also makes control and distribution of narcotics within Sixfields extremely lucrative to the region's middle market wholesalers.'

The detective paused. Milner was still listening. His eyes had lost some of their intensity – as if a switch had been flicked inside his head. Crosby had to push on. 'A recently formed drugs consortium have been attempting to eliminate all major dealers on the Sixfields estate under a smoke-screen of serial killings. To divert attention, you were set up as chief suspect. The consortium also engineered last week-end's riots, during which several more key players were targeted and eliminated. In the resulting chaos and its immediate aftermath, they intended to set up their own infra-structure and supply network.'

Grace Taylor frowned and looked sideways at Crosby. 'Where has all this come from Sir?'

'I'm filling in a lot of gaps Grace,' the senior detective replied. 'And it's very recent. Nothing confirmed.'

'I could have been briefed about it this morning?' Taylor said. 'In the car.'

'Just stay with me Grace.' Crosby concentrated on Milner who was making his way back into the stall. He looked calm. A different person.

'Yes Inspector!' Milner stood in front of them. 'You have my full attention. How were Stephen and Lucy involved?'

'It would be easier to talk if these hand restraints were removed,' the detective said.

'No!'

Crosby didn't have the time to pursue it. 'When the consortium were looking for ways of unsettling Sixfields they used the attack on your son to introduce a serial killer onto the estate,' he paused. 'I believe Lucy's role was to supervise a contract gunman, hired to carry out the murders.'

'Why would they implicate me in them?' Milner asked.

'The syndicate knew that you carried out the attack on Stephen,' Crosby replied, 'and that you were already under suspicion from the police. You made it easy for them to point the finger your way.'

'How would they know that I was responsible for attacking Stephen?'

'Because one of their organisation was aware of your behaviour and routines,' Crosby replied. 'She would have realised you were responsible.'

Milner nodded. 'Lucy!'

'She also used your house as a base at weekends.' the detective said. 'Traces of sedatives were found in the coffee mugs there. To make sure you slept.' Crosby turned his head towards the policeman sat alongside him. 'Lucy used PC Stewart to ferry her around Sixfields when she was checking out various locations and sites.'

'And how was Stephen involved?' Milner asked.

'He was probably recruited by Lucy,' Crosby replied. 'To advise on where their targets could be located. She might have promised him a position with the consortium's future operation in Sixfields.'

'Why was he killed?'

'He'd become a liability,' Crosby said. 'The business with Janet Sterne had attracted too much attention from the police, and he knew about his sister's position within the consortium. They couldn't trust him.'

'Would it have been Lucy's decision to have him killed?'

Crosby shrugged. 'Probably!'

A shadow passed across Milner's eyes. 'And how much of what you've been telling me is guesswork Inspector?'

'Some!' the detective admitted.

Milner didn't look totally convinced. 'Why didn't you act on it before?'

'It didn't really make sense, until you said that Lucy was involved at Shurville Gardens.' Crosby paused. 'Were you actually in the house when Stephen was killed?'

Milner nodded. 'I'd been following him.'

'Did you witness the shooting?'

'No! Stephen was already dead when I got to him. Lucy was in the room with another man.'

'The hired gun!' Crosby said.

'My daughter was very angry at me being there.' Tears began to well up in Milner's eyes again. 'I didn't know her. She was a stranger.'

'You would have been in shock.' The detective strained his ears for sounds of the station wagon being started up. Why the hell hadn't Roberts left the barn – Milner had come in from the walkway at least five minutes ago.

Crosby looked across at him. His eyes had glazed over again. The detective needed to keep him focused. 'What happened after you found Stephen?' he asked.

'It's a bit hazy now.' Milner frowned as he tried to recall events. 'I think someone must have knocked me out.'

'How long were you unconscious?'

Milner shrugged. 'Don't know. When I came round my hands had been tied.'

'Were you still in the same room?'

Milner nodded. 'There was no-one else around and I managed to work my hands free. When Lucy came back in I was able to overpower her and take the gun.'

Crosby was only half listening. He was getting concerned. Still no sound of the station wagon being started. A sudden thought planted itself. The detective didn't want to entertain it.

'We eventually left the house.' Milner was still rambling. 'Lucy's car was parked outside. I remember forcing her to come with me. The gunman had disappeared.'

'How did you end up here?'

'My daughter had often talked about the farm.' Milner shook his head. 'It was the only place I could think of that would get us far enough away.'

'Your daughter drove?'

Milner nodded. 'I put the gun to her head. She was frightened. I remember a lot of shouting during the journey. Probably me.'

'You can still walk away from this.' Crosby said. 'It isn't too late.'

'And what about my state of mind Inspector? Can I walk away from that?'

'Your illness is treatable.'

Milner shook his head. He looked around him. 'They'll be back tomorrow. And when I sit down with them to talk about clearing vermin from the streets I'll consider it perfectly normal. Is that a treatable illness Inspector?'

Both men turned towards the sound of footsteps hurrying from the barn. Milner quickly moved out onto the central walkway but didn't pursue them. The footsteps faded. Crosby listened for sounds of a vehicle pulling away. Silence! He should have acted sooner.

'Mister Milner!' the detective tried to inject some urgency into his voice. 'We may be in danger. Drugs enforcement indicated there was a substantial backer within the consortium who they hadn't yet identified.'

Milner looked across at him.

'I should have considered the possibility earlier,' Crosby said. 'It might be Lucy's step-father.'

'Her step-father?' Milner repeated.

'He could have also recruited Lucy into the consortium,' Crosby added.

It got a reaction. 'This is all due to him?'

Crosby tried not to let the panic show in his voice. 'Mister Milner! We need untying. I don't want to continue sitting here if there's a possibility that he's involved in all of this.'

Stewart and Taylor shifted nervously alongside him.

Milner remained out on the walkway.

Above them the building's overhead strip lights suddenly went out, plunging the barn's interior into semi-darkness again.

Peter Stewart panicked, his shouts for help echoing through the building. Crosby swore at the PC before turning to Taylor. 'On top of the ledge. There's a small penknife attached to my keyring.'

A powerful flash accompanied by a huge bang shook the ground underneath them. Out on the walkway Milner dropped his gun and fell to the floor.

'Shit!' Crosby swore. 'That was a fucking shotgun. Get the penknife!' he hissed at Taylor.

The policewoman scrambled to her feet and fumbled along the ledge for Crosby's keyring. As she located it Henry Roberts appeared out of the shadows, his shotgun levelled at the three occupants.

He wasted no time in pointing the barrel at Peter Stewart.

'Don't!' was all the young policeman could say. 'Please don't!'

Another loud explosion reverberated around the barn.

Stewart's look of abject fear quickly disappeared. His body was slammed backwards as several balls of lead-shot struck him full in the face. The projectiles' penetrating shockwaves caused the policeman's head to violently expand, bursting apart at its weakest points.

Roberts snapped open the shotgun. Pulling two cartridges from his pocket he calmly and unhurriedly reloaded each barrel. Crosby realised he intended to kill them all. Roberts swung the shotgun back round towards Grace Taylor. His finger tightened around the trigger. At the same time, in quick succession, three separate events occurred – set into motion by the piercing screams of Penny Roberts, echoing across the yard.

Henry Roberts, momentarily distracted, turned his head towards the barn's entrance. Almost immediately the indistinct outlines of two small children appeared out on the walkway.

'What the fuck!' Crosby said out loud. Both children wore loose fitting nightshirts, their thin, bare legs exposed to the elements. Holding each other's hands they looked directly into the stall.

Crosby later dismissed what he'd seen – putting it down to shadows and the near-dark interior. It didn't explain the fact that Roberts must have also seen something because he discharged both barrels at the two children. They continued to stand there. A sudden breeze gusted through the barn's open doors, gently ruffling their hair and billowing the loose fitting nightshirts. Still holding hands they moved effortlessly away, disappearing into the dark shadow.

As Roberts loaded more cartridges into his shotgun, another movement caught the detective's eye – Milner's outstretched hand closing on the steel baton that Crosby had dropped earlier.

When Roberts turned back, Milner had pushed himself up onto one knee. Swinging his arm upwards he smashed the baton's thin rod of solid steel directly into Roberts' exposed windpipe. The intricate, fragile bone structure immediately cracked and disintegrated.

Henry Roberts' screams were soundless as he dropped the shotgun and pawed at his mangled voice box, desperately trying to suck air past it.

Staggering out onto the central walkway he lurched towards the building's exit doors. Milner hauled himself upright. Badly wounded, and unsteady on his feet, he picked up the double-barrelled shotgun and followed Roberts out of the barn.

It took Grace Taylor a few seconds to react. Finding the penknife on Crosby's keyring she turned back to her DI and sliced through the thin plastic around his wrists.

Stiff and cramped from sitting in one position the senior detective was slow to regain his feet. 'See what you can do for Stewart and Lucy,' he said. Picking up Milner's abandoned handgun Crosby hobbled out of the stall.

A deep, booming report sounded from across the yard.

Outside there was still some daylight. It took the detective a few moments for his eyes to adjust. Halfway across the yard he could just make out the figure of Henry Roberts lying face down on the damp concrete.

Crosby approached slowly as Milner held the shotgun over Roberts' motionless body. Smoke drifted from one of the barrels. A gaping hole smouldered in the back of Roberts' jacket.

Milner stepped to one side, his unruly mop of white hair lifting in the wind. He turned and levelled the shotgun at Crosby's chest. 'It would appear that I am capable of killing Inspector.' A moment of understanding passed between the two men before Milner raised the gun up and jammed both barrels into his mouth.

Crosby instinctively turned away as a fine spray of blood and brain matter splattered his face. Forcing down a surge of bile he kicked the shotgun away from Milner's lifeless hands, before moving across to Henry Roberts. He stooped to pick up his wrist. The pulse barely registered.

Crosby didn't waste any time searching for Robert Milner's vital life signs. There was very little left of his head. Inside the station wagon Penny Roberts had begun to scream again.

Taylor appeared next to him. Her features were chalk-white and she was shaking. Crosby took off his coat and draped it around her shoulders 'What about the other two?' he asked.

'Lucy's still alive. I can't find a pulse for Stewart.'

'Do you need some time?'

Taylor shook her head.

'I'll start on the preliminaries then,' Crosby said. 'You'll have to take the car back down until you can get a mobile signal.'

Taylor was finding it difficult to look away from the two bodies.

'Will you be able to manage?' Crosby asked.

She nodded, moving away towards the farmhouse.

'Take Penny Roberts back down with you,' Crosby called after her.

He watched Taylor make her way across the yard and up towards the house. Crosby could see she was in a state of delayed shock. It wasn't surprising. She'd come within a hair's breadth of being shot. The full realisation would come later.

Crosby dug out a twelve-week-old unopened pack of cigarettes from his inside jacket pocket. The detective took one out and placed it between his lips, trying to control the tremor in his hands. 'Fuck!' Crosby muttered, unable to flick the wheel of his lighter.

Crosby waited for the Freelander's rear lights to disappear from view before he knelt down beside Roberts to take his pulse again. There wasn't one. Pushing himself up Crosby headed towards the farmhouse – to get blankets for Lucy. He didn't feel particularly steady on his legs either.

CHAPTER 32

Dryffed's Farm: Tuesday 27 February 2007: 5.30 pm

Crosby tracked the two headlights as they climbed slowly up the hill. He waited on the farmhouse steps as Taylor coasted towards him. Pulling up alongside she switched off the Freelander's engine and lights.

He opened the driver's door for her. 'Any problems?'

Taylor climbed out. 'I managed to get a signal at the first village we reached. Emergency services are on the way.'

'Are you OK?' Crosby asked.

Taylor shrugged it off. 'I've had better days. What about Lucy?'

'I've made her comfortable,' Crosby said. 'Nothing much I could do for the other three.'

Taylor looked around the yard. 'Any more surprises here?'

The senior detective shook his head. 'I did find both cars. Tucked away behind one of the outbuildings.' He glanced inside the station wagon. 'What have you done with Penny Roberts?'

'Being checked over by the local doctor. She was very distressed, almost hysterical. Claimed to have seen a child's face staring in through the car window.' Taylor shrugged. 'The mist playing tricks I expect.'

'You didn't see anything then?' Crosby asked.

'Like what?'

Crosby shook his head. 'Doesn't matter. Did you speak with the DCI?'

Taylor nodded. 'Briefly! He's on his way. By helicopter.'

'Were you able to give him any details?'

'A few!' Taylor replied. 'He wasn't happy. PC Stewart's involvement could be awkward for the department apparently.'

Crosby nodded. 'Having your head blown apart is a lot less embarrassing presumably.'

Taylor looked up at him. A brief pause. 'The DCI seemed unaware of all the stuff you were telling Milner earlier.'

'I said before. A lot of guesswork.'

Taylor didn't look happy. 'Most of it true though.'

He didn't reply.

'I'm not very impressed to be honest Sir,' Taylor said. 'You put me at risk. If the possibility existed that Henry Roberts was involved we shouldn't have been here in the first place.'

'I didn't know about Roberts.' Crosby replied. 'But you should have been briefed about the other stuff. It was poor judgement on my part.'

'It was irresponsible,' the policewoman replied. 'And Milner ended up here because of what you told him about his son.'

Crosby couldn't look her in the eye. The repercussions from that continued on. Even Milner's suicide hadn't put an end to it.

Taylor shook her head. 'I came very close to losing my life in there.' An awkward silence. The policewoman eventually turned away 'I'll check on Lucy.'

Crosby went to call her back but thought better of it. She crossed the yard and disappeared into the barn.

The detective went to his pocket and pulled out the crumpled pack of cigarettes again. As his hands had finally stopped shaking he was able to work the lighter. Dragging acrid smoke deep into his lungs he headed towards the farmhouse.

A sudden clatter of helicopter blades echoed around the surrounding hills, intermittent flashes lighting up a dark sky. Crosby swore softly under his breath. Halfway up a mountain in the company of DCI Rees-Bramley wouldn't have been his evening of choice.

He'd have to ring the wife at some point and cancel their dinner date.

CHAPTER 33

Sixfields Estate: Monday 5 March 2007: 9.00 am

As he stood watching the removal lorry parked outside Milner's house, Donald's bulky frame rocked rhythmically from one foot to the other.

He remained standing on the grassy common as two removal men went about their business of transferring number sixty-nine's contents into the lorry's interior.

A small, black Labrador puppy sat impatiently at Donald's feet, pawing his trouser leg. The puppy had been delivered by a local veterinary practice, three days after Donald's discharge from the Royal West Midlands.

Donald's mother had to read him the accompanying note. It simply said: 'This is Ben. He needs someone to take good care of him.' The note had been signed: 'Your good friend Robert Milner'.

Donald's parents had initially refused to accept the puppy. They only relented after the veterinary representative had assured them that all necessary inoculations and insurance plans had been fully pre-paid.

Donald and his new charge spent every waking moment together. The puppy was already in danger of becoming overweight – spending most of its time lodged inside his owner's coat whenever they left the house.

Across the road a blue-overalled figure slammed shut both rear doors of the removal lorry. Stooping down, Donald slipped a hand underneath the puppy's bulging stomach and picked him up. After carefully tucking Ben into the crook of his arm Donald crossed the green and made his way towards Milner's house.

Standing on the opposite side of the road Donald placed Ben carefully at his feet.

Another overalled-figure came out of Milner's front door and slammed it shut behind him.

'This is Ben,' Donald called out to the removal man, his childlike voice barely carrying across the road.

The man ignored him.

'When is Mister Milner coming back?' Donald asked.

'Fuck off!' the removal man said. 'You're a bloody nuisance.'

The man walked around to the lorry's front passenger door, pulled it open, and got in. After a few seconds the vehicle rumbled into life and pulled slowly away.

Donald remained. He stood looking at the empty house.

At the far end of the street a commotion of noise caused Donald to turn. A small group of youths were making their way along the path towards him. He quickly scooped the puppy up and tucked him inside his coat.

To raucous shouts from the approaching youths Donald shuffled awkwardly back across the common.